I0681159

DEEP SECRETS

A Cold War Thriller

By Gerry A. Young, Captain USNR (Retired)

ISBN: 978-0-9965962-2-0

Library of Congress Catalog Number: 2015911238

Published by DBF Publishing

Dedication

To my wife Joyce, who encouraged me while I worked (for a long time) on this book. Without her support, it wouldn't have happened.

Preface

THIS book is a work of fiction. Any coincidental similarities between characters, companies, or other elements in this book and the real world are just that—coincidences.

"Outlaw Shark," an actual defense program from the 1970's, is a key element of the plot. This program, now declassified enough that you can find information about it on the Internet, began in the 1970's. The impetus of the project was the advent of the Harpoon missile, giving our submarines long-range attack capability. The goal of Outlaw Shark was to enable our submarines to generate a valid attack at these ranges. This would be done by providing data downloads identifying surface ship targets "over the horizon." Until the advent of cruise missiles, submarine attacks on surface ships had been limited to torpedoes aimed at targets visually classified and confirmed.

As a Naval Reserve officer, I had a peripheral involvement with this program. My Reserve colleague and I assisted as outside advisors helping to identify and solve the constraints imposed by the submarine environment.

The functionality Outlaw Shark was designed to provide is now supplied by other means. If you're interested in what our current targeting systems are, search online for information on "TADIXS."

This novel focuses on what might have happened if the Soviets had taken an interest in this technology, either to steal it for their own use or to sabotage its usefulness, making their own surface navy safer from our submarines' anti-ship missiles. These were the days before personal computers and cell phones, so the technology may seem crude, but this provides some insight into technology's effect on espionage operations.

All the primary characters in this book are completely fictional, and do not represent any actual person. The company "Federated Aviation" is wholly fictional and is definitely *not* intended to represent Lockheed Aviation, the company which was actually involved in Outlaw Shark.

The Homebrew Computer Club was real, and included some of the key founders of the computer industry in Silicon Valley.

Descriptions of the interior layout of the *LOS ANGELES*-class submarines are based on unclassified sources only, as are descriptions of submarine fire control procedures. I should also note that *LOS ANGELES* was commissioned later than this book indicates. Some liberties were taken with the geography of San Mateo County's Memorial Park.

The cover image of *USS LOS ANGELES* is a US Navy photo, obtained with the Navy's permission from the *www.navy.mil* website.

I would like to express my appreciation to Captain Bill Green (USN Retired), my commanding officer on *USS TUNNY* (APSS 282), and a former naval attaché in the USSR, for help in making the descriptions of espionage tradecraft more authentic, as well as for good plot advice. Any errors regarding tradecraft are entirely mine. My thanks also to Warren Branges, who served on *USS TUNNY* (SSN 682), for unclassified technical assistance, and to Carroll Ann Kimsey and my sister Nancy Burley for their very detailed editing work. Gary A. Young (my Naval Reserve colleague on the Outlaw Shark project), Gene Lasater, Harlan Sager, Phil Murray and Russ Hardgrove also provided very helpful suggestions.

Prologue

8:02 pm, 13 November 1975 (near La Honda, California)

THE PATH was worse than I'd expected. The rain had softened the ground to the point where my boots sunk in deeply, forcing me to pause to pull the boot out of the mud with each step. It took me until a few minutes before eight to reach the small cabin.

I intended to walk up to the door and knock, but a figure emerged from behind a tree. "Hold it right there!" he said sharply. It was someone I hadn't seen for years. "Hand over your weapon."

I handed him the 9 mm pistol butt-first.

"Come on in," I heard from inside the cabin. I stepped forward and the sentry fell into place behind me. It was a cramped and shoddy little space, probably not the actual lair of my long-time enemy.

Behind the table, a burly man was smiling. "Let's see the proof."

"I've got to reach into my pocket," I said, not wanting to be shot for making a move for a weapon. I turned slightly so the sentry could see I was reaching into the breast pocket of my shirt; he was holding the pistol I'd surrendered, but pointing it at the floor. I pulled out a sheaf of color Polaroid photos and turned back to the desk.

"I did what you said I had to," I said, and placed the first photograph face up in front of him. It was a close-up of a young woman's head and upper body. Her eyes were staring vacantly at nothing; around a hole in the side of her skull was a mess of blood and brains. Her mouth was agape, and a trickle of blood was running down her chin. I heard the sentry gasping behind me.

"That's the exit wound," I explained. "Here's a photo of the entrance wound. It's a lot smaller and cleaner."

"Jesus," the man behind the table hissed, staring at both pictures. "That's her, all right. I never thought you'd have the guts to do this."

"You didn't offer me much choice. The alternative was that you'd do it over a few days, throwing in torture and rape. This seemed a much better end for her. She never saw it coming."

I tossed on a couple of other photos, showing her lying face-down on the forest floor.

"What'd you do with her?"

"We were in a remote area of one of the county parks here—a place way off the paths where almost no one ever goes. The park was completely empty when I was there. There were no cars in the parking lot, probably because of the crappy weather. Anyway, the ground around the redwoods is soft and easy to dig, so I buried her about three feet deep. I moved a big fallen branch and some good-sized rocks on top to keep the critters away." I flipped down a final picture showing the grave site.

Both men stared at the pictures.

"Now it's your turn," I said. "You promised me the documentation—complete documentation—once I delivered my end of the deal."

"Just a minute, lad. What'd you do to make it look like she ran off on her own?"

"Her car's still at her house and she hadn't told anyone that she and I were going anywhere tonight. I told her it was a secret and she had to keep it quiet. Tomorrow they'll wonder why she's not at work, but nothing will happen during the weekend. Maybe early next week they'll get worried enough to send someone to check her house. It'll be a mystery. Now give me the documentation."

He hesitated, and then reached behind him and pulled up an accordion file from the floor.

"Here's all the stuff for the two of them. The first half is for one of them and the second for the other, and the sections are labeled indicating whether it holds check copies, transcripts of telephone conversations, actual data handed over, and so on."

I leafed through them and was impressed. The identities didn't totally surprise me; one was my prime suspect and the other had been number three on my list. If this was valid data that'd check out, I had plenty to nail the guilty bastards.

"When do you plan to turn this stuff over to your boss?" the man asked. Now for the dangerous part. Some of us in the room were about to die. If my planning and preparation weren't perfect, it'd be me. I really wasn't prepared for a situation like this. I'd spent the last seven years, up until a few months ago, as a submarine officer. I'd been in some tricky situations, but nothing remotely like this. How did I come to this? I'll tell you.

Chapter 1

A LOUD *BWANGG* noise reverberated against the submarine's hull, echoing around the control room. It got my attention and that of everyone else in the compartment. If we could hear the "ping" of the Soviet sonar through the hull, there was a decent chance the destroyer would get a return echo, giving them our bearing and range.

I was the OOD[1] as our 'long-hull' *STURGEON*-class[2] submarine crept silently through the cold black Pacific on a southerly course, riding the slow subsurface countercurrent to give us an "over the ground" speed of about four knots. Our sonar could clearly hear the relentless pinging of the Soviet *KASHIN*-class destroyer, designated as contact Sierra 42, hundreds of feet above us. For the last twenty minutes, it'd seemed to be moving away from us, perhaps drawn off by a false contact. Now it was back.

We were on the last phase of our mission. We'd successfully snuck into the Soviet submarine base at Rybachiy, near Petropavlovsk. It hadn't been easy; the Soviets believed in using extensive minefields to protect their bases. But we'd made it in without being detected. For five days, we'd carefully reconnoitered the large harbor and taken photos of the facilities and the submarines. With the long summer arctic days, we'd had almost twenty hours a day of good visibility. Overhead satellite photos were well and good, but a view from inside at close range provided details we might need if the balloon went up.

---

[1] Officer of the Deck—the officer in charge of the submarine's operation during his watch period.

[2] In 1975, this was the newest and largest class of 'attack' submarines in the US Navy. The "long hull" *STURGEON* class was ten feet longer than earlier submarines of that class.

"What was that, Mr. Halsted?" asked the Chief of the Watch. He looked worried. Anxiety isn't something I like to see in a senior watchstander. But since he was a Machinist's Mate, I couldn't expect him to know the characteristics of Soviet sonar systems.

"Oh, you heard that?" I asked, trying to sound nonchalant. I heard a few nervous chuckles. "I'm only guessing, Chief, but it sounds like Soviet surface sonar. Probably an MG-311—the NATO designation is 'Wolf Paw,' if I recall correctly. It's a medium-frequency sonar. Not as good as what our destroyers carry, but a pretty decent system."

The chief turned his attention back to the ballast control panel, probably wondering what violent maneuvers we'd have to execute to escape a hostile torpedo.

That ping hadn't been good news, but as OOD I had to be sure no hint of nervousness could be seen. Putting on what I hoped was a calm expression, I strolled over to the chart table and used a pair of dividers to measure the distance between two randomly chosen points, trying to show I wasn't concerned about the chance of us being detected.

I glanced at the XO[3], who seemed not to have heard anything. Although I was OOD, the XO would be making the tactical decisions so long as he was in the control room. He walked over to stand next to me. The quartermaster of the watch hovered within earshot. Glancing at him, the XO suggested this would be a good time for him to get a cup of coffee in the crew's mess. "Take your time," he told the QM. That left just the two of us in relative privacy. Absolute privacy doesn't exist on a submarine, except possibly in the CO's stateroom.

"XO," I asked quietly, "what about that ping? It sounded like he might have us nailed."

"It's one of two things, Rick," he said thoughtfully. "Either it was a final ping before putting a weapon in the water or it was a fluke that got down through the layer but didn't get back to him. Since we haven't detected a weapon, I'm guessing it was the fluke." I hoped I looked as calm as he did.

The XO went on, "Suppose they'd put a weapon in the water, I'd suddenly succumbed to a heart attack and the CO wasn't available. What would you have done?" This was a legitimate question. The CO and XO tested and pushed the junior officers to make sure we could handle an emergency. One day, after all, we might become XO or even CO of our own submarine.

I'd been thinking about this since I'd come on watch, so I had a ready reply. "Well, so far as we know, the Soviet anti-submarine torpedoes on their surface craft use either passive homing, which vectors in on

---

[3] Executive Officer = the second in command under the Commanding Officer.

cavitation noise[4], or active homing, which goes after any non-stationary target. I'd put us dead in the water and set 'ultra-quiet,' shutting down most of the rotating machinery. At the same time, I'd launch a MOSS[5] from Tube 4. It'll draw the Soviet fish away from us while we just sit here quietly."

"Not bad," the XO said. "That'd about cover it, except for the part where you fall on your knees in prayer." I managed a smile as he went on, "You know, that bastard's been trying to nail us for three days. It's a good thing he hasn't got dipping sonar or he'd probably have us."

"Come on, XO, we're way out in international waters now. Let him ping. I don't think he's even sure there's a submarine out here. And if he did get a good track on us, so what?" My fingers were firmly crossed.

He frowned. "You really think that if he got a good fire control solution he wouldn't put a weapon in the water? Maybe they'd do a *SCORPION*[6] on us. I think we might have tickled some passive system when we were sneaking out of Petro. They probably didn't get a firm classification, but maybe enough to wonder if someone was there who shouldn't be. That might be why they sent this guy out. If he finds us, he'd probably shoot—who'd ever know what happened?"

I didn't have a good answer to that. The *SCORPION* had gone down just a few weeks before I was commissioned and sent to Nuclear Power School. Its loss had caused two of my classmates to decide against volunteering for submarine duty.

Fifteen minutes passed in tense silence as we waited to see if a torpedo would be launched at us. Then the 27MC speaker came to life. "Conn, Sonar. Contact Sierra 42 appears to be turning away and speeding up. They've stopped pinging."

The atmosphere in the control room eased. Turning to leave for his stateroom and some well-deserved rest, the XO paused. "Rick, stay on this course another thirty minutes. If the Soviet doesn't show up again by then, come back to our base course to Pearl, speed up—carefully!—and go

---

[4] Cavitation noise is produced by a ship's propellers when they rotate fast enough to form steam bubbles, which produce a popping noise as they collapse. It can be eliminated by slower screw speeds and/or going deeper, where the increased water pressure inhibits the formation of the bubbles.

[5] MOSS = Mobile Submarine Simulator. A torpedo-shaped device ten inches in diameter; these were fitted in tandem racks that fit a standard USN submarine torpedo tube (21 inch diameter). MOSS is designed to produce sounds that mimic those of a US submarine. The launching submarine, staying as quiet as possible, can use a MOSS to draw away homing torpedoes.

[6] In May of 1968, the *USS SCORPION* sank in the North Atlantic. The official Navy finding, based on photos of the wreckage, was that the sinking was due to a battery explosion in one of their torpedoes. Many submarine officers suspected the Soviets might have had a hand in the sinking.

deeper." He paused for thought and then went on, "Before we make any course or speed changes, have Sonar search all around to make sure there aren't any other bad guys lurking in the area. And leave at least two hundred feet underneath us; I don't totally trust that bottom contour chart. Banging into an underwater pinnacle wouldn't be a good thing, right? Stay at eight knots or less until we can go down to at least 600 feet." He left Control, heading aft for his cabin a few feet away.

It looked like we were getting away cleanly. We'd come away with a lot of data about their submarine force that they'd just as soon we didn't have, and then slipped back out into the Pacific, hopefully without them realizing they'd been penetrated.

As the adrenalin rush I'd been on for the past six days slowly faded, I realized I was exhausted. Maybe I needed more than two hours sleep a day.

Half an hour later, the *KASHIN* was much further away, barely registering on our sensitive sonar. It was time to add some turns and get out of this unfriendly neighborhood.

I toggled the 27MC[7]. "Sonar, Conn, search all around—report all contacts."

"Conn, Sonar aye."

After what seemed a long wait the 27MC came to life. "Conn, Sonar. Completed search all around. No contacts except for Sierra 42, which we still hold faintly, bearing 348."

I went over to the SINS[8] console and noted the submarine's estimated position, marking it on our bottom-contour chart. The water depth here was supposedly 450 feet, getting steadily deeper to the southeast. We could go a little bit deeper now, but it'd probably be better to wait half an hour so we could go even deeper. Bottom contour charts aren't 100 percent accurate.

"Rig in the towed array[9]," I told the Chief of the Watch. The towed sonar array, almost 800 feet long, didn't like to be deployed at more than about six knots. Bringing it in would reduce our passive sonar capability, but that couldn't be helped—our priority now was to get out of this very unfriendly part of the ocean.

---

[7] The 27MC is a two-way circuit between sonar and the control room.

[8] SINS = Ship's Inertial Navigation System. This system keeps accurate track of a submarine's position based on integrating accelerometers that accurately measure direction of movement and distance traveled.

[9] A submarine towed array system is a long cable with passive hydrophones mounted along it. It trails behind the boat and is very effective detecting contacts while the boat operates at low speed. At higher speeds, or in situations where radical maneuvers are needed, the submarine has to rely on its hull-mounted sonars.

"Towed array sonar is housed, Mr. Halsted," the Chief of the Watch reported fifteen minutes later.

"Very well, Chief," I acknowledged and turned to the Diving Officer. "Make turns for eight knots and come left to 127. Tell Maneuvering to build up the turns slowly." The big submarine banked slightly as it swung onto the new course. Even after years of this, it was a thrill to have a 10-million pound submarine responding to your commands.

Now that *BOWFIN* was coming back to our homeward course, I double-checked the SINS navigational readout and, going to the chart table, carefully re-plotted the submarine's position. The first thing you learn in the submarine force is to keep double-checking—yourself and everyone else. That'd been a tough lesson for me, but now it was a habit.

Fifteen minutes later, I checked the water depth on the chart. Before going deeper, I needed to make sure the water was as deep as advertised. "Single-ping sounding on the fathometer, Chief," I told the Chief of the Watch.

The fathometer told us we had 375 feet of water under us, not counting the almost three hundred feet of ocean above us. "Chief, make your depth four five zero feet."

"Four five zero feet, aye sir," the chief torpedoman serving as Diving Officer replied. He gave quiet commands to the two men seated in front of him at the plane controls. *BOWFIN* tilted gently downward toward a depth that'd make us even more difficult to detect, wrapping us in the sheltering depths of the cold Pacific.

I re-read the Captain's night orders, concentrating on his directions for our stealthy exit from this Soviet-dominated area. Once we could safely go below 600 feet, we'd increase speed to fifteen knots as we continued our escape. On this course, we'd cross the Kuril Trench in about ninety minutes, which would give us more than enough water to go deeper and faster.

The control room personnel were feeling good, pleased with themselves after having completed the stealthy penetration of the secret and well-guarded Soviet submarine base. With things currently under control, I allowed myself to relax a little. We'd had a tense time up at Rybachiy, but Chuck Schneider, our commanding officer, had carried us through it with calm and cheerful professionalism. I doubted the CO had gotten as much sleep as I had, hard to believe as that was, and was glad he'd taken a chance to rest up.

Probably just to demonstrate he didn't actually need rest, the Old Man[10], wearing a ratty old Naval Academy bathrobe, materialized in the

---

[10] The commanding officer of an SSN would typically be in his late thirties. Submarining is largely a young man's game. Except now there are young women submariners as well.

Control Room. I called out "Captain in the Conn" and everyone stiffened slightly to a position remotely resembling the military definition of "attention."

"As you were," the CO smiled. "How's it going, Rick?" He still looked exhausted.

"Fine, Captain. XO probably told you the *KASHIN* went away about forty minutes ago. We just pulled in the towed array, went to eight knots and down to 450 feet. We should hit the Kuril Trench at about 0400. Then we can go deeper and get up to fifteen knots."

"Sounds good. Once we get a hundred or so miles further away from Petro, we'll need to come up to periscope depth, link up to the SSIXS[11] satellite and see what the message traffic is. Also, I want to get a report off to COMSUBPAC[12] so he'll know we exited safely. I'm going to amend the night orders now, but be sure to tell your relief—is it Jim?—that once we hit this point here ..." the Captain marked a position on our projected course line "... to slow down, redeploy the towed array for a thorough search, start coming up to PD[13] and to wake me up. Draft a message to the Admiral with our projected position at that time and the news that we completed the mission satisfactorily. Keep it short. When I get up I'll check it, update the position, and then send it out." The captain headed back to his stateroom for another nap as I began drafting the message.

A few hours later, I was relieved as OOD by Jim O'Clarey and, after the required bow-to-stern inspection of the submarine that the off-going OOD performs, went to the officers' head to wash up before getting some badly needed sleep. I headed for my bunk and collapsed into it without bothering to take off my poopy suit[14]. For the past two weeks, we'd all been sleep-deprived because of the high state of alert inside the tightly guarded Soviet submarine base. We were approaching a zombie state.

It seemed I'd barely fallen asleep when a messenger holding a clipboard was shaking me gently. "Mr. Halsted? Mr. Halsted, sir? I've got a message for you to read and initial." I dimly realized we must have come up to PD and established radio communications, so I must have gotten a couple of hours of sleep.

I raised my head blearily, careful not to bang my head on the bottom of the bunk above me, and read the message by the light of a red-lensed flashlight the messenger was holding. As Weapons Officer, I wasn't routed on routine messages, but this one wasn't routine, at least as far as

---

[11] SSIXS = Submarine Satellite Information Exchange Subsystem, a satellite-based system allowing US submarines to send and receive communications traffic with relatively high security.

[12] Commander, Submarines Pacific—the admiral in charge of all submarines operating in the Pacific Ocean. His Atlantic counterpart is COMSUBLANT.

[13] PD = Periscope depth

[14] A one-piece blue cotton coverall worn by submariners at sea

I was concerned. It was from BUPERS[15]. It advised me that my orders to report to the Naval Postgraduate School in Monterey next month had been canceled and that I was to be detached from *BOWFIN* immediately upon arrival at Pearl Harbor to proceed "with no delay" to Washington. A street address in Arlington, Virginia was provided as a "report to" location. Below that was some BUPERS gobbledygook saying the orders "were in accordance with ..." followed by several improbably long strings of numbers and letters.

If I hadn't been an officer and a gentleman, I'd have said something rude. I scribbled my initials on the message and fell onto my back, considering this unwelcome surprise.

I'd been looking forward to two years in PG school, where I'd have been studying for a master's degree in physical oceanography, with a specialty in underwater sound. This had been a key part of my career plan. After over five years of sea duty following eighteen months of nuclear power and submarine training, I was more than ready for some time ashore. I'd been commissioned seven years earlier, so in a year or so, I'd be in the "zone" for promotion to Lieutenant Commander. My advanced degree would've helped me in my mission to be assigned as XO of a submarine. That job would be the last step before being considered to command a submarine, my long-time goal and my idea of the best job in the world.

What these new orders would mean for my plans I couldn't tell. "Good thing I'm a bachelor," I thought sourly; a disaster like this would be tough to explain to a wife who'd probably already be house-hunting in the Monterey area.

That brought my thoughts back to Natalie Montaigne, the girl I'd loved and lost during my senior year at Cal Berkeley. She'd seemed the only real chance I'd had for "true love," a concept on which I was still a little fuzzy.

The submarine service, I'd learned, was great for providing technical challenges but came up short on offering opportunities for developing serious relationships with young women. Over the past two years on *BOWFIN*, I estimated I'd been at sea or on duty in port for about eighty percent of those seven hundred plus days, and my earlier sea time on *PERMIT* hadn't been much different. What was worse was that the boat's schedule often changed without warning, usually while we were already at sea, leaving me unable to contact my current girlfriend. I'd learned that desirable young ladies have a low tolerance for suitors who apparently vanish from the face of the earth, only to reappear weeks later with a lame story about a mission they can't discuss. Postgraduate school would have given me a couple of years in Monterey, where I might have been able to resume the hunt for "the one," but now that was off the table.

Still exhausted, and now a little depressed, I decided to talk with the XO in the morning and, if necessary, the Captain, to find out what this meant and if I could get these mysterious orders reversed. Worn out from the weeks of frantic operational work, I fell asleep again almost instantly, into pathetic dreams of Natalie and what might have been.

Chapter 2

"**X**O, have you got a minute?" I asked, tapping lightly on the open door to the XO's stateroom just aft of Control. After more than three hours of uninterrupted sleep, I felt much better.

"I'll bet this is about those message orders," the XO said, beckoning me in. "Shut the door, Rick."

He came straight to the point. "I've seen orders like these—once. When you see an address like that, you know it's the spook side of the house that wants you. When they want you, they get you. So you might as well relax and enjoy the ride."

"But what about post-grad school? I wanted that master's degree to give me a leg up on getting an XO job not far down the road," I objected, uneasy at this hint I might be working in intelligence, a part of the Navy I'd always wanted to avoid.

"Lieutenant, there's a reason they call these 'orders' and not 'requests.' Now, you've got your orders and you'll damn well carry them out," the XO told me, a smile softening the message.

"Look," he went on. "My guess is that if you do a good job on whatever mysterious chore they have for you, you'll be in better shape than you'd have been with the Master's degree, so cheer up, for Christ's sake. Orders like this tell me this job must be important to someone very senior in this Navy. Now, come on—the Old Man wants to talk with you." He knocked on the connecting door to the CO's stateroom. Turning to me before he opened the door, he reminded me, "Remember, if you can't take a joke ..."

I interrupted him and finished, "... you shouldn't have joined the submarine force." I think I heard that for the first time in Nuclear Power School, and probably a dozen times since. Sometimes I'd been the one saying it to a shipmate who'd thought he'd been dumped on. The XO offered a sardonic smile and shut the door behind me as he returned to his pile of paperwork.

I found myself sitting in front of my commanding officer, hoping he'd have some miracle fix for the orders that might destroy my carefully laid plans for promotion and eventual command of a submarine.

"Look, Rick," he began, "the first thing you should understand is that these orders aren't necessarily bad news. I don't have any idea why they want you so badly, or what you'll be doing. But it's probably something important, so that tells me that if you do a good job, you'll be in better shape for an eventual XO slot than if you'd gone to PG school."

I nodded politely, but didn't believe this for a minute. It was a Navy tradition, probably going back to John Paul Jones in the Revolutionary War, that an officer who got a bad set of orders received, along with the paperwork, a pep talk on what a great break this particular set of crappy orders was.

"The second thing," the captain went on with a wry smile, "is that I may have had something to do with this. About three months ago, all the submarine CO's in the Pacific fleet, and probably all of them in the Atlantic as well, got a request from the Naval Investigative Service[16] to let them know if we had a Weapons Officer who was really sharp on the Mark 113 fire control system[17] and who might have aptitude for 'sensitive and independent' work. I gave you very high marks and it looks like that carried some weight."

'It probably would,' I mused to myself. Captain Schneider had a top reputation for what the Navy called "special operations"; the most sensitive and secret work assigned to submarines. I resented being put in this position, but he had, as usual, only done his best to help the Navy and the nation. NIS was definitely *not* where I wanted to be, for a variety of reasons.

"And there's some good news buried here," my CO said. "One of the references at the bottom, once you decipher it, gives you a spot promotion to Lieutenant Commander. It's like the promotion to Lieutenant Commander for getting the Chief Engineer job as a Lieutenant—theoretically you might not be confirmed by the selection board when you come up for your normal permanent promotion, but it's almost unheard of not to select someone who's already holding the rank. That'll indicate to command selection boards that you're way above average."

---

[16] Now, of course, titled "Naval Criminal Investigative Service" (NCIS)

[17] The fire control system on a modern Navy ship has nothing to do with putting out fires. It's the computerized system that tracks targets and sets the commands in the weapons systems to intercept and destroy the target. As of 1975, the Mark 113 was the most modern system in the US submarine force.

Still not certain whether I was really being screwed by these orders, I thanked Captain Schneider and went down to the wardroom to catch up on my departmental paperwork, still confused about whether my new career path was really as good a deal as the Captain was trying to portray it.

Chapter 3

TWELVE days later *BOWFIN* moored at the Pearl Harbor Submarine base just after dawn. I'd seen pictures and movie clips of World War II submarines coming back from a successful patrol—the band and the Admiral would be waiting on the pier to congratulate them, with newsreel cameras rolling. But the kind of missions SSN's had in the Cold War weren't publicly acknowledged, so we'd tied up at 0630 met only by half a dozen sleepy line handlers on the pier.

My rushed departure half an hour later deprived me of the usual going-away celebration. "I missed out on the plaque and the present, not to mention the free drinks at the going-away party," I complained to the XO as I rechecked to make sure I'd packed everything. It wasn't much—just uniforms, a few civilian clothes, underwear and a toiletry kit. You don't carry much in the way of personal belongings on a submarine.

"Don't sweat it—we'll package that stuff up and send it to you, except for the free drinks. We'll mail it to your home address in California," the XO told me as we shook hands. His expression sobered. "We'll miss you, and we wish you luck. You've been a great shipmate." He looked at his watch. "You'd better hurry; your flight from Hickam leaves in less than an hour. Best of luck, Rick—we all know you'll do a great job."

Forty-five minutes later, I was in the air on a non-stop MAC[18] flight to Andrews Air Force Base, just outside Washington. As soon as we reached cruising altitude, I tried to sleep, but found Natalie Montaigne in my thoughts again. As the plane headed toward the mainland US, I realized I might be about to enter what would seem like "normal life" to a civilian, with a chance to start a social life again. With this looming in front of me, I couldn't help musing over my too-brief love affair with that maddening girl.

---

[18] MAC = Military Airlift Command. Run by the Air Force, this provides military or chartered civilian aircraft to move military personnel around the world. Coach class on a real airline would be a big upgrade from the travel experience MAC provides.

I'd met Natalie in 1967, early in my senior year at Berkeley, at a mixer in my fraternity house. I was living in an apartment, but still went to most of the social functions at the house in search of my next temporary relationship. At this time in Berkeley, the hunting was easy. The famous "Summer of Love" in San Francisco had happened only a few months earlier, so let's just say that loose morals were common.

A slender long-legged young woman was standing off by herself; I'd watched her rebuff overtures from a few of my fraternity brothers. I found her striking, although my usual type was more on the voluptuous side. She had reddish-brown hair cascading thickly around her face, in what I guessed might be a pageboy hairstyle, hanging above her shoulders. Her huge emerald-green eyes and soft lush mouth caught my eye immediately. I decided to risk a snub. I was a long way from being the best-looking guy in the room, but my face didn't cause women to turn away in disgust, and at a fraction of an inch under six feet, I was tall enough to make a decent first impression.

Walking up to her, I smiled and said, "Now it's my turn to get rejected."

"Why would you think I'd do that?" she asked curiously. Her voice was intriguing—low and husky.

"Well, I watched you shoot down the last two guys in flames," I said. "Just so you can call me by name while you're doing it, I'm Rick Halsted."

She smiled. "I'm Natalie Montaigne. Fetch me some punch and we'll see how things go."

I came back with a cup of the horrible punch for each of us. Looking over the rim of the glass as she took her first sip, she said, "We might as well get the formalities out of the way. I'm a sophomore majoring in computer science. My father's a professor of sociology here; we moved here two years ago from Ann Arbor, where I grew up. Your turn."

Not offering my opinion that sociology was a waste of time, I said, "I'm a senior in electrical engineering. I'm a California native, brought up in San Mateo, over on the Peninsula. When I graduate in June I'll be commissioned as a naval officer, since I'm here on an NROTC scholarship." The rituals were completed.

She blinked and looked away for a moment. Then she turned the full force of those lovely green eyes on me. "You should probably know I'm active in the anti-war movement," she said hesitantly. I wasn't surprised; the various leftist movements seemed to constitute a solid majority of the undergraduate student body at Berkeley.

"That's OK," I said solemnly. "I'm anti-war too, but the way I choose to express it is to help the US be strong enough that no one wants to get into a war with us. Of course, if anyone's stupid enough to do it anyway, I'd reluctantly have to help kick their ass."

Natalie laughed, an infectious bubbly sound of pure joy that drew curious glances from around the room. An anti-war girl who'd be amused by something like that would be interesting to be with.

Not much later, we slipped out of the house and headed for a crowded local pub where ID's weren't checked carefully and the liquid refreshments were better. Within a few minutes shouting over the din, I found I was surprisingly at ease with Natalie, as if we'd known each other a long time. I learned she shared an off-campus apartment with another girl, and she found out I was also off-campus, in an apartment with another guy. I explained, "Jim's a football player, so I really don't see him much in fall term. He travels a lot with the team, and between games, practices, and study tables over at the Athletic Department, he basically just sleeps in the place."

"Look," she said hesitantly, "it's too noisy here. Would it be OK if we went over to your place so we could talk without having to shout at each other? Just don't get the wrong impression; I'm a girl who likes to take things slowly."

Later I decided she probably was inclined to go slowly, but we'd built up such a strong mutual attraction that within half an hour of getting to my place we were kissing feverishly. Unable to resist the urge, I'd leaned over and kissed her gently, moving slowly enough that she could have made it clear she wasn't interested. But she was. The first kiss stunned me with its passion and power and, it appeared, had the same effect on Natalie. Neither of us seemed able to stop. Her kisses were intoxicating, and I realized she'd already become an important part of my life. I found myself happy just holding her and kissing her, with no need to try to push things further, very unlike my usual tactics. I suppose the traditional thing to say was that I fell in love with her because of her incredible kisses or her lovely face, but it wasn't that—it was my sense of who she really was, and that she was the one I'd been looking for. That may sound trite, but that's what I believed then. Unfortunately, almost eight years later it was what I still felt.

From that evening on, we were a couple. Our relationship deepened quickly, and two weeks later we made love for the first time. I was many times removed from being a virgin, having had an unusually early sexual initiation let alone being in Berkeley during the Bay Area free-love era. But my previous encounters hadn't prepared me for the intensity of the feelings Natalie evoked in me. After our first lovemaking, we'd stared at each other in mutual amazement before she burst into tears, which she assured me were from joy. I laid there stunned—I'd had my fair share of good sexual experiences, but this had shaken me with its intensity.

On first seeing her, I'd thought she was on the thin side, but her nude body was lush and silky smooth, bewitching me. Her sexual persona was an invigorating blend of playfulness and ardor. I was hopelessly in love. Her passion was blissful, but I craved to be with her even when all we could do was talk. When I'm with her, I feel complete, I told myself, amazed I could feel this strongly about anyone. Deep inside, I realized an attachment like this didn't fit well with my long-term plans, but I had to be with her.

I'd had enough experience that I shouldn't have been overcome by the fever she'd awakened in me. I was a long way from being the best-looking guy at Cal—probably near the 50th percentile—but my first sexual partner, an older girl, had made sure I understood how to make a woman happy, so I'd ended up with more than my share of opportunities once the girls passed the word around. Making love with Natalie, however, was at a different level of ecstasy altogether.

We spent every spare moment together, and Natalie even slept over a couple of nights when my roommate was out of town for away games. We avoided the word "love," but she seemed as enthralled with me as I was with her. And that was saying a lot.

We began talking hesitantly about the future. At graduation in June, I'd be commissioned as a regular Navy officer and most probably would be off immediately to a year and a half of nuclear power and submarine school, followed by lots of time at sea. This bothered both of us but Nat never suggested that I try to find a way out of my naval obligation, despite her fervent anti-war beliefs. Other than the worries about how we'd stay together after I was commissioned, this time was complete bliss to me. I couldn't imagine being with another woman, and the idea of Natalie making love to another man was unthinkable. It was too ideal a situation to last.

About two months after we'd met, Natalie and I had arranged to meet at the Student Union on Sproul Plaza on a Tuesday. It was NROTC drill day, so I was in my "working blue" midshipman uniform. Natalie loved to twit me about it, especially the ribbons I wore. I'd spent my last midshipman cruise during the preceding summer on a diesel submarine, the *TUNNY*, which operated with UDT and SEALs in the Vietnam War zone. By being on board out there, I'd earned the Vietnam Service ribbon, which seemed to amuse her even as it infuriated the lefties who recognized it. The National Defense ribbon (aka "I was alive in '65") came along with it. Plus, I'd received combat pay for two months for being in the Zone, making the cruise even sweeter, and distinguishing me from other midshipmen at Berkeley.

I responded to her sarcasm about my "war" experience by teasing her about her affiliation with the Free Speech Movement. It was one of the loudest leftist organizations on campus, and that was saying a lot when the campus was Berkeley. Natalie, I'd learned to my chagrin, was well known in the radical community, and was even a member of the powerful Coordinating Committee, which planned most of the major demonstrations on campus. By tacit agreement, I never asked her what went on in those meetings.

I got to the Union early that day and found a table to camp out at while waiting for Natalie. A few minutes after I sat down, a noisy group of hippie types came in and claimed a table next to me. I knew the leader of the group, who called himself "Giovanni Rossi." Natalie had told me his name was actually Johnny Ross and that he'd Italianized his name to evoke memories of Mario Savio, the founder of the Free Speech Movement a few years earlier and a legendary figure at Berkeley.

I'd first become aware of Rossi in January of the previous school year. He'd been a speaker at one of the anti-Reagan demonstrations. The governor, according to campus gossip, had forced the firing of the president of the University of California statewide system, Clark Kerr. Emotions had been running high around campus. Kerr, I had to admit, had had a decent sense of humor for a lefty—he'd explained that the purposes of a university were to provide "sex for the students, sports for the alumni, and parking for the faculty." Not bad. Ironically, I found out later that Kerr had actually been fired by a majority vote of the university Regents after Kerr himself forced a vote of confidence. Reagan, as Governor, had a vote on the committee, but he wasn't the driving force behind Kerr's termination. Kerr's insistence on the vote of confidence had caused him to lose his job. None of this had dampened the left-wing student movement's enthusiasm in blaming Reagan for the whole thing.

Rossi had garnered a lot of attention for his speech, most of which was shouted into a bullhorn. Even though his talk had consisted mostly of stale slogans, he somehow got a reputation as a decent speaker. Giovanni's style, which leaned heavily on yelling at the top of his lungs, was surprisingly effective in inciting a mob demonstration. Apparently, chanting "Ho, Ho, Ho Chi Minh—the NLF[19] is gonna win!"evoked strong emotions, even among students who thought the NLF was a professional football league. Who'd have guessed just shouting the name of the elderly mass murderer would excite a crowd? I gave Rossi as little attention as possible, but now here he was sitting next to me.

---

[19] NLF = "National Liberation Front," a Communist insurgent movement in South Vietnam that had been set up by the North Vietnamese.

Giovanni was always accompanied by a couple of beefy thugs, and today he also had a couple of lefty-losers trailing along, probably hoping to gain prestige by being seen with him. I'd watched him at a couple of campus protest meetings, and knew his speaking skills and intelligence were far below Savio's flaming brilliance. Rossi and the others like him, who were thick on the ground in Berkeley, styled themselves as Marxists but, I was sure, had no idea what real Marxism was like. If they did, they wouldn't be pushing for it. Or maybe they would; some people liked the idea of a totalitarian government, so long as they could be among the few at the top.

Rossi called out to me, "How's it going, stooge?" In the radical chic world at Berkeley in those days, "stooge" was shorthand for "stooge of the fascist government."

"Just fine, scummie," I answered without looking up from my textbook. The full title of "leftist hippie scum" was reserved for more formal occasions.

The niceties having been observed, Giovanni and his crowd settled down to discuss planning their next public protest meeting while I leafed through my text on semiconductor theory.

A few minutes later, I heard coarse chuckling from the lefty table. "Now that chick is something. When you first look at her, you don't realize how hot she is. I'd really like to nail her, and I bet she'd love it," I heard Giovanni murmur. Looking up, I saw Natalie approaching my table. As always, just the sight of her gave me a thrill. She gave a friendly wave to the lefties and then leaned over to kiss me softly before sitting down. Realizing Giovanni had been trying to taunt me, I tried to ignore what he'd said.

"Hey, sweetheart," she said with a naughty grin. "What were you thinking about? Was it something sexy?"

Actually, I'd been thinking about punching out Giovanni, but had managed to hold my anger. A uniformed midshipman starting a fight with a well-known campus agitator would be a local scandal. And I'd probably get the shit kicked out of me by the two bodyguards. All in all, it'd be a bad idea. "You know those guys?" I asked, trying to stay calm.

"I know who they are. At some of the planning meetings for the protests, they show up. I'm on the Committee, so I've talked with Giovanni and a few of his friends at the meetings. Why?"

"No reason," I lied. "Are we all set for dinner tonight?" Natalie had promised me a special home-cooked meal at her apartment.

"You betchum, Red Ryder. Just bring a nice bottle of Chianti and whatever else strikes your fancy. Six-thirty—OK? Gotta run—I've got a COBOL class coming up." She kissed me again and left me wondering what "COBOL" was.

I was at her apartment on time with the Chianti and, because I loved to make her happy, a nice bouquet of roses and some small flowers I couldn't identify. But I was still in a foul mood, Giovanni's crude comments about Natalie having festered in my jealous mind for hours.

My lovely girl was delighted with the flowers, kissing me so passionately that dinner was almost shelved. She finally broke away, flushed with arousal. "You can have your way with me, sailor-boy, but not until after dinner," she laughed. "Sheila's out of town on a field trip, so the place is ours."

"What are those little flowers?" I asked. "I recognized the roses."

"Those are impatiens."

"Wow! A flower named after me." At least I got another laugh.

Natalie's infectiously cheerful attitude helped me get through dinner ... and afterward. It wasn't until after we'd made love and were lying entwined on her bed that I brought up Giovanni.

"I was pretty mad about something when I saw you at the Union today," I told her.

"Mmmm," she sighed, snuggling closer. "And what could that have been?"

"That jerk Giovanni said something sexual about you," I mumbled.

"What'd he say?" she asked drowsily.

"He said he'd like to nail you, and he'd bet you'd love it," I said tightly.

"Fat chance," she said indignantly, sitting up to look down at me. "I've already found a guy who makes me completely happy. I don't need or want anyone else, especially Giovanni." She paused for suspense, and then smiled. "It's you I'm talking about, by the way."

"I know, honey," I said, my jealous anger ebbing. I pulled her back down, taking her more firmly into my arms.

"Oh, Jesus, not again," she sighed with a smile before kissing me deeply. After another long, slow lovemaking, both of us fell soundly asleep.

When I woke up, my anger about Giovanni's crudity had evaporated. Everything seemed to be fine with Natalie, and therefore in my world.

Early the next Monday morning I was sitting in the Union again, doing a last-minute review for a mid-term exam in my integrated circuits class, when I realized someone had come up to my table. Giovanni smiled down at me, his bodyguards looming behind him.

"Hey, stooge," he smirked, "I wanted you to know I banged the shit out of Natalie yesterday evening. It was just like I thought—she couldn't get enough. I love those cute noises she makes when she comes hard." He laughed and added, "But maybe you've never heard that." Then, looking at his watch, he said, "Sorry, gotta go. You know—governments to overthrow and all that." He strolled off, leaving me seething behind him.

19

I hadn't been with Natalie on Sunday. She'd planned a birthday party lunch for her father in the afternoon and had told me she had a Coordinating Committee meeting that evening. Since I had a Monday midterm, I'd spent Sunday getting ready for it. But now this lout was making me wonder if she'd lied to me so she could have a tryst with Rossi. The whole thing seemed unlikely, but Rossi's crude remarks had seemed strangely believable.

I went through my exam in a fog, not even sure I'd finished all the problems when I turned my paper in. I wanted to confront Natalie with my doubts, but had no idea how to do this without looking like I assumed she'd cheated on me. One more class and a three-hour lab period later, I still wasn't sure what to do. I decided we needed to talk in person, so I headed for her apartment.

As bad luck would have it, Sheila opened the door. I'd been hoping Natalie and I would have the place to ourselves for this possibly awkward talk. Sheila had made it clear from the time we first met that she wasn't in favor of my romance with Natalie.

"Sheila, it's nice to see you. Is Natalie in?" I was as polite as my stress level allowed.

"Sorry, Rick," she smiled maliciously. "She's at a friend's place. But I don't think you know him."

Was she gloating because she knew something I didn't want to? "Do you have a number? I need to get in touch with her." I was sure I was starting to sound desperate.

She smirked at me, then disappeared and came back with a scrap of paper on which she'd scribbled a phone number. "Goodbye, Rick," she said with a trace of smug finality that worried me. She'd sounded like she didn't expect to see me again.

Back at my apartment, I nervously dialed the number. A gruff male voice answered, "Yeah?"

Trying to sound like a faculty member, I said, "I understand Miss Montaigne may be at this number? Miss ... Natalie Montaigne? It's important I speak to her before her afternoon class tomorrow. Is she available?"

"Hold on."

A few minutes later, Natalie came on the phone. "This is Miss Montaigne. How may I help you?" she asked tentatively.

"Nat, it's Rick. Look, it's important I talk to you tonight. When you're finished over there, can we meet somewhere?"

She hesitated. "I suppose we should. How about we meet at the Union in an hour and a half or so? That'd make it about seven o'clock. See you then." She hung up, but not before I heard a man laughing in the background.

On a suspicion, I opened my East Bay telephone directory and looked up Giovanni Rossi. The phone number I'd dialed was his, but under the "Johnny Ross" name. So I knew she'd been meeting with him without telling me, but still didn't know whether she'd actually had sex with him. I had no idea how to handle this situation. I was desperate not to lose Natalie, but couldn't tolerate the idea of her being with another man—especially that crude slimeball.

Naturally, I was at the Union early. Natalie got there on time, looking solemn and worried. Before I could say anything, she blurted out, "I don't know how to say this, but ..."

My expression, I later realized, must have revealed all my fears. "Oh, baby," she whispered, "I don't want to hurt you. You have to understand that."

"What are you trying to say?" I asked, trying desperately to keep a whine out of my voice. "Are you with Giovanni now?"

"What? Oh, I see what you're thinking. No—I was at his place for one of the Committee meetings, that's all."

"He told me this morning that you and he had sex together yesterday," I managed to say. "I didn't want to believe him, but when I realized you were with him again tonight ..."

"Look," she said firmly, "I have not had and will never have sex with that man. He's a pig. But there *is* a problem and you and I have to talk about it." I'd learned years ago that when a woman said that we "had to talk," bad news was on the way.

Trying to get a grip on my turbulent emotions, I braced myself and waited.

"You're not making this easy for me," Natalie managed to say with a nervous laugh. "I ... I think you know how much you mean to me. I've never been as happy with anyone as you've made me, and I hope you understand that. But I've been thinking about us and what kind of future we might have. I know you'd do your best to make it work, but ..." Her voice trailed off and she lowered her head to stare down at the table, unable to meet my desperate gaze.

I seized her hand in mine. "What is it, Natalie? You know I'd do anything for you—what's the problem?"

She sighed and raised her head to look into my eyes, tears glistening in her lovely green eyes. "The problem is that I don't see a future for us. In June, you get commissioned and head off to nuclear power and submarine training, and then you'll have sea duty and spend most of your time away for years. There's no way for us to really be together. I think it'd be better if we were just friends from now on."

"Just friends" was, of course, girlie code for "I never want to see you again," but young women seemed to think it was a diplomatic way to drop the axe, as I'd already learned—several times. The male way was better—just stop calling them and ignore any messages they leave.

Now I was groveling. "Natalie, you should know how important you are to me. Please don't do this—I need you in my life. I know we can find a way to work this out. If it'll make you feel better, I won't volunteer for submarines. I can just go surface Navy and we could be together more." Of course, this would break the long-term plans that had been made for me, but she was more important to me than anything else in my life.

Staring down at the table, she murmured, "But you'd be giving up what you've dreamed of since you were a kid. You'd be on sea duty anyway and we still wouldn't be together the way we need to be. Rick, I wouldn't be a good Navy wife—I know that much about myself. I'd be unhappy and I'd make you unhappy too. Let's just end it now before we get too involved."

I'd been prepared for bad news, but this was a disaster. I took her hands and insisted, "We're already involved! You *are* my life, Natalie. You're more important than the Navy, or my engineering degree, or anything else. I need you. Tell me what I have to do to keep you."

Now she was crying openly. "This is the worst thing I've ever had to do, but I have to walk away from you. I'd ruin your dreams for the kind of life you want to live, and we'd end up desperately unhappy and maybe hating each other. Let's stop now before we spoil things."

"Stop now? That'd ruin everything for both of us forever, Natalie—don't you see that?" I could hear the whiny tone I'd been trying to suppress.

She shook her head mutely, got quickly to her feet, and rushed out of the Union, leaving me stunned and desolate. I didn't understand—I'd been sure she loved me as much as I did her. And the reason she gave didn't make sense to me. We'd discussed the amount of sea time I'd have, and she'd seemed to accept it as a necessary cost of marrying a naval officer. Now she insisted she couldn't do it. All I could do was to try to win her back.

Over the next week, I tried to phone her and to meet with her, but when she heard my voice on the phone, she'd hang up and when we encountered each other in public, she'd ignore me. After a few weeks, I had to admit I'd lost her. I adjusted my routes around campus to minimize the chance I'd run into her. If I couldn't be with her, I was better off not seeing her at all.

I sank briefly into a lethargy of despair until I realized I was jeopardizing my future. If my grades tumbled, Rickover[20] might not let me into the nuclear power program, and I absolutely had to get into that. I channeled all the energy I'd devoted to Natalie into my studies, planning to set aside my social life. Ironically, my lack of interest in chasing girls seemed to make me more attractive to them. Instead of having to identify and charm young ladies as I had my first three years, they were calling to ask me out. "If only I'd realized this a few years ago," I'd mused after agreeing to meet a shapely blonde the next evening.

All that had been over seven years ago, and I still couldn't get Natalie out of my mind. Now I'd be back in the States for a while. Maybe I'd have a chance to find someone just as entrancing and possibly more dedicated to me. After all, Natalie couldn't be unique, could she? If I worked my way through a large enough number of young women, statistically I should find someone who'd make me just as happy. With these thoughts, I fell into an uneasy fitful doze.

---

[20] Admiral Hyman Rickover, the eccentric founder of the Navy's nuclear power program, insisted on interviewing each officer candidate for nuclear power and personally approving him or, as happened frequently, rejecting him. The interviews were legendary for the often profane abuse Rickover would heap on each applicant. He was sarcastically referred to as KOG—the Kindly Old Gentleman.

Chapter 4

I LANDED at Andrews just after midnight local time, disoriented by the five-hour time zone change and dazed by my inability to sleep well on airplanes. Since it was too late to report in, I got a room at the BOQ[21] and fell into my bunk as soon as I'd stowed my gear. I was awakened from a deep sleep an hour later by a pounding on my door.

"Lieutenant Commander Halsted!" I heard foggily. "Are you in there?"

I stumbled to the door and opened it. A stocky captain in khakis pushed through the door, forcing me out of the way.

"I heard you were on that flight. Why didn't you report in?" the captain demanded. I saw he had three rows of ribbons, including one I thought was the Distinguished Flying Cross, below his gleaming gold naval aviator's wings.

"Jesus, Captain, it was after midnight when we landed. I figured on being there at 0700 tomorrow ... I mean, today," I corrected, realizing it was now the next day.

"Your orders said to report immediately on arrival. You're off to a bad start, Commander," the captain growled. He produced a bottle of Jack Daniel's. "But let's put that behind us and get acquainted a little bit before you report tomorrow. There are a couple of things you need to know before showing up at the office. Why don't you go down the hall and get us some ice?"

"Why don't you get it, Captain?" I snarled, still muddled by the wake-up call. "I'm still in my skivvy shorts." I realized, too late, that I'd just stepped over the invisible line of deference to a senior officer.

The captain laughed. "Let me give you a tip, son—don't try to boss me around. But just to be a nice guy, I'll get the ice and be right back. By the way, my name's Sammon—Jack Sammon—and I'll be your new boss." He handed the bottle to me and strolled down the hall as I struggled into my khaki pants and pulled on a T-shirt.

---

[21] BOQ = "Bachelor Officers' Quarters," known in the more politically correct Navy of the 21st century as "Unaccompanied Officer Personnel Housing," or UOPH. This is NOT high-quality housing.

A minute or so later Sammon was back with a plastic bucket of ice. He took a glass from my washstand, threw a few ice cubes in, poured four inches of Jack Daniel's into the glass, then repeated for his own drink.

"Now tell me," Sammon asked after taking a slug of his drink. "What makes you think you can work in naval intelligence?"

"Nothing, actually. I never asked for a job in intelligence. I wanted to go to PG school and get my master's degree in physical oceanography. But I got dragooned here, and I still don't know why."

"Well, ain't that the saddest story I ever heard," Sammon smiled. "Look, bubblehead[22], if you can handle the job I've got for you, you'll be able to write your own ticket—you may even be the first guy in your year group[23] to get command. But it's gonna be a tough job, especially for someone like you who's been sheltered from the rougher side of life."

I was getting tired of the repartee. "I'll tell you what, Captain. Why don't you just explain what the job is and I'll tell you why I am—or am not—the right person for the job."

Sammon eyed me appraisingly for a moment. "OK, here's the deal. We brought you in because we need a qualified submariner who's smart, can work hard on his own, and is sharp on submarine weapons systems. Now, what do you know about the submarine-launched Harpoon[24] missile?"

"What's your clearance level?" I asked. I actually didn't know much about Harpoon, other than what I'd learned from a one-hour presentation to a group of submarine officers in Pearl Harbor several months earlier. That dog-and-pony show had raised a lot more questions than it'd answered, but this was a good opportunity to stick it to him a little.

"You're going over the line, Commander! My clearance level is higher than anything you've ever heard of."

"So you say," I answered with a straight face. "But all I know about you is that you showed up in the wee hours of the morning dressed as a Captain and claiming to be the guy I'll be working for. You could be anyone; you might not even be a naval officer. Let's defer the Harpoon discussion until later, when I can get some proof about who you are and what I can tell you."

---

[22] A derogatory nickname for submariners, used by jealous surface ship sailors ("targets" or "skimmers") and aviators ("zoomies" or "airdales"). "Bubblehead" refers to the necessity for submariners to control the "bubble"—a device like a curved carpenter's level which displays the up or down angle of the submarine.

[23] An officer commissioned in 1968, for example, is in the 1968 year group, along with all other officers commissioned that year.

[24] The Harpoon missile, which would be introduced to the fleet in 1976, would be the US Navy's first deployable anti-surface ship cruise missile.

This earned me an icy stare from Sammon for a few seconds until he lost control and began laughing. "Maybe you'll work out after all. I like people with a suspicious mind; it's an asset in our kind of work. Let's just get acquainted for a few minutes and then I'll go away and let you sleep. I'll tell you what—sleep in a little. I won't expect you until 0800 instead of 0700. But it's at least an hour's cab ride, and the traffic around here sucks. So take that into account. By the way, it's civilian clothes—do *not* show up in a uniform. Now let's sit and get to know each other for a few minutes. Tell me about your early life—before you were in the Navy."

I explained I'd been born in northern California, just north of Bodega Bay. "That's an area the Russians tried to colonize back in the early 1800's, so there are a lot of people there who are ethnic Russians, which is what I am—at least five generations back. My dad died in an accident in a lumber mill, and my mom and I moved down to the Peninsula. She ended up remarrying. I took my stepfather's last name—I was only about twelve at the time."

Sammon looked at me speculatively. "Vy govorite po-russki?" he asked.

Laughing, I said, "I caught the word 'Russki,' but I don't speak the language, although my mom says I had a few words when I was little, like a lot of kids in the area did. I speak some German and a little conversational Spanish."

My potential new boss gave me a brief summary of his naval career. "I graduated from the Academy[25] and went straight into Flight School. After basic flight school, I decided to fly EF-10 electronic surveillance aircraft. A few years later I transitioned to the EA-6B[26] aircraft. I did OK and commanded a squadron operating out of Yankee Station in the Tonkin Gulf. We flew a lot of combat missions in that shitty war and I lost some guys out of my squadron. After my command tour, I drew an assignment as naval attaché in Moscow. I spent a year learning Russian before I went over. Had some interesting times there playing with the Commies."

Not a word about what he was doing now or what I might do. I let it lie—he'd have to tell me at some point what these mysterious orders were all about.

We traded a few sea stories, finished our drinks and then Sammon turned, gave a mock salute, and left, taking the bottle with him. Looking blearily at my watch, I figured I had time for a three-hour nap before I'd have to start getting ready for my new job, whatever it was.

---

[25] This meant Sammon was an IFNAG. (an Ignorant Naval Academy Graduate).

[26] The EA-6B was a variant of the A-6 Intruder. It was configured for electronic jamming and carried a crew of four.

Chapter 5

A T 0700 I showed up, in a civilian suit, at the address specified in my orders. I'd spent a fortune in cab fare—over $15!—to get from Andrews to Arlington, and hoped I'd be reimbursed through the Navy's unpredictable travel pay process. I was still a little pissed at Sammon and didn't want to be late, despite my new boss giving me some leeway.

The building looked like an ordinary office structure populated by commercial clients. There was no indication in my paperwork as to the name or suite number of the organization I was to report to. Maybe this was a test in which I had to display the intelligence and initiative Sammon told me he was looking for. Before approaching the guard at the desk, I scanned the names on the board in the lobby and saw "International Security Associates" in suite 501. That sounded like a good cover name for a bunch of spooks.

Walking up to the guard, I said, "My name is Rick Halsted. I have an appointment with Mr. Sammon in 501."

He consulted a list. "You mean 703. You're on the list to see him. I'll call him for you." Looking over his shoulder, I saw the company in 703 was "Motivational Consulting, Inc."

A few minutes later Sammon, wearing a business suit and looking like he'd had a full night's sleep, came out of the elevator. "Rick," he said with a polite smile, "I'm glad you could make it. Thanks for coming in at this early hour."

"My pleasure, Mr. Sammon," I assured him for the guard's benefit. It was harder than I'd imagined not to address him with his rank as proper naval etiquette demanded, but being irritated with him for interrupting my sleep last night helped.

"Well, come on up and let me show you our digs," Sammon said heartily. "I think you'll be impressed with our layout."

"I understand your company is doing great work in the motivational area," I offered, not having much else to say, but feeling it'd be nice to leave the guard feeling this was a legitimate business visit. Sammon winked at me as we headed for the elevators.

As we entered the elevator, he put a finger to his lips and we rode in silence up to the seventh floor. The office suite for "Motivational Consulting" was, I supposed, typical for a small company.

A tall blonde receptionist greeted us with a smile. "This must be Mr. Halsted," she said. "I'm Debbie. Can I get you anything—coffee, tea, a Danish ...?"

"Hot tea and a Danish would be very nice, thanks, Debbie, and please call me Rick," I managed to say before Sammon pulled me down the hall and into a corner office, shutting the door behind us. I'd been told I was one of the three officers in the United States Navy who weren't coffee addicts. I never found out who the other two were.

"Before we start," he said with a sardonic smile, tossing a file folder onto the desk, "here are my security clearance credentials. If you'd like to make sure they aren't forged, Debbie can give you a Pentagon telephone directory and you can call the Naval Intelligence office there. Dial it yourself so you can be sure you're talking to the right people. Ask for the director—Admiral Robards—and identify yourself. He's my reporting superior and will verify my clearance."

"Thanks, Captain," I managed to say, scanning the papers quickly. I had no idea how to identify fake security clearance documents. "But would it be OK if I called him after you've given me some idea as to what you're looking for? Maybe after you tell me exactly what has to be done we'll agree I'm not the right person for the job."

Debbie came in with a large mug of tea and a plate with pastries on it. I thanked her and added some sugar to my tea. After she shut the door, Sammon began, "Here's a five-thousand foot view to get you oriented. After all, we know everything about you, but so far you don't know anything about us."

I was sourly amused at how far off Sammon was. He *was* correct that I didn't know anything about his organization. But nobody knew everything about another person.

He went on, "First of all, I'm a counter-intelligence officer. I work with the Naval Investigative Service—NIS[27], but don't belong to it; I'm on loan from ONI[28]. I'm sure you've heard that NIS offices handle primarily criminal matters and are staffed with civilian Special Agents. My operation is a special counter-espionage unit focused on a specific mission. This operation is special, and is outside the normal purview of NIS. Are you with me so far?"

---

[27] Since 1992, known as NCIS.

[28] Office of Naval Intelligence. As well as gathering intelligence on potential enemies, this organization is also responsible for identification of spies and saboteurs.

I nodded, and Sammon continued, "You've probably heard of a big company called Federated Aviation Systems. In fact ..." He paused to leaf through a folder in front of him. "Yes, I see you actually visited them on your senior engineering field trip from Cal. As you know, it's headquartered in Sunnyvale, not far from where you grew up, and has factories scattered around the country. It's the lead contractor on a new program for the Navy. The code name of this project is Outlaw Shark—that title is classified Secret, by the way. The idea is to give SSN's an over-the-horizon[29] missile targeting capability by downloading ocean surveillance data from a communications satellite into a new module that'll tie into the fire control system. Next year they'll start shipping the new Harpoon missiles to the fleet, and it'd be nice to be able to use them effectively. Do you see where I'm going with this?"

I nodded again—the submarine community had been buzzing with talk for over a year on exactly how we could employ an anti-ship missile with a range of over sixty miles. There was no way a submarine using its onboard sensors could be certain that a surface target at that range was an enemy combatant. And at sixty miles, a sonar contact would have to be via the second convergence zone[30] path, adding more uncertainty to the firing solution. It didn't seem prudent to lob a missile out hoping it'd land on a bad guy instead of a neutral or even a good guy, but no one I'd talked to had figured out how to solve this target identification problem.

"OK," Sammon said, "naturally the Soviets found out that we're working on how to solve this problem and, to put it mildly, they're very interested in finding out how we do it, so they can either sabotage Outlaw Shark or adopt it for their own use against us—or maybe both, the bastards. We don't want them to do that." The last sentence had, I thought, a patronizing sarcastic edge to it.

"I understand the Soviets getting this technology would be a Bad Thing," I acknowledged, ignoring his condescension and trying to pronounce the capital letters distinctly.

---

[29] The Navy abbreviation for this is "OTH"

[30] A "convergence zone" sonar contact is achieved at long distances because of the bending of sound waves first down and then back up in an deep-water environment. CZ's occur at ranges that are multiples of roughly 30 nautical miles. In a given situation, the first CZ might be at about 28 miles, the next at 56, and the third at 84 nautical miles. The actual interval width depends on the sound velocity profiles in each area. In between those ranges, you wouldn't have any CZ sonar contact on the target.

Acting as if I hadn't said anything, Sammon went on, "The problem is that our sources indicate that the Soviets—more specifically, the KGB[31]—may have already set up an operation in the Bay Area to penetrate this project. So your job—or the job of whoever we end up selecting in the event you don't get the job—will be to work on the project team as a civilian employee of Federated. As far as anyone there will know, you're a former naval officer named Rick Halsted. Your cover story is who you really are, except they'll be told you got out of the Navy because you were dissatisfied with your career prospects. Your job will be to discover if information from that program is being leaked, and to identify the people involved in those leaks."

I must have looked skeptical, because he said, "Look, Rick—if I can call you that—if you feel this isn't something you're comfortable doing, just say so. We can probably get your PG school orders reinstated, and you can leave with no hard feelings."

But I'd have a black mark in my record to reflect I'd turned down an important assignment. And, of course, I'd lose my spot promotion. It looked to me I had to go through with this.

"Why couldn't I work there as a naval officer—what I really am? I could be assigned there as a liaison to make sure the project was coming along as expected."

"We thought about that," he conceded, "but decided it'd be better if you were an insider, rather than an outside liaison type. That way you'll be working with the other people in the department on a daily basis. We considered setting up a false identity for you, but since you're from the Bay Area, there's a good chance you'd run into someone who knows you, so that'd be too dangerous." I nodded.

"We need someone who seems to be a civilian working this deal— for one thing, you'll be accepted more readily by the people you'll be working with. As an expert in submarine fire control systems, you're a logical person for Federated Aviation to hire."

"Why don't you use one of your own guys? You must have people who've already been trained in intelligence. I don't know anything about it, so they'd be bound to be better at this kind of work," I argued.

---

[31] *Komitet Gosudarstvennoy Bezopasnosti,* or "Committee for State Security," the national intelligence and security organization, operates in competition with the GRU. The KGB (aka "The Sword and Shield of the Party") and the GRU (military intelligence) are natural rivals, the first working for the Communist Party (Government and Communist Party Politburo) and the other for the military. Within the KGB, the First Directorate is responsible for gathering foreign intelligence.

"They wouldn't have any credibility—there's no reason why Federated would hire someone without specialized knowledge in this area. It'll be easier to give you training in the kind of intelligence work you'll be doing than to teach them enough about submarines and their fire control systems to make them believable. It has to be you or someone else with a similar background. And you came highly recommended by your CO, although I'm not sure why." That last phrase may have been an example of his sense of humor.

After a long silence, I finally asked, "What kind of training would I need?"

"Well, that'll be the fun part—maybe not for you, but at least for us," Sammon smiled. "We're going to cram a year's worth of training for new NIS types into a couple of months for you. You'll learn basic security procedures—how to shadow someone, how to keep from being trailed, and methods to obtain and analyze information about the people you'll be working with. We'll train you in safe and lock work, and, just for fun, some hand-to-hand combat and weapons training. You'll be educated on how the Soviets organize their espionage activities in the U.S. and what seems to work best in counter-espionage. When you finish training, you'll be a semi-spook—not quite the real thing, but close enough for this mission. But you're going to have to put in a lot of work—probably a minimum of twelve hours a day, six or seven days a week—to get all this done. Are you up to it?"

I had to admit it intrigued me—it'd certainly be more interesting than postgraduate school. Captain Schneider might have been right about the upside to this assignment. A twelve-hour day would be a piece of cake compared to my eighteen and twenty-hour workdays on an SSN. Finally, the upside from doing well in this assignment might be enough to propel my career upward. "All I can say is that I'll give it my best, sir."

Sammon sat back and surveyed me for what seemed like minutes, although it was probably only a few seconds. "Let's go for it," he finally said and stood, holding his hand out. "Welcome to our team, Commander." I shook it, wondering if I'd made the right decision. I'd been offered a way out, but since backing out might have hurt my prospects, this was probably my best career alternative. Besides, I had to admit, the spot promotion felt good, even if I couldn't talk about it to anyone.

"Next," Sammon said, seeming relieved the decision had been made, "Admiral Robards will grant you an SCI[32] clearance for this project based on your SBI[33], which is still current. That'll take a day or two to come through. In the meantime, you've got some logistical issues to take care of. Today you'll move out of that BOQ and into an apartment we have available here in Arlington—you won't have time to waste on a long commute, and the apartment's only a few blocks from here. Debbie will run you back to Andrews to pick up your gear and then to the apartment. The price is right—it's free for the time you'll be using it, since we prepaid the lease for use on another project that we just wrapped up."

Sammon went on, "You'll also need to do some clothes shopping so you can fit in at Federated. We'll advance you money for that, and Debbie will help you pick out what you need. You can do that this afternoon."

"I can choose my own clothes, sir," I said, irritated by the insinuation that I didn't have good taste. I mean, I was wearing what I thought was my best suit. Most of my civilian stuff was still at the BOQ back in San Diego.

"Based on what you're wearing, I think you might find her advice very helpful," Sammon grinned. "Just accept her judgment and everything will go fine. She's a California girl, and knows these kinds of things. Oh, one more thing."

"Yes?" I asked suspiciously.

"Actually, I think you'll like this part. You'll still be getting your Navy pay, although it'll still be as a Lieutenant—the spot promotion doesn't affect your pay. You'll also have your salary from Federated. They're bringing you in at about $14,000 a year. So as long as this assignment lasts—probably at least six months—you'll be legally double-dipping. You'll have some extra expenses to take care of, like the clothes you're buying and some other stuff we'll talk about later. This'll be a lot easier than having to submit expense reports. Your Navy pay will be automatically deposited in your Navy Federal Credit Union checking account in San Diego." He seemed to know a lot about the details of my life, but I supposed that was his job. No problem, just so long as he didn't know too much.

---

[32] SCI = "Sensitive Compartmented Information." A "compartmented" clearance is at Top Secret level, but access to SIC material is limited to those who have been admitted to the compartment itself, which often has a special code word or phrase identifying it.

[33] SBI = "Special Background Investigation," a very intensive (and intrusive) in-depth probing of the candidate's background, including interviews with people who knew the candidate well at various stages of his or her life.

Sammon was right—having the two salaries was good news. I'd been worried about paying for my new wardrobe, as well as the cost of living in California, but it sounded as though I'd have more than enough cash coming in to support what would be a strange new lifestyle. My civilian pay would be almost exactly what my Navy pay was as a lieutenant (not counting submarine pay), so I was effectively getting a temporary doubling in salary.

On the way out of Sammon's office, I stopped to ask Debbie for the phone directory. I memorized Admiral Robard's phone number; years ago I'd been trained in memorization. Although I was taking Sammon at his word so far, it'd be nice to be able to contact someone higher in the food chain if things started to go south on me.

Chapter 6

DEBBIE whirled me around Washington for the rest of that day and most of the next. Within two hours of leaving the office with her, I found myself in a small and sparsely furnished apartment in Rosslyn which, I was stunned to learn, rented for over $300 a month. I was starting to understand the DC area was even more expensive than California. Then it was time for my new wardrobe.

Equipped with a credit card, Debbie pushed me through three or four men's clothing stores. I ended up with eight suits, three pairs of dress shoes, at least two dozen shirts and an equal number of ridiculously expensive silk ties, as well as belts, socks, and so on. Surveying my existing everyday wardrobe with a raised eyebrow after we brought the new suits and accessories back to the apartment, Debbie said thoughtfully, "I think I'd better give you a hand with some casual clothes also. I mean, you've got to pass as a California guy."

"I *am* a California guy," I insisted defensively. "I went to middle school and high school just south of the City and graduated from Cal Berkeley. Besides, most of my civilian clothes are still in San Diego; this is just what I had on the boat." I decided not to tell her that these were what I believed were my best casual clothes.

"You've been out to sea a while. Things have changed," she smiled. "Come on—this'll be fun." It wasn't. I'd never enjoyed shopping and detested clothes shopping in particular, which may have been one reason my wardrobe had amused Debbie. At the end of the day, I had what she called "the basics" of what I should wear in California. "Just buy stuff like this when you get out there," she told me firmly, "and you'll be fine."

I looked at my watch. "I should get back to the office. Maybe my security clearance has come through."

"On the way we'll pick up a car for you out of our motor pool. It won't be much, but it'll do, especially because you can walk to the office. When you get a few days to spare, you can fly to San Diego, pick up your own car and whatever else you have there and drive it up to the Bay Area. That way it'll be ready when you move out there in a few months. Captain Sammon can arrange military flights in both directions. Do you have somewhere in the Bay Area to put the car and your stuff?"

"My folks live a little south of SFO. I'm sure it'll be OK to leave everything there for a while."

"You'll need some other stuff that has to do with the training," she smiled. "More shopping! Let's go." Off we went again, this time buying athletic shoes, workout clothes, and some free weights, which she assured me I'd use enough to make the purchase worthwhile.

At the end of the day, I was holding a stack of credit card receipts showing me I'd spent about two months of my Navy salary on stuff I hadn't thought I needed. This would, I was sure, be withheld from my Navy pay until I'd paid it back. Debbie assured me I was well equipped, at least sartorially, for my assignment.

Then the training began. Many of the daytime hours—and some night hours too—were devoted to activities such as learning the principles of tailing someone without being spotted, and of reversing the technique by making sure you weren't yourself being trailed. I did this on foot, in cars, on city streets, on interstate highways, and in sparsely populated rural areas. Finally Sammon grudgingly proclaimed me "barely capable" in this area.

I worked on breaking and entering techniques, including lock-picking and safe work, and in parallel with that, methods to set up traps in my own rooms so I'd know if someone had entered in my absence.

Probably just because Sammon had a sadistic streak, I spent at least two hours a day on hand-to-hand combat training, progressing slowly and very painfully from complete ineptitude to the point where my instructor told me I might be able to subdue a drunken midget. I shot at least fifty rounds from a 9 mm pistol almost every evening, starting with regular targets and progressing to a pop-up combat range. To my surprise, I became very good at making quick accurate shots at the pop-ups. When I completed that satisfactorily, I began practicing with an M16 rifle. I ran miles each day, with my times recorded and merciless pressure to run faster and farther. I had no idea how this stuff related to my job; I suspected it was hazing.

In my spare hours, I studied the history and management structure of Federated Aviation and classified documents on ocean surveillance systems. I took to ordering in from take-out restaurants and spent most evenings studying in the apartment. I had to get through this as quickly as possible so I could get out to Federated and start the real work on my assignment.

I was tutored at irregular intervals by mysterious gentlemen whose names I was never told. Their areas of expertise varied, but all were focused on counter-espionage techniques. I learned common methods of espionage used by Soviet bloc countries inside the US, and which methods had been used to try to counteract them. None of our counterespionage methods, I was told, had actually worked very well, and my tutors didn't seem to have many examples of where the espionage had been totally thwarted. "In lots of ways," one of my instructors told me glumly, "the Soviets have it all over us in espionage. They probably know things that we think we've kept perfectly secure. If it ever comes to a shooting war, we're pretty likely to get some very unpleasant surprises." He was probably right.

These experts told me that the most likely Soviet group trying to penetrate Outlaw Shark would be the KGB. "But there's a GRU[34] contingent based out of the Soviet Consulate in San Francisco, so you might run into them too," I was warned. On the bright side, I was advised that "Those guys don't like each other much, by the way, so they may wind up causing each other problems while they're trying to spy on us."

I also learned techniques for communicating back to Sammon. I wasn't to use my office or home phone to call Sammon, but at the same time, I should avoid raising suspicion by being seen using the same payphone too frequently, so I'd have to be careful to be careful to choose a different one each time. Sammon handed me a phone number. "That's a toll-free number to let you call here from payphones without a bucketful of quarters. Now, about telephoning—I won't talk to you on your personal phone. If I need you to call me, I'll page you. You'll go to a payphone and call back. As far as passing physical items, I have a guy in Sunnyvale who can pass hard-copy material back and forth. I'll tell you about him later."

The only recreation I'd had was a few nights spent picking up young ladies. The DC area seemed to have a surplus of attractive young women, so I didn't have much trouble finding temporary relationships. After the intensive sea duty on *BOWFIN*, this was definitely a change for the better. Happily, none of these young women seemed to have any interest in a serious liaison; they were in it for the fun, just like I was.

A serious relationship didn't seem to be in my near-term future; I wouldn't be at Federated long enough for that to happen. If I did my job properly, I couldn't see any way I'd be there longer than six or so months. If I hadn't solved the problem by then, I was pretty sure Sammon would yank me out and ship me back to the Submarine Force with a bad fitness report[35]. Either way, there didn't seem to be much point in getting into a serious relationship with a young lady out there. For it to be meaningful,

---

[34] *Glavnoye Razvedyvatel'noye Upravleniye,* or "Main Intelligence Directorate of the General Staff," the intelligence and special operations directorate of the Soviet military. A major thorn in the side of the KGB, and vice versa.

[35] Officers receive regular fitness reports written by their commanding officer. These are the primary basis for making promotion decisions, so an officer's career flourishes (or not) based on these reports. A single negative report can ruin a career.

she'd have to be at least as alluring as my lost Natalie. What were the odds on that? I decided the DC way—casual sex with no commitment—would be the way to go in the Bay Area.

After about six weeks of training, Sammon called me into his office on a Monday morning. "How's it going so far?" he asked. I was sure he already knew very well how it was going, but wanted to see what I'd tell him.

"Other than getting the crap beat out of me on a daily basis in the hand-to-hand combat training, it's a hell of a lot easier than qualifying in submarines. I think I've got a good handle on what you wanted me to learn."

"So you think our training is easy?" Sammon asked sarcastically.

"Come on, Captain—what if I suggested it was easy to get naval aviator's wings? Other than the physical stuff, what I've done here is butt-simple compared to what a submariner has to master. The book learning—and the weapons training—have gone fine. What else do I need to get done before I head out to Sunnyvale?"

"Ideally, there'd be more training on the counter-espionage aspects. From what I hear, you've acquired a solid knowledge of how the KGB and GRU work, and on methods to find out how information might be leaking. And from whom. Let me ask this—do you feel prepared to go out there and do this assignment? There's some personal danger involved in this—the Soviets don't mind leaving a few bodies around, as long as they can't be traced directly to them."

I gave this some serious thought, but finally shrugged it off. If the Soviets wanted to kill me, they'd probably succeed. I didn't see any way Sammon and his group could provide enough additional training in a few weeks to help my odds much.

"I think I'm set," I told Sammon. "If there's anything I need, it's probably more practice on tailing and making sure I'm not being tailed myself, but we could probably do that in a day or two."

Sammon looked at me thoughtfully. "I'll set that up. Today's September 22. Let's say you'll start at Federated two weeks from today. I'll let our guy there know so he can prepare the paperwork accordingly. That should give you time to finish up here and then get settled out there before work starts. Debbie's arranged a going-away party for you next Tuesday. You'll fly west the next day." He'd apparently anticipated I was coming to the end of my training, but since he'd certainly been getting regular updates on my progress, that wasn't a surprise. I didn't particularly like the man, but he was efficient.

I was pretty sure going-away parties weren't normally associated with intelligence training, but since I'd missed my farewell soiree on *BOWFIN*, this might be a nice substitute. I'd gotten along well with my instructors, although I was still a little pissed about what I considered the unnecessary roughness of my hand-to-hand combat instructor. The man seemed to get a little more pleasure than was polite out of slamming me around.

During the last few days, Sammon passed detailed information to me regarding people I'd contact locally. The most important, a former aviation electronics technician who'd been in Sammon's squadron, was now Chief of Detectives in the Sunnyvale Police Department. He was going to be my document-passer, among other things.

"His name is Norm Connors," Sammon explained. "I already contacted him and let him know your general situation, so he'll be expecting to hear from you. Use him as a go-between when you have something important. Make sure you aren't being tailed when you meet him. You can pass him a document and he'll get it to me. Use him sparingly, but he's absolutely trustworthy. If you have to get something here as reliably as possible, use Norm. Keep in mind he doesn't need to know the details of what you're doing."

My contact at Federated would be Dick Detweiler, a manager in the Personnel Department. Sammon explained, "He already has the paperwork set up so you look like a normal new hire. He's making copies of the personnel records of everyone who's involved with the Outlaw Shark project—both the regular records and whatever classified stuff they have on these people. Pick those up from him a few days before you start work so you have time to go through them before meeting your new co-workers. Here's his office phone number; when you're ready, call him from a payphone and set up a meeting. You'll need to go through those files thoroughly so you know all you can about those people—one or more of them may be feeding information to the Soviets, or be vulnerable to blackmail so they can be forced into doing that. You know what to look for, right?"

I nodded. I'd had days of training on how the Soviets recruited agents, and on how they used blackmail, money, or sex to "persuade" someone into betraying the US. Besides the ones who were coerced into helping, there were "volunteers" who wanted to help World Communism. My instructors had gone through dozens of case histories on how we'd caught some of these people by investigating details of their private lives.

"Remember, even though Detweiler has a higher position at Federated than yours, he's working for you on this project. Don't take any crap from him, and make sure he does whatever you need to have done. He has a bit of an attitude, so if you have any trouble with him, let me know. I'll bring him back into line." Clearly, Sammon had something on the unfortunate Detweiler.

41

My going-away party Tuesday was more elaborate than I'd anticipated. It was held in a private room at the Fort Myer's Officers' Club in Arlington, and was attended by almost everyone I'd had contact with over the past few months, including my sadistic hand-to-hand combat instructor and excluding the nameless people who'd taught me counter-espionage.

Sammon gave me the medals and ribbons for Expert Pistol and Expert Rifle. "Add those to your measly collection of awards," he said with a straight face.

Lastly, he asked Debbie to come up. "Rick, we'll miss you," she said, and kissed me on the cheek. "Here's a little something to remember us by." She handed me a nicely wrapped and surprisingly heavy package. I opened it to find a new 9 mm Beretta pistol, complete with a shoulder holster and a cleaning kit.

"Just thought it might come in handy," Sammon laughed. "You never know. Besides, it'd be a shame to let you get sloppy with your weapons skills after all your training."

The party broke up shortly after the awards. I was pleased to get what seemed to be sincere best wishes from everyone. The last to shake my hand was my combat instructor. He wished me the best of luck and apologized for his overzealous attitude. "I had to make sure you can handle yourself," he said. "You'll do fine."

The next morning I took a United flight to San Francisco International.

Chapter 7

MY FLIGHT landed at San Francisco International in early afternoon on Wednesday. From there it was a short cab ride to where my mother and stepfather lived in San Mateo.

They were glad to see me and happy I'd be in the Bay Area. I'd already told them I'd gotten out of the Navy and was taking a job at Federated in Mountain View. They'd been surprised I'd suddenly decided to quit the Navy. In fact, my mom pulled me aside to ask if I was sure I knew what I was doing. I assured her I did, but she was still upset at my decision.

"Talk to your Uncle Peter when you get a chance—he may have some good advice for you. Right now he's away on a trip somewhere, but I know he'll want to see you when he gets back." I promised I'd talk to him at my earliest opportunity, but I intended to wait for him to contact me. Pete, who was only an honorary uncle, wasn't easy to fool, and I wanted to make sure I had a good story before meeting him.

A month earlier, I'd taken a few days to fly from DC down to San Diego to bring my car and personal belongings up to San Mateo, so I now had the little I owned in one place. I'd withdrawn some funds from my savings account at the Navy Federal Credit Union in San Diego, so I had more than enough cash to handle immediate expenses.

The first item on my list was to find a suitable apartment. Drawing two salaries, I could afford something nice, but to avoid raising suspicions, I'd have to pick one that I could clearly afford just on my Federated salary. But whatever I picked was almost sure to be luxury compared to a BOQ room.

The next morning I drove down to Sunnyvale. I was looking for a location convenient to Federated Aviation with lots of single tenants, so I could blend in. Within a few hours, I found what I was looking for. The Carillon Apartments was a "singles only" complex of about five hundred apartments. It included two large swimming pools, several outdoor hot tubs, and a large recreation facility with banquet rooms, pool tables and a two-lane bowling alley. It was just off the Lawrence Expressway, only a few miles from Federated.

There were several apartments vacant. I wanted an apartment above ground level to minimize security issues, such as having KGB or GRU agents coming and going in and out of my apartment as they pleased. Luckily, there was a unit available on the third floor of one of the buildings. It was a one-bedroom furnished apartment and had a balcony overlooking one of the pools. I'd have preferred not to have the balcony, as it offered a possible way for someone to bypass the front door and get into the apartment, but I could find a way to discourage that sort of behavior.

"It gets a little noisy at night by the pool, especially on Friday and Saturday," the manager warned me.

"That won't be a problem," I assured her. If I could sleep on a submarine, I could sleep with a little pool noise, and this place was nice. Better than anywhere I'd lived since starting college, but since I'd been living in Bachelor Officer Quarters, that was a low bar. I put down two months' rent in advance and a cleaning deposit, and was handed the keys and a brochure showing the layout of all the buildings and parking areas along with information on activities within the complex.

The next morning in San Mateo I loaded almost all my personal belongings into my car. I left anything suggesting a current association with the Navy; there couldn't be any sign of that in my apartment. The normal souvenirs—ship's plaques, commendation letters, framed photos, and so on—I could display in the apartment without raising any eyebrows. I'd received my "going away" package from *BOWFIN*, including a plaque and a large framed color photo of the submarine running at high speed on the surface, signed by the entire wardroom. All that could be put on a wall in my apartment. I'd hidden my Navy ID card at the bottom of a box of uniform accessories that I'd left at home.

I drove down to Sunnyvale and stowed my clothing in the closet and bureaus. Most of the rest of the day was spent buying towels, sheets, cleaning supplies, food staples, and a few cooking and eating utensils in addition to the basic inventory the apartment came with. On the way, I stopped at Wells Fargo and opened a checking and a savings account, using an NFCU cashier's check for $3,000. There was still over $29,000 in my NFCU savings. Navy salaries aren't high, but living expenses are low when you live in government-provided quarters and spend most of your time at sea, so I'd had most of my pay automatically deposited in savings.[36]

---

[36] Rick had also benefited from "Nuclear Continuation Pay," a monetary incentive for nuclear-trained officers to stay on active duty beyond their minimum commitment of five years.

Using a temporary check, I bought my small mountain of supplies. It took an hour to unload my supplies and put them away. Once that was done, I sat with a beer and flipped through the brochure the manager had given me. I discovered that each weekend night there was an informal get-together in the main clubhouse. Maybe that'd be an opportunity to find an understanding—and temporary—young lady.

I spent a few hours getting my WestPac[37] stereo system set up and organizing the apartment well enough that if someone happened to visit I wouldn't have to apologize for all the mess. That made it time for dinner, so I headed out to a steak restaurant on El Camino. "Enough for one day," I told myself aloud as I came back from dinner.

---

[37] "WestPac" = Western Pacific, where Pacific Fleet naval vessels routinely deploy. In the 1960's and 70's, port visits to Japan, Hong Kong, and the Philippines offered the opportunity to buy excellent audio electronics at very low prices.

Chapter 8

I WOKE in a good mood; no one had shaken me awake in the middle of the night to tell me it was my turn to stand a watch. Today's priority was to get security arrangements set up for my apartment. I'd start by talking to Norm Connors, the Chief of Detectives in Sunnyvale. My phone had been activated, so I called the police department and was soon connected to Connors.

"This is Rick Halsted," I said. "Jack Sammon suggested I should get in touch with you when I got into town. I was wondering if you had any time free so we could talk briefly. I know you're pretty busy, but ..."

Connors interrupted me. "Sure, Rick. Glad you called. How about we meet for lunch? Maybe 11:30?" He suggested a restaurant called "The Jury Room" near the Sunnyvale Courthouse on El Camino and hung up. I realized—too late—that I should have called Connors from somewhere other than my apartment. In fact, hadn't Sammon told me that? It'd be nice if there were some way to call people without using your home phone or driving to a payphone. You'd think with all these electronic geniuses in the Bay Area, someone would invent some kind of phone you could carry around. But that was a little too "Buck Rogers" to hope for. You'd have to plug it into a phone outlet wherever you were. And would anyone want to receive telephone calls anywhere at any time? Not such a good idea.

Next, I started flipping through the Yellow Pages to find an alarm company. I wanted the apartment secure as quickly as I could. Sammon's people had taught me not to leave anything in the apartment that could damage my cover story of being an ex-naval officer or worse, anything that might indicate I was at Federated for something other than a legitimate job. I found several alarm companies listed, but realized Connors might know which company was best.

My next step was to set up a safe deposit box under a false name. Sammon had given me some excellent false documentation that I could use to set up a different bank account and, more importantly, a safe deposit box. On the way to meet Connors, I went to a Bank of America branch and opened up another savings account under the name of Larry Unfeld, presenting a California driver's license and Social Security card as identification. I chose the largest size safe deposit box they had

47

available, since I had no idea how bulky the file copies Detweiler was making for me would be.

I got to the Jury Room a few minutes before 11:30, and walked in, looking around for someone in police uniform. A tall dark-haired man who looked to be in his forties, wearing a well-tailored gray suit, stood up and waved. "Rick—over here," he called.

We shook hands and I sat down. Norm said, "Glad to see you. I talked to Jack last week, and he said you'd be calling. Naturally, Jack being Jack, he didn't tell me squat about what you're supposed to be doing, but I didn't expect him to. How can I help you?"

"Well, he told me that if I needed to get something to him quickly, I could do it through you. I have ... other means, I suppose I'd have to say, for routine stuff, but something may come up where I need help. He told me you're a busy guy, so I don't plan on bothering you very often."

"Sure, I'll be glad to do whatever I can. Here's my card; my pager number's on it so you can reach me any time. I understand you won't be doing this often, but I'm thinking that when you do need my help, it'll be important you can get in touch with me quickly, right?"

"Absolutely. By the way, I'm now living in your jurisdiction. Here's my address and phone number." I handed him a notepad sheet with my contact information.

"The Carillon Apartments," Connors smiled as he read the address. "I assume you're single. If so, you'll have a good time at the Pussy Palace—that place has quite the reputation. When did you move in?"

"Just yesterday. I'm still getting settled." I explained that I'd set up a safe deposit box under an assumed name, and that I was planning to have an alarm system installed.

"OK," Connors said, pulling a notepad out of his jacket pocket. He wrote on it, tore out the sheet and handed it to me. "Call this alarm company and ask for Wes Sheeley. Tell him I recommended his company, and that you need a 'special' alarm system installed. That'll protect you a lot better, and the price will be fair."

Over lunch, Connors explained how, when he got out of the Navy after a five-year hitch, he'd started as a patrolman in the Sunnyvale police and rapidly made his way up the ranks in the detective department, which he currently headed. "I worked for Jack Sammon for most of the time I was in—I was a new air-crewman and he was the pilot on the EA-6B I crewed on. Once I proved I could do the job, he dropped a lot of his hard-ass attitude and we got along well."

I asked Norm about his job. "Sounds like it might be pretty interesting," I offered.

"Not as much as you might think," he shrugged. "Most of the crimes around here are burglary or other petty crap. We get a few murders, but almost all of them are domestic—wife killing a husband or vice versa. A

48

rape or a burglary now and then. There's no organized crime to speak of, except for a few small-time guys peddling grass. And with all the single chicks here, there's very little prostitution—too much free competition. San Jose and Oakland and, naturally, the City, have big-time problems with hard drugs, but that hasn't hit us yet. On the other hand, the way this area is building up, that probably won't last long."

Connors didn't ask any personal questions, probably understanding that whatever I said would be fiction.

"Where are the restrooms here?" I asked.

He jerked a hand over his shoulder. "Back there. Make sure you use the right one," he smiled.

I didn't know what was so funny until I saw they were labeled "Hung" and "Split"—not bad for a tavern called The Jury Room.

"Do you have a personal weapon?" he asked me as the waitress brought the check. I grabbed it and put down a twenty to cover both of us with a generous tip.

"I have a 9 mm Beretta," I answered. "Should I register it or get a license of some sort?"

"Do you have it with you?"

"Don't have a carry permit yet. Right now it's in the apartment. I was trying to figure out where to put it so it'd be secure but I could still get to it in a hurry."

"I've got something out in the car that'll help you with the 'where to put it' problem. Jack sent it to me last week," Connors said. "Follow me out and I'll give it to you. Come by my office this afternoon with the weapon. I'll get the paperwork done to get you a concealed carry. How'd you get it, by the way?"

"Uh, it was kind of my going-away present from Jack," I admitted.

"Typical Jack," Connors laughed.

We went out to Connors' car. "If your car's not nearby, you should drive it over. This thing would be difficult to carry around the parking lot," Norm told me.

"I'm right there," I said, pointing to my car a couple of spaces away.

Connors opened the trunk on his car and hauled out a wide flat box. I could tell it was heavy as he levered it out of the trunk and set it upright on the ground. "What is it?" I asked.

"It's a wall safe. Jack wants you to install it in your apartment. It has an electronic lock, so it's more difficult to break into than a traditional tumbler safe. Wes will be able to install it for you. One hint—every time after you close it, wipe down the keypad with a damp cloth. A clever burglar will dust the keypad so see which keys you hit—that makes it easier for him to find the five-digit combination to open it. Don't leave it in plain sight—put a big picture or a mirror over it. You might as well

49

make the intruder work a little." I already knew this from my training at NIS, but Norm didn't need to know that, so I nodded appreciatively.

I opened my own trunk and went back to pick up the safe. The package weighed about sixty pounds and had no handles. I was straining to carry it over, but was determined to do it and make it look easy. I set it into the trunk with a sigh of relief and shut the lid.

"Thanks, Norm. Is there a good time to come by this afternoon?"

"Unless something comes up, I'll be there doing paperwork, so pick your own time."

A few minutes later, I was back in the apartment with the safe, which I'd lugged to the elevator and then slid along the carpeted hallway down to my apartment. I called the alarm company and left a message for Wes Sheeley with my phone number, mentioning Norm Connors had recommended me. Then I grabbed my pistol and headed back out to see Norm again. An hour later, I was the owner of a permit to carry a concealed weapon in California. Connors had told me that the normal requirement was to complete a firearms training course, but Sammon had assured him that I'd gone through the NIS training. "He says he wouldn't have given you the weapon if you hadn't done well in the training," Norm shrugged. "That's good enough for me."

On the way back to my apartment, I decided to buy a device I'd heard about and was intrigued by—a telephone answering machine. You've gotta love new technology. I didn't want to have to stay tied to the apartment for fear I'd miss a call, and was already hoping I hadn't missed Sheeley's return call. I stopped at a familiar office supply store and bought a simple one. Back in the apartment, I started to set up the machine and my greeting. Before I could finish, the phone rang.

"Hello?"

"This is Wes Sheeley from South Bay Alarms. I'm returning your call."

"Hi, Mr. Sheeley. I'm Rick Halsted. I just moved into an apartment here in Sunnyvale, and Norm Connors recommended I call you to get what he called the 'special' alarm system. Also, I have a safe that needs to be installed."

The line was silent for a moment. "Why don't I come over and look at your place? We can decide what you need. Give me your address." I did and Sheeley chuckled. "Carillon Apartments, huh? Well, get the broads out of there so we can talk. I'll be there in about twenty minutes."

And he was, toolkit in hand. After introducing himself Wes asked, "So how do you know Norm Connors?" He was looking intently around the apartment as he spoke.

"Friend of a friend. Can you let me know what's so special about the special alarm setup?"

50

He had a good sales talk. I ended up with alarms on the entry door, the sliding door to the balcony, and one that would go off if any glass was shattered, as well as a motion detector. He explained in detail how it'd be monitored, how I'd be contacted (by pager), and how to get information about who'd gotten in using my alarm code, so I could be sure no one had figured out the code and snuck in. He promised to come back the next afternoon to install the safe.

I set my new alarm code as Wes pointedly turned his back on me, paid the man, and promised I'd see him the next day. "Tomorrow," he told me, "I'll bring along a peephole I can install in your door and a deadbolt lock that works from the inside only."

Now I had a functioning alarm system, a pager, and had picked my emergency code word ("Heisenberg," to remind me of all the uncertainty I was facing with this project. Physics joke).

Chapter 9

ONCE AGAIN I'd had a solo dinner and a good night's sleep. It was Friday, so I decided to call Detweiler at Federated Aviation and arrange to get the copies of the personnel files. Wes wasn't due back until the afternoon to install the safe, so I had plenty of time.

The nearest payphone was just outside the Carillon complex, but I purposely drove down to El Camino and then north for several miles, watching carefully for a tail. After a few random turns, including going through a subdivision with a lot of curvy streets and several exits, I stopped at a payphone outside a gas station on a side street. These are harder to find than you'd think—a gas station owner wants to be in a high traffic area.

I'd memorized Detweiler's number; it was 9:30 as I dialed. "Mr. Detweiler's office," a chirpy female voice announced.

"Is Mr. Detweiler available?" I asked.

"May I say who's calling?"

I'd already realized I didn't want to leave my own name and have someone else at Federated know I was contacting the personnel manager. "This is Jack Sammon," I told her. "Mr. Detweiler should be expecting my call."

After a few moments, Detweiler was on the line. "Mr. Sammon, this is Dick Detweiler. How can I help you?"

"This isn't Jack Sammon. I'm Rick Halsted—I think you know who I am."

"Yes, Mr. Sammon. Thanks for calling." Someone must have been within earshot and Detweiler was clever enough to cover on his end for me.

"I need to set up a meeting so you can hand over those files you copied for me. Can we do that today?"

"One moment," Detweiler said. A few seconds later, he was back on the line. "We can talk freely now; I shut my office door. How about 3:30 this afternoon? There's a McDonald's on El Camino near Mathilda Avenue—I'll meet you there."

"See you at 3:30," I answered and hung up. If Wes wasn't finished installing the safe by the time I had to leave, he could let himself out.

53

On the way home, I passed a shop that sold framed art and picked up a large framed Ansel Adams photo of Half Dome at Yosemite, along with the hardware to hang it. I'd always liked his work, and it was large enough to hide my new safe.

A few hours later, the safe was installed in the wall between the living room and bedroom of my apartment, and I'd been shown how to set the five-digit code I'd use to open it.

Sheeley installed the door peephole in about sixty seconds, then reached into his bag and produced a deadbolt assembly. "You could use this to secure the door better when you're at home," he suggested. "It only works from the inside—there's just a blank plate on the outside. An intruder can break through it, but they'll make enough noise to alert you before they'll be able to get in. If you want it, I'll put it in for $20." I agreed, and was pleased with my security arrangements when Sheeley was done. It occurred to me (too late) that the apartment management might not have wanted me to put a safe in their wall, or even the alarm system, but I could argue it enhanced the value of the apartment for future renters. Maybe they'd agree.

An hour later, I was sitting impatiently in the McDonald's on El Camino in Sunnyvale. It was already fifteen minutes past the agreed time. "Why can't the man be on time?" I muttered to myself over the shrieks of kids who were merrily throwing bits of food around the almost empty restaurant, ignored by their bored moms. "And somewhere we could talk without shouting would be nice."

Finally, I saw a portly man in a tan business suit carrying a leather briefcase step through the door. After a quick glance around the restaurant, he headed directly for my table, having cleverly decided none of the moms watching their brats could be the man he was supposed to meet.

"Mr. Halsted?" he asked, with the snarky air of someone assuming he's in charge. "I'm Dick Detweiler."

"You're late," I told him flatly. Sammon had made it clear that I was in charge of the operation, not Detweiler, and I wanted to establish this from the beginning.

"I brought the material you asked for," Detweiler said, ignoring my remark and a stray French fry that bounced off his head, thrown by a squealing toddler. He opened his briefcase and handed over a stack of file folders. "These are copies of the employee files for everyone on the project and some material describing the project itself."

I flipped through them to get an idea of their content while Detweiler waited, fidgeting nervously. After taking enough time to irritate him, I looked up. "So far, so good. Now, just to be sure, these are the complete employee files for everyone who has access to classified data about the project?"

54

Detweiler started to nod, but then stopped. Embarrassed, he muttered, "Those are the unclassified files for everyone in Andy Malone's group, which you'll be in. I forgot to include the file for the IT manager who supports the project; she doesn't report to Andy. She has a few analysts working for her who also have access."

"I'll need those files. I also need whatever classified information you have on each of these people, besides the data on the IT people. I expected to get the whole package today. When can I get the rest?" I made sure I sounded exasperated at his inability to perform a simple task.

"It'll take me a couple of days. I have to wait for a chance to get the file and copy it without anyone else in Personnel knowing. Sorry about that." Detweiler seemed nervous, and he should have been. Sammon had made it clear to him that he had to give me all the files I needed before I started at Federated. He must have good leverage on Dickie.

In a magnanimous mood, I said, "Get the rest of the files to me by Tuesday afternoon. I've got a lot to read right here. Now, what do I do when I show up Monday at Federated?"

"Just show up at the security desk and give them your name; tell them you're a new employee. One of the folders has your offer letter and some other correspondence from the company. Show that to the guard. Someone from my department will come down and take you to fill out all the forms. That'll take an hour or so; when you're finished with that, you'll get your photo ID card with the proper clearance on it so you can enter all the areas associated with the project. Then you'll be taken to meet Andy Malone and the rest of the team you'll be working in."

"What will the people from Personnel know about me?"

"So far as they know, you're a normal new hire. I've already set up a file. All the material in it shows you were interviewed and hired through normal channels. Is that satisfactory?" Detweiler finished sarcastically.

"Tell me—what's my salary on this job?"

"Standard for a new engineer on a job like this--$14,400 per year, plus health plan, stock purchase plan, and so on. The details will be in the package you get Monday."

That checked with what I'd been told. I said, "Now the only remaining item is to set up some way I can contact you if we need to talk. I can't just stroll into your office, so what do you suggest?"

Detweiler pulled out a business card and scribbled on the back of it. "There's my home address and phone number. If you call me, don't use your own name; just tell me a time and I'll meet you here. I know how to make sure I'm not being followed." I wasn't so sure he did.

"Let's go somewhere else next time. There's a Thai restaurant on Fair Oaks just this side of El Camino. We'll meet there; there's a better chance of some privacy there at any time of day. Don't be late again." Detweiler nodded grudgingly.

"One more thing," I added, having just realized I couldn't use my own name when calling him in his Federated office. "When I call you in the office—or at your home—I'll use the name Ray Spruance." Detweiler didn't show any reaction as he made a note of the name, so I assumed he wasn't aware of the hero of Midway. Another downcheck.

Watching Detweiler leave, I sighed and wondered how much cooperation I could expect from the man. Where did Sammon find these people, and what leverage did he have over them to make them cooperate? It was probably none of my business.

Chapter 10

L UCKILY, I got home before the terrible rush hour. I spent a couple of hours going through the personnel files to get an idea what the contents were. The files were thick and, based on the first one I riffled through, contained biographical information, resumes, the unclassified security investigation results, employee performance evaluations, W-4 forms, salary history, and other miscellaneous data. No credit reports were included, so I'd have to send the names and Social Security numbers to Sammon to get those run. The credit information would, I hoped, help identify anyone who had financial problems severe enough to consider selling secrets to the Soviets, making them vulnerable to bribes or blackmail.

I sat back to think a moment—it'd probably take me all weekend just to go through everything I had. My weeks of training on counter-espionage had included exhaustive analysis of the various factors that could make someone vulnerable to foreign agents, and this would be my first chance to use those techniques on a real case.

I decided to make up a grid listing the names of the various people associated with the project along with the key information categories associated with the likelihood of stealing classified information—education, income, credit rating, and so on. This wasn't a technique I'd been taught, but it seemed a reasonable way to organize all this information. I jotted down some notes on what those categories might include. After finishing, I looked at my watch; it was almost six pm.

Time for a break. After all, this complex was apparently renowned as a great place to meet young ladies, and I deserved a reward for all my hard work. I put all the folders and notes into my new safe, wiped off the keypad, re-hung the Adams photo on the wall over it, and went to the bathroom to brush my teeth, put on after-shave, and make sure I looked presentable. I made sure to wear some of the casual clothes Debbie had picked out for me.

I walked out my door and almost bumped into a man of about my age who'd just left his own apartment. "Hey, you must be my new neighbor. I'm Billy Samuels," he said as he shook my hand.

After exchanging names, I asked him what the deal was on this social event "Most Fridays there'll be a hundred or so, basically 50-50 guys and girls. I think a lot of the girls show up regularly, unless they're involved with someone, but some of the men don't bother, so it usually turns out pretty even. Overall, this place is probably about two-to-one male."

As we approached the clubhouse, he went on, "The committee that runs these get-togethers sets out some bottles of wine and glasses. There's a jar for the men to put in a couple of bucks to cover the cost. Then just hang around and decide how you're going to play it. Some of the girls are pretty aggressive, and you're a new guy, so they may approach you, or at least give a signal they wouldn't mind if you came over to them. The only warning I'll give you is that a fair portion of the women who live here are husband hunting. If you're not looking for a serious relationship, keep your ears open for signals."

I walked with Billy to the clubhouse as I thought about tonight. The ideal situation would be to meet a young woman who had the same commendably free-spirited attitude as the girls I'd met in DC. Avoiding women focused on finding a mate seemed a good tactical decision.

When we got to the clubhouse, there seemed to be about fifty or sixty people there, roughly divided between the sexes evenly, as Billy had predicted. All, I guessed, were between their mid-twenties and early thirties. Some of the men were wearing what Debbie had called "leisure suits." They were polyester, came in weird colors, and required a gaudy open-collar shirt underneath. Debbie had made it clear I should *never* wear one, a promise I found easy to keep.

Everyone here was still mostly in same-sex groupings—presumably the pairing off hadn't started yet. Billy led me over to the bar.

I put a few dollars into the jar and poured red wine into one of the glasses lined up there. Looking over Billy's shoulder, I could see several groups of young women studiously keeping their gazes away from the men at the bar. Trusting my new neighbor's advice, I sat and waited to see what might happen. People were still coming in, so I could take my time.

A few minutes later, I noticed a fine-looking young lady looking in my direction. I offered what I hoped was a charming smile and she smiled back. "Show time," I said to myself and began what I hoped looked like a casual walk toward her.

"I'm Beth Haggerty, and I believe you're new here," she said as I stopped in front of her. She was blonde, about five inches shorter than I was, and seemed to have a very nice figure indeed. "Look at her eyes, not her chest," I reminded myself mentally.

"Hi, Beth. I'm Rick Halsted. I was just trying to figure out what the etiquette is here."

"It's pretty simple. The idea is to find someone you think you could get along with and then see how it goes."

I found a table and brought over a bottle of wine, which we shared. Beth was easy to talk to as well as to look at. We exchanged the usual biographical information and found common interests in golf and, of all things, history. She had an American history degree from San Jose State and was working as a secretary at Hewlett-Packard in Palo Alto. After about thirty minutes, I decided Beth was ready to make a decision, and suggested we go to dinner. She accepted happily and we were off.

She was not only a very attractive woman whose charms had become more obvious as we talked, but was bright and fun to talk to. As I suspect is the case with many men—could it be most?—I was strongly attracted to women with voluptuous figures. On the other hand there was my obsession with Natalie.

As we talked further, her conversation focused on her goals. "I really don't want to keep working at Hewlett-Packard until I retire," she told me frankly. "I hope in a year or so I'll have found the right guy and can settle down." Warning bells began going off in my head, but I decided to persevere for a while. Maybe it was just bad phrasing on her part.

After dinner, I dropped her at her door in the complex. If I was reading her signals correctly, a goodnight kiss wouldn't be out of order. The kiss was very nice, but I got the feeling that going any further would tell her I was serious about her. I wasn't, not yet, so I played it safe. "How about a movie and dinner tomorrow night?" I asked after we broke apart. Maybe I was misreading her, and I did like her.

"I can't," she said. "I'd really love to, but I already made a date. Can we do it next weekend?"

We agreed on the dinner and a movie for next Saturday. In the meantime, I could make up my mind on whether or not it was wise to take a chance on getting seriously involved with any young woman.

Chapter 11

MY OBJECTIVE for Saturday was to build the matrix to summarize the information about the people working on the Outlaw Shark project. It would obviously have been better if Detweiler had included the classified data and the files for the computer systems people who were involved with the project. The employee files seemed to be organized in a standard fashion; if that was true for the other files, the matrix would work for them too. If I needed to add categories based on data in the classified files, I should be able to do that easily.

I realized I needed a very large sheet of grid-lined paper to put the matrix together. Colored markers or pencils would be nice, too, and a long ruler. I made a short list of what I'd need for the day and headed for the office supply store again. On the way, I went through the procedure to detect tails—none—and stopped at a random payphone. Hoping Sammon would be in the office on a Saturday as he usually was, I dialed the toll-free number and pulled a slip of paper out of my pocket.

"Motivational Consulting; this is Mr. Sammon."

"It's Rick. I've got a list of names I need a credit report and a criminal background check run on."

"Wait a second. OK—go ahead."

I dictated the list of names, giving an address and a Social Security number for each. "This is a partial list. The stuff Detweiler gave me yesterday didn't include the computer software people who have access to the project, and was also missing the classified part of the employee files. I should have that info in a few days. Let me give you my mailing address, phone and pager number."

"Anything else?" Sammon asked after he'd noted my contact information.

"Thanks for the safe, I guess. I have an alarm system and a deadbolt installed, the safe's in the wall, and Norm set me up with a concealed carry permit. I've set up a separate safe deposit box at a different bank under another name."

"Excellent. About the safe—there's a shallow hidden compartment set into the inside of the safe door. You can pry it open with a very thin blade, like a small screwdriver. There's not much room in it, but that's where you should put anything that might compromise you, including your fake ID's. Keep your pistol and any valuables you have in the main compartment of the safe; hopefully an intruder would think they're the reason for the safe. Also, find a gun club in the area, join it, and set up a routine of shooting on weekends. That'll keep you sharp and give you cover on why you have the pistol. I'll fax the credit report stuff to Norm and he'll call you, but it'll be at least a week. Any questions?"

"One more thing. If someone's leaking information from the project, they might be getting paid for it. If I could get the last four or five years of federal income tax filings, we'd have better information on their cash situation. I could compare their declared income with what the credit reports suggest they're spending. Someone's who's cheating on their taxes might have something to hide."

After a slight pause, Sammon answered, "Sounds like a good idea. I can do that, but it'll take a little longer—maybe more than a week. Now—any more questions?"

"Actually, yes. To get this apartment I had to sign a six-month lease. That was the shortest lease I could get; after that I can renew month-to-month. So if I wrap up the project before the six months are up, can I get any help from NIS on paying off the rest of the lease?"

"Nope. That's one of the reasons you're getting paid by both Federated and the Navy." He hung up without a further word. I shrugged and headed for the office supply store and a hardware shop.

Half an hour later, I was back at the apartment. I spread out one of the 24" by 18" grid-printed sheets I'd bought on the kitchen table. Using the notes I'd taken regarding the categories I wanted to fill in for each, I drew in grid lines and labeled the columns with notations including credit score, annual salary, total income declared for taxes, estimated monthly expenditures, dependents, political background, hobbies, age, college attended, degrees and GPA, a couple of blank columns for later ideas, and "notes."

Then I set up rows for each of the six people on whom I had information so far:

Andy Malone (Manager)
Owen Langston (Electrical Engineer)
Arnold Kunz (Electrical Engineer)
Wayne Girard (Software Engineer)
Phil Boyce (Technician)
Yolanda Ramirez (Administrative Assistant)

I allowed five more rows to fit in the computer support people; Detweiler hadn't told me how many there actually were. With eleven rows, each vertical block was almost an inch and a half high, so I could put a fair amount of information in each cell if I lettered carefully.

By the time this was laid out, it was almost noon; now to figure out the safe's secret compartment. Opening it, I peered at the inside of the door but couldn't see any seam or joint. I prodded the door in various places, but couldn't feel it give anywhere. Frustrated, I used a flashlight to examine the door. I found that by pressing on the center of the door, a narrow slit running around the inside of the door was revealed. I quickly popped off the compartment cover with my smallest screwdriver, revealing a cubby about a half-inch deep and eight by twelve inches on the sides. The personnel folders could never fit in there. I couldn't even get the contents of one of them in; the sheets would have to be folded double. If the damned compartment had been an inch wider, I could have put a complete file in without folding the paper. The folders could go in the safe for the time being, but I'd have to find somewhere more secure as quickly as I could, probably my safe deposit box. That meant I had to extract all the data I needed as soon as possible so the folders could be stored at the bank. I considered destroying them once I'd recorded the information I wanted, but decided I'd keep them in case I wanted to go through them again for additional information.

I slid my worksheet into the main compartment of the safe, shut and locked the safe, wiped off the keypad, and re-hung the Ansel Adams photo over it. Then I set the alarm for "*Away*" and headed out for lunch.

After lunch—a beer and a burger at a nearby tavern—I came back to restart my work on the chart. Going through each personnel folder, I found the data I needed and entered them neatly into the corresponding box on the chart. "God bless Engineering Drafting class," I murmured as I worked.

By late afternoon I was finished. Should I go to the clubhouse and try my luck again? I decided not to. Getting seriously involved with anyone made no sense, since I hoped to be gone in a few months.

Dinner was at a steakhouse. I came back to settle down for the night. I set the alarm on "Stay," pulled out a John D. MacDonald mystery, and sat comfortably reading while my stereo system played quiet jazz. Sunday would be a quiet day, I decided as I shut the book to go to bed.

Waking at eight on Sunday, I mentally outlined my tasks. First, I wanted to spend a couple of hours refining my chart and listing any thoughts for other categories that should be added. I also needed to go through the material on the project that Detweiler had given me. Some of it was new to me, despite having read what NIS had on the project. I wanted to have that memorized so I'd have enough background to detect any cover-ups or misleading statements I might get from my new colleagues on the Outlaw Shark team.

That kept me busy until mid-afternoon, including a short break for lunch at the tavern I'd gone to the day before. I was just putting my work back in the safe when my pager buzzed, displaying Sammon's number. Now to a payphone so I could return the call.

"A cheery good afternoon to you," he said. "Norm told me you must have chosen your apartment based on the number of single women who live there. I hope you saved a little effort getting ready for tomorrow."

Ignoring his comment, I explained what I'd done, going into details on how the chart was laid out and how I expected to use it. "Good idea," Sammon said. "When you get it filled in further, see if you can copy it and send the copy to me."

"Anything else?"

"I should have those credit reports within a week, or at least I hope so. I'll send them to Norm and he'll give you a call when they get there. The tax returns will take longer. Good luck—keep me informed."

I took myself out to dinner again, driving up to Palo Alto to prospect for a new restaurant, and settling on a nice Italian place. A few glasses of wine with an excellent Lasagna Bolognese and I was ready to head back home. I'd need a good night's rest before starting my first day of civilian work.

Chapter **12**

S TEPPING out of my car, I looked across the parking lot at the six-story headquarters of Federated Aviation. I was wearing what I thought was the best of my new suits, with a carefully chosen shirt and tie. "Let the games begin," I murmured as I checked my briefcase for the third time to make sure I had all the required papers. There's nothing like the submarine service to train you in checking absolutely everything over and over. It's kind of like having obsessive-compulsive disorder; it's not optional in submarines.

The portly security guard at the reception counter looked up as I approached. "Can I help you, sir?" he asked in a monotone.

"I'm Rick Halsted," I told the guard, sliding my job offer letter across to him. "I'm a new employee, starting today."

"May I see some identification, Mr. Halsted?" the guard asked. I handed him my driver's license. As I waited, I reflected sourly on the contrast between this fat middle-aged guy and the armed Marines who'd guarded every naval facility I'd ever been on. It didn't make me feel any better about Federated's security procedures. The guard handed me back my letter and identification and asked me to take a seat.

While I was waiting, I looked around the lobby and saw it was arranged so everybody leaving the building had to go through a checkpoint, which included something that looked like an X-ray machine. That was good for security, but a possible problem for me. I'd have to consider how to get things out of the building that Federated would prefer stayed on the premises. If this guard was typical of the security staff, I was sure I'd find a way.

After a few minutes, a young brunette woman emerged from one of the elevators and headed toward the security desk. "Mr. Halsted?" she asked, after talking briefly with the guard. "I'm Bernice Lindstrom. If you'll come with me, we'll get your paperwork processed so you can go to work. Welcome to Federated Aviation." Her disinterested tone took any warmth out of the greeting.

I took her ice-cold hand and shook it briefly. Bernice was a slim and very plain woman with a no-nonsense manner. Her demeanor didn't encourage friendly remarks, so I waited for her to question me.

Walking toward the elevator with me, she asked, "What made you choose Federated as a place to work?" This must have been on the list of polite questions to ask new hires. Bernice obviously didn't care what I said; she wasn't even looking at me.

I made some noises about what a great reputation the company had, what a challenge it'd be to work here, and so on. She was so clearly uninterested in my answer that I could have said almost anything.

An hour later I'd filled out a stack of paperwork, gotten my photo taken, and was now the bearer of a plastic security badge with a black band across it under my name and photo.

"All the work areas here at Federated are color-coded to indicate the security level that's required to get in," Bernice explained, handing me a list of the colors. "Each card scanner has a color bar above it indicating the minimum level necessary to enter that space. The scanners won't let you through unless your color is at least at the appropriate level, and you have to wear the badge in plain sight so everyone can see you're authorized to be in that area. Black is the third highest level—only silver and gold are above it. And when you leave the building, you have to scan your card so the system will know you've left."

I noticed that Bernice's badge had a green band. "Is there any other kind of restriction on entry to a space, or is it all based on the color code level?" I asked.

"Just the color," Bernice answered, looking puzzled. If this were true, there weren't any "need to know" restrictions in effect, making it possible for anyone to wander at will into projects he had nothing to do with. That would make it easier for a spy to find information on a wide range of material. Worse, a bad guy who had a lower-level entry permit might be able to figure out how to change the magnetic information embedded on the card to "upgrade" the security level. If so, and if he could spoof in a new color, there might be serious risks. I made a mental note to raise this issue with my new boss. Bernice might not know much about restrictions on highly classified material, so maybe things were tighter than they appeared.

"OK," she said briskly, "I'm going to bring you up to the area where you'll be working and introduce you to your team leader, Andrew Malone. He'll do the rest of the first-day orientation—introduce you to the people you'll be working with, set you up with a place to work, and so on."

We rode the elevator to the fifth floor, where a reception desk sat, flanked by sets of closed doors that clearly required card access. "Bethany," Bernice said coolly, "this is Rick Halsted. He starts work today in Mr. Malone's group."

Bethany was younger and friendlier than Bernice. She favored me with a warm smile. "Just have a seat, Mr. Halsted. I'll call Mr. Malone;

he'll come out to escort you into your work area." I turned to thank Bernice for doing a chore she'd so clearly disliked, but she'd already vanished into an elevator. Apparently, her idea of introducing me was to leave me at the reception desk.

Malone kept me waiting for ten minutes before he appeared. He was an inch or so shorter than I was, and carried himself with what he apparently thought was an air of authority. To me it looked more like arrogance. His expression was grim as he approached. "Mr. Halsted, I take it?" he asked without extending his hand or introducing himself. I thought I knew why he was taking this attitude, but decided to play it straight.

Forcing the issue, I held my hand out. "That's right," I said cheerfully. "Thanks for coming out to meet me."

Malone reluctantly took my hand. "I'm Andy Malone, the manager of the project team. Let's go over here and sit down. I'd like to discuss a few things before I take you back to our work area."

I followed my new boss over to a grouping of chairs near the receptionist's desk. Malone examined me for a moment. "I don't appreciate having someone assigned to my group without my being involved in the hiring process," he told me. What a nice start for our working relationship.

I started to respond, but Malone held up his hand. "I'm not finished. Now I want you to tell me exactly what the deal is here. Somebody pulled some strings to get you onto this project, and I want to know why." Bethany was staring at us in shock.

Sammon had warned me Malone might be a little pissed about someone joining his department without him having had anything to do with the selection process, so I was ready for this.

"Mr. Malone," I began politely, "the last thing I'd want would be to make you think anything strange went on with my hiring." That was, of course, a true statement. I went on, "While I was getting out of the Navy down in San Diego, I went to the officers' club one night and ran into a man named Harris Booth; I understand he's a retired naval officer with some connection to Federated. We got to talking and he asked me what my plans were. I actually didn't have any, although I was thinking of applying to Berkeley or maybe UCLA for an MBA program. He said Federated had a project going that I could be useful in and ... well, he talked me into it. He said if I wanted to go for an MBA at some point that'd be fine, but some "real world" experience would help by showing I'd worked in the private sector. So I contacted the personnel department, filled out an application, and here I am." My story was a lie, but Malone would never learn that.

Booth, to whom I'd been introduced by Sammon back in DC, was a member of the board of directors of Federated Aviation and a retired Rear Admiral. He'd gladly agreed to claim he'd recruited me into the company, especially after Sammon pointed out that unless the Navy was sure the project data was secure, Federated might lose the project and its potential profits. It was obvious Andy Malone was aware of who Booth was.

"Well," Malone said quietly after a long pause, "thanks for explaining that to me. I'm sorry for pre-judging the situation. I'm sure you could be a great help here. Why don't you tell me a little about your background?" He could eat crow without gagging on it.

I spent a few minutes outlining my electrical engineering training, the curriculum in nuclear power and submarine school, and some of the duties I'd had on the boats, emphasizing my familiarity with the Mk 113 fire control system, which was one of the systems Outlaw Shark would have to tie into. The new *LOS ANGELES* class submarines, which were being built now, would eventually have a new system designated as the Mk 117 FCS, but my understanding was that much of the software and user interfaces were the same as the 113. The early boats in the class would start with the 113, and would later convert to the 117.

"It sounds to me like you can contribute quite a lot to the project, Rick. I'm glad to have you on board. Come on in and I'll introduce you to the rest of the group."

I decided to push him a little more. "If you're not entirely comfortable with me being here, I can just let Harris know. I'm sure he can help find a place for me somewhere else in Federated." Letting him think I was on a first-name basis with a director of the corporation seemed a good tactical move.

"No, no," Malone said hastily as he led me toward a door that presumably led to the working spaces. "I was just taken a little off-guard when you were assigned to my department without me having interviewed you. We can really use someone with your background. Now follow me and you can meet your colleagues." At least one of whom, I believed, might be working for the Soviets as well as for Federated. Maybe it was Andy.

Chapter 13

M ALONE swiped his badge through the card-reader, which had a red label, and made sure I did the same.

"The rule is that everyone has to swipe their badge going into a controlled space, even if the door's already open. This keeps someone from tagging along behind a person who's authorized and getting into a space they shouldn't have access to," Malone explained. "It also produces a record of everyone who's entered the space."

"Does the system actually enforce that somehow, or could someone walk through without swiping once the door's open?"

"It's up to each person going through to make sure everyone in front of him has swiped the card. The last person is kind of on his own, so the practice here is that the senior person lags behind so he can see that the people in front of him use their cards," Malone answered. This seemed to be a complicated way of answering "yes" to my question about someone being able to get into a classified space without swiping a card. So it appeared that someone *could* get into a restricted space without swiping a card, and if people weren't observant, into a space he wasn't cleared for.

Malone led me down a hall with closed doors on both sides, all armed with card-readers. I noticed with interest that the readers had different colored security requirements. The lowest level I noticed was the red that had been on the main corridor entry scanner. That made sense.

About halfway down, he keyed his card into a door with a purple label and led me in. We'd entered a space that had a large conference table in the middle and cubicles set around the perimeter of the space. Most of the cubicles had the desk arranged so the occupant sat facing the wall when working, allowing anyone to look over his shoulder at what he was doing. There were ten of these cubicles, but only six of them seemed to be currently occupied. One of the cubicles was significantly larger than the others and had better furniture. Also, its desk faced the central space, probably so no one could see what the occupant was doing on his terminal. No doubt that was Malone's.

He led me to a cubicle that had a terminal, but otherwise seemed to be unused. "This'll be yours. We'll have the computer passwords and access set up by this afternoon. Let me take you around and introduce you to the other people on the team." I made a mental note to rearrange my cubicle so my back wasn't to the room. I suspected this was a Malone preference, so he could literally look over the shoulder of the people in his department as they worked.

I'd already studied the files of each of these people, and probably knew more about the details of their personal histories than Malone did, but was curious to see what they were like in person. Malone himself had a bachelor of arts and an MBA from Stanford; his undergraduate major had been political science. After having gone through his personnel file, it wasn't clear to me how Malone was qualified to lead an engineering project, but I supposed I'd find out how well he could manage it in the next few days. The man hadn't even taken calculus, let alone any advanced math, and his only science course had been what appeared to be a "descriptive physics" (without math) course for liberal arts majors. He'd gotten a B in that course. I suspected C's and below were endangered species at Stanford.

The two electrical engineers—Owen Langston and Arnold Kunz—had each been working at Federated for over five years, but otherwise had little in common. Langston was tall and lanky, with a self-assured manner. His specialty, I already knew, was in data systems, particularly in engineering a system to ensure data integrity. Kunz was below average height and above average weight. He wore thick glasses and was almost a stereotype of the nerdy engineer, complete with the pocket protector and the slide rule clipped to his belt. His expertise was in setting up communications protocols for uploading and downloading data. Langston, I decided, was an extroverted engineer, meaning he looked at *your* shoes while he talked to you. Kunz was not.

Wayne Girard, the software engineer, had an Industrial Engineering degree and had also taken a number of courses in computer languages, ranging from machine language up through FORTRAN, something called "C," and PL/1. Wayne was the team's main liaison with the computer systems people, whom I so far knew nothing about. He was stocky and athletic, and didn't seem particularly pleased to have a new person coming onto the team. It's possible I'm not as likable as I prefer to believe.

Phil Boyce, the technician on the team, was the hands-on person who was doing the assembly and testing of the prototype models for the system. He was average height and stood out from the rest of the group mainly by being better dressed than anyone, including Malone and possibly even me in my Debbie-selected clothes. Phil seemed to have a high degree of self-confidence and, I suspected, regarded himself as a ladies' man. Interestingly, he had a purple card, while the three engineers had black.

"And this is our administrative assistant, Yolanda Ramirez," Malone said. I'd seen the facial photos of all these people, but wasn't prepared for the visual impact of Yolanda. She was a classic Latin beauty—long dark hair, huge brown eyes, and a very lush mouth—all that I'd seen in her photo. The head shot hadn't included her voluptuous figure, which she apparently liked to show off. Today she was wearing a too-tight sweater displaying breasts of my favorite size—almost too big—and a very short skirt proving that her legs were long and sleek. She was several inches taller than I'd expected—about 5'9", I estimated, which made her a lot of woman.

Trouble, I decided. I was sure she was a huge distraction to the rest of the staff, probably especially for Phil, who was undoubtedly trying to hustle her, and for Arnold, who I suspected lusted after her in a not-so-secret fashion.

"Rick, would you give the team the summary of your background and qualifications that you gave me earlier?" Malone asked.

I'd been expecting this, and was ready with a somewhat longer version of what I'd told Andy, going into detail about my experience with the Mk 113 fire control system. I finished with, "On my last assignment on *BOWFIN*, which is one of the newest submarines in the Navy, we installed the latest software upgrade to the system a few months before I got out of the Navy. Without being immodest, I can say that I have a thorough knowledge of the capabilities and limitations of that particular system. I hope that'll be helpful to our team in completing this project successfully."

My little talk seemed to be well received; I hoped Malone was coming around to regarding me as a valuable, although unasked for, addition to the team.

"May I ask a question?" I asked.

"Go ahead," Malone said magnanimously.

"Has anyone here actually been on board a submarine to see how this system would be integrated into the submarine's electrical and fire control systems?" There was general head-shaking.

I volunteered, "I have some contacts in San Diego. It might be helpful to arrange a tour of one of the boats." Sammon and I had gone over this, with his main concern being whether it'd be possible to avoid someone inadvertently revealing that I was still in the Navy. We'd decided we could set up an "after hours" tour so only the duty section would be on board. Someone from naval intelligence would pre-brief the CO, XO, and duty section to treat me as a former naval officer, rather than one still on active duty. I was sure this wouldn't be a problem; submariners have lots of practice in cover stories and tactical deceptions.

A stray thought crept into my mind as I visualized Yolanda boarding a submarine in the provocative outfit she was wearing. Sailors, and maybe some of the officers, would be fighting at the bottom of the vertical ladders to be standing under her as she descended in that micro-skirt. This was why women were encouraged to wear long pants when visiting a submarine. Contemplating her trying to make her way down a crowded passageway didn't bear thinking about. It'd be like the top-heavy nurse in that Cary Grant submarine movie—but even worse, I decided.

"Sounds like a good idea," Malone agreed condescendingly, "but I think we have a pretty good handle on what kind of environment we have to install this system in." I'd have been glad to bet Malone had never been on a submarine, and that he had no idea of the space constraints in that environment.

"Is there a prototype of the system you want to put into the boats?"

"You mean *ships*, don't you?" Phil asked with a slight smirk.

"Submarines are always referred to as boats, even though the missile submarines, for example, displace more than a World War II light cruiser. It's a tradition," I explained, trying for a heavy Russian-Jewish accent in the last sentence. Apparently, no one here had seen the movie, as they all stared at me blankly, probably wondering why I'd used that strange accent.

Owen spoke up. "We have the computer we're going to use over here." He led me, with the rest following, to the rear corner of the room. A gray tarpaulin was draped over an object there. Langston swept off the cover to reveal an electronic assembly almost four feet high with a footprint of about three square feet.

"That looks like a UYK-7[38]. We had one on my last boat to run the fire control system," I said. "Where's it supposed to go in the boat?"

"We've been told it'll go in the 'sonar equipment space.' This'll be connected to an external tape drive for data storage and to a display system near wherever the torpedo firing controls are. I think it's somewhere in the forward part of the ship," Owen responded.

"Boat," I said reflexively.

Malone looked at his watch. "We can talk more about this later. Our Monday meeting's about to start."

---

[38] The "state of the art" 1970's military computer. It had 256K of memory, weighed several hundred pounds, and had less computing power than an electronic watch in 2015.

Chapter 14

ANDY took a seat at the head of the conference table, and the rest of us chose our own. The door buzzed open and I turned my head to see who was joining us. The first person I saw was Natalie Montaigne. She looked superb, to my eyes—just as I last remembered her, but even lovelier. I didn't see a wedding ring, raising a desperate bubble of hope in my heart. Suspicion also arose—was this just a coincidence? Would Sammon have put me here if he knew the history—the sad history—between us? It didn't seem likely; she could only distract me from my mission. Only a tiny fraction of my mind was functioning; most of it was directed on staring at my lost love.

I sat there stunned as she walked in, followed by two men and a woman, presumably the other members of the computer team working on the project. If that stupid bastard Detweiler had given me all the files he was supposed to, I wouldn't have been taken so badly by surprise.

"Natalie," Malone said, "I'd like to introduce you to our new team member, Rick Halsted."

She turned toward me and stared in disbelief. "Rick! What are you doing here?" She was successfully suppressing the joy she must have been feeling at seeing me again.

"I got out of the Navy a few weeks ago, and started at Federated today," I managed to say, lying with the first sentence I'd spoken to her since the breakup.

"You left the Navy? But that was your lifetime dream—to be a submarine officer."

"It's a long story. It's nice to see you again, Natalie," I managed to say, trying to look calm.

"You two know each other?" Malone asked, obliviously stating the obvious.

Natalie, blushing with embarrassment, explained we'd dated briefly at Berkeley. My memory was that we'd had an intense love affair, but she didn't seem on board with that concept. She recovered her composure and introduced the people on her team to me. Her lead analyst was Greg Jeffries, and the two other analysts were Tammy Drake and Fred Ward. I was still in a mental haze, and didn't form a strong impression of any of the three except that Tammy was a petite redhead with a very nice little body. And a wedding ring, a fashion accessory that Natalie wasn't wearing.

"Rick, we should talk later," Natalie said. "If it's OK with Andy, maybe you and I could go down to the cafeteria for a little while after the meeting, just to catch up." The last time she'd said we had to talk, it'd turned out very badly. At least she couldn't dump me again.

I nodded mechanically, still having trouble accepting that Natalie was back in my life. But was she really? Just because she was working on the same project didn't mean we'd be together again. If she was overjoyed—or even mildly pleased—at seeing me again, she'd hidden her emotions quite well.

The meeting began. Natalie and her group delivered a status report on the software debugging. "We're having some trouble with the graphics display from the UYK-7," she noted. "It isn't giving us the definition we want, and we still aren't sure exactly what the users on the submarine will want." She paused. "Perhaps Rick could spend some time with us. His background may help us design the user interface better." She didn't sound excited about this.

"Good idea," Malone nodded. "Rick, would you mind working with Natalie's group—in addition to your duties here, of course—to help with that?"

"Not at all. Natalie, I'm familiar with the fire control systems, the attack procedures, and so on. If that'd be helpful, I'd be pleased to work with your people."

She avoided making eye contact, but answered, "That'd be fine. I think we could use your help."

The meeting moved on. I noticed Phil had slipped in next to Natalie and was whispering to her. She seemed to ignore him, but it still irritated me.

Most of the discussion was over my head, despite my studying the materials Detweiler had given me. It'd probably take me at least a week to get enough up to speed to be able to start contributing.

As the meeting went on, I tuned out and tried to understand Natalie's presence here. Why—and how—would an avid anti-war activist end up working for a major defense contractor on a highly classified project? I was going to have to contact Sammon to get a copy of her background investigation to see what the FBI had concluded about her political background. I hoped nothing negative was in there; I didn't like to think my lost love might be the part of the problem I'd come here to solve.

The meeting ended after about an hour, and Natalie approached me as we were getting up from the table. "Let's not talk here—wait until we get to the cafeteria," she said quietly.

Chapter 15

W E GOT into the elevator, which already had two people in it; she pushed the button for the basement level. "The cafeteria actually isn't too bad," she said, keeping the conversation innocuous until we had some privacy. "I think most of the employees eat lunch here—there's a decent selection and it's a lot cheaper than going out. Plus you don't have the hassle of going in and out through security."

Natalie got a cup of coffee, I got a Coke and we found an isolated table. She didn't waste any time getting to what was apparently bothering her. "Rick, did you research me to find out where I am and then manage to get a job here so you could 'accidentally' meet me again?" she asked, looking me straight in the eyes.

"Absolutely not. I was as surprised as you were when you walked in. Look, when I was getting out of the Navy I ran into someone who I guess is on the board of directors here. He told me Federated was working on a project that I could be of great help on. I was planning on getting an MBA from Cal or UCLA, but I took him up on the offer. I had no idea you'd be working here, let alone on the same project." Three of those five sentences were true. If "absolutely not" counts as a sentence.

"So all this time—over seven years now—you didn't think about trying to get back together with me?"

"Well, I was guilty of thinking about it," I admitted. "But I never took any steps to try to find out where you were or what you were doing. I mean, you were pretty definite about calling it quits between us."

"I'm sorry. I guess I sounded like I thought you'd snuck around trying to find a way to be with me," she apologized. "I know the breakup was tough on you. It was pretty bad for me too, but I was sure—I guess I still am—I did the right thing for both of us."

"You'll have to allow me to disagree with that."

"OK," she said reluctantly. "So tell me—what's been happening in your life?"

I gave her a truthful summary of my time in the Navy, up to the time when I got the message orders for my present assignment. From that point, sticking to my cover story, I said, "I got a lot of enjoyment and a

75

sense of accomplishment from my time in submarines. But I finally realized I didn't really have a life like most people do. It was kind of like what you were worried about—I was spending so much time at sea that I basically didn't have anything else going on in my life. It wasn't an easy decision, but I decided to give civilian life a shot."

"Did you enjoy being on submarines? I mean, you were so enthusiastic about it when we were together."

"It had its ups and downs," I said solemnly. This extremely witty comment sailed over her head. "Now it's your turn."

Natalie took a sip of coffee. "That's what I said to you when we first met. Good memory. Well, there's not that much to tell. I finished my degree in computer science with pretty high grades. I was interested more in software than hardware, so I looked for a job where I had some chance for advancement working on software systems. I ended up here at Federated, starting as an analyst, then made lead analyst and last year got promoted to manager and given this project."

"Married? Kids?" I asked, although imagining her married was painful to me.

"Nope. I actually don't even date much. I'll probably end up as an old maid with a bunch of cats." That was hard to believe. I knew very well Natalie had an enthusiastic sexual nature, and was sure she'd find someone to make a life with.

"Look, I have to ask this. How did someone who was very involved in the anti-war movement at Berkeley end up working for a big defense contractor?"

"And how did I manage to get a Top Secret clearance? I suppose you'd like to know that too." But she was smiling for the first time. "In a way, you had something to do with that. You probably guessed that I caught a lot of flak from the crowd I ran with when they found out I was dating a midshipman. But you weren't the stereotype military guys were supposed to be, so I'd started wondering about whether we had assumed a lot of things that just weren't true. I think things really started to turn for me in early '68," she said tentatively. "Remember the Tet Offensive and how everyone was screaming that it showed we were losing in Vietnam and had to get out?" I nodded. That had been after she booted me out of her life.

"A few months after Tet, a Marine officer who'd been in those battles was giving a talk on campus about the Tet Offensive, and some of us on the Coordinating Committee decided to go. We wanted to know what the 'enemy' was going to say, so we could prepare arguments against whatever they were saying.

"Well, it didn't turn out the way I'd assumed it would. The Marine explained that the North Vietnamese had broken a cease-fire they'd agreed to, committed a large portion of their regular army, and hoped to take over the northern part of South Vietnam, and maybe Saigon, to bring a quick end to the war. He told us how the VC and NVA slaughtered thousands of civilians. And he told us how, despite the North Vietnamese violating the truce and staging a surprise attack, the Marines and the Army were able to bounce back from the surprise and whip them, destroying large elements of the North Vietnamese Army. He'd brought along maps, photos of some of the combat, and data on our losses and theirs, which were twice as much as our side's. If you looked at just fatalities, the North Vietnamese and Viet Cong lost five times as many. When it was over, we started talking about how to rebut what he'd said. I realized that what he said could be checked out by looking at the various news stories, press releases, and so on. So I volunteered to do that."

"And you found he was telling the truth—that we'd not only overcome a surprise attack by a numerically superior force, but damaged them so severely that they couldn't operate effectively for a long time. But the news media, starting with 'Uncle Walter' Cronkite, spun it as a disaster for us. Too bad you and I weren't still together—at the NROTC unit, we got together with the Army people and had a briefing from a Marine major. Maybe it was the same guy."

"Yep," she agreed, leaving me to wonder whether she was also agreeing that it was too bad we hadn't still been together. "So I started disengaging from the Committee and all the protests. Some of them had connections—I don't know with whom—and were getting inside info from North Vietnam. I heard things about how they were treating American prisoners that turned my stomach, while my 'friends' were laughing about how the POW's deserved it. I saw some things that convinced me that a lot of my former friends were lying through their teeth to support a radical agenda. I realized I really didn't agree with a lot of their goals and especially not with their tactics."

"The same goals and tactics you'd helped to plan and orchestrate in the past," I couldn't resist saying. I was still upset about the fall of Saigon a few months ago, after the Democrats in Congress cut off our promised military support. The "boat people" were dying by the hundreds of thousands trying to get away from the new Communist regime in the South as a result of the US breaking our pledge to them.

"What can I say? I was young and idealistic," she said with a shrug.

"So you joined Young Americans for Freedom, and voted to re-elect Reagan for governor and Nixon for president, right?"

"I didn't go quite that far," she laughed. "Let's just say I'm more middle of the road now. I didn't vote in the last presidential election—I couldn't bring myself to vote for Nixon and thought McGovern was naïve. Now that the war's over, about the only political issue I'm interested in is global cooling. Anyway, I suppose my change of heart helped me get a clean enough record for the background investigation. Good thing too—you can't go very far at Federated without a high-level clearance."

"I appreciate your telling me all that," I said. I paused a moment. "Just what is 'global cooling'?" I'd never heard of it, and shouldn't have asked, because it set her off on a too long explanation. She finally wound down after about five minutes of telling me how all the important scientists had proved we were heading for another ice age, and that everyone was going to have to make sacrifices to avoid this horrible possibility.

Time to get back on track. "Look, Natalie—are we going to be able to work together? If our history is a problem, just let me know, and I'll figure out some other way to get submarine tactical input for your group. For example, we might fall back on some of the submarine-qualified Naval Reserve officers in the area.[39]"

"Rick, I realize you're new on board here, and you have a lot to learn about this project. The Outlaw Shark capability is primarily designed for the new *LOS ANGELES* class submarines. They've made provisions in the design of those boats to set aside room for the equipment. It's possible that the newest of the existing boats will get this also, but any submarine more than a few years old is out of the picture for this project. So what are the odds that we'll find a reservist with experience on one of the newer boats, and who's willing to devote time to this project?"

"Probably not very good, but you still didn't answer my question as to whether you're comfortable working with me or not."

"It won't be a problem. I mean, we're friends, right?"

No, we're ex-lovers, I thought, but nodded agreeably. I really didn't want to be "friends" with Natalie, but there didn't seem to be any alternative but to treat her platonically despite what would probably be regular contact at work. She certainly wasn't showing any interest in rekindling our relationship. If only to maintain my pride, I'd keep my distance and let her initiate any meetings between us.

"So tell me what some of the important factors are that we have to take into account in making this software work," she suggested.

I'd brought a writing pad with me and started by sketching what the attack center of the *BOWFIN* looked like. "Let's start with physical constraints, based on my last boat, which is fairly new. This is the Control Room, and this area is where the fire control analysis and decisions take place, so it's the best place to have the Outlaw Shark terminal. It's about nine feet long, and there's not much spare room, either for the equipment

---

[39] This actually happened. I was one of the two Reserve submarine officers brought in to help on the Outlaw Shark project. We could only put in a few hours a month on it. The project, I have to emphasize, was managed much more professionally in real life than in this fictional story.

itself or for another operator to sit. It's already jammed with three or four people on consoles that are used during an attack."

Natalie nodded. "This is good stuff. Someone should have told us this before. By the way, I think we have some preliminary specs on the *LOS ANGELES* submarines. They should be in our technical library, in the classified section. You might want to check those to see how their control room is different than what you're used to."

I made a note on that and went on, "At some point we need to talk about how the targeting information from the Outlaw Shark system gets into the Harpoon. If the missile was designed for submarine operation, it'll probably have the same capability as a torpedo to accept data from the fire control consoles." I paused a moment. "Is there a Harpoon expert here, or do I have to go somewhere else? Here's the issue—shooting the missile in a straight line toward the target means the target—if it's a warship—can counter-target the submarine by firing a surface-to-subsurface weapon right back down the line of the missile track. It'd be nice to be able to program a zig into the weapon so it couldn't be easily traced back to the submarine."

Natalie gave me a rueful look. "I didn't understand much of what you said there. But I don't think Federated has any Harpoon experts on staff. Some other company—was it McDonnell?—designed the missile. But I'm sure we have some preliminary operator manuals on it. So far as I know, the missile isn't actually in production; I think they're planning on rolling it out next year."

We talked for another half hour about some of the other issues regarding the program, and then I excused myself to go back up to the fifth floor. She didn't say anything about meeting again, either for work or socially. Maybe it was best that way.

It was almost time for lunch by the time I got back to my own area. Yolanda was waiting for me. "Rick, you need to get your desk accessories and supplies, and I've got some forms for you to fill out, mostly for computer access." Although her spoken English was quite good, I detected a slight "j" sound on words beginning with "y," and my name came out like "Rrreek."

She turned me around and took me down to the second floor, where there was a large room filled with various types of office supplies. I loaded up with in and out trays, pads of paper, binders, pens and pencils, a stapler, and so on. Yolanda helped carry all this; I walked behind her as we went back to our area so I could appreciate those luscious legs in the mini-skirt. Not very subtle, I concede.

Yolanda helped me store the supplies, and then looked around to make sure no one was near my cubicle. She leaned in closer, offering a better view of her lush cleavage. "You and I need to talk sometime outside the office. It's important." She'd suddenly lost her accent.

79

"About what?" I asked, wondering if she was coming on to me.

"About why you're really here, Commander," she said. "But it can keep until next week." She strode out of my cubicle, her hips swinging rhythmically.

"What the hell was that about?" I muttered aloud. Sammon hadn't said anything about other Navy agents being on the case. Who else would address me with my supposedly secret rank? And what happened to her Hispanic accent?

After stowing my office supplies, I spent a few minutes turning my desk around so I'd face the room rather than having my back to it. Andy came by, saw what I was doing and frowned, but didn't say anything.

Chapter **16**

A FEW MINUTES later Malone, Owen and Phil asked me if I'd like to join them for lunch in the cafeteria. "Absolutely," I said, and locked up my desk per company rules, even though there was nothing in it but office supplies.

Naturally, all of them had submarine questions, so I spent most of the lunch telling submarine stories, many of which were true. I tried to give the impression that I'd gradually become disillusioned with a Navy career. I ended up answering so many questions that most of my food was left when the others finished. Apparently lounging in the cafeteria wasn't encouraged; the other three left when they'd finished eating, saying they'd see me upstairs.

After finishing my lunch, and seeing no reason not to, I used a payphone outside the cafeteria to call Sammon. When he answered I said, "I'm calling from a payphone at Federated. Two things. First, I just met the person managing the software team. Her name is Natalie Montaigne, and I know her from Cal. I don't have the file on her yet from Detweiler, but could you start a check on her? She was very active in the anti-war movements back in Berkeley, and I'm a little surprised to see her working for a defense contractor on a job that requires a Top Secret."

"Spell her last name. OK. I'll run a national agency check on her, but before I can do credit reports and so on, I'll need the Social Security number. I can send what we've got over to DIS[40] for a background investigation and see what they come up with. But she must have a TS or she wouldn't be read into this project."

He paused then asked, "How well did you know her back in the day?"

"Actually, we were a couple for a while," I admitted.

"And then she dumped you?"

"I wouldn't put it that way."

"I'm sure you wouldn't. Have you been in contact with her since?"

"Today was the first time I've seen or talked to her for almost eight years."

---

[40] DIS = Defense Investigative Service. This was established in 1972 to centralize security clearances and security investigations.

"And she pops up as a key person in a counter-espionage assignment," Sammon mused out loud. "Okay, what was the second thing?"

I related the strange remark Yolanda had made. "It was like she was from NIS or ONI. She addressed me as 'Commander' and made me feel she knew exactly why I'm here. Also, she lost her accent, I suppose to let me know she was playing a role in her regular job."

"She's definitely not Navy," he said emphatically. "And no other federal agency should know about this operation. It's compartmented material and as far as I know, no one outside our organization has been read into it. I'll tell you what—I'll bump this up to the Director and see if he can find any trace of this woman or someone like her in the FBI, NSA, DIA, CIA and so on. Give me a physical description—that'll help."

"Well, she appears to be Mexican or maybe Central American, but speaks English with no accent, at least when she's not using one on purpose. Long black hair, light tan complexion, dark brown eyes. She may be in her mid to late twenties, and is probably about five feet nine inches tall and about 130 pounds. Let's see—she's a very good-looking young lady. Excellent figure, very nice legs."

"I see your powers of observation have improved since your training here," he said sarcastically.

Ignoring this, I said, "Captain, you said you might ask the CIA. I thought the CIA couldn't operate domestically."

"And I thought the tooth fairy left me money, Halsted. I'll get back to you." Having had the last word as usual, he hung up.

Carrying a Coke, I headed back up to my cubicle, planning to dive into all the material I could find on the project. Malone was waiting for me. "Where have you been?" he asked impatiently.

"Well, let's see," I said slowly. "I had lunch with you, Owen and Phil, but you know that. After lunch, I got a cold drink before coming back here to read up on the project. Was that OK?" I brandished the soft drink.

"Someone saw you on a payphone down by the cafeteria," Malone said, frowning.

"I'm sure they did. I was calling my landlord to make a complaint about the air conditioning in my apartment." I'd made up that lie on the way back up. Was I being spied on everywhere I went in this building. Could the payphones be tapped? That'd be awkward.

"Why didn't you use your desk phone?"

"Because I assumed we couldn't use company phones for personal calls. And I was down in the cafeteria anyway. If it's OK to use company phones for calls like that, just let me know."

"You can use your desk phone for personal business as long as it's a local call and doesn't take more than a few minutes," Malone said grudgingly. "And we need to talk about your clearance."

It turned out I wouldn't regain my Top Secret compartmented clearance until Federated's personnel department completed the paperwork, including checking with the Navy to make sure my special background investigation was current. It'd be interesting if whoever they contacted at BUPERS said I was still on active duty.

All I could do until the clearance came through would be to spend my time reading and studying the unclassified and Confidential material Malone gave me. The culture in this office, I learned, was to stay past five pm, except for Yolanda. She arrived promptly at 8:30 and left on the dot of five. For the rest of us, it seemed like a contest, with the last person to leave the office each evening being the winner. On the other hand, no one seemed to be working very hard. Strange. I decided to try to be the first one in each morning and the last to leave at night. This would increase my odds of spotting suspicious behavior among my co-workers, and being alone after everyone left would also give me an opportunity to snoop in my colleagues' desks and personal safes.

Chapter 17

TUESDAY afternoon I realized I still hadn't received the additional personnel files from Detweiler, nor had he contacted me to set a new delivery date. Assuming that calls from my phone at work might be monitored, I decided to call him at home during the evening. After leaving work at six-thirty, I dodged around Sunnyvale until I was sure no one was tailing me and picked another random payphone.

A woman's voice answered, "Detweiler residence."

"This is Ray Spruance," I said. "May I speak to Dick, please?" I hoped his wife wasn't a WWII history buff.

"He's not here now, Mr. Spruance. I'd be glad to take a message." She wasn't.

"Would you let him know that I'm still waiting for some information he was going to furnish me? I hate to bother him at home, but if you could let him know it's important I get it as quickly as possible, I'd really appreciate it."

"Can you give me a number he can reach you at?"

I gave her my phone number, thanked her again and hung up, frustrated that I couldn't reach Detweiler.

When I got back to my apartment, I found I had a message from Beth, wanting to know why I hadn't called her "all week." In fact, it had been only a few days since we'd been together, but apparently I was expected to call or see her regularly. Like the atmosphere control systems on *BOWFIN*, she seemed to be high maintenance. I called her and apologized half-heartedly, explaining I'd been working late. This didn't seem to satisfy her. Maybe I could placate her later. Or perhaps it wasn't worth the effort. Since Natalie had reappeared, I was less interested in other women, which was foolish. Natalie had shown no indication she was interested in me.

When I still hadn't heard from Detweiler by Wednesday evening, I decided I'd had enough. I got up early on Thursday and left the apartment, driving a different route and checking carefully in the light traffic for anyone tailing me. Pulling over at a payphone off Sunnyvale-Saratoga Road, I checked my watch. It was five-thirty here, so it'd be eight-thirty at Sammon's office.

When he answered, I explained that Detweiler hadn't returned the call I'd made and was several days late on supplying the files for the computer systems people and the classified personnel data for everyone involved.

"And that includes the file for this Montaigne broad?" he asked.

I didn't like him referring to Natalie as a "broad," but answered "Yes" curtly.

"You don't need to know what I've got on him," he said, "but I'll call him in a couple of hours when he's in his office. I can guarantee he'll be salivating to get them to you as quickly as he can. When you see him, make it clear that if he doesn't keep you *very* happy about his cooperation, things won't go well for him. If you don't have that material in a few days, let me know—but first, let him know how pissed off you are."

I acknowledged and hung up, curious about the leverage he had over Detweiler. Being already up and dressed, I headed into work early. Maybe I could leave sometime before six if I got an early start.

I was deep into researching the unclassified data on the project when, at ten, my desk phone rang. "Rick Halsted," I answered.

"This is Detweiler. I can deliver the material you want tonight. When can you be at the restaurant?" I couldn't believe the man was stupid enough to call my office phone from his own office, but the mistake had been made.

"You must have dialed the wrong number," I said, and hung up. Maybe that would confuse anyone who might be recording the intra-company calls. From there I headed down to the cafeteria payphone, called the dumb bastard back, and told him to meet me at 6:30 that evening. "Bring everything I asked for," I emphasized, and reminded him our rendezvous was the Thai restaurant.

Naturally, I was there before he showed up. It was more crowded than I'd hoped, but I'd found a table with no one sitting within earshot. A few minutes after 6:30, he finally slipped through the door and headed to my table. I'd decided to use my "rude and overbearing" personality to get him back into line. It came to me easily.

"Do you think you're in a position to ignore specific instructions?" I hissed. "You promised those files by Tuesday. You didn't deliver, and then you dodged my phone calls. Today you were dumb enough to call me from your office on my work phone, and now you arrive late. Is this some kind of joke to you, or should I tell Sammon you refuse to cooperate?"

"I've got the files here—it just took me a little longer to have time alone to copy them than I thought," Detweiler said hesitantly.

"Maybe you could have stayed at the office past five," I suggested sarcastically. "But we'd hate to cut into your leisure hours. Now, let me see those files so I can make sure I have what I need."

"They're right here," Detweiler stammered, opening his briefcase. He passed over a set of folders.

I leafed slowly through them. After taking enough time to irritate him, I asked, "Where's the classified data associated with these people? Remember me asking you for it?"

"That ... that takes a little longer to get," Detweiler said, looking down at the floor.

"Look," I said firmly, "your performance has been unsatisfactory. I don't think you understand what'll happen to Federated if we can't solve the security issue in the Outlaw Shark project. The Navy will pull the project and there'll be very little chance the company will ever again get work from us. We'll make sure the blame will land on you. Not to mention what Sammon can do to your career." I was making all this up, but judging by the expression on his face, it seemed to be working.

"So, right here and now, you make a firm commitment as to when you're going to get me the rest of this information," I told him firmly. "Or else ... well, you know what the alternative is." I hoped he knew, because I sure as hell didn't. But since Sammon was clearly holding a figurative gun to Detweiler's head, there must be something he could do that Dickie wouldn't like.

"Don't do that," he pleaded. "Give me a couple of days and I'll have that for you."

"So by Monday evening, you'll be able to give me everything?"

"Yes—absolutely," Detweiler said desperately. "I'll even stay late to make sure I get it done." What a sacrifice—staying past normal business hours.

"Be here with *all* that material by no later than 7:30 Monday evening," I told him. "Now get out of here." After he stumbled out, I ordered spicy beef Kow Pad and Singha beer and flipped through the files.

Chapter 18

FRIDAY morning Malone let me know my Top Secret clearance had been reinstated, only two days later than promised. Now I could start doing some of the work Federated was paying me for. I'd already gotten a decent start on the work the Navy was paying me for—the counter-espionage investigation of the project.

I headed down to the classified library to start learning more about the Harpoon missile. I already knew there were three versions of the missile planned—one to be launched from aircraft, one from surface ships, and one from submarines. The submarine model would be encapsulated so it could be launched from a standard 21-inch torpedo tube, float to the surface, and then ignite and fly away.

As I'd mentioned to Natalie, one of my concerns, in my capacity as the submarine expert on the project, was the flight path of the missile. If it headed directly for the target, it'd create a line of position from the target to the firing submarine. I flipped through the preliminary manual issued by McDonnell-Douglas and couldn't find any mention of a capability to insert a zig into the missile's course. I found an appendix citing possible future enhancements; one of them would allow waypoints to be created so the missile's path could be programmed. I made a note to find out who to contact at McDonnell to see when this upgrade would be available.

Next, I found the plans for the new *LOS ANGELES* (also known as "688 Class") SSN's. The schematics indicated there'd be more room for computer hardware than in previous boats, which might be good news, depending on how much capacity would be left for the Outlaw Shark system after the standard submarine sonar and fire control system hardware had been installed. The attack center area in the control room was larger than what I was used to in *BOWFIN*, which had, along with its sister long-hull *STURGEON* boats, the most spacious attack center of any active American SSN. The Navy had a compulsion to cram equipment into whatever cubic footage is available, so the only way to know for sure would be to have more detailed specs or, ideally, to visit a 688-class boat that was basically complete. The *LOS ANGELES* herself had been launched over a year ago and should be fitted out with much of her equipment, although her commissioning was still several months away. She was in Norfolk; I decided it'd be helpful to organize a visit.

As an ostensibly former submarine officer, I was hardly in a position to request such a visit. The request would have to come from Federated or whichever flag officer in the Pentagon had responsibility for the Outlaw Shark program. I considered calling Sammon from the payphone in the cafeteria, but shelved the idea. I didn't want Malone wondering why I was making calls from down there, now that I officially knew I could use my desk phone for personal calls.

Looking at my watch, I saw it was almost lunchtime. The best thing to do, I decided, would be to go out for lunch and seize the opportunity to call Sammon. I had some other things to discuss with him, including the Detweiler problem.

I left the building at 11:45 and headed on a circuitous route. Once I was sure no one was tailing me, I found a payphone a few blocks off El Camino and dialed the toll-free number.

"Captain, this is Rick," I began. "I've got a few things to discuss. Do you have a minute to talk?"

"Go ahead—I've got a meeting in about fifteen minutes, so make it quick."

"First thing—can you arrange with whichever admiral back in DC has authority over this program to set up a visit to *LOS ANGELES* for some of the people from Federated? She should be in Norfolk and, I hope, almost fully fitted out. We need to see whether the gear from this project will actually fit into the boat and how it might be integrated into the attack center."

"Who would you want to go on that visit?" he asked.

"I think Andy Malone would insist on going, and he should be asked to pick someone else in addition to me. Also, Natalie Montaigne should go, since one of the issues is fitting all the necessary computer hardware and terminals onto the boat."

"So you want me to set it up so you and your ex-girlfriend can go on a cross-country trip on the Navy's dime?" he asked.

Refusing to rise to the bait, I answered, "Yes, sir. You can decide not to include her, but this is squarely in her area of responsibility. She has the best handle on how much room the computer hardware will require, and you know how tight space is on a submarine. We'll want to set it up the same way we discussed earlier—the crew is briefed ahead of time so no one identifies me as an active-duty naval officer. Also, we need to make sure this looks like an initiative of the program manager, rather than something I might have asked for."

"OK, just jerking your chain a little about Natalie," Sammon chuckled. "I think we can arrange that. I'll get back to you on the timeline. What else have you got?"

"Did you hear anything back yet about Yolanda and what outfit she may be associated with?"

"The Director sent requests, along with your description of her appearance, to all the agencies we talked about. You got their attention by emphasizing her looks, so I'm certain they're looking through their files, if only to have an excuse to look for hot young women. My guess is that she's FBI, but none of these agencies, including the Fish and Wildlife Service, are likely to own up to having put her in place. The Director says he's pushing hard, and that he has SecNav[41] behind him on this, so maybe we'll get some results. Don't hold your breath for a quick answer. Now, tell me, how's our friend Dickie Detweiler doing?"

"That was my last topic," I said. I described the meeting of the previous evening, and Detweiler's promise to have the rest of the material to me by Monday. "That's almost a week after he promised," I told him angrily. "What do you have on him, anyway?"

"You'll never know. I'll try to reach him today. Talk to you later." he hung up.

On the way back to work, I went through a McDonald's drive-through and came out with a quarter-pound cheeseburger, an order of fries, and the largest Coke they had. I ate in the car as I drove back to the office in time to be at my desk less than an hour after I'd left. This didn't stop Malone from quizzing me, obviously irritated that I'd left the building instead of eating at the cafeteria. I assumed Malone's attitude was based on annoyance at me doing things my way, rather than any suspicion about my activities. In our brief acquaintance, I had yet to be impressed with his intellect. Or his management skills.

I was still in the office at six when Malone finally called it a week and left without saying anything to me, the last occupant. This rudeness was, I supposed, his way of showing his disapproval of my daring to go out for lunch without asking permission.

I spent the afternoon writing up two reports, one on the issues regarding the Harpoon missile; the other was my preliminary conclusion on the compatibility of the 688-class submarine with the Outlaw Shark system. Based on the highest classification of the information I'd referred to in the reports, each was classified Secret. Both were written in longhand. I planned to hand them over to Yolanda on Monday to type a draft version of each that I could mark up. I put the drafts into my personal safe and locked it.

I waited half an hour to make sure Malone wouldn't come back and then went to his cubicle and examined the lock on his safe. Everyone in the office, except Phil, had a safe to lock up classified material when away from the desk. Phil didn't have the privilege of storing written material

---

[41] Secretary of the Navy, the civilian head of the Navy and Marine Corps

above the Confidential level, and therefore had no need for a safe. You may think it was odd he could access Top Secret compartmented data but not be authorized to store it. I certainly did, but I was a newbie in the civilian world.

"Time to try out my safe-cracking skills," I muttered as I slowly rotated the dial of Malone's safe. I quickly learned I had little hope of getting in this way. My own safe had the old-fashioned rotary wheels that provided audible and tactile clues to the numbers in the combination, but Malone's seemed to incorporate lightweight wheels that were so quiet I couldn't detect the numbers that had been set. This made it impossible to use the techniques I'd been taught to identify the numbers comprising the combination. After twenty minutes, I abandoned the effort, making a mental note to call Sammon to see what options he might have for getting into this safe. I took a quick look at Owen's safe. It was built like mine, and I was able to get into it in short order, but found nothing of interest. Quick examinations of the contents of the other safes didn't yield anything interesting either.

I returned to Malone's desk and began rifling through its drawers. They were locked, but manipulation with my lock-pick set opened them up quickly. I worked on one drawer at a time, first carefully examining the contents to memorize the arrangement of the contents so I could put everything back properly. Besides trying to find anything that might indicate Malone was siphoning out secrets of the project, I was also looking to see if my boss was stupid enough to leave a note with his safe's combination. After forty-five minutes, I hadn't found anything suspicious, nor had I seen anything resembling a safe combination. There was a voice muttering at the back of my mind about finding the combination, but I couldn't make it surface. I shrugged and looked at my watch—seven-thirty. Time to go, even though I had no plans for tonight, to one of the "mixer" nights at Carillon. But should I?

Chapter 19

S HOULD I go to the mixer again? I decided not. I'd committed to a
date tomorrow night with Beth, and didn't see any particular point
in trolling for new possibilities. Natalie's reappearance had made it
difficult to get interested in another woman, despite the fact that she'd
made no effort to see me again—our talk on Monday morning had been
our last conversation for that entire week.

On Saturday morning, I decided to go to a gun range I'd located
through the Yellow Pages. It was up in Cupertino, and promised a variety
of target types, including pop-ups. I was just loading my gun bag when
the phone rang. It was Beth, wanting to discuss tonight's activities.

"I'm going shooting this morning," I told her. "Would you like to
come along? I can take you to lunch after and we can talk about what to
do tonight. Then I need to get some work out of the way before we go out
this evening." She didn't want to shoot, and made it clear she was upset
that I had to work in the afternoon. I'd already realized she was high
maintenance, for which I didn't have the time or patience. If we
continued to date, both of us would end up pissed off, so it might be best
to put our relationship to a merciful end after this weekend.

The range was well-equipped and laid out, with decent separation
between the shooting stations. This was my first time shooting my new
pistol. I went through six clips of ammunition before I felt comfortable
with it. After lunch at a tavern in Cupertino I went back to the apartment
for more work.

I went through Natalie's file first. She'd graduated from Cal with
honors and a 3.65 GPA; higher than mine, the bitch. I read her
performance reviews from her start at Federated in 1970 up to the
present. They were all quite glowing, showing why she'd already been
promoted twice. I saw with a stab of something—was it envy?—that she
was making considerably more than I was at Federated, and slightly
more than my total even after I added in my Navy pay. Her address had
changed after her last promotion from an apartment to an address in
Cupertino that might be a private home. Pulling out my map of the South
Bay Area, I located the address, just west of the 280 freeway. I marked
the site with an "N" and decided, now that I had the basic files for
everyone on the project, to place their initials at their addresses on the

map. Most everyone lived in or near Sunnyvale, except for Phil Boyce, who lived down in Gilroy, about forty miles south of Federated and off the map, for that matter.

"Interesting," I muttered once I had all of them plotted. I made a notation on the margin of the map of the monthly take-home pay of each person, based on the latest pay stubs. I decided it'd be helpful to take the information from each credit report, work out mortgage and property tax payments, and then compare that to each person's take home pay. For those living in apartments, it should be easy to get the rental figures and do the same comparison. Maybe that'd reveal people who might, at least based on their Federated pay, be living beyond their means. Or maybe I was over-analyzing. But it was submariners who put the "anal" in "analysis."

I looked at my watch and saw it was about time to put my work away and pick up Beth. She'd decided tonight's movie would be "One Flew Over the Cuckoo's Nest." From what I'd heard, it sounded depressing. But if a gloomy movie where the main character—her favorite actor—had a frontal lobotomy and became literally a complete idiot would make her happy, that was fine with me.

So it was dinner and a movie, followed by an abbreviated make-out session in Beth's place. I was proud of myself for not pushing her for sexual favors, since I'd already decided our relationship had reached a point of no return. I told her I had more work to do on Sunday, and had to go into the office. Naturally, I'd lied—my real plan was to just take the day off and go somewhere to relax and think about the project. I'd have to stay away from my apartment in case the suspicious girl decided to see if I was home. I didn't attempt to schedule our next date, leaving her obviously disappointed in me. That'd make the upcoming breakup much simpler.

Sunday worked out fine. I took a lot of my material to the local public library and spent time cross-indexing addresses and phone numbers, and looking up whatever personal information about each person I could find in the local papers. I didn't find much—after all, there was no way to look up newspaper articles based on a person's name. I got a few nuggets, including some society articles on Andy Malone's wedding, which appeared to have been a very posh affair. I understood that the bride's parents traditionally ponied up much of the cost of what seemed to have been a very elaborate wedding, but wondered how Andy had ended up in such an elevated social circle. If he'd married into wealth, it seemed less likely he'd be spying for cash. For some people, there was never enough money. Even if it wasn't money, ideology might be motivating him.

Chapter 20

I GOT to the office early on Monday. Now that I had my security clearance, I'd be able to make progress both in my real job—finding out whether classified data on the project was being leaked to the Soviets—and my nominal job of working as an engineer on the project.

I pulled the two draft reports out of my safe and used the first hour to go through them and make some minor corrections. I handed them to Yolanda for draft typing. Federated had invested in mag-card typewriters—the new generation of office equipment—so work could be saved and easily modified.

"Why didn't you dictate these to me?" Yolanda asked peevishly. "You aren't supposed to spend your time writing things out in long-hand." There was the accent again.

One reason I hadn't used dictation was that I'd found my thoughts came better when I was writing rather than talking. The other was that having Yolanda displaying her long sleek legs and deep cleavage as she took shorthand notes might have made it more difficult for me to think clearly. I only offered the first reason to her, but she was still irritated. "I'll have them for you after lunch," she told me sullenly. Considering she, like everyone else in the department, would have to spend several non-productive hours in the weekly meeting, this would be an excellent response time.

The weekly meeting started promptly on time. But this time there was a uniformed naval officer—a Lieutenant Commander wearing an insignia I'd never seen before. From where I was sitting, it looked vaguely like submarine dolphins, but clearly wasn't. "This must be that brand-new Surface Warfare insignia I'd heard about[42]," I mused. The Navy's surface community had been jealous for decades that naval aviators, submariners, and UDT were allowed to wear a distinguishing pin, but

---

[42] Actually, the Surface Warfare pin wasn't instituted until a few years later; I couldn't resist putting it into the story of the Outlaw Shark project. In about 1979, I got a letter from BUPERS telling me that I could turn in my submarine dolphin insignia for a Surface Warfare pin. But surface warfare officers couldn't upgrade to a submarine insignia, indicating that the degree of difficulty was much higher for submarine qualification.

they weren't. Now they had one, but I was guessing the qualification requirements were a lot less rigorous than for us who had gone before. Was I disparaging my fellow naval officers who happened to be in the surface Navy? Sadly, yes. I was a strong believer in the adage that if you transferred the stupidest man in the Submarine Force into the surface Navy, the average IQ of both groups would go up. Do the math and you'll see I'm right[43].

Next to Andy Malone was a well-groomed man in perhaps his late forties, wearing an elegant charcoal pinstripe suit. Malone beckoned me over and introduced us.

"This is Lee Greenwood, Rick. Lee, Rick is the newest addition to our team. Lee is the Vice President in charge of all our military-related products, and is my boss." I remembered that Andy's wife's maiden name had been Greenwood. The plot seemed to be thickening, to overuse a cliché. But if they weren't overused, they wouldn't be clichés.

Greenwood gave me a perfunctory handshake and led me into a corner of the room. "I understand you're good friends with Harris Booth."

"Not really," I answered. "I met Mr. Booth briefly down in San Diego and he suggested I apply to Federated for employment on this project. That's the only time I've spoken to him." The "not really" was true.

"I see," Greenwood said with a condescending smile. His tone of voice indicated he assumed I was being modest. "If by any chance you find yourself talking to Harris, please give him my best wishes. I guess I'll be seeing you at Andy's pool party this Saturday."

"I don't think so. I haven't been invited." Nor had I heard anything about the party, for that matter. You can see how well I was bonding with my co-workers.

"I'm sure that's an oversight, since you're new on board. Andy put out the original invitations a couple of weeks ago. I'll mention it to him."

I was about to ask Greenwood not to bother, but realized I might get better insights into my colleagues (or should I call them "suspects"?) in an informal setting, hopefully with lots of alcohol to loosen their tongues and inhibitions. I looked around and noticed that Natalie and her people were already seated. Since starting at Federated, this was only the second time I'd seen Natalie. I didn't even know where her office was, although I supposed her working space number in the company phone directory would give me a hint. She gave me a friendly smile, pointed at her watch, then pointed down. I interpreted this to mean she wanted me to join her for lunch down in the cafeteria after the meeting. Not wanting to appear

---

[43] To enter the submarine force, every volunteer, whether officer or enlisted, must be well above the average score on the Navy's written entrance tests. Now do the math.

too eager, I shrugged and put on what I hoped was a puzzled look. I probably succeeded, if only because I was confused as to why she'd want to have lunch with me. Our brief contact last week had convinced me she had no interest in me.

Malone called the meeting to order. "As you can see," he began, "we have Lieutenant Commander Tim Nielsen here from the program office in Washington. He hasn't been with us for several weeks so we'll use this as an opportunity to catch him up on our progress since then. Natalie, will you start, please?"

Her presentation was succinct and made it clear that although substantial progress had been made over the last several weeks, there were still software and computer hardware issues remaining to be settled. Nielsen asked a few questions which she answered easily.

Then it was Malone's turn. It seemed that meetings that included Nielsen and Greenwood required recapping everything that had gone on since the two of them last attended. This appeared to be a waste of valuable time to me—couldn't weekly summaries of each meeting be sent to each of these men? Since I wasn't in management, presumably this was none of my business.[44]

Andy talked for about twenty minutes. I tuned him out as soon as I realized I'd heard all this before, even though it was only my second weekly meeting. When he wound down, he suggested a ten-minute break. Most of the people left the room to head down to the cafeteria for a refill on their coffees. I lagged behind and found myself walking toward the elevator with Nielsen.

"So you were a submariner," Nielsen said, having noticed the miniature gold dolphins on my coat lapel. I gave a brief summary of my naval career. I had no particular interest in surface warfare, but was curious about what it took to get the new insignia. Not surprisingly, I learned that the qualification requirements didn't compare well to the rigorous submarine qualification procedure.[45]

The meeting reconvened, and Malone finished his description of the status of the hardware side of the project was and what issues it faced. He threw the floor open for questions and discussion.

Nielsen raised his hand. "I heard from the O-8[46] who heads up this group of projects. He decided it would be productive to have some people from the group here visit the *LOS ANGELES* in Norfolk. He's thinking a two-day visit—one day for a thorough tour of the submarine, and the

---

[44] Decades after all this happened, someone who must have worked for Andy created the "Dilbert" cartoons. You get to guess which character represented Andy.

[45] See footnote 42 in the previous page.

[46] Nielsen is referring to a Rear Admiral (upper half). Navy officer ranks begin with an "O-1" for an Ensign and go up to an "O-10" for a four-star admiral.

second day in the trainers, watching the crew practicing attack procedures. He wants the group kept down to no more than four people if we can." It sounded to me like this might be the fruit of the bug I'd put in Sammon's ear, happening much more quickly than I'd expected.

Malone adopted an expression apparently intended to simulate deep thought. "Well," he finally said, "as the team leader I should go. Natalie should go, as head of the software side of the operation. I think Rick should go, as our resident submarine expert. Everyone who has questions or issues should funnel them to me and I'll make sure we get answers while we're out there. Tim, when will this visit be laid on? And will we use government transportation, or should we travel commercial?" It was telling that he didn't attempt to pick a fourth person, when clearly almost everyone, including Yolanda, was interested in being included.

Nielsen answered, "It'll take a couple of weeks to get it set up. You'll fly commercial into DC and then get a connecting flight to Norfolk. I'll call you when we have a definite date so you can get the flights set up. For your overnight in Norfolk, we'll set you up with rooms in the VOQ[47]."

I spoke up. "I think Tim's suggestion on the trainers is a great idea. It'll give us a chance to see the physical limitations of a submarine attack center, and maybe some ideas on how and where to position the console—if it turns out actually to be a separate piece of equipment—so it can be in the middle of the action without getting in the way. One thing though—because of the time difference, we'll probably have to spend two nights at the VOQ—we won't get in until late on the first day of travel. Even if we got a 7 am flight out of SFO, we wouldn't get to a DC airport until about 3 pm their time and we'd still have to connect to Norfolk."

"What's the VOQ like?" Natalie asked curiously.

"Ever stayed at a Motel 6?" I responded. She seemed to shudder, but favored me with a tentative smile. I'd never actually been to Norfolk, but this was a safe guess based on what I'd seen of VOQ's.

"Anybody else have anything to add?" Malone asked perfunctorily, obviously ready to shut down the meeting.

It was time to step up. "I know I'm the new guy here, but I just wanted to get something straight. So far as I can tell from everything I've studied since I started here, the Outlaw Shark program is completely focused on attack submarines—SSN's, right?"

Malone answered curtly. "Obviously. What's your point?" I had the feeling my boss was acting out, maybe to impress Greenwood with his management skills. I wasn't sure it was working on Greenwood, but it wasn't doing a thing for me.

---

[47] VOQ = Visiting Officers' Quarters. The quality of these rooms are usually a notch above the BOQ for bachelor officers, putting them on a par with a low-end motel room.

"Well," I replied, "this is probably in Commander Nielsen's bailiwick. But it seems to me that the Navy ought to consider putting this system into SSBN[48]'s as well."

"I don't understand," Malone said pompously. "SSBN missions don't include attacking surface targets." He should have stopped after his first sentence. Andy must have gotten a Cliff's Notes for basic submarining and not read it all. Actual submarine doctrine was that SSBN's, if they survived their missile launch, were to take on the role of an attack submarine—hunting down and destroying enemy ships and submarines.

"Not as their primary mission," I agreed. "But they're *very* interested in remaining undetected when they're on patrol. I've never served on a boomer, but I think I have a good handle on their operating philosophy. It can be summed up as 'never let yourself be detected.' If they could tap into the ocean surveillance database via Outlaw Shark, they'd have an early warning system about what ships might be in or coming into their area. And after an SSBN fires their missiles, they'd have to fight their way out against the Soviet forces that would be vectored onto them. Outlaw Shark and some Harpoon missiles might be a good way to do that. I'm sure any SSBN CO would be very happy to have this system available to them. And their attack centers have lots of room compared to an SSN."

All heads turned to Nielsen, who was either thinking deeply or making a good show of it. Finally he said, "I'll ask the program manager to contact COMSUBPAC and COMSUBLANT to see what they think. They'll bounce it back to OP-02[49] in the Pentagon for a final decision. This won't be a fast-turnaround item—it'll take some time to formulate the question for the submarine force commanders and longer to get an answer. I'd guess it'd be at least a month before we know what they think. But this is definitely worth pursuing."

I saw that Malone and Greenwood understood that if the SSBN's also used the Outlaw Shark technology, Federated would more than double their sales volume on this project. They were talking happily, with occasional approving glances toward me.

---

[48] SSBN = Submarine (SS) Ballistic Missile (B) Nuclear powered (N). In the 1970's, the US Navy had forty-one of these big submarines. They spent most of their time at sea, with two different crews ("Blue" and "Gold") alternating, so the submarine's time on patrol could be maximized. These boats were also known as "boomers." In "real life" 1976, my reserve colleague and I suggested to the Sunnyvale Test and Evaluation Detachment that the Outlaw Shark system would be more valuable as a defensive tool for SSBN's than as an offensive tool for SSN's.

[49] The OP-02 was a vice admiral with the title Deputy Chief of Naval Operations (Submarine Warfare). He reported to the Chief of Naval Operations, the Navy's most senior officer. There were similar billets for surface (OP-03) and air (OP-05) warfare; each was referred to as a "Platform Baron."

The meeting paused when Malone announced lunch was being brought in. The doors opened, revealing two servers who arranged trays of sandwiches, salads, and soft drinks on a side table. I looked ruefully at Natalie and shrugged, getting a disappointed smile in reply. Was that platonic?

"Come up here, Rick," Malone called out, and I trudged up to sit between Greenwood and Malone. All I'd been thinking about was how helpful the technology Federated was putting together would be for the SSBN's, but my boss and my boss's boss seemed to think I'd been focusing on the company's profit margins. I decided whatever got me more believability couldn't help but give me more opportunities to do my real job.

When I sat down, Malone asked me excitedly, "What do you think about the possibility of extending Outlaw Shark to surface ships?" What I thought was that Malone needed a much deeper understanding of naval operations than he'd demonstrated so far. Greenwood was regarding Malone with what seemed like amusement.

"I think we need Commander Nielsen for that, but my understanding is that the surface Navy uses a system called NTDS—the Naval Tactical Data System—to exchange targeting information like that," I told him.

Malone's face fell, but he asked Nielsen over and hesitantly offered his idea. Nielsen tactfully explained that surface ships wouldn't have any use for the Outlaw Shark system. "But," he went on, "Rick's idea on the SSBN's is excellent—I don't see any reason why this wouldn't be approved. Assuming the data in the ocean surveillance system is good, this seems like it'd be invaluable to them, not only when they're on station, but when they're transiting to and from their patrol area."

My boss—a word I was starting to feel queasy about when it applied to Malone—remained cheerful. "I have to apologize," he told me, "for forgetting to let you know there's a pool party at my house this Saturday. You—and a guest if you'd like to bring one—are very welcome to join us. Yolanda will provide you with my address and a map showing how to get there." Even when he was trying to be friendly, the man couldn't help but sound as though he was reading a speech.

Chapter 21

A FTER we'd all eaten, the meeting broke up and we returned to our work routine.

As promised, Yolanda produced the smooth copies of my two reports. Clipped to them was a note with the name of a local tavern—the "Brass Rail"—and the notation "Meet me there at 5:30. It's important!" She also gave me a photocopy of a hand-drawn map to Andy's house and an invitation to the party on Saturday.

I decided to show up at the tavern. Maybe I could find out more about Yolanda and why she seemed to know too much about me. I tried to figure out how to respond if she directly challenged me on who I really was. Since I couldn't admit that I was at Federated under false pretenses, I'd have to divert the conversation away from anything related to that. Hopefully I'd come up with an effective tactic to do that. I didn't have one yet.

Even though having left work at the official quitting time for the first time since I'd started, I arrived at the tavern to find Yolanda already waiting at a secluded table. Most of the men in the place were staring at her; they gave me resentful looks as I took a seat next to her. She came to the point as soon as I sat. "I know you're working for Navy intelligence. Your boss is Jack Sammon and you're here on a counter-espionage mission." The Hispanic accent was missing.

Shaken, but trying not to show it, I decided to deliberately misunderstand. Maybe I could bluff my way out of this. "Yolanda, I've never heard of this Joe Trout, or whatever it was you said." I signaled one of the waitresses for a draft beer.

Yolanda glared at me. "It's Jack Sammon, as you know very well. You're being deliberately obtuse, Commander, but I know exactly who you are and what you're doing here."

"Why would some secretarial person like you know anything like that? And I used to be a lieutenant, so at least you should use the right rank if you're trying to impress me with how much you know."

"I'm *not* a secretary. I'm a Special Agent in the FBI," she hissed, pulling an ID card out of her purse.

I snatched the card out of her hands and held it out of her reach, studying it carefully. "Wow! Where'd you get this made up? It looks almost real." It showed the name of 'Maria Vega' under her photo, and I was able to read a serial number ending in '2226' before she jumped to her feet and grabbed it back.

"Just what do you think you're doing? You need to listen to me—Sammon isn't what he seems and he's not a good guy." she told me angrily as she resumed her seat.

Perhaps the best way was to try to turn the whole thing into a joke. So I smiled and gave it a whirl. "You're saying there's something fishy about Sammon? I guess that's kind of funny. Look, Yolanda, or whatever you want to pretend your name is—if this is some way of trying to get me interested in you, all you have to do is say so without all this secret agent bullshit. I mean, you wouldn't be behaving the way you do—showing yourself off and inviting me out for drinks—if you weren't interested in me, right? Let's go back to my place. Then we can have some fun without you playing 007."

She snarled something that sounded like 'buck view'—I couldn't make out the words—and stomped out. I tried to figure out what to do. I was worried about her allegation regarding Sammon. Obviously I couldn't report this directly to him, in case he really *wasn't* what he seemed, as Yolanda had insisted.

I sat for a moment nursing my beer. Maria, I mused. I just met a girl named Maria. And that brought the key question to my mind—how could I solve a problem like Maria? Then I realized I was humming aloud and was getting inquisitive glances from the male patrons around me. They were probably pissed I'd driven the voluptuous beauty out of the bar, eliminating their chance to ogle her and, at the same time, wondering what I was doing mumbling to myself. Time to leave.

As I left the bar, my thoughts came back to more serious considerations. Yolanda—or Maria, or whatever her real name might be—knew way too much. I couldn't believe she was an FBI agent, but maybe that was just male chauvinism. I *was* impressed with her ability to fake a Mexican accent so well at work.

I had to report this back up the line, and not to Jack, at least not until I'd passed the word on to people above him in his chain of command. I was going to have to jump over his head and call Admiral Robards, the Director of Naval Intelligence. I'd call early the next morning; it was too late on the East Coast to call him now.

Chapter 22

RATHER than go back to work, I headed to the Thai restaurant for my rendezvous with Detweiler. He was supposed to deliver the rest of the files to me this evening, and if I was going to keep him under control, I needed to be there when he showed up.

He was, naturally, a few minutes late. "Were you followed?" I asked him before he could say anything.

"I don't think so," he stammered, as if he hadn't imagined that was possible. He wasn't filling me with confidence.

"What have you got for me?"

Detweiler opened his briefcase and pulled out a stack of slim manila folders. "Here's all the classified data on the people in both departments."

I leafed through them quickly. At first glance, the contents looked disappointing, but maybe I'd find some nuggets after going through them more carefully.

"This looks OK," I said grudgingly. "Now I'll need all the files on Lee Greenwood, and on that Navy lieutenant commander, Nielsen."

Detweiler stared at me stupidly, one of his favorite facial expressions. "But Greenwood's a vice-president. And Nielsen's not an employee, so we don't have anything on him."

"I know who Greenwood is," I said patiently. "But he has as much access to the information on this project as anyone in Malone's and Montaigne's groups."

"Look," he said nervously, "I've done a lot to help you out here, but it'd be worth my job if I were found snooping around the senior executive files. Those are kept in a separate area that I don't have routine access to."

"Here's where we are," I said forcefully. "Your task—which you were supposed to have completed *before* I started work—was to get me all the relevant files on anyone at Federated who had access to this information. Greenwood is one of those people. You've screwed up twice now on not having all the data. Get the Greenwood information and whatever you have on Nielsen. Then, so far as I know, you'll be off the hook." Of course, Sammon might have other ideas, or more suspects might surface, but Dickie needed some assurance now that his work might be over. And how dangerous could copying personnel files be? It wasn't like he was putting himself at any real risk.

Detweiler glared at me, but didn't have the nerve to actually speak.

"I almost forgot," I told him. "I'll also need a complete set of organization charts for the company, so I can see who else might have access to the project information."

He actually sneered at me, the insubordinate bastard. "The secretary in your department—Yolanda, isn't it?" He cupped his hands in front of his chest to make sure I knew which Yolanda in our seven-person department he was talking about. "She has a complete set—just have her make a copy for you."

"When will you have the Greenwood and Nielsen files?" I asked, ignoring the opportunity to say something sexist about Yolanda's 'complete set.' I needed to regain the upper hand.

"Let's see—today's Monday. I have to be careful getting Greenwood's. I'm pretty sure we don't have anything on Nielsen except some correspondence with the Navy; I'll check on that. I should have an opportunity in the next day or two. How about Wednesday?"

"Fine. Don't be late," I said and turned my attention to the files. He got the idea and slunk out. After another decent Thai meal, I headed back home. It took only a few minutes to get back to my apartment. My answering machine was blinking; the lights indicated I had one message. The message was a brief one from Norm Connors, telling me he had some information that I could pick up at any time; he'd leave it at the front desk.

Now seemed as good a time as any, so I made the quick run to and from the Sunnyvale police department, coming back with the credit reports.

Before I started on them, I decided to see if the alarm company could give me a list of the times they showed the system had been activated and then turned off when I re-entered. Any times I didn't recognize might represent an intruder who'd gotten around the alarm system.

I called and reached someone who identified herself as a "customer service representative," a title I'd never heard. I explained that I wanted to verify that no one else had disarmed the alarm system over the past ten days or so. "From Sunday night through Thursday of last week," I explained, "all you should see is me putting the system on "*Stay*" late at night, putting it on "*Away*" early in the morning, and disarming when I come back in between 6:30 and 7:30 pm each night. And it should be the same for today, except I got back a little earlier."

"That checks out, sir," she said after a few seconds. "But starting on Friday night, there's a lot more variability." She read off for me the times the alarm was reset from Friday afternoon until Sunday night; I jotted them down and thanked her. It looked like all the times for last weekend were consistent with my comings and goings. Maybe I hadn't yet popped onto the radar of any bad guys. I decided to start a new routine of keeping the system on "*Stay*" whenever I was alone in the apartment. Now was as good a time as any to start this habit, so I did.

Before I could start on the credit reports, my phone rang.

"This is Rick," I said into the phone as I finished punching in the code numbers to re-alarm my system.

It was Beth. She started with "You sneaky bastard," and went downhill from there. I sensed she was upset.

"What's wrong?" I asked when she paused, probably short of breath. I was trying to sound sensitive and in tune with her feminine feelings.

"It's you, you ... you son of a bitch. You've been telling me you've been working late, but it turns out you're hanging out with some cheap Mexican girl after work."

"One of your friends saw me at the Brass Rail today after work today, I suppose. Beth, that was a business-related meeting with a woman I have no interest in having any sort of relationship with. She's the secretary in my department." The "no interest" part was almost true; a few sneaky sexual fantasies sometimes popped into my mind because of Yolanda's enticing beauty. But how could anyone blame me for that?

"What kind of business meeting takes place in a bar with a girl dressed like a slut? Why couldn't you talk at work?"

"Beth, please trust me on this. It was work-related, and it's nothing to worry about."

She was silent for long enough that I wondered if she was still on the line. "No," she finally hissed. "I won't trust you. I think you took advantage of me. I think you've been lying about your work hours all along so you could see other women. I don't want to see you anymore. Don't try to contact me again." She hung up, leaving me wondering whether that last sentence meant. Could it actually be a feminine-coded plea to call her in a day or two to try to rehabilitate our relationship? That would naturally involve groveling on my part, so I wasn't interested in pursuing that option. Since I'd already realized she wasn't "the one," despite her good looks and intelligence, it was probably best to take her literally. And I'd been very careful *not* to take advantage of her, so where did she get off whining about that? The more I thought about it, the better this development was. I'd been looking for a tactful way to terminate the relationship, but Beth had pre-empted me. Good enough.

So far, since leaving work today I'd had Yolanda (or Maria) claim she was an FBI agent, had a confrontation with Detweiler, and then gotten dumped by Beth. Tomorrow I had to go over my boss's head to tell the Director of Naval Intelligence that I'd been told Sammon wasn't to be trusted. Busy busy.

I looked at my watch and at the stack of papers Detweiler had brought me, and decided to loaf through the classified files he'd brought before tackling the credit reports. Flipping through them, I saw that most of the material consisted of the FBI summary of the background investigation on each person. I didn't understand why these were considered to be classified, but I already knew some of Federated's internal practices seemed to be what an engineer would consider FUBAR'd.

I'd never seen an actual background investigation report, although several had been performed on me. The documents Detweiler had supplied were summaries of each person's financial status, criminal record, employment history, associations with organizations, education history, and so on.

Skimming rapidly, I saw that Andy Malone had gotten several negative comments regarding his ability to pay his bills on time. This was interesting, in light of his father-in-law's wealth. Presumably his credit report would shine some light on this.

I naturally went to Natalie's file to go through a report in detail. They'd all seemed similar, with brief comments in most of the sections indicating that no problem existed. The exception was in Natalie's file, where in the "Associations" section, the note said "Waiver obtained from ..." then a redacted section, then "... in accordance with the National Security Act of 1947."

"What the hell does that mean?" I murmured. I flipped quickly through the other files and didn't see any other notations like that. Going through them in more detail could wait.

Now it was time for the credit reports. Opening the packet, I saw a handwritten note from Jack explaining that the copies of the income tax returns wouldn't be ready for at least another week.

I pulled out my large spreadsheet and filled in the credit scores for each person. The lowest score was for Andy Malone, the highest paid person. Interesting, but not a surprise, based on the notes in his classified files about his bill-paying habits. Maybe I'd find out more about Andy at his pool party, to which I'd be arriving without a date, unless I persuaded Yolanda to come with me. Phil Boyce also had a relatively low score; everyone else had acceptable levels. Looking at the details, I saw that many of the recurring expenses for each person—mortgage or rent, utilities, car payments, insurance—were listed. I could compile these and compare the total with the take-home pay for each and see who might be desperate for some extra cash. In a burst of energy, I made a duplicate copy of the entire spreadsheet. I could give that to Norm so he could send it to Sammon. Unless, of course, my call to the admiral tomorrow pushed me out of Sammon's organization.

Enough, I decided, realizing it was past 10 pm and I'd been working since before 7 am. I might as well still be on sea duty. Checking to make sure the alarm was on "*Stay,*" I set the deadbolt in the door, and took my pistol out of the safe so it'd be at my bedside. I was going to have to make a very early start tomorrow.

Chapter 23

TUESDAY was going to be a ticklish day. I was nervous about calling the Director of Naval Intelligence—my boss's boss—directly. Since I'd been sworn in as a midshipman I'd never actually spoken with an admiral, unless "yes, sir" qualifies as a conversation.

My alarm went off at 0415, and I was out the door—showered, shaved, and in one of my best suits—half an hour later. I'd had trouble getting to sleep as I mentally rehearsed, over and over, how to explain this situation to the admiral.

There was almost no traffic as I drove out of the Carillon complex, making it easy for me to make sure I wasn't being tailed. I drove a long roundabout route and went north almost to Palo Alto, using mostly secondary streets before stopping at a payphone on a side street.

Before I started the call, I mentally rehearsed the short message I'd decided on. This call would only be the first step. A public payphone was a very unsuitable medium for the discussion that needed to happen.

I punched in Admiral Robards' direct number and then fed in a few dozen quarters. Why couldn't the admiral have a toll-free number like Jack's? As I'd expected, the phone wasn't actually answered by the admiral. Instead, I heard "Yeoman First Class Myers, sir. This is an unsecured line. How may I help you?"

"Petty Officer Myers, this is Lieutenant Commander Richard Halsted. I'm calling on an unsecured line, and need to arrange to speak with the Admiral on a classified topic."

Yeoman Myers, who'd clearly been well-trained, said, "Hold the line, Commander. I'll get right back to you." For someone who'd been a Lieutenant a few months ago, it was sweet to be addressed as "Commander."

As promised, he was back on the line within a minute. "Commander, the Admiral wants to know if you're in the vicinity of Moffett Field NAS[50]. " It appeared the yeoman somehow knew the number I was calling from. All the detective shows I'd seen indicated it took quite a while to trace a call. Did the Navy have technology the civilian sector didn't? Or maybe the yeoman knew I worked in Sunnyvale.

---

[50] NAS = Naval Air Station

"It's about six miles from here," I told him.

"Our clock shows 0813 Eastern Standard Time, or 0513 Pacific Time. Sir, can you get to the main gate at Moffett by 0545 your time?"

"That's affirmative."

"When you get to the gate, show civilian ID, like a driver's license, and ask for the Sergeant of the Guard. He'll escort you to a place where the Admiral can phone you on a secure line. The Admiral will call at 0600 your time." He hung up.

By 0550, I was ensconced in the office of the senior Captain who commanded the Naval Air Station. I wanted to get out of there before the CO showed up, but that'd depend on the Admiral. The Marine lance corporal who showed me in demonstrated how to punch the scrambler button. "Do that after you pick up the handset, and before you start speaking," he told me, adding "sir" as a reluctant afterthought before he left to stand outside.

The phone rang at 0559. "Lieutenant Commander Halsted," I answered after punching the scrambler button.

"This is Petty Officer Myers. Hold for the Admiral."

A few seconds later I heard, "This is Admiral Robards, Commander. Kindly tell me why you're calling me." The old gentleman didn't sound pleased to hear from me.

"Admiral, as you know, I report to Captain Jack Sammon. Yesterday I was meeting with a woman who works with me at Federated, where I'm on NIS assignment. She claimed to be an FBI agent. More importantly, she warned me that Captain Sammon 'isn't what he seems and isn't a good guy.' I couldn't very well call him and pass that on, and decided you had to know about it."

"Describe the circumstances under which you met with this person who claims to be an FBI agent, Commander." At least he didn't sound angry yet, which I took to be a good sign.

"She works at Federated, in an administrative support role in the group I'm assigned to—the Outlaw Shark team. Federated believes her name is Yolanda Ramirez. The day I started work—a week ago yesterday—she addressed me privately as 'Commander,' which got my attention, since everyone at Federated should believe I'm a former naval officer who got out as a Lieutenant. Also, when she did that, she didn't have the Hispanic accent she normally speaks with at work.

"Yesterday afternoon she slipped me a note asking me to meet with her after work. I decided to see what she had to say. She showed me what seemed to be a legitimate FBI identification card identifying her as 'Maria Vega.' I didn't get a long look at it, but the last four digits of the serial number on the card were '2226.' That was when she made her comment about Captain Sammon."

"What did you do then, Commander?"

110

"I felt it'd be a bad move to get drawn into a conversation about my mission, so I treated it as a joke, and acted as though I assumed she was trying to seduce me with a foolish story. She got angry and left."

I waited as the Admiral considered what I'd told him.

"OK," he finally said. "You did the right thing in this particular case by bypassing Jack and calling me directly." I felt pleased until he went on in a much colder tone, "Don't do it again. Now let me make a few points that you need to understand. First, I have the utmost faith in Captain Sammon's integrity and loyalty to this country. I feel sure I know what this 'Yolanda' person based her comment on, and I can guarantee you that although she may sincerely believe Captain Sammon 'isn't what he seems,' he continues to enjoy my complete confidence and trust.

"Secondly, we need to resolve two issues regarding this woman. We need to find out how she learned you're still an active duty naval officer, and we have to find out whom she's working for. Do you have any opinions on that?"

I thought for a moment. "Admiral, as you probably know, my background isn't in counterintelligence. I'm hoping she's working with a rival US agency. But it could be Soviet, Israeli, Chinese—anything ..."

Robards cut in. "What do you think we should do?" Nothing like being put on the spot by a senior officer.

"I think we should start with the 'who she works for' question. We should be able to quickly either verify or disprove the FBI ID—that'd be a big first step. Maybe we could work with each other if she's genuine. So far as finding out how she learned I'm still on active duty, I don't think we'll be able to find that out until we answer the 'who' question. I should also say that Captain Sammon has already started on identifying this woman and finding out who she's working for."

"Commander Halsted—Rick, if I can call you that—the FBI doesn't work *with* other federal agencies. They make other federal agencies work for *them*. This is our deal—it's a Navy project and we have to be the lead agency. I will contact the Director and see if he's inclined to at least let us know if this young lady is one of his. Either a firm 'yes' or 'no' would help us, but what I think we'll get is some bureaucratic weaseling while the FBI tries to figure out how to manipulate us on this. Maybe you and she can work together on this if she's a legitimate agent of a US agency, but that'll happen only if I feel comfortable that the FBI won't try to take the leadership on this away from us."

I was trying to visualize working cooperatively with Yolanda/Maria, or whatever her real name was, and was having difficulty imagining that working out well.

"Tell you what," the Admiral said. "I'll start the ball rolling on this young woman. I want you to call Jack now. Tell him everything, including why you called me first. OK?"

"Aye aye, sir," I said, having learned that's a phrase flag officers enjoy hearing. The Admiral hung up without saying goodbye. A privilege of rank, I supposed.

Checking my watch, I saw I still had over an hour before I planned to show up at work. I went to the door of the NAS CO's office and found the Marine corporal waiting in the anteroom. He didn't actually have his pistol in his hand, but looked as though he wished he were holding it. "I'm finished in there," I told him. "Is there another phone I can use to make another call? This one won't need to be on a scrambled line."

He led me to a phone on a desk in the CO's anteroom, and I dialed Sammon's toll-free number as the Marine relocked the door to the CO's office. The conversation started awkwardly, as I suppose it had to when I told him I'd gone over his head to the Director of Naval Intelligence because I wasn't sure I could trust him. I recapped the whole conversation for him and realized by his questions that he was taking this a lot more equably than I'd expected.

"All right," he said when I'd finished. "I understand why you had to call the Admiral. Someday we'll get drunk together and I'll tell you what this chica might have found out that led her to make that comment. In the meantime, what else do you have?"

"I got your credit report info yesterday." I explained how I planned to use it, building a separate data sheet itemizing take-home pay for each person and comparing it to the known monthly expenses revealed on the credit report. He seemed to like that concept. I gave him the Social Security numbers for Natalie's group, and was assured I'd have their reports in a few days.

I related how I'd learned yesterday that at least two more people were in a position to acquire classified data on the project, and that I'd asked Detweiler to get me their files. "You might be able to find out more about this Nielsen guy through Navy files," I suggested.

On a roll, I then went to a question. "Captain, I also got the background investigation reports from Detweiler last night; about ten days late. Most of them looked clean, but Natalie Montaigne's had a note in the 'Associations' section that seemed to indicate she'd been in groups that raised some eyebrows, but she got a waiver on it. The reason for the pass was partially blacked out." I pulled a slip of paper from my pocket on which I'd copied the wording on Natalie's BI and read it to Sammon.

He promised to check into it. "I should be able to at least find out which agency approved the waiver. I'm guessing its name starts with a 'C.' Probably the associations they're referring to go back to Montaigne's time at Berkeley. She was pretty active in the lefty movements there, wasn't she?"

I agreed she had been and terminated the call. After getting off the phone, it was still only 6:30. I stopped at a nearby café for a quick breakfast. As I ate my cholesterol-heavy breakfast, I pondered what to do next in my counter-espionage job.

Chapter 24

FEELING I'd already done a full day's work, I got to work shortly after 7. Dealing with the admiral had turned out to be more mentally stressful than I'd anticipated. My talk with Jack afterwards hadn't been a walk in the park either.

Wayne Girard was already at his desk, but no one else was in yet. He was apparently in a good mood, as he grunted at me in response to my cheery "good morning," rather than ignoring me as usual.

There was a phone message on my desk from 6:00 pm the night before. Owen must have still been here and been nice enough to answer my phone. Natalie wanted to see me first thing this morning. I'd wait until nine to make sure she was in.

Yolanda strolled in promptly at 8:30 as usual, favoring me with a malevolent glare that I took to be related to our meeting the previous evening. I offered a genial smile and a wink, turning her frown even nastier.

I spent a few minutes outlining the tasks I wanted to accomplish and then walked over to Yolanda. "Yolanda, can you please make me a copy of the complete set of Federated organization charts? This afternoon would be fine. I have a meeting with Miss Montaigne now, so I'll probably be out of the office for maybe an hour. Thanks for your help."

She looked around to make sure there was no one within earshot. "You shouldn't have tried to make a joke out of this whole thing yesterday. This is serious stuff. We need to meet and talk about it."

"Yolanda, I already have a girlfriend," I lied. Beth had voluntarily removed herself from that status, saving me the trouble. "I agree that having a fake FBI ID card probably is serious. But don't worry—I won't turn you in." Of course, I'd already kind of turned Yolanda in when I called Admiral Robards. Despite my reassurances, she still seemed annoyed. Strange woman.

I headed down to Natalie's office, guided by her office number, which indicated it was two floors below. The layout in her space was much like my team's, with cubicles surrounding a central conference area.

She saw me as I came in and beckoned me over to her desk. "Thanks for coming down, Rick. I wanted to get your reaction to some issues we're having with the data downloads from the ocean surveillance system. I need to know how the submarines generally communicate, how often they uplink to the satellite, what's the typical amount of data transferred, and so on. We'll have to build a storage buffer into the system to allow for each update, and I need to get an idea how much data might accumulate before a download."

We'd just started on this when one of the mailroom clerks showed up with an envelope for Natalie. "You're supposed to tell your people about this. Right away," he told her over his shoulder as he walked away.

She opened the envelope, pulled out a sheet of paper and read it. Her eyes widened.

"What is it?"

"It's from Warren Hodgkins, the CEO. It's about a manager in Personnel named Richard Detweiler. This says he was shot and killed on his way to work this morning. I've got to tell my people." She got up and called her analysts together to give them the news.

I sat there in shock. I hadn't liked the man, and he'd done a piss-poor job of getting me the information I needed on a timely basis, but I hadn't had any desire to see him dead. More importantly, he still owed me information.

Then I realized that if he'd been stupid enough to keep notes containing my name, something I wouldn't bet against, I might be one of the people questioned by the police. That would be awkward. If anyone at Federated found out I'd been in contact with Detweiler I'd have some 'splainin to do, just like Lucy Ricardo.

An even worse possibility surfaced—if Detweiler's murder was connected to the Outlaw Shark project, my name might also be on the hit list. Carrying my pistol around, even if I could take it everywhere, wouldn't make me invulnerable.

She came back and sat across from me, her eyes moist with unshed tears. "I didn't know the guy, but this is horrible news," she said softly.

After a moment of respectful silence I suggested to Natalie that we restart our discussion, but she was clearly shaken by the news. "Maybe later," she sighed. "But there was one other thing, Rick."

I nodded encouragingly.

"You know about this pool party at Andy's place on Saturday, right? I have a favor to ask, and I don't want you to take it the wrong way," she began hesitantly. "I realize you may have someone you want to bring to the party, but if you don't, I'd really appreciate it if we could go together."

This was definitely a shock. "Why would you want me to go with you? I mean, I didn't expect we'd have any sort of relationship outside of work."

Now she was blushing, and very prettily too. "I know, Rick, and it's really not fair of me, especially given what I've put you through. But I

116

thought that since we always got along well, it'd be ... well, look, it's about Phil Boyce. He keeps coming on to me whenever we see each other, and it'd be much easier for me if he thought you and I were a couple so he'd leave me alone."

So she really didn't want to be with *me* so much as to not be hassled by Phil. How flattering.

"I've got a better idea," I said cheerfully. "Since all you really need is someone to shield you from Phil, how about a blind date? My neighbor Billy is a bright presentable guy, and that way you won't have to worry about past history." As soon as I'd said that, I realized that if she accepted this offer, I'd have to skip the party rather than skulk around watching her and Billy enjoying each other's company.

"I want *you* to take me. Do I have to beg?" That might make this proposal more appealing.

"I'll think about it," I said curtly, standing up. Last week I'd realized I was still in love with her, but escorting her just so some other man wouldn't hit on her was too demeaning. I left, trying to salvage some pride.

Back in my cubicle, I saw a phone message on my desk. Apparently the Mountain View Police Department wanted to talk to me. It had to be related to Detweiler's murder. It'd been thoughtless of him not to manage to get himself killed in Sunnyvale, where at least I had a connection inside the detective bureau.

I dialed the number and gave my name. In a few seconds, I was connected with a Detective Fehler. His first sentence was, "You're what we call a person of interest in the Detweiler murder today." I didn't say anything, so he went on, "When we went through his briefcase we found a note indicating he was going to visit you last night. Did you and he actually meet?" You're supposed to like a guy who comes right to the point, but I was having a hard time with that.

I admitted we'd met last night. Fehler, now that he knew I'd been in contact with Detweiler in the hours before his murder, insisted I come into the Mountain View department for what he called a friendly discussion. I decided to take a very early lunch. I couldn't let anyone at Federated know where I was going, since I had no good answers as to why I'd known Detweiler, let alone him visiting me at home. If Yolanda realized what the phone message meant, and if she were really an FBI agent, she'd understand that she now enjoyed a tactical advantage over me. I walked out, leaving my suit coat hanging on the hook in my cubicle to give the impression I was still in the building.

By 10:30 I was at Fehler's desk. Detweiler, the detective told me, had been shot in the head by someone in a car who'd pulled up next to him at a stoplight on El Camino. The shooter had shot just before the light turned green, and then drove off.

117

"The shooter used a .45," Fehler told me. "Made a hell of a mess; almost took off the poor guy's head. Now, let's get to the point here. First of all, we want to eliminate you as a suspect."

"Sounds good to me. What time was the shooting?"

"It was 8:12 this morning. We got a call right away from a motorist who saw it happen and pulled over to call us."

"OK. I checked in at Federated at about 7:15. We have magnetic cards that are scanned to show when people come in and out. I didn't leave the building until about twenty minutes ago. You can call security at Federated to get that verified." I was hoping he'd take my word for it. I didn't want the security people at the company finding out I was linked with Detweiler's murder.

"I'm familiar with how Federated's security systems work. We'll check that out. And what time did you meet with him last night?"

"We met at a restaurant at around seven; it took about fifteen minutes."

"What was the meeting regarding?" I'd hoped this question wouldn't be asked, but of course, it had to be.

"I can't answer that, but I can assure you it has nothing to do with his murder." Another lie: I believed it was possible that Detweiler's role in supplying internal company information to me was linked with his death. Telling Fehler that would just lead to more questions I couldn't answer.

"Look, Mr. Halsted, you know I can't accept an answer like that. Just let us know the *why* about that meeting and that'll be that." His words were friendly; his ice-cold tone was not.

"I can't do that, for security reasons. I'll tell you what—you could call Norm Connors in the Sunnyvale police department. He should be able to give you assurances that I'm holding back that information for a good reason." At least I hoped he would.

"The lieutenant in charge of their detective bureau? I know him. But why should I bother him, when all you have to do is answer a simple question?"

"Detective, I'm in a situation where I can't let you know the details of why Mr. Detweiler met with me. But Norm can vouch for the fact that I'm doing something related to national security."

He shook his head, but picked up the phone and dialed. After a few minutes of tense conversation, the detective hung up, still frowning. "Norm said you were OK, and not to press you for information you shouldn't give me. If the security data from Federated validates what you told us, we'll know you couldn't have been the killer. I suppose we're finished here. Thanks for your time." He clearly wasn't happy with this situation, and would probably have loved an excuse to interrogate me more thoroughly. I made a mental note to minimize the amount of time

I'd spend in Mountain View and, when I had to be there, to carefully observe all the traffic laws. Fehler would love to have an excuse to haul me in for another friendly discussion.

On the way back to the office I realized Sammon needed to know about Detweiler's murder. I went through my usual routine to detect possible tails before stopping at a payphone on Fair Oaks. Debbie answered the phone at Motivational Consulting.

"Debbie, it's Rick. I need to talk to Captain Sammon."

"He's out all day for a meeting, Rick. I can take a message."

"Let him know that Dick Detweiler was shot and killed this morning. I'll give him more details when I speak with him." Debbie repeated the message and promised to relay it to Jack when he called in. I'd call back at around 8 pm Eastern time, since Debbie told me he planned to come back to the office after the meeting.

I stopped at a drive-through Mexican place and went back to work, getting back to our area shortly after noon. Malone confronted me as soon as I walked into the space. "Where were you?"

"Personal business," I said as I continued walking toward my desk.

"What kind of personal business?"

"The kind I'm not going to tell you about. That's why they call it personal."

Malone's face reddened. "You should have told me how long you'd be gone."

"Andy, I've been gone for about an hour and a half on something I had to take care of. I got in today just after seven, and have been putting in extra work time every day since I started. I think I'm entitled to take my lunch a little early once in a while. OK?"

He stared at me, apparently stupefied that I hadn't knuckled under to him. I felt sorry for Andy; he had the management skills of a kindergartner and knew almost nothing about engineering or technology. I continued to wonder why Federated had put him into a management position. Even with an influential father-in-law, you'd think they'd have minimum standards for managers.

I sat and pretended to work while I was really thinking about Detweiler's murder. It was always possible, I suppose, that it had been a random act of violence or that the poor guy had made an enemy of someone willing to kill. But from my point of view, I had to assume it was connected with Outlaw Shark. If I knew what Sammon had been holding over him, I might get a clue. That would have to wait until I could talk to the captain later today.

Chapter 25

THE AFTERNOON seemed to crawl by. I welcomed the interruption of a call from Natalie at about 4:30. "Can we meet down in the cafeteria? I feel bad about how we left our conversation earlier today."

I agreed and earned myself another dirty look from Andy as I left my desk without asking his permission. Yesterday I'd been his favorite person after suggesting the project be expanded to include SSBN's.

She was waiting for me at a remote table in the almost-empty cafeteria. As I sat down, she offered a wan smile. "I need to apologize for the way I put things when I asked if you'd come with me to the pool party. I made it sound like the only reason was to keep that little shit Phil away from me."

That was exactly what it'd sounded like. But I wanted to meet her halfway, especially if this gave me a chance of getting her back into my life. "Don't worry about that. But I still have no idea why you'd want me to escort you."

"Let's just pretend it's a first date and take it from there," Natalie suggested.

"What's your major?" I asked. "I'm in engineering."

"Cut the crap, Rick," she smiled. "Just concentrate on us enjoying the pool party together." Then she looked at her watch. "I've got to get going—there are a couple of things I have to get done before I leave tonight." She seemed to be assuming I'd gratefully agree to be her escort to the party. She was probably right.

"Before you go, tell me something. Last week, after we had our little talk in the cafeteria, you pretty much avoided me. Now you seem to be interested in seeing if we can get back together. What happened?"

She lowered her eyes. "When I saw you last Monday it was a big shock to me. I didn't know how to react or what to do. And ... well, I had a date this past weekend and I wanted to see how that went. It was a man I thought I might be interested in. But on the date all I was doing was comparing him to you, and I realized I really wanted to be with you, not him."

Hopefully that was an impressive display of honesty, rather than a lie. "I guess it's up to me to prove you were right."

That earned me a radiant smile. "How about you come over to my place for dinner tomorrow night? It'll give us a chance to get to know each other again."

"I'd like that."

"Let me give you my address," she offered. I almost told her not to bother, as I already had it, but that would make it sound like I'd been stalking her. She wrote it on a page from her notebook and listed the streets to turn on. "Head south on Sunnyvale-Saratoga Road past the 280. About a mile after the freeway, take a right on Stevens Creek until you cross Highway 85. About a quarter-mile later you'll see a turn on your right—that's my street."

I looked at my watch as she left. It was a few minutes after five and I'd promised Debbie I'd call Sammon at about this time. The cafeteria was almost deserted, with only a few people behind the counters desultorily cleaning, so I headed for the payphone. I'd been taught to avoid using payphones in areas where people could see me, and had already broken that rule on the same phone. But if I waited to get out of the building, I might miss telling Sammon the dirty details of Dick Detweiler's death, I realized alliteratively.

He answered immediately. "Motivational Consulting. This is Jack Sammon."

"Captain, it's Rick. I'm talking from a payphone in the Federated cafeteria, but no one's anywhere near me."

"OK, we'll keep it short. Debbie gave me your message from this morning. How'd it happen?"

"The police told me he was shot while driving to work. A .45 round to the head." I went on to tell him about my interview with Fehler and how I'd had to pull Norm Connors into the picture to avoid telling the Mountain View police department why Detweiler was visiting me.

"Yeah," he said unhappily. "Norm called and left a message and I was able to catch him on the phone just an hour or so ago. He told me the whole thing. I have to say he wasn't thrilled about getting called by the Mountain View cops."

"I wasn't glad it went that way either, Captain. The other choice was to tell the Mountain View detectives why Detweiler had my name and address on him when he was killed, and why he met with me last night. Or I could have said nothing and be locked up right now. Why don't you tell me what I *should* have done?"

"You could have made up some story ... like, you two were friends and got together for a beer or something. Use your imagination, for Christ's sake!"

Now I was getting pissed. "Maybe we should continue this call from a more secure phone. In the meantime, I'll try to figure out exactly how I could have come up with a fake story about Detweiler that couldn't be disproven by what he'd told his wife, by notes he'd made, or some other evidence. Detective Fehler seemed like someone who'd carefully check out whatever I told him. And a story that didn't prove out would make me a suspect."

A long silence from the other end, until Sammon finally said, "Call me tomorrow morning before you go to work. Use a payphone you know is secure." He hung up, as usual.

Chapter 26

I WENT back up to my office at about 5:20. Everyone except Yolanda and Phil was still there, so I went back to work. Keeping an eye on who was leaving, I worked on an outline detailing what we should accomplish during our two-day visit to the *LOS ANGELES* out in Norfolk. The goal was to get Andy and Natalie to understand the space limitations that the submarine environment would impose on the Outlaw Shark equipment. Time in the tactical trainer would also be helpful, so they could see the crowded reality of a submarine at battle stations. As a plus from Federated's viewpoint, the visit might result in an opportunity to sell more hardware to the Navy—after all, they'd need the equipment in all the submarine tactical trainers, of which there were at least ten I was aware of. I should be working in sales.

I'd gotten about halfway through my outline when Andy appeared in the doorway to my cubicle. "I just wanted to apologize," he said awkwardly. "I realize you're putting in a lot of time on the job. I don't want to micro-manage, so I'll leave it to you to manage your time. Cindy and I look forward to seeing you at the pool party on Saturday. Are you bringing a date?"

It was unexpectedly gracious of Andy to apologize. "Actually, Natalie and I will be coming together," I told him.

He seemed confused by my news, but managed to say, "That's a surprise, but I realize you knew each other at Berkeley. Well, see you tomorrow."

I left about twenty minutes later. As I got into my car, I reminded myself that if Detweiler had been somebody's target, I could also be on that list. I looked around the Federated parking lot but didn't spot anyone lurking with a .45. It'd be nice to have my own weapon with me whenever I was outside my apartment, but I didn't see how it could save me from Detweiler's fate. If someone pulls alongside your car and shoots you, your pistol won't do much good unless you're driving with it loaded, a round in the chamber and beside you on the passenger seat. And with the window already rolled down. Even then, I wasn't sure my reaction time would be fast enough.

Luckily, I made it home without being shot at. I looked around the parking lot near my apartment but couldn't see anything suspicious, not that I'd recognize it until it was too late.

The first thing I did after entering my apartment and changing the alarm from "*Away*" to "*Stay*" was to engage the deadbolt. The second was to take my pistol out of the safe, eject the magazine, dry-fire it a couple of times to check the action, slap the magazine back into the grip, and work the slide to chamber a round. The third was to call South Bay Alarms and verify that my apartment hadn't been entered since I left early this morning. Lastly, I poured myself a healthy slug of Jack Daniel's and sat down to think about what Detweiler's murder really meant, as far as my naval mission was concerned.

Two sips of the Jack relaxed me. I'd just started wondering what I was going to do for dinner, the cupboard being empty, when the phone rang.

"Rick Halsted," I answered.

"It's Jack. Look, I'm sorry for biting your head off about calling Norm to help you today. I've considered your actions and decided you chose the best of a few very poor alternatives you had." This was the first conversation I'd had with Jack in which anything like an apology had surfaced. Apologies from each of my bosses within a few hours of each other! And Jack had called here instead of using my pager to make me call him. Maybe he realized I wasn't too keen on leaving my apartment right now.

While I was recovering from my surprise, Jack went on, "I talked to Norm again. Now that he has a better idea what the situation was, he's not as pissed at you as he was initially." But he was still somewhat pissed, I gathered. I had a bridge to repair. Hopefully it was shovel-ready.

"Also," Jack told me, "you need to give some thought about personal protection. Obviously we don't know who killed Detweiler or why, but it's possible you could end up on their list too."

"I'm already worrying about that," I told him. "But I've got to drive to and from work, and I can't think of any effective way to stop someone doing a Detweiler on me—pulling up alongside and shooting. Any ideas?"

"Not really," he sighed. "If I thought an attack was probable, I'd pull you off this job. Right now, we don't know why Detweiler was killed. It might not be related to you at all."

"If you'd tell me what you were holding over his head to make him cooperate, maybe I could figure out what might have irritated someone enough to kill him."

"OK," Sammon said grudgingly. "The FBI found out during his background investigation for a security clearance that he'd lied about his college degrees. He claimed to have a bachelor's from Stanford and a master's degree from USC, but he didn't have either of them, just a few

Chapter 27

AFTER a fitful sleep, I woke at about six. I'd been jerking awake every time I thought I heard a noise. As I shaved and showered, I realized I probably shouldn't carry the personnel files into Federated. If I was caught in one of the random searches on the way out there'd be no good explanation for them. When I parked at Federated, I left the files in my trunk.

I'd decided to take a mid-morning break and put the files into the safe deposit box. I double-checked like a good submariner to make sure I had my Larry Unfeld ID papers and my key to the box and went into work.

At ten, I left without telling anyone where I was going. Again, I left my suit coat behind so they might assume I was somewhere else in the building. Within half an hour I was back, the files safely deposited. Just before lunch I remembered my bridge repair issue and called Norm from my desk phone. We set a time for lunch despite his obvious lack of enthusiasm at meeting with me.

I made up with him over a quick lunch at the Jury Room. I explained that my options had been very limited. "What else could I do?" I asked him and finally received a reluctant nod of agreement. He was still annoyed about being called, but didn't seem to be blaming me.

I spent the rest of the day working hard at my desk, making up for the time I'd been away, taking only a short break around noon to pick up some food in the cafeteria and bring it back to my desk, making up for the time I'd been away. Natalie wanted me at her place at 6:30, so I needed to leave shortly after five to go home, take a quick shower, change into casual clothes, and drive to her place.

Remembering our last dinner together and how happy Nat had been with the flowers, I stopped en route to pick up a large bouquet of what the florist lady called a 'fall color ensemble,' a fancy name for a bunch of flowers with different colors. I brought a decent bottle of wine, so I was all set. Except for nervous thoughts about how this evening might go. Would it be a platonic dinner between former lovers or a rekindling of the romance of my life? On the bright side, maybe I'd be assassinated on the way to dinner and wouldn't have to worry about it.

I found her home with no problems, and was surprised and impressed. It was a California-style home, based on the old mission architecture, on a hill with a good view of the valley below. I knew that home prices in the Bay Area were approaching stratospheric levels—a small starter home in a dicey neighborhood might cost over $45,000! Surely they couldn't go much higher, or nobody could afford to buy one.

Natalie answered the door with a smile, which faltered when she saw the flowers I was carrying. "You shouldn't have," she frowned. There are two ways to say this phrase. I'd been hoping for the grateful tone that meant the opposite of the words, but what I heard was more like 'Johnny, you shouldn't have flushed the gerbil down the toilet.' She no doubt remembered the last time I'd brought her flowers and didn't want me assuming we'd have a repeat of that very passionate night.

"I hoped you'd enjoy them," I said hesitantly.

"They're beautiful," she said with a forced smile. "I'm sorry for not saying so at first. Come in—I'll show you my house. Would you like a drink?"

"If you have any, a Jack Daniel's on the rocks would be fine," I said, handing her the wine. A few minutes later, we each had a drink as she led me around the house.

She proudly showed off her home, which I knew she'd bought for about $85,000 a year earlier. The place was impressive. Besides a spacious living room, dining room and kitchen, she had three bedrooms; a large master suite and two decent-sized smaller bedrooms, one of which she'd converted to a home office. From the little I knew about housing, it seemed to be a well-built home with lots of extra features to make it more comfortable. The house sat on what looked like almost an acre of wooded property, with a nice shady patio out back.

In her home office, I stared at her desk, where a large plastic typewriter with a small viewing window sat. "What's that, Natalie?"

"That's my computer," she said proudly. "It's an MCM/70, and I can program it in APL." I had no idea what "APL" was. I later learned she'd paid almost $10,000 for the thing—not long ago you could buy a house for that.

I stared at it. "You actually have a computer in your house—but why? What do you do with it?" The only civilian computers I'd seen took up thousands of square feet in special air-conditioned spaces with raised flooring for cable runs, and ran on programs using decks of punch-cards.

She told me happily about how she spent a lot of time trying out new programming ideas or solving programming puzzles. She belonged to a group called, believe it or not, the Homebrew Computer Club, whose members apparently spent a good deal of their spare time trying to figure out how to create what they called a "personal computer." Now that, I was sure, was an idea that would never take off. I mean, why would anyone need a computer at home? Would people line up to learn APL so they could write programs at home? And what would the programs do? A real loser of an idea, I concluded.

Dinner, which she'd already prepared, was a tasty cold shrimp and pasta dish. We ate on her back patio, with a view of the steep hills of the Coast Range. Natalie seemed nervous, but finally got to the point.

"Rick," she said, "I had a reason for asking you to dinner tonight."

I offered what I hoped was an encouraging smile; a leer wouldn't have been appropriate. She went on. "I think—I hope—you understand that the day I told you we couldn't be together anymore was one of the worst of my life. Ever since then, I've wondered if I did the right thing. But I don't really know how you feel. I always assumed you moved on and found someone else, but I couldn't just let this lie."

She was clearly waiting for me to respond. I wondered if I should go tactical or be honest and admit my true feelings.

I took a deep breath and made what I hoped was the right choice. I'd already lied to her enough, and would probably have more lying to do in the future. Why not be honest now? "Natalie, that was a horrible day for both of us. Nothing's been the same since, but I have to say that you might have been right about the difficulty of us being happily married while I was in the submarine force. Most of the married guys I was with in nuclear power and submarine training tried to get onto the 'boomers'—the missile boats. Those have set schedules, and provide a lot more family time. The attack boats, which I chose, had some married officers, but I saw a few divorces and I suspect there were big problems I never learned about. You know—wives cheating on their husbands when they're at sea, husbands renting prostitutes in a foreign port—that type of thing. Anyway, to answer your question, I have to say that in the limited time I had available to socialize, I met a number of young women but never developed a serious relationship with any of them."

"Did you think of me at all?" she asked hesitantly.

Here was another chance to make Natalie think she'd have some work to do to win me back. But I stuck to the truth, enjoying the ability to be honest. "A lot," I admitted. "Work days are long in the submarine force, but there's usually time in each day, even when standing a watch, when things are calm enough to allow some daydreams. And you were in mine—regularly."

"So you still have feelings for me?" she asked, fixing those gorgeous green eyes on mine.

"Always have, always will," I confessed. "I guess I'm no good at playing hard-to-get. And you?" Now that I'd laid it all on the line, everything would depend on how Natalie responded.

Looking at me shyly she said, "I believed when we broke up—when I left you—that I'd eventually find someone else who made me feel as happy as you had. But I never have, and it's been eight years. So I guess what I'm saying is that I'd like to give us another chance. I can't use the Navy as an excuse, now that you're out, so maybe we can make a go of it."

That put me in a fine kettle of fish, as Laurel—or was it Hardy?—would have said. If I kept operational security, I'd be lying to the woman who might be the love of my life, or at least had been, years ago. But if I told her my real status and the romance didn't work out—or, worse, if she was involved in any of the espionage we suspected was going on—I'd be jeopardizing my mission. The best thing, I decided, was to keep my still being in the Navy my little secret until I was sure Natalie and I would stay together. Sometimes, kids, the easy way is the best solution. I still had to figure out what to do about the biggest secret of all, the one I'd never told anyone. If Natalie and I were to be together, she'd have to know that at some point, even though revealing it might destroy our love. And perhaps me, at the same time.

"Come over here, sweetheart," I suggested, and she moved over to sit next to me, one arm around my neck and the other hand stroking my face. With what felt like a gravitational pull, our mouths came together. I was afraid my memory of how glorious her kisses had been was exaggerated, something that had never really existed, but as soon as our lips touched I was lost again. We continued kissing passionately for what seemed simultaneously an endless period and one that was all too short.

"Wow," I whispered, cuddling Natalie close to me. I heard her sigh happily.

"So, big boy," she murmured, "are we back together?"

"Definitely. And Natalie, I have to say this is the best thing that's happened to me for a long time. But we have a lot of catching up to do."

"Yes, we do," she agreed, leaning in to kiss me again. That wasn't what I'd meant by having a lot of catching up to do, but it'd serve for now.

A few minutes—or maybe an hour?—later, we broke apart.

"Look, Rick," Natalie said, "this may seem strange, but I'd like us to stop for the time being. I think you know how important you are to me—again—but I'd like some time to think about us being back together before we end up in bed. Does that seem too weird?"

Actually, I not only understood what she meant, but felt the same way. A little time to think before we resumed our sexual relationship might be a good thing. Of course, I was thinking of a delay of a day or two, while my perhaps re-found love might have something on the order of several months in mind.

I decided to maintain momentum. "Why don't you come to my place tomorrow night? You wouldn't want to eat my cooking, but there are some nice restaurants in the area."

"Where do you live?"

"Not far from work; it's a complex called the Carillon Apartments, just off Lawrence Expressway. I'm in Unit 4, Apartment 3C. It's on the third floor."

"Oh my," she smirked. "I've heard a lot about the Carillon and the type of people who live there. I should have known you'd choose that place."

Ignoring her insinuation, I suggested, "How about six p.m. tomorrow? You can come straight from work." She agreed happily and slid back into my arms.

After another immeasurable blissful interval of passionate kissing, I managed to stagger out, more than a little confused about exactly where Natalie and I stood.

Less than thirty minutes later I was home, had bolted the door, reset the alarm, and verified with the alarm company that my alarm hadn't been touched since I'd left. My answering machine was blinking with a message.

Curious, I pushed the button and heard Beth asking angrily why I hadn't called her. "Because you insisted I *not* call you, you stupid cow," I muttered, erasing the message. It was too late to return the call. Besides, the best strategy was to pretend the call had never happened.

I got my pistol out of the safe, ejected the magazine and the chambered round and dry-fired it a couple of times, imagining I was aiming at an intruder. Then I locked the slide back, slapped the full magazine back in and chambered a round before setting it on my bedside table and getting into bed. The last two days had been too hectic for my peace of mind, but it looked like I had a chance of having Natalie back in my life. I fell asleep happily, again dreaming of her.

Chapter 28

THURSDAY went smoothly at work, although most of my thoughts were focused on dinner tonight with Natalie. Andy seemed to be cutting me more slack, although I really didn't need it. I was putting in more hours than anyone else in the department and, I thought humbly, was being more productive than any of the others, including our manager.

A lot of my concentration was on how things might go tonight with Natalie. I'd have to leave early to make sure that my apartment was fit to receive a special young lady. It'd been fine when I left, but another look would make me feel better. There's that submariner nit-picking again.

Driving home, I had to admit I was a little nervous. A casual girlfriend like Beth was one thing, but if I screwed up with Natalie, our suddenly revived romance could die as quickly as it had restarted.

Paranoid as always, I checked and double-checked the cleanliness and order of the apartment, and made sure, for the third time, that the alarm system was muted. Natalie hopefully wouldn't realize I had an alarm system when I let her in. I'd stocked white and red wine, the former of which was chilling. I'd even bought some cheese and crackers to serve as hors d'oeuvres, which I hoped I wouldn't have to spell.

I was checking, for the third time, that the bathroom was spotlessly clean and had fresh hand towels when I heard a knock at the door. Praying fervently that it wasn't Beth, I tiptoed over and peered through the peephole. There was Natalie, staring at the peephole as though she'd never seen one.

I paused a few seconds to show I wasn't over-anxious, although I was, and opened the door. "Natalie, please come in." She probably wondered why I had a peephole in my apartment door, but came in with a smile.

She took her time surveying the living room and kitchen area. "Nice apartment," she finally said. "But you've got some work to do to make it habitable."

"Like what?" I'd assumed it was already livable.

"More art on the walls, some bookshelves—you know, something to give the place personality. I don't even see anything to show you used to be a submarine officer."

"Let me show you that." I led her to the bedroom, where the "I Love Me" wall was set up with the various certificates, plaques and photos showing what an all-around submarine stud I was.

She looked at each of the items carefully. "What's this plaque mean? It says 'Plank Owner' on it." I explained that a member of the commissioning crew of a ship was, and forever would be, a plank owner. In my case, it was for *BOWFIN*.

"Get me a glass of white wine, if you have it, and then let's sit down," she suggested. "I have a few questions, if that's OK." She was in a more serious mood than I'd expected, but I couldn't very well refuse.

She didn't waste any time. "Rick, do you have anyone else—another woman—in your life now? I need to know that before we get too involved."

"I met a young women who lives in this complex and had a couple of dates with her. But nothing serious happened, and we're not together anymore. There's no one else. You can thank the Navy for that."

"I hate to ask this, but did you have sex with her?"

"I did not." I said, pleased to be telling the truth. "And should I assume I can ask you similar questions?"

"I'll answer whatever you ask; I just wanted to know. After all," she said, "I think we're trying to decide whether we'll be together again or not. Anything else you should tell me?"

"Well, to be honest, I should let you know that I did have sex with a few young women during my time in the fleet," I admitted.

"But no serious relationships?"

"Not really. With one, I thought it might turn serious, but I missed a big event in her life when we got extended at sea, and that was that."

It was time to change the subject to her. "How about we continue the questioning, but now I get to ask you a few things, OK?" She nodded.

Where to start? "Natalie, how many guys would you say you dated over the past eight years, not counting the ones you went out with only once or twice?"

She thought for a few seconds. "I'd say between twelve or fourteen. And before you ask, I ended up in bed with just two of them, and only once in each case. I suppose I was trying to see if it could be the same with another man as it was with you." And apparently it hadn't been, I supposed, or she would've had more than one session. That's assuming she was telling me the truth, of course. But "the women always lie so easy," as I recalled from a folk song years ago.

Deciding to go for complete candor, I said, "Nat, no woman I've ever known can thrill me like you do. I don't know why, but you strike a chord in me that no one else can. If you feel anything like that about me, I think we need to try our romance again. Now, can I take you to dinner?"

"Just one thing first," she murmured as she slid toward me and into my arms. "A little kiss to show how we feel about each other."

With Natalie, I'd never experienced a "little kiss"—hers were all major erotic productions, and this particular kiss was so intense I was completely overcome. What made her so special? Maybe it was her intense focus on the kiss itself. Or maybe it was just her.

We finally broke apart, but stayed in each other's arms. "Another kiss, or shall we do dinner?" she asked mischievously.

"One more kiss like that and we can forget dinner," I said, echoing her remark eight years earlier. She blushed happily.

I realized that when we left, she was going to find out I had an alarm system installed. The only alternative was to leave for dinner without arming the system—not an appealing idea, with Detweiler's murder still fresh in my mind.

I decided to get a decision on dinner while I pondered this problem. "How does Italian sound?"

"It soundsa like-a thees," she said in an atrocious Italian accent. Then she relented. "Italian food will be fine."

I was belatedly coming to realize that there was more depth to Natalie than I'd remembered. If our love was resurrected, I could look forward to an extraordinary experience. But if she turned out to be on the wrong side in this espionage scenario, she'd be difficult to handle.

Chapter 29

SHE WENT to the bathroom on a needless trip to make sure she looked all right while I called the restaurant and made sure we could get in.

"Let's go," I said as she came out. "Just let me set the alarm system first."

"Why do you have an alarm system? And a peephole in the door? And that deadbolt?"

"Natalie, you should have a good security system too. This area's more dangerous than you think, and the system doesn't cost much to install or monitor. In fact, I'll be glad to pay to have one installed in your house so you'll be safer."

She shook her head but actually seemed to give it some thought. "Let's talk about that later. Right now I'm hungry, so get me to some food—fast."

Fifteen minutes later, we were at Salvatore's enjoying a pre-dinner drink. I was trying to think of something romantic to say when Natalie beat me to it.

"Rick, I know I should play hard to get, but I have to tell you how happy I am to have you back in my life. You are back with me, aren't you?" That was, in many ways, a very brave thing for her to say.

"For as long as you'll have me," I promised. Which would probably be right up to the point when I explained I was still actually in the Navy and investigating her, among other people, as a suspect in Soviet espionage activities.

"We should celebrate," she declared as she finished her drink. "Would you like to invite me for a sleepover tonight?"

You have to like a forward woman, right? "Absolutely. But you have to promise to respect me in the morning."

"Don't worry about that. Just keep your strength up, because I'm planning to wear you out tonight. And switch to iced tea or something else with a lot of caffeine. You wouldn't want to leave me frustrated, would you?"

My mind was busy boggling. It had only been two days ago that she'd asked me to escort her to the pool party just to keep Phil away from her, and now she was throwing herself at me? This was what I'd been dreaming of for eight years, but I really wasn't that irresistible. What if Natalie was trying to use me? But why? And should I just calm down and enjoy it while I was finding out? Was I asking too many rhetorical questions? Answering "yes" to the last one, I did my best to relax.

As dinner began, I decided to do the sensitive masculine thing and find out what had been happening in her life. That seemed the thoughtful and proper course of action, even though women might say that "sensitive" and "masculine" are oxymoronic.

"Natalie," I began, "it's been a long time since we've been together, and I need to catch up on what you've been doing. What about your family? How's your dad doing?"

She sipped her wine and looked up. "He died five years ago, just a year or so after I graduated from Berkeley." I mentally kicked my own ass for putting my foot firmly down my throat in my very first sensitive question. Now there's an awkward mixed metaphor.

"I'm so sorry," I managed to say, although I'd only met the man a few times, and never really had a conversation with him, other than falsely assuring him I wouldn't molest his daughter. "That must have been horrible."

"I'll miss him," she said quietly, "but he wasn't really my father; I was adopted when I was a baby. He treated me very well, especially after his wife died. I was only about eight then, so he pretty much raised me on his own."

"He did a hell of a job," I told her. "You're a very special woman."

"You're biased," she smiled. "I suppose we weren't as close as a real father and daughter, but he did what he could. When he died I inherited the house he'd bought in Berkeley when we moved out from Ann Arbor, and was also the beneficiary on the life insurance he got through the university. After it seemed I'd be with Federated for a while, or at least working in this area, I sold the Berkeley house and bought my own place."

"How did you get promoted so fast at Federated?"

"Some of that was luck. I'd been here for a couple of years when my supervisor got promoted to manager, and I was picked to step in as lead analyst supervising a group. Then when this project came along about a year ago, the VP in charge of the department asked me to set up a group to handle the IT end of it. A promotion to manager came with that."

"Good work—I'm very impressed. And, of course, honored to be allowed to socialize with someone in higher management."

"We're *not* socializing—we're restarting our love affair. And I hope you know the difference, or it's going to be a short one," she said with a saucy grin.

"Yes, ma'am," I said obediently.

"Hey," she said brightly, "do you remember Giovanni Rossi?"

"I do, but not fondly." My last memory of Giovanni was his bragging about having "banged" Natalie. Not one of my favorite moments.

"Well, he finally graduated from Berkeley, and he's working in Oakland."

"Doing what?" I couldn't imagine anything useful Johnny could do.

"He's called a community organizer," she smiled. "And before you ask, I have no idea what that means, but I see his name in the paper now and then. He's still a rabble-rouser. He's tied in with the Black Panthers somehow. Maybe it's because his degree was in African-American Studies."

"I didn't know Cal offered a degree in that," I laughed. Nor could I figure out what anyone would do with such a degree, especially a pallid fake Italian. But it appeared the answer was to become a "community organizer." Good for old Johnny. The bastard.

"They didn't offer it as a major when you and I were there. But Giovanni was a part-time student for about eight years and in 1972 or so he took a few extra courses after they set up this new program, and finally got his degree."

I was trying to picture Giovanni dealing with the Panthers and trying to talk "black." Maybe they'd get tired of his pasty white ass and terminate him—the hard way. "Can we change the subject? I don't like Johnny and don't want to talk about him."

"Fine by me. But now it's your turn to tell me about your exciting times in the Navy. Wasn't it dangerous—I mean, in a submarine?"

"It was days of boredom punctuated by a few minutes of absolute panic," I said with a straight face.

She smiled but pressed me. "Come on, you must have some exciting stories. Tell me some of them."

So I regaled Natalie with a short explanation of the training I'd had and what the qualification standards mandated, and then a much longer set of sea stories that had her laughing helplessly.

My favorite was one that was actually completely true. Not that any sea story is ever actually *false*, just exaggerated for effect. I'd had a shipmate on *PERMIT*, an officer named T.J. Watson. He was in my year group, and junior to me by lineal number[51]. The problem was that he

_____

[51] "Lineal numbers" are used to identify each naval officer's seniority. They're initially based on an officer's grade-point average and military aptitude ratings from midshipman days for people with the same date of rank. The lower the number, the more senior you are. Until and unless you get promoted before

thought it was hilarious to habitually relieve me late as EOOW[52]. In those days we were standing four-hour watches[53]. Naturally, everyone was expected to relieve on time so the off-going watchstander can attend to his other duties or maybe even have a short nap. Being late to relieve once or twice in a month or so was frowned on but tolerated, since anyone can slip. But with T.J., it was every damn watch—late.

Complaining to the XO or the Senior Watch Officer[54] about it was just too childish. This was something I had to handle on my own. For lack of a better idea, I took to having T.J. called earlier and earlier, until the messenger of the watch was shaking him awake more than an hour before his scheduled relief time. He still showed up late, smirking to show how superior he was.

My chance to get even came when *PERMIT* made a port visit to Yokosuka. Our CO, Commander Joe Blair, had been stationed there several years earlier on the staff of Submarine Flotilla Seven, which manages submarine operations in the Western Pacific. He'd become somewhat fluent in Japanese and decided to give daily language lessons to the officers after lunch each day. Joe even made up his own flash cards. Any officer who was interested could attend. We did this for about a week while en route to Japan.

Naturally, no one got fluent, but we got good enough to communicate with waiters, taxicab drivers, and hotel staff. We didn't have to worry about the bargirls; all they could say was "Buy me drink. I love you—no shit!" and we didn't have to speak Japanese to get what we wanted. But you had to have a yen to do that. Actually, thousands of yen.

For whatever reason, T.J. had skipped all the language lessons. I'd known he was a lazy bastard, but hadn't seen why he shouldn't learn a little Japanese. We arrived in Yokosuka and had mail call[55] just after we

---

Jack, who has a lineal number lower than yours, you'll always be junior to him.

[52] EOOW = Engineering Officer of the Watch, the officer in charge of reactor operation, main propulsion, electric power, and so on.

[53] The submarine force changed to six-hour watches in the early 1970's. This meant your watches were two hours longer, but you got four hours more off-watch time afterwards. Usually you stood one watch on and two off, called a 'three-section rotation.' No matter how long each watch is, a three-section rotation means you average eight hours on watch per 24-hour period. The other sixteen are spent on all-hands evolutions, managing your department, collateral duties, meals and sometimes even sleep.

[54] The Senior Watch Officer is the third officer in seniority on the submarine, junior to the CO and XO, neither of whom stand watches. He sets the officers' watch schedules and is responsible for officer training. In addition to SWO, he'll also be a department head, usually Navigator/Operations or Engineer.

[55] On Navy surface ships, which regularly have underway replenishment for fuel and stores, mail is transferred every few days. For submarines, mail call has

came in. Immediately afterward T.J. came up to me. Why he'd come to me for a favor, I'll never figure out. It was, of course, a colossal error on his part. He confided that a girl he'd dated at Ohio State was teaching at an American school in Yokohama, about thirty miles away. She wanted to see him and had enclosed driving directions written in Japanese. But she'd warned him that the cab drivers often drove recklessly fast.

"How do I tell the cab driver to slow down?" T.J had asked.

This was too good to be true, and I took full advantage. Now I could get at least partially even for all the late reliefs and consequent lost sleep. I told him, "Well, shipmate, all you have to do is say *hayaku*[56] and they'll slow right down." Of course, *hayaku* means "go faster," which he'd have known if he'd showed up for any of the lessons.

T.J. must have had a very interesting ride to Yokohama, apparently breaking all known land-speed records for that route, and this was in the day when it was all secondary roads through villages. I cherished the mental image of him frantically shouting *hayaku* to the driver, who'd obediently go even faster. Engineers call this "positive feedback"—a very bad thing in mechanical or electrical devices, but a good thing in interpersonal relations. So he was very pissed off and I was extremely happy.

Natalie was laughing so hard she had to leave the dining room; I think she was afraid she'd pee her pants. Coming back, still gasping for breath, she said, "Those are great stories. But are they true?"

I explained that, by long-standing tradition going back to the days of sail, all sea stories had to be based on fact. "You see," I said solemnly, "a fairy story always begins 'once upon a time,' and a sea story always begins 'this is no shit.' That's the rule."

That set her off again, but she managed to calm down enough to finish dinner.

"Dessert?" I asked politely, ever the gentleman.

"It'll be back at your place, and it won't involve food. You've got a long night ahead of you, so if you need something to give you enough energy, get it now." She waggled her eyebrows at me. "I intend to take advantage of you, sailor."

Was this all my dreams come true? I hoped it was. "Come on, honey. Do we need to drop by your house?"

"Silly boy," she smirked. "I have an overnight bag in my car. I was planning on spending the night with you all along."

"I think I can muster up the energy, but I'm a little worried about you."

---

to wait until the boat's in port.

[56] I later learned that "*isogu*" would have been a better way to say "hurry up," but how much Japanese can you learn in just a few days of one-hour lessons?

"Why?"

"It sounds like you're a little out of practice. Maybe we should start with some basic lessons and then give you a day or so off before you try to swing for the fences."

"You bastard. I'll bet I can have you crying for mercy within an hour."

"Big talk from a woman who claims to have had almost no sex in eight years."

"Let's get out of here and we'll see what happens. I may surprise you."

I actually *was* worried about what might happen. Maybe my memory was malfunctioning and I'd been mentally exaggerating how marvelous it was to make love with her. Maybe she had elevated expectations I wouldn't be able to meet. It seemed very possible that the night would end in disillusion, making it a losing proposition for me and for Natalie.

But looking back on that long and emotionally charged night we spent together, I think we both won. I once again found the magic that Natalie brought and, judging by her reactions, she found happiness also. The word "love" wasn't spoken by either of us that night, but it was certainly in my heart. Time would tell whether it was in hers as well.

The lovemaking, interspersed with cuddling, went on for several hours. I hoped I'd done well in satisfying her, but worried it still might not have been enough. After all, this was our first time together sexually in a long time, and she might have had higher expectations than I could meet.

But before she drifted off to sleep at about three am, she murmured, "Not bad, sailor boy. Not bad at all."

Chapter 30

NATALIE left early Friday morning with a passionate kiss and an invitation to spend the weekend at her place. She'd decided to go by her house before showing up at work, even though she'd brought her overnight kit. I was about ready to head out the door myself when my phone rang.

"Hello?"

"Is this Rick Halsted?" The caller introduced himself as Special Agent Ryan Philpott from the NIS office in San Francisco. "We got a call from Captain Sammon. He asked us to provide a little help for you, so I came down to Sunnyvale. If you have some time available, I'd like to come over."

He was there within ten minutes. Ryan, a tall husky blond, looked to be in his mid-thirties. He had an air of calm confidence as he checked out my alarm system. "This looks decent," he finally told me. "And I like the deadbolt. That'll buy you some time if you're here when they try to break in. Do you have a weapon?"

"It's in the safe," I said, taking the print off the wall and opening the safe. I handed him the pistol. He ejected the magazine, worked the slide to throw out the chambered round, and inspected the barrel. I suppose he was checking to make sure I cleaned it regularly.

"You any good with this?"

"I'm OK. I qualified on the combat range back in DC and I've started shooting at a gun club near here."

"Next thing," he said. "Let me check your phone and make sure it hasn't been bugged." He unscrewed the phone mouthpiece and peered in.

"Nothing here," he announced. "Open up the mouthpiece like I did. It should look like this. If you see anything else in here, let me know. It might also be in the base." He removed the base plate of the phone and showed me where it might be, and described what one might look like. "If you find one, leave it in and be careful what you say. Removing it will just prompt the bad guys to try something different you might not notice."

He walked around with what looked like a transistor radio for a few minutes. "No bugs," he said, and handed it to me.

"I'm going to leave this with you, so you can check your apartment from time to time." The device was supposed to give an audio signal when a bug was detected.

"So this'll find any bug?" I asked hopefully.

"Not really," he admitted. "The federal government can authorize taps at the telephone company central office. There's no way to detect those. But unless the Feds are after you, this should do the job.."

Ryan walked out on the balcony, looked around, and nodded. "It'd be pretty tough for someone to get up here, plus you've got the sliding door alarmed. Worst case is someone comes here when the place is empty—everyone at work—and just breaks down the door. If he did that, what might he find?"

"Well, first of all, the alarm should go off, so he couldn't stay long. He might be able to get into the safe, but he'd have to find it first. It locks down for an hour after three failed attempts. If he got that far, here's what he'd find for all his work."

Other than the pistol and its accessories, all I had in the safe was a set of star sapphire studs and cufflinks—bought in Hong Kong two years ago and the only valuable jewelry I owned. Ryan looked closely at the inside of the safe door and, in a few seconds, pried off the cover to the hidden compartment. "Most intruders would miss this," he said, shuffling through the papers I had in there. "But if they found this stuff, I'm guessing it'd blow your cover, whatever that might be."

I nodded. "But it doesn't seem very likely someone would get into the apartment, find the safe, be able to open it, and then find that hidden compartment, all before the police arrive in response to the alarm." Philpott looked skeptical and shrugged noncommittally.

"Also," I said, "I check with the alarm company every day to make sure no one else disarmed the alarm. If someone sets it off during the day, they page me right away. Or so they promised, anyway."

It occurred to me—way too late—that this guy might not even be from NIS. "Can I see your ID and a business card?" I asked.

He smiled and handed them over. "Shouldn't you have done that right off?"

I ignored the sarcasm and looked at the card, which gave a phone number for the NIS office in San Francisco. Rather than dial the number on the card, which might have been phony, I dialed "O" and asked the operator to connect me to the Naval Investigative Service office on Treasure Island.

"NIS San Francisco. This is Petty Officer Martinez, sir. This is a non-secure line."

"Ryan Philpott, please. This is Lieutenant Commander Halsted."

After a short pause, Martinez told me "Commander, Special Agent Philpott is signed out to visit you in Sunnyvale. Has he arrived yet?"

"Can you describe him?"

"He's about six feet one inch, sandy blonde hair and light blue eyes. He has a USMC tattoo on his left shoulder. His ID card serial number is 31850." I peered at the ID card; the number matched.

"Thanks, petty officer. He's here. I appreciate your help." I hung up.

Philpott went on, "Next step is your car, Commander. First, I'll search it for booby traps, like a pipe bomb, and then I'll run a check to see if I can detect any tracking equipment. That may take several hours. Would you like me to drop you at work? I can phone you when the car's ready."

"I'd appreciate that, Agent Philpott." I handed him one of my business cards. "If you're done around lunchtime, I'll be glad to take you out to lunch."

"I'll probably be done by then, but I've got to get back to Treasure Island. I'll also make some notes on how to minimize the chance you'll get an unpleasant surprise."

The morning went relatively normally. I spent most of my time reviewing the technical specs for the power supply and cabling connecting the system to the consoles in the control room.

At about eleven, Philpott phoned and said my car was ready. I met him outside the building and he drove me back to the Carillons and left me at my car. On the ride, he explained some ways to find bombs, but warned me that a clever bomber could install one that would take time and expertise to find. "There are no bugs in the car," he said, "but it's kind of the same thing—it could be there tomorrow and you'd never know it without going through all this again." He handed me a few pages of handwritten notes with hints on how to avoid being shot. I should have my pistol with me at all times, should have eyes in the back of my head and incredible reaction time with my own weapon. Very helpful.

Natalie phoned me to ask me to meet her in the cafeteria for lunch; she'd apparently decided our newly revived relationship could be on public record. Her behavior at lunch somehow indicated we were a couple, without her doing anything overtly affectionate. I have no idea how women convey subtleties like that. Maybe the Y chromosome inhibits that ability in men.

"Tonight," she said with a smile, "I'll take you to dinner at a place near my house. My treat this time."

"Sounds fine," I told her. "Should I bring anything special?"

"Your shaving kit and a change of clothes for the pool party tomorrow. And whatever you wear to run in. Saturday mornings I like to run at the local high school."

"Does this mean I'm a kept man?"

"Not yet, sailor. You're still on trial. Be at my place by 6:30, OK?"

"Well, if I must, I must," I sighed. "But please try to treat me gently and with respect. I do have feelings, you know."

She grinned at me saucily. "Just do your job like you did it last night and we'll both be very happy people."

She changed the conversation back to work. "How are you getting along with Andy?" she asked.

"OK, I suppose. He's anal-retentive and doesn't seem to have much in the way of management skills, but I suppose I'll eventually figure out why he's managing this project."

"I can tell you why he's managing it, or at least why he's assigned to manage it. Or you can wait until the pool party on Saturday to find out."

"Just tell me, OK?"

"You remember meeting Lee Greenwood earlier this week? The vice president?"

I nodded.

"Well," she said with a knowing smile, "Lee Greenwood has one child—a daughter. And she's married to Andy Malone."

I already knew this, but didn't want to divulge that. "Wow," I said. "Now it all makes more sense." It also made me wonder if a man who had low enough self-esteem to rely on his father-in-law to find a job for him would peddle secrets to the Soviets for some extra spending money. I decided the answer might be "yes."

"You know," she told me, "you should be the one in charge of this project, not Andy. Besides having no managerial skills whatsoever, he also knows nothing about the Navy, or engineering, or anything else that's important for the project."

"Come on, Natalie—this is my very first civilian job and I just started last week."

"Actually, I overheard Greenwood and Andy talking after our Monday meeting. Andy may be moving to another project and your name came up to head the group."

"That's crazy," I said. "Owen and Wayne have each been here years longer than me." I didn't bother mentioning Arnold as a candidate. A manager who couldn't say anything without blushing in embarrassment probably wouldn't succeed in business, whether he was really trying or not.

"Those guys will never be considered for management. I've heard talk about them at some of the quarterly meetings the company holds for people at management level, and they're not what Federated is looking for. They hunker down and do their job, but they don't venture an opinion and never volunteer for anything. What Federated wants in management are people who are competent, but keep questioning assumptions and trying to make things better. I think you're just what they're looking for. My guess is nothing will happen for a few weeks, maybe even as long as a few months. But sometime soon they'll move Andy over to another project. Then we can keep seeing each other without it looking like I'm using my authority to coerce you into sex."

"You're just worried that people will think you're dating below your appropriate level," I offered, trying to turn this topic into a joke.

I put in a good afternoon's work, since I had to leave early. I needed go back to my apartment, put together clothes for the weekend and a shaving kit, and make it to Natalie's in time for dinner.

I put together my overnight kit and, just for the hell of it, took my pistol out of the safe along with two boxes of ammunition and my range bag. Maybe Natalie would enjoy going to the range with me—we could do it tomorrow morning, have a nice lunch somewhere, and then go to Andy's. Remembering she'd mentioned running, I also brought my running shoes and clothes.

Chapter 31

I WAS AT Natalie's exactly on time, just as you'd expect from a naval officer. I'd had to kill seven minutes driving randomly around her neighborhood to accomplish this. En route, I'd bought flowers, earning me the traditional passionate thank you.

"I thought we'd try a French restaurant up the 280," she suggested after breaking away from our kiss. "I can drive so you can save your energy; you're going to need it. Would you like a drink before we leave?"

"How about I stow my stuff and we can go to the restaurant. Where's the guest room?"

"Don't be intentionally stupid. You know very well where my bedroom is." That was a good sign, but not surprising after our lunch conversation. Hopefully I'd pass my qualification exam tonight.

A few minutes later we were heading north on the 280. "Where exactly is this restaurant?" I asked.

"Woodside. It's a little place that only holds about twenty people, but I got a reservation last week." That was interesting—had she been planning to be with me tonight, or was the reservation originally planned for her and someone else, like the suitor she'd told me about on Tuesday? There was, unfortunately, no way to ask her without appearing paranoid-jealous.

The restaurant was on Whiskey Hill Road, in a grove of redwoods. As she'd warned, it was quite small and, I saw when we walked in, almost full. The maître d' murmured to me, "Do you have reservations, monsieur?"

I leaned in closer, surveying the room carefully. "Yes," I whispered. "But we're really hungry, so we'll settle for eating here." The man didn't even smile.

Natalie elbowed me sharply, but was smiling. "It's under 'Montaigne'—a reservation for two at seven-thirty," she told him. He bowed politely and led us to a table at a window.

I shouldn't have been surprised to see Natalie speaking what sounded like fluent French to our table waiter. I heard the words "Jack Daniel's" as she ordered the drinks, dinner, and, as far as I knew, discussed my sexual performance with the waiter.

Reaching across the table to hold her hand after the waiter left, I murmured, "We'll always have Paris, Ilsa."

"Since you're already Rick, that works out nicely," she laughed, squeezing my hand.

I smiled at her. "It's nice to be back in Woodside. When I was in Boy Scouts we used to do campouts in Huddart Park, just a mile or so north of here."

"This is a beautiful area, but it's impossibly expensive to buy a home here," Natalie said. "If I could afford it, I'd love to be living here."

This started me wondering how interested Natalie might be in earning more, perhaps by selling secret tidbits to the Soviets. This was an awkward thought to be having in a romantic moment, but I still wasn't sure about Natalie.

"Look," I began, "what are your long-range plans? You're obviously doing fine at Federated, but if you could have your dream job, what would it be?" What I wanted to find out was if money—or something it could buy—was her goal, or if she had less ambitious goals.

She pondered for a moment, and then fixed those huge emerald eyes on me. "This may sound selfish, but what I'd really like—what I dream about—is finding some way to make it big while I'm still fairly young and not have to work after I'm forty or so. I don't need to have houses all over and fancy cars and all that, but I want to have a house I love in a nice area and enough to travel whenever I want. And, most of all, not to have to worry about money."

"Nice dream."

"This is actually a good time to accomplish it," she told me. "At our Homebrew meetings, I meet people who're trying to start new computer companies. One of them, a little guy named Steve, is actually working with another guy on building a personal computer that he thinks will appeal to a lot of people. Getting a job at one of those places could end up being worth millions if I could get stock options. If I don't want to take the risk of a startup, I can see if there's something available at Intel or some other high-tech company. If I stay at Federated, or even move to an established high-tech company like Hewlett-Packard, I'd make a decent living, but I couldn't make myself financially independent, at least not until I'm an old woman."

I must have looked skeptical. She asked, "Why don't you come to next week's Homebrew meeting? It's Tuesday night in Palo Alto, at the Linear Accelerator auditorium. You're an electronics engineer after all, so you might be able to contribute some ideas. And if you're nice to my friends at the meeting, I might reward you."

Before I could decide what kind of reward I'd prefer, the appetizers arrived. I stared at them, remembering I'd heard "escargot" when she was placing our order.

"Never eaten snails?" she asked cheerfully. "Try one—you'll like it."

Actually, they weren't bad, although they had more garlic than I was used to. I ate three. Then the main course arrived—a small steak for each of us, with a mushroom sauce that must have been incredibly fattening. But looking at Natalie, I decided it couldn't be.

"Do you like horse meat?" she asked, cutting a piece of her own steak. If that was really horse, all we'd need was frog legs and we'd have the French Trifecta. She might have been joking about Trigger.

"Dessert will be at my place," she announced as she paid the bill. "You get to guess what it'll be." It turned out to be the same "dessert" we'd enjoyed the night before.

I woke up twice during the night. More accurately, Natalie woke me with gentle hints that I had more work to do. After the very pleasant second wake-up call, I could have sworn I heard her murmur, "I love you." That brought me fully awake. I vaguely understood that a woman expected exactly the right reply to a declaration like this, and that not answering or giving the wrong answer could lead to seriously bad consequences. During our passionate liaison years ago in Berkeley, she'd never used the word at all, making this even more significant.

I thought rapidly, discarding answers like "Of course you do" or "That's nice." I fell back on the truth. "I love you too, sweetheart," I murmured into her ear. I was rewarded with a soft buzzing snore. I could have said anything.

Lying there, I pondered the mysterious rules of behavior that all women seemed to know, and no man seemed to understand. Exactly where did they all learn these rules? Were they written down anywhere? Or did each woman make up her own and change them around at will? The last choice seemed the most likely answer, I decided as I drifted off to sleep.

She woke me at 6 am. "Time to run a few miles," she chirped happily. "Assuming you can handle it."

Chapter 32

WITHOUT any overt grumbling I brushed my teeth and pulled on my running gear. Natalie looked at the ratty shirt I was wearing. "I found a shirt yesterday I thought you might like."

She handed me a folded T-shirt. Unfolding it, I saw printed in large letters over the chest, "*Southeast Asia War Games, 1961—1975: Second place,*" superimposed on a map of Vietnam. Very amusing.

Smirking, she told me, "Wear it this morning and lunch will be on me."

I agreed more or less graciously; she drove us to a high school track a few miles away. "I like to do four miles on Saturdays," she explained. "My goal is to make it in half an hour. Is that OK with you?"

She took off and I stayed beside her with no trouble. Compared to the muggy DC summer climate, running here was a breeze. We were on the last lap with about 200 yards to go when she suddenly accelerated. "See you later," she taunted as she left me behind. With a little effort, I passed her with thirty yards to go. Maybe more than a little effort.

We headed back to her house for a friendly two-person shower and breakfast. At breakfast, I told Natalie I wanted to go to the gun range this morning. "We should have plenty of time for that, a nice lunch, and still get to the pool party on time. Do you want to come along to the range?"

"Don't mind if I do, sailor-boy. Who knows—I might enjoy shooting."

It sounded like she was a novice, which would give me the chance to tutor her. We both might enjoy that.

Before we left, I held a range safety class for Natalie. I loaded my pistol with a clip of snap caps—inert rounds used just to practice trigger pull—and handed it to her. She took it carefully, ejected the clip, smoothly jacked the slide back to eject the chambered round, and caught it neatly in mid-air. Locking the slide back, she then carefully inspected the breech and the barrel, nodded to herself, and slapped the clip back in. She released the slide with her thumb to chamber a snap cap and then adopted a crouching stance, with her left foot slightly forward and both hands grasping the pistol in an interlocking grip. What was that about? The Navy insisted on a one-handed grip and an upright stance.

"Where'd you learn that?" I asked.

"Former boyfriend," she smiled. "Long gone. Nice trigger pull," she commented after squeezing it. She jacked the slide to eject the top snap cap, and then repeated the shooting routine several times. "What's the recoil like?"

"Not bad—certainly a lot less than the .45's the Navy made us shoot," I answered, trying to hide my surprise at her apparent expertise. Where had she learned this? Weren't far-left liberals supposed to be anti-gun?

At the range she shot very well. I did better than she did, but suspected she could actually shoot more accurately and might be trying not to show me up.

"I like that pistol," she commented as she watched me field-strip and clean it.

"Me too. Are you interested in having one?" Maybe it'd make a nice getting back together present. Nothing says "I love you" like a lethal weapon. That'd be a good movie title.

She shrugged. "Maybe. Where am I taking you for lunch?" It turned out she had some suggestions, so we ended up at a place that featured gourmet burgers. My burger was covered with hot sauce, jalapenos, and spicy cheese, and Natalie's was avocado-laden. She'd turned into a true California girl since she moved here from Michigan.

"What's this pool party going to be like? Is Andy as stiff and unnatural at home as he is at work?"

"Rick Halsted, I can't believe you're asking me how stiff Andy is at home. That's between him and Cindy," she said with a straight face.

"Extremely funny," I assured her. "Now answer my question. For starters, what's his wife like?"

"About all you need to know about Cindy is that her family is, and I think always has been, very well off financially, she went to the best prep schools, and she signs her name with a little heart over the "i" instead of a dot. And I found out that the money isn't Lee's—it's her mom's. She's a Hopkins."

"Wow," I murmured. Besides being the namesake of the eponymous hotel, Mark Hopkins was one of the four founders of the Central Pacific Railroad[57], all of whom had made large fortunes[58].

"And," Natalie confided, "what's interesting is that Lee had to sign a pre-nuptial agreement when he married. If they get divorced, he gets virtually nothing." I'd never heard of a pre-nuptial, but this tidbit told me Lee might not be averse to doing something nefarious to get some money of his own. How did Natalie know all this?

---

[57] In the twentieth century, this was known as the Southern Pacific Railroad.

[58] The others were Collis Huntington, Charles Crocker, and Leland Stanford, who founded the famous university (actual name—"Leland Stanford Junior University") in memory of his prematurely deceased son.

She went on, "Anyway, Cindy really is a nice person, or at least I think so. I've only met her once."

"So how'd a little rich girl end up with a schlub like Andy?"

"I understand Andy actually came from money himself, but his dad lost most of it somehow. Andy was used to living the good life up to that point, so I suppose he looked for a girl whose family had plenty. As for why Cindy went for Andy, let's just say that she wasn't deluged with suitors and she settled on him."

I gathered that Cindy might not be the best-looking woman we'd see at the party. I'd already known that, since Natalie would be number one if I had the deciding vote and Yolanda—especially in a swimsuit—would lock down a top place as well. The wives of my co-workers were a mystery to me, since no one in my group displayed family pictures in their cubicles. That was a little weird, but it seemed to be part of the Federated corporate culture.

"Do you know any of the other wives?" I asked.

"Fred Ward, in my group, is married and I've met his wife Mimi. Tammy's husband is Charlie. In Andy's group, I think Owen and Wayne are married, but I've never met either of their wives. I know Phil's single, and I assume Arnold is also." So did I. It was hard to imagine Arnold getting up the nerve to even talk to a woman.

"How about Yolanda?"

Natalie frowned. "I'm pretty sure she's single. She's kind of a mystery; no one seems to know what she does outside of work." Neither did I, but I hoped I'd find out soon from Jack.

"Have you ever been to one of Andy's parties?"

"Last year he had a party before Christmas. The only people he invited were those at manager level in our group. I'd just been promoted, so I was there. There were five or six other managers and their spouses there and, naturally, Lee Greenwood and his wife."

"Well, come on—tell me what the party was like."

"Andy wasn't much more relaxed at home than he is at work, so everything was too formal for people to really have a good time. Whenever Greenwood's around, Andy gets very nervous. He seems to keep worrying that he'll do something wrong, so the whole party seemed scripted. Not much fun, really. The liquor flowed freely, but I didn't see anyone get drunk."

"Sounds like we don't have much to look forward to," I thought out loud.

"It may be OK. Greenwood usually arrives a little late and leaves early, so maybe people will relax enough to enjoy themselves before he gets there. Speaking of that, it's time for us to get going."

Chapter 33

W E GOT to Andy's about ten minutes after the official start time of 1 pm and appeared to be the first guests. The house looked from the outside to be large—I was guessing well over three thousand square feet with maybe four bedrooms. I already knew what the mortgage payments were (over $2,000 a month), what the house was assessed at ($260,000), and how far in arrears Andy was on the mortgage (three months).

Natalie had made me stop en route so we could buy flowers and what she called a "nice bottle" of wine. The nice wine was $25, which struck me as too expensive, but I'd learned not to reveal opinions that contradicted those of my female companion.

I rang the doorbell and the door opened, revealing a rather tubular woman of indeterminate age. She wasn't ugly, but didn't seem to have any individually attractive features. When she smiled her face lit up, making her almost pretty.

"Natalie!" she said with what seemed to be real pleasure. "It's so nice to see you again. And I'm guessing this is Rick Halsted, the new boy genius in Andy's department. You brought flowers and wine! How thoughtful." To my surprise, I liked this woman. She seemed to be what she was, with no pretension. And she had the cross of Andy to bear, although he might be a better husband than a manager. I hoped so, for her sake.

The two women hugged and pecked each other on the cheek. When they pulled away from each other, I shook her hand. "It was very nice of you to invite me," I said. "Natalie and I are looking forward to this."

That sounded clumsy, but it seemed to make Cindy happy.

"Come on in—you're the first ones here." She took us into the living room and down a hall. "This room on the left is where the ladies can change if they want to swim, and the one over here is for the gentlemen. Now let me take you out to the pool. Andy's putting the drinks together."

On the way, she said cautiously, "Rick, Andy was telling me that you and Natalie actually knew each other years ago in Berkeley."

"We did," I agreed. "Until a couple of weeks ago, I not only hadn't seen her for almost eight years, but had no idea where she was. We met again at work, and we're getting reacquainted."

"Very *closely* reacquainted," Natalie said with a wink. Cindy blushed as she led us out to the patio.

"Andy," she called, recovering valiantly, "Rick and Natalie are here."

"Hi, it's great to see you both. Thanks for joining us," he said enthusiastically, with a big smile on his face. He and I shook hands and he kissed Natalie on the cheek as I wondered where he'd suddenly acquired a personality. So far, a nice one.

"I'm mixing up a batch of sangria. There's a keg of beer on ice over there, and a couple of ice chests with soft drinks. I have the hard liquor set out inside, at the bar. In a couple of hours we'll barbecue some ribs, steaks, and burgers."

I heard the doorbell ring and saw Cindy trotting toward the door. In a few minutes, she came back with Owen Langston and a tall lanky redhead, who turned out to be his wife Ginny. She seemed nice and Owen, in a social setting, was more friendly. He was very interested in learning that Natalie and I had arrived together. "So," he murmured, "dating management now, huh?"

"We're just good friends," I said, and heard Natalie chuckle quietly.

I was talking with Owen and Ginny when Phil Boyce showed up and headed straight for Natalie. He'd just started to open his mouth when Natalie said, "Honey, Phil's here."

"Great!" I said enthusiastically. "Good to see you, Phil. Sweetheart, what would you like to drink?"

"I think just a Coke right now, honey. Maybe later I'll try something stronger." We might have overdone the endearments, but Phil seemed to get the point.

He wandered off disconsolately, muttering to himself. But he perked up when Yolanda appeared. She strolled onto the patio wearing some sort of lightweight knee-length wrap; I presumed she had a swimsuit underneath. So far, she was the only one who'd shown up already dressed for the pool. Or almost dressed, as I saw when she dropped the wrap onto a chaise lounge. She'd decided a skimpy bikini would be just the thing. It was bright yellow and apparently made out of some miracle fabric—the tensile strain being put on the top must have been enormous. And the bottom barely covered the essentials. "Attractive," I murmured in a massive understatement. Ray Charles would have been impressed with her looks.

"Get your eyes off her, you pig," Natalie whispered in my ear. I couldn't tell if she was pulling my chain or was really irritated.

"Of course, dear. I was just checking to make sure she didn't have any concealed weapons."

"I see two fairly large ones, but I wouldn't call them concealed. Now could you pay some attention to me?" I could and did.

Within twenty minutes everyone except Greenwood had arrived. People wandered around talking to whomever they encountered and, in the case of the females, casting annoyed glances at Yolanda. The men were looking at her too, but didn't seem upset with what they saw.

Wayne Girard came up to talk to Natalie and me briefly, introducing his wife Lillian. As usual, he showed very little interest in talking to me, but he was friendly to Natalie. Lillian was a rather plain-featured brunette with what I judged to be a very nice figure, if you like full-bodied women. Which I do, despite my love for Natalie.

I was talking to the very cute Tammy Drake and her husband Charlie when someone tapped me on my shoulder. I turned around to find Lee Greenwood smiling at me. "Can you and I talk for a moment?"

Excusing myself, I followed him. He led me over to the other side of the pool, away from everyone else. "I wanted to thank you for your help at the meeting Monday. It took someone new to the group to point out the advantage of expanding the program to include SSBN's." I looked around uneasily, uncomfortable with him bringing up classified aspects of the project in this setting.

"Thanks, but it was just something that popped into my mind."

"Rick, my point is that Harris Booth made an excellent call in persuading you to join Federated. Andy and I are both very impressed with your intelligence, experience, work ethic, and your willingness to speak up." In Andy's case, he was probably also impressed by my insubordinate attitude.

I had no idea what the man was getting at. "I'm glad Federated is pleased. It's my first civilian job, so I'm still kind of feeling my way."

Greenwood leaned in closer to speak more quietly. "Andy's probably going to be moving on to a different project in about a month. Keep this to yourself, but we'll move you up so you can start taking over the project. It'll be probationary, but if you work out, we'll make it permanent."

"Shouldn't Owen or Wayne be promoted?" I asked, trying to sound naïve. "They've been here a lot longer than I have, and probably deserve it more."

"They aren't management track, and you are, as I think you probably realize. Just don't tell anyone yet." He winked and strolled away, presumably to join his wife, whom I hadn't yet seen. Despite his warning, I passed his remarks on to Natalie as soon as I had her alone.

The party went on pleasantly enough, although Greenwood and his invisible Hopkins wife had disappeared shortly after our little talk. Just like an admiral, but without the personality, I thought; last to arrive and first to leave, so everyone else could relax and enjoy the party. I went into the kitchen and made myself what looked like a stiff Jack Daniel's on the rocks, but was iced tea. I'd heard Sinatra did this in live performances, to fool the audience into thinking he was slugging down the booze.

No one, at least by the time dinner was served, seemed to be getting particularly drunk, although Owen and Phil were on their way.

I made an effort after dinner to spend time with all my Federated teammates, especially after they'd downed a few drinks to loosen their internal control systems. I had come up with questions that might reveal personal problems, which in turn would make that person interested in a moneymaking opportunity. Like selling secrets to the Soviets.

I started with Arnold, but couldn't get him to hold a conversation with me. To be fair, his eyes were so fixated on Yolanda and her body's effort to burst through the bikini fabric that I wasn't sure he registered that I was talking to him.

Next I tried Phil. I sidled over and engaged him in a conversation about the horribly high cost of living in the Bay Area. Phil, who was commuting over eighty miles a day so he could afford housing, opened up freely. He made it clear he wasn't being paid what he believed he was worth, and even told me he'd looked for a part-time opportunity to help with his costs. "The gas alone to get back and forth to work costs me a fortune," he bitched. I could sympathize with this—regular gas now cost almost sixty cents a gallon. I knew Phil was making just over $11,000, which seemed to me more than fair for a technician without a degree. Cash payments from the Soviets would be tempting to Phil.

I moved on to try again to get Wayne Girard to talk to me, something I hadn't been able to do at work. Now that he had a few drinks in him, and believed I did also, I might stand a better chance. His wife had moved off to talk with Natalie and Cindy, so I went over and tried to start a conversation.

He turned out to be drunker than I'd hoped, but was in a bad mood. His greeting was "Rick, don't take this personally, but I hate your guts." I did my best, but I was still taking it personally.

"What's the problem?" I asked politely.

"The goddamn problem is that I hear they're going to promote you to acting manager. You haven't even been here two weeks."

"Where'd you hear that?"

"I was standing near Cindy a little bit ago and she was babbling on about how Andy was getting moved to a different project and getting a pay raise, and that you'd be promoted so you can take over the group when he left." Greenwood's daughter had spilled the beans he'd wanted to keep on ice. Sorry for the clashing clichés.

Maybe my best tactic was to help Wayne along, if he really wanted to buck for a management position. "Wayne," I began, "I realize I'm new at Federated, but I notice that during the weekly meetings you never speak up with a question or a suggestion. If you did that more often, you'd have better visibility when they start thinking about who to promote." If

162

Wayne were politically clever, he might realize it'd be in his best interests to act a little deferential toward his possible future manager.

"Go screw yourself," he muttered. "The last thing I need is advice from you." I should probably mark him low on "gets along with co-workers" for his next evaluation.

All the trouble I went to didn't earn me much. The people I targeted either were too drunk to communicate any further—Phil and Owen—or didn't open up while talking to me—everyone else. Maybe I needed to work on my interpersonal skills.

The party began to wind down around ten pm; Natalie gave me a significant look and I was bright enough to decipher it. We gave our thanks to Andy and Cindy, waved goodbye to the people who were still there, and headed out.

"My place or yours?" Natalie asked.

"Mine, unless you'd rather be at home." I wanted to check my alarm system and phone messages, which I hadn't been able to do since the previous evening's brief stop there.

"Fine by me, big boy. But let's go by my place so I can pick up what I'll need overnight."

Chapter 34

MY ALARM was still armed when I opened the door, which I took to be a good sign. As Natalie was putting away her stuff, I called the alarm company to see if anything unusual had gone on in the last twenty-four hours. They assured me the last event before I arrived back today was the arming I'd done before going to Natalie's the previous evening.

The answering machine was blinking. The first message was from San Mateo. I heard my stepfather's voice ask if I could come to dinner tomorrow. "And bring a friend, if you'd like," he'd hinted. The next was from Jack Sammon, although he didn't leave his name: "Hi, Rick, sorry I missed you. Give me a call when you get a chance. I have some of that information you were looking for." That couldn't be too important or he'd have paged me.

The last was a plaintive message from Beth asking me to call her. Not much chance of that.

As Beth's message ended, Natalie came back into the living room, now wearing a virtually transparent negligee. Or was it a peignoir? I had no idea what it was called, but I was very much in favor of whatever it was.

"Who was that?"

I explained that Beth and I had met a couple of weeks ago and dated once, but that I'd decided she wasn't a keeper. "She got angry at me for not paying enough attention to her, like calling her every night during the week, and so on. Since I already knew we wouldn't be dating much longer, I decided to take her at her word when she said not to call her anymore. Now she seems to call every couple of days whining about me not calling."

"I actually meant the first call," Natalie smiled. She'd apparently heard them all and wasn't interested in Jack's anonymous call, which would save me another devious explanation.

"That was my stepfather. As you may have heard, they want me to come up for dinner in San Mateo tomorrow afternoon. Would you be interested in coming up and meeting everyone? Not to put any pressure on you, but I'm not going without you."

"Who's everyone?"

"My mom, my stepfather—Byron Halsted—and maybe his two children. Actually, they're adults; his daughter Shannon is two years older than I am and Eric is four years older. They're both married, so their spouses would probably be there too. I should let you know Byron's pretty well off financially."

"So you have your stepfather's last name?"

"Yep. I changed it after my mom married him. I was about thirteen at the time. My original last name was Burke."

She turned away slightly and then back. "Are you sure you want me to be there? I mean, we just started seeing each other again and they might think ..." Her voice trailed off.

I pulled her against me, kissing the top of her head as she snuggled in. "If they think I brought you because you're important to me, that'll be fine with me. But I won't push you to do something you're not comfortable with."

She slid her arms around me and hugged me. "I guess I'm just afraid things are moving too fast," she murmured into my chest. This from the woman who'd asked *me* out eight years after we broke up, initiated a torrid make-out session on our first night together again, and then invited herself for a sleepover at my place the very next night.

"Honey, I lost you once and I don't intend to let that happen again. Let's give this our best shot. Come with me to dinner—meet the family and charm them. I'd be very proud if you could be there with me."

"It's too late to call them now," she suggested. "Come to bed with me and we'll talk about it in the morning." She could be very persuasive. Especially the way she looked in whatever she was almost wearing.

She was in a good mood when we woke up; almost as good as mine. We'd made each other happy during the night, and were now comfortable with spending the night together. I'd heard the word "love" whispered several times. At least one of them was from Natalie. I was beginning to wonder if I needed to go on a vitamin regimen. And someone had told me oysters helped.

As she was ransacking my kitchen for breakfast food, she asked what time dinner would be. I took this to mean she'd be coming up to San Mateo with me. "Around three, I think. I'll wait until nine or so to call to make sure I don't wake them up. They like to sleep in on Sunday."

"Remember we need to stop at my house so I can get into some decent clothes. What'll everyone be wearing?"

"No one's going to dress up—casual will be fine."

I looked at my watch; we had almost five hours to get there. Natalie was already putting scrambled eggs and sausage on the table.

"Sit and eat," she smiled. "You're going to need your strength."

After I'd eaten and helped Natalie clean up the kitchen, I called up to San Mateo and got Byron on the phone. "I got your call, and I'm planning on coming up," I told him. "If it's OK, I'd like to bring someone up with me." Within a few seconds my mom was on the phone. Byron had quickly understood I was bringing a female, and that he wasn't the best person to discuss this.

"Is it a young lady?" she asked hopefully.

"Yes, Mom," I said patiently, resisting the impulse to tell her I was bringing a young man of whom I was very fond. "Her name is Natalie. I'm sure you and Byron will like her. Who else will be there?"

"Today it'll be a small group. Shannon and Eric can't make it. What time will we see you?"

"How about around two? That'll give us time to relax before dinner." After hanging up, I noticed Natalie looking at me expectantly.

"Take a seat," she suggested. "We have to talk."

A look of terror must have briefly surfaced on my face; this sounded too much like the kiss-off eight years ago. She smiled and sat on the couch, patting the seat next to her. "Relax, this won't hurt."

I sat cautiously. She leaned over, kissed me gently, and then sat back. "Let's start with the easy stuff. Have you noticed anything unusual about our relationship so far?"

"Other than the total bliss?" I asked rhetorically, earning me another smile. "Well, it's all happened kind of fast, not that I'm complaining."

"That's almost what I'm getting at. What you *should* have noticed is that I've taken the lead in everything so far—I asked you out, I set up the situation for our first kiss, I almost had to drag you into bed, not that I'm complaining about the results. I'm starting to wonder how committed you are to this relationship."

"Committed? Natalie, what you and I have is the absolute center of my life. As far as you taking the initiative, keep in mind that you dumped me eight years ago and left me with the definite impression I wasn't to contact you at all. Then we end up working together, and, from the way you behaved at first, I figured you didn't want me to try to renew what we had—the marvelous love we had together." Too long a speech, but Natalie had been listening raptly.

With a wicked grin, she said, "So you're admitting you didn't have the nerve to get us back together, and had to leave it to me?"

"I said no such thing. Keep in mind that since we got back together I've been doing most of the work while you just lie there and enjoy yourself."

That earned me a nasty look. "The point I'm trying to make, you nitwit, is that I'm deeply and permanently in love with you. What do you have to say to that?"

"That I fell in love with you eight years ago and have never stopped loving you. That you're all that gives meaning to my life." I realized with surprise that this was true.

She slid into my arms and kissed me again with soft passion, laying her head on my chest afterward. Was that a sigh of contentment I heard? "Thank God," she murmured. "I've been kicking my own butt for eight years over walking away from you. That was a bad decision—not that I had much choice at the time."

I wondered what that meant as she went on, "The only obstacle I'd have been worried about would have been the Navy, but now that you're a civilian, I don't see any problems for us. Now we can just be happy together."

OK, it was decision time. Should I take her at her word that she truly loves me and reveal the truth about my Navy status to her, or wait until I'm certain she's not mixed up in whatever espionage may be going on?

If I revealed my actual mission to her and she turned out to be involved in the transfer of secrets to the Soviets, not only would the mission be blown, but I'd probably be in some physical danger. And my Navy career would be in the crapper. That seemed incidental right now.

But I couldn't believe Nat was mixed up in any of that mess, and I had to trust her if I loved her. Didn't I?

Chapter 35

"**H**ONEY," I began tentatively, "there's something I have to tell you."

"Mmm," she said into my chest. "And what would that be?"

"You'd better sit up for this one," I suggested.

Natalie reluctantly disentangled herself. "What is it?" she asked warily.

"I haven't been completely frank with you about my leaving the Navy," I began. That sounded better than telling her I'd outright lied to her.

She looked at me narrowly. "Go on."

"Actually, I'm still in the Navy."

She stared at me. "Then how can you be working at Federated as a civilian?"

"Federated thinks I'm out of the Navy. I'm actually here on a classified assignment regarding the security of the Outlaw Shark project."

"So you lied to Federated to get hired, by telling them you were a civilian?" She seemed to be irritated, but who can figure women?

"Look," I said, "just let me outline the whole thing from the beginning and then you can ask whatever you want. I don't want to have secrets from you, and I hope you'll see that there were good reasons I didn't tell you all this at the beginning." I went briefly through the surprise orders I'd received, the training (without mentioning NIS specifically), and the likely Soviet interest in this project. Partway through this speech, I realized I'd violated several security rules that could land me in a Federal slammer for a long time. But only if Natalie told someone about it, so I shouldn't have to worry. Right?

Ten minutes later I'd said all I could. I finished, "I hope you can understand why I wasn't able to tell you this when I first met you again—after all, you weren't behaving as though you were pleased I'd shown up. In fact, you were suspicious I might have tracked you down and taken a job at Federated just to be near you."

She stared at me for a while before gathering herself. "How about you go somewhere for an hour or so? I need some time alone to think about this, OK?"

It didn't look like I had a choice, so I explained to her how to lock the deadbolt after I left. "I'll knock when I come back; you can look through the peephole to be sure it's me before you open the deadbolt." She pushed me gently out the door.

For lack of something better to do, I drove to a nearby park and walked around ... and around ... before heading back home. Natalie let me in, but didn't look directly at me. Not a good sign.

"I have a lot of questions, Rick. Is that OK? I mean, I need to trust you and I need to find out if there can be a life for us."

"Go ahead, honey. I'll tell you anything I can." That was true, although I intended to continue to conceal some things from her that she didn't really need to know. I'd already told her enough to destroy both my assignment at Federated and my Navy career.

"First of all," she said, "I don't understand how you actually got a job at Federated—I mean, who hired you?"

"Ever heard of Harris Booth?" She shook her head.

"He's on the board of directors at Federated. My boss for this project introduced me to him; Harris is a retired admiral and agreed to say he'd recommended me to the company. Then one of the managers in Personnel set up fake files with my employment application and so on. Greenwood heard from Andy that Harris had gotten me into Federated, and he's been sucking up to me ever since. That's probably the reason he was recommending me for promotion."

Natalie was more interested in the Personnel issue. "So someone in Personnel was working for the Navy? Why would he do that?"

"It wasn't voluntary. The government uncovered something they used to put pressure on him, so he had to cooperate with us. He set up the files so it'd look like I'd been hired through the normal process." I didn't mention he'd given me copies of all the project's personnel files, including Natalie's.

Her eyes widened. "This wouldn't be the manager who was killed last week, would it?"

"Dick Detweiler," I admitted.

Natalie absorbed this sobering fact. "Does that mean you're in danger?"

"I don't really know. I've thought about it, but figured there's not much I can do about it, so I'll take some reasonable precautions—keep my eyes wide open, and so on. Other than that, I'll just hope I'm not on their list."

"I don't want to lose you ... again," she said, almost to herself.

"Honey, I don't think it'll ever come to that," I told her, gathering her into my arms. "I just have to get my job done here."

"And then you'll leave me to go back to sea, I suppose," she said.

This had been on my mind. "I'm not really sure. Now that you and I are together again, the idea of going back to sea duty isn't as appealing as it used to be. If I don't succeed in finding out if someone's actually leaking secrets to the Soviets, I probably wouldn't get a good enough fitness report out of this to give me a chance of getting command. So there'd be no point in sea duty—I'd be better off just resigning my commission." And there was at least one other reason that I wasn't yet ready to reveal to her; it could short-circuit my career no matter what I wanted.

"Getting command?"

"Command of a submarine. That's been my long-term goal, although you might remember I was willing to not volunteer for submarines if that would have made a difference in keeping you."

"Let's take a break from this for a while," Natalie suggested. "I've got way too much data to process right now. And a lot of questions to ask, but not right away."

"Honey, do you understand why I couldn't tell you this until we were pretty sure we'd be together from now on? I mean, even now, if you told anyone what I've told you, I might be court-martialed, and I'd certainly get tossed out of the submarine force."

"Okay, Lieutenant," she smiled. "I promise no one will hear any of this from me."

I was tempted to reveal my actual rank, but didn't see the point. "Frankly, although I've been working hard at it, I still don't have anything showing me who at Federated might be slipping classified information to the Soviets."

"Shouldn't you start with the "why" of it?"

"That's the angle I've been pursuing. Money, ideology, or being blackmailed are the usual motivators. I started by trying to identify people within the project who seem to need extra cash. It could be someone who has trouble maintaining the lifestyle they want, or who has a lifestyle that could make him susceptible to blackmail. The trouble is that with inflation being what it is, and the cost of living in this area, everyone could use an extra few thousand bucks a month." Of course, the most likely person in the Outlaw Shark group to be spying because of ideology was probably the woman I was talking to.

"Well, how about the 'what'? What particularly about Outlaw Shark would the Soviets be most interested in?"

"I've given that a lot of thought. At first I thought it'd be the guts of the system –the hardware and software the SSN's will use for targeting Harpoon missiles. But I've changed my mind on that. I'm not saying they wouldn't snap up that information if they were offered it, but I don't think that's the crown jewel they're looking for."

"Why not?"

"It seems to me it's too specific to US systems and weapons to be of much good to them. As far as I know, the Soviet Navy is much less computerized than our Navy is, so it's not as though they could actually use what they steal. I suppose it'd be helpful to know our capabilities, but that's about all they'd get from that source."

"So if that's not what they could use, what is?"

"I think it's the uplink and downlink for the SSIXS system, and the data itself. If they could get into that, they'd—at the very least—have access to our ocean surveillance data, which would be bad enough, believe me. The worst case would be if they could get access into the system and change the data or corrupt it. Plus, SSIXS carries other highly classified traffic that they'd love to get their hands on. Outlaw Shark might provide them the info they need to crack into SSIXS. Then we'd really be screwed."

"But I thought that system requires a specific identification of the submarine. I think it's hardware-based—something like a serial number that's built into the radio transmission system and that's unique to each submarine. And isn't all the message traffic encrypted?"

"Sure, but there might be a way to spoof the hardware verification, or even create a fictitious submarine ID that the system would accept. I'm sure the Soviets have been after our encryption systems for a long time, although I have no idea if they've succeeded in that[59]. Anyway, that's where I think the most dangerous breach of security would occur."

"That'd mean Arnold Kunz is the guy who could cause the most danger. Most of his job on the project deals with downloading SSIXS data—establishing the uplink, and so on."

"And he's such a quiet little nerd. The only person he seems interested in talking to is Yolanda, and she's not interested in him," I mused aloud. But if he were the leaker, she'd be an excellent choice for whoever wanted the data, I decided—he'd probably tell her everything she wanted without asking for a dime.

Natalie smiled. "He was the highlight of the pool party with his constant staring at Yolanda."

"And she was well worth staring at," I said unwisely, earning an cold glance from Nat.

She paused long enough to worry me before going on. "I guess we should check him out to see if he might be the one," she finally said,

---

[59] By 1985, ten years later, the Navy would learn that John Walker (aka "Johnnie Walker Red") had been systematically selling information about Navy cryptographic systems in general and specifically submarine crypto systems to the Soviets. With this information, it'd be much more possible the Soviets could break into the SSIXS system once they knew more about the hardware elements involved.

generously foregoing any sarcastic comments about men and their fascination with voluptuous women.

"We?" I asked. "Sweetheart, you shouldn't get involved in the investigation. It could be dangerous."

"Look, if you're going to put yourself into danger, why can't I do the same thing?" I was smart enough not to answer, assuming that "because you're still a suspect" wouldn't go over well.

"Let's get ready to head up to dinner," I temporized. "You said you'd need to get a change of clothes on the way." I looked at my watch. "It's almost one now. How about we go to your place and then head up the 280 to San Mateo? We can take the scenic route."

"You didn't answer my suggestion. Can I help you on this or not?" Natalie persisted.

"We'll talk about it later."

Chapter 36

WE STOPPED at Natalie's, where she took only the promised few minutes to change clothes. When she reappeared and announced she was ready, she looked great, but to me she always did.

"What's the dinner going to be like?" she asked as I helped her into the car. "Are your folks formal?"

"They're pretty informal. Byron's a nice guy, and he's been very good to my mom since they married. His first wife died fairly young in a car accident; I think Eric was twelve and Shannon was ten when she died. A few years later, after my mom and I moved down from Fort Ross, she met Byron. I think they got married about a year after that, so Eric was probably sixteen or so then and Shannon fourteen."

"Do you get along with them OK?"

"I think both of them resented me and my mom at first, but she won them over pretty quickly. Eric's an attorney. He's a little stuffy, but I'm repeating myself. Shannon's kind of a typical California girl—blonde, interested in outdoor sports—just what you'd expect. Her husband's an orthopedic surgeon; I think he's at least ten years older than she is. Neither of them will be there today." I wondered if she'd noticed I hadn't answered her question.

"You said Byron was well off. What does he do?"

"He inherited a good chunk of money and could have lived nicely off the income from it. But he's the kind of guy who enjoys doing things. He started an office supply business in San Mateo and later added stores up and down the Peninsula and a few in the East Bay—Hayward, Fremont, places like that. The stores do pretty well, and he spends most of his time in general management. He has managers who run the individual stores." In fact, I'd bought many of my household supplies, including my answering machine, from one of Byron's stores in Mountain View. I hadn't asked for a family discount.

We reached the poetically titled Halsted homestead just before two. "Nice place," Natalie observed. It was high in the hills above the swank Peninsula Golf and Country Club, with a view of the Bay and Mount Diablo, at least on a smog-free day, which was rarer in the Bay Area than it should have been. It sprawled over an acre of land and featured excellent panoramas of the Bay from a lot of the rooms. I could see my old high school below us.

Naturally, we'd stopped en route to buy flowers and a bottle of wine. I'd barely gotten my finger off the doorbell before my mom opened it, smiling happily. "It's about time you came to visit the old folks," she said, leaning forward to kiss me on the cheek.

"Mom, this is Natalie Montaigne. Natalie, this is my mom, Emily Halsted. And the big guy looming behind her is Byron, my stepfather."

The women exchanged air kisses in the vicinity of each other's cheek. "Thank you so much for letting me join your family dinner," Natalie smiled, handing Emily the flowers. Then she stepped forward to shake Byron's hand.

"This is for you," I smiled, giving Byron the wine.

"Good to see you," he said as he shook my hand. "We'd expected to see you more often now that you're back in the Bay Area. It's been a couple of weeks."

"My fault, but I have to plead that I've been working some long hours trying to get used to a civilian job."

"Yep," he told me with a grin. "No more lollygagging like in the Navy." He may actually have been serious. Byron had always seemed to think a military career consisted mostly of goofing off. I'd liked to have see how Byron would've enjoyed my seven day a week, sixteen to twenty hour a day working schedule when we were at sea, especially at my puny Navy salary level.

"Come on in," he said, ushering Natalie and me into the large living room. "Drinks? I know what you like, Rick, but I'm not sure about your lovely lady."

"White wine would be fine, Mr. Halsted," Natalie said.

"It's Byron and Emily to you," he assured her. In a few minutes, everyone had their drinks and we were seated, admiring the spectacular view. Today was one of the smog-free days, and Mount Diablo loomed clearly thirty miles away across the blue waters of the Bay.

"Natalie," Emily started hesitantly, "this is the first time in a long while that Rick has brought a young lady to meet us. How long have you two known each other?"

"About eight years, actually," Natalie smiled. "We dated for a while in college, but we hadn't seen each other since ... I suppose late 1967. It turns out I'm working on the same project Rick is at Federated, but neither of us had any idea we'd run into each other there. We've been seeing each other since shortly after he came to work."

Emily's eyes widened. "Were you the one who left Rick during his senior year? He was absolutely devastated when you two broke up! And now you're back together?" She seemed upset at Natalie's revelation, but I had no idea why.

"I'm afraid the breakup was my fault, Mrs. Halsted. I was young and made a mistake, but now we're together again."

"I've already asked you to call me Emily. Well, this all sounds like a soap opera, but Rick looks happy, so I'm very pleased you two are together again." She looked more worried than pleased. Puzzling.

We chatted for a half hour or so, with me being probed about my job at Federated interspersed by social questions to Natalie, most of them apparently designed to see how long it'd be until we announced a wedding date. I excused myself, letting everyone assume I was going to the bathroom. Instead, I went up to my room on the second floor, shuffled through a couple of boxes there and retrieved my Navy ID card. I'd decided to bring it down to Sunnyvale and put it in the safe's secret compartment. Just in case, I murmured as I slipped it into my wallet and headed back downstairs.

I hadn't been back long when Emily looked at her watch. "My goodness, dinner should be on the table. Byron, will you get Rick and Natalie seated? I'll be right there."

We arrived at the table to see it was set for five people. "Are we missing someone?" I asked. She'd specifically told me we'd have a small group for dinner.

"Uncle Pete's joining us, but he said he might be a little late and we should start without him," Byron told us. Too bad—I could have gone longer before having an encounter with Pete. Since my mom knew that, she'd probably decided to let me think he wouldn't be here. If I'd known he would, *I* wouldn't be here.

"Is he your brother, Emily?" Natalie asked.

"Oh, no—he's not really related at all. Just a friend of the family. I'm sure you'll like him." I wasn't at all sure Natalie would like him. I certainly didn't.

We were starting the main course when I heard the front door open and close. Pete felt free to walk in like a real family member. Heavy steps clomped toward the dining room and Pete appeared in the doorway, displaying his unique sneering smile. He was somewhere in his fifties by now, I guessed, and looked overweight, but wasn't—it was all muscle. He claimed to be Irish and might well have been, for all I knew. Pete had told me he'd been in the Official IRA, which I'd learned was the Communist faction of the IRA. From unpleasant experience, I knew him to be both dangerous and ruthless, using his friendly Irish mannerisms as a mask. His expression changed from the phony smile to confusion as he saw Natalie.

She was staring at him in what looked like horror. She pushed her chair back and fled, going out the other side of the dining room to avoid

Pete. "Please excuse me," she managed to say as she ran out. I got up and followed her, catching up with her near the front door.

"We have to leave. Now!" she said, tears gathering in her eyes.

"What's wrong, sweetheart?" Obviously it was something to do with Pete.

"That man—that awful man! I can't be anywhere near him."

"Wait here," I told her, and went back into the dining room. I explained that we had to leave early. "Natalie apparently came down with something. I need to get her home. My apologies and all that, but I'm sure you understand." They didn't, but pretended they did, which was almost as good. Pete favored me with a smirk, hinting he knew very well why Natalie had bolted from the table.

"I need to meet with you, Rick. Soon," he said. "I'll call you to set a time." I ignored him and left the room.

Chapter 37

I HELPED her out the door, walking past what I assumed was Pete's car. It was a classic 1962 Studebaker Gran Turismo Hawk with a license plate reading "DSY 682." I made a mental note of the plate for further research. If he was reinserting himself into my life, I might need to take action against him.

Once we were in the car, I drove only a few blocks and then pulled over, taking the sobbing Natalie into my arms. "What is it, honey?"

"I've been wanting to tell you this ever since we got back together, but kept putting it off," she managed to say before starting another crying jag.

I waited until she calmed down. "Let's go somewhere we can sit and talk," she finally managed to say. I drove to a coffee shop down on El Camino.

I ordered an iced tea and she asked for hot tea before heading to the bathroom to repair her makeup. "OK," I said after she returned, still red-eyed from weeping, "will you please tell me what's going on and why you're so upset?"

"That horrible man—your Uncle Pete—is the reason I left you eight years ago." That was a conversation stopper.

"I don't understand," I managed to say. A massive understatement.

"I'd never met him until the day before I had to break up with you. After the Coordinating Committee meeting ended on Sunday, Giovanni insisted I go to his apartment. I thought he was just trying to get me into bed—which I'd never do with him, of course—but he told me there was someone there I needed to meet. I still didn't want to go, but he finally badgered me into agreeing.

"We got to his place and Peter was waiting there for us. Giovanni seemed to know him pretty well, so I suppose the two of them were working together somehow. He was actually polite and almost charming at first. He told me he was a friend of your family. In fact, he said he was your godfather."

"That's a lie. I doubt Pete's ever been into a church in his life, except maybe to bomb it. But lying is one of his primary ways of communicating." The other relied on threats.

Natalie smiled wanly. "I didn't believe everything he said; maybe not even any of it. Anyway, he told me I wasn't the right kind of girl for you, that'd I'd never make a good Navy wife and I'd end up hurting your career. He said, 'You'll have to cut this romance short, for Rick's sake.' I told him there was no way I was leaving you—that we loved each other and that I was sure our relationship wouldn't hurt you in any way." This was interesting, as Natalie, during the time we were together at Berkeley, had never used the word "love," even at our most passionate moments. Maybe she'd been a shy girl, afraid to speak her mind. Or perhaps she was lying to me for some reason.

"So what did he do?" I asked.

"He tried threats. He said that he had some information about my father that would get him kicked out of his job at the University, and that if I didn't break up with you, he'd make sure it got to the dean of his department."

"What could that have been?" I asked curiously.

"It was about him having an affair with one of his students when he was in Ann Arbor," she explained hesitantly. I didn't think that was all that damning, especially since Natalie had already told me that her adopted mother had died quite a while ago, eliminating the issue of adultery.

"Come on, Natalie, having a fling with a co-ed years ago wouldn't have been that bad. He'd been widowed for years when that happened, right? I don't think he'd have gotten much more than a warning not to let it happen again."

"It wasn't a co-ed, Rick," Natalie said, blushing. The light dawned. The University probably had a low level of tolerance for homosexual activities—this was back in the 1960's, a long time before everyone at a university was pressured to be enthusiastically in favor of this sort of conduct. Maybe this explained why Natalie's adoptive parents hadn't had any kids of their own. If Tab A had never been inserted into Slot B and you wanted a child, adoption was your only choice.

"OK, so you had to agree to break up with me to save your dad's position. I can understand that. It wasn't really my Navy obligations and all the sea time that was the reason."

"Actually, that worried me, but I wouldn't have left you because of it. I told Pete I appreciated his concern for you, but I was sure you and I would do just fine. I figured I could warn my dad and he could let his dean know; probably he'd just get a reprimand of some kind. I made it clear I didn't want to leave you."

"And what did Pete do?" I asked warily, knowing violence was his preferred method of solving problems.

"He slapped me across the face," she said softly, beginning to tear up again. "Really hard—it knocked me down and hurt a lot. I started crying, got up and tried to leave. He grabbed my arm with one hand and squeezed until I screamed. Next, he started groping me with his other hand—squeezing my breasts so hard it hurt. He said, "I guess I'll have to show you I'm serious about this. I didn't know what he meant. Then Pete told Giovanni to lock the apartment door."

I was starting to realize why Giovanni had bragged about having had sex with Natalie on that horrible day when I lost her. "What then?" I managed to ask.

"He punched me in the stomach. I fell down again and was having a hard time breathing. I was in a lot of pain, and couldn't resist much. He flipped me over so I was face-down. He pushed my skirt up over my hips and ripped off my panties. Then he pulled my hips up into a kneeling position. He told Giovanni to watch what he was going to do."

I feared what might come next. "Honey, you don't have to tell me any more if you don't want to. I already know what a scumbag Pete is."

"No, you need to know," she said stubbornly. "I should have told you before, but I was afraid you'd be disgusted with me."

Before I could say anything more, Natalie went on. "You can probably guess what happened. He pried my legs apart and ... well, he just crammed into me. Rick, I'm not talking about normal sex here. I think I howled out loud, it hurt so bad. I never thought I'd be violated like that. He kept on for what seemed like a long time. I was sobbing and trying to fight him off, but there was no way I could. It seemed to go on forever. Finally he finished and got off me."

That may have been the background for Giovanni's smirking at me the following day, and making comments about the cute sounds Natalie made during sex. I couldn't see anything cute about the way Natalie had described her rape.

"That's horrible," I muttered. Most of my thoughts were on how to terminate Uncle Peter in the most painful way possible. A red-hot fireplace poker was an element of my plan. It might give Pete, in his last moments, a different perspective on anal rape.

Natalie went on, "I was lying there sobbing, and heard Giovanni asking Peter if he could go next. Peter just laughed and said that'd be wrong. As if him having raped me that way was just fine."

"That son of a bitch! I'll get him for this," I hissed. I couldn't help remembering how Giovanni had described the sounds she made when she was sexually pleased.

She went on, "I managed to get up and get my clothes straightened out. Pete slapped my face again and told me I had to come back the next night to tell him I'd broken up with you. I was back over there trying to get him to understand when you called. You know what happened after that. Please understand—I didn't want to leave you, but I couldn't stand the thought of what he threatened. It was going to be both him and

181

Giovanni raping me, and every night they'd bring me back there for more. So when you called and asked to meet, I knew I had to get it over with." I suppose one alternative might have been for her to call in the police, but could see why she'd decided to minimize the chance of more brutality from Pete. If she'd brought the police into it, it'd only have increased his determination to abuse her.

"I understand, honey. I don't know what else you could have done, and I have to admit that I couldn't have taken on Pete at that point. Now I may be able to."

"Rick, don't! He's a brutal and very strong man. I think he enjoys giving pain; he might really injure you."

"I can take care of myself," I told her, wondering if my rudimentary hand-to-hand combat lessons would be enough to take on Pete. I remembered a few instances in high school where I hadn't satisfied the ambitious goals he'd set, and how much he'd seemed to enjoy beating the crap out of me. But if motivation would be the deciding factor in this, I could definitely kick his ass.

Chapter 38

IT TOOK a while for Natalie to calm down and I could understand why. It had to have been humiliating for her to relate the horrible things Pete had done to her. As we merged onto the 280 southbound, I was wondering whether we needed to protect Natalie from Pete—maybe an alarm system for her house, a pistol for her? I should keep us together as much as possible so he couldn't get her alone.

"Honey, tomorrow I'm going to call my alarm company and get your house set up. I'd feel a lot better if you had a little protection there. After work tomorrow, we can find a handgun for you. Maybe something like mine, but with a smaller grip to fit your hand better?"

"I suppose," she said absently; her mind was clearly on another track. "Rick, why would you and your family be close to someone like Pete? It just doesn't seem to fit who you are and who Byron and Emily seem to be."

Was this the time to reveal the big secret? The one nobody—except Emily and Pete—even suspected? I was disgusted at what Pete had done to her, and she hadn't given me any reason to believe she wasn't truly in love with me. The longer I waited to tell her what she'd regard as an astonishing and almost unbelievable revelation, the more trouble I'd be in for not telling her sooner. On the other hand, if I did reveal my past, she'd have a fatal hammer to use against me. It seemed both choices were bad.

"I'm waiting for an answer," she said impatiently.

I tried to stall her. "Honey, I didn't pick Pete as an honorary uncle—I inherited him. I hate that bastard, and have for a long time, so please don't say I'm close to him, OK?"

"You're not paying attention. Tell me what's really going on here. I think you owe me that." It sounded as though I had to tell her the truth or risk losing her. That made the decision easier than I'd feared.

"Natalie, first of all you have to understand how much I love you. If I tell you any details about what you're asking, I'm giving you the power to absolutely destroy me."

"Then I guess this is where I find out if you really trust me," she said firmly.

"OK. I'm going to tell you a story. Maybe it'll help you to understand the situation." I paused to gather my thoughts. We were getting close to the Pulgas Water Temple, so I pulled off the 280, parked, and led her to a bench by the pool overlooking Crystal Springs Lake. We had the place to ourselves—surprising on such a beautiful Sunday.

"Think of this as a fairy tale gone bad. Once upon a time, in a small town in Russia not far from Yekaterinburg, there was a little boy named Pavel Nikolayevich Ulyanov. He was a happy boy. His mother and father loved him and did as much as they could for him and his beautiful little sister Larissa. Now, it came to the attention of the KGB—that's the Committee for State Security—that Pavel had an unusual talent for languages. It was mandatory in those days that children be taught rudimentary English, since America was the main enemy of worldwide socialism. Pavel's abilities were good enough to attract attention from the government. I suppose one of his instructors must have alerted those goons. They probably had teachers acting as talent scouts all around the country.

"By the time Pavel was about ten years old, which was when the KGB became interested, he was speaking good basic English without much of an accent. His vocabulary wasn't extensive yet, but it was clear he was a fast learner. He was also good in math and science, which made him even more valuable to them. They decided to take him to a special school, far away from where he lived. Naturally, they didn't give him or his parents a choice on this. So he was taken away from his mother, his father and his sister, all of whom he loved very much, and never saw them again."

"What happened to them?" Natalie asked hesitantly.

"In this story we'll say the KGB rewarded them somehow—maybe getting better jobs for both of his parents or even letting them move into Yekaterinburg itself, where there was ballet, a nice orchestra, and football. But probably they were done away with—sent to a camp in Siberia or maybe killed outright. If they made it to a camp, the guards probably would have used Pavel's mother as a whore; maybe his little sister too, once she got old enough to be interesting. They would have just worked his father to death. You see, the KGB wouldn't want it to get around that they were taking children for a special purpose." I didn't mention the other possibility—that the KGB might take good care of them to use them as leverage against me.

She was clearly upset, but managed to say, "Tell me about the special school, Rick. Or should I call you Pavel?"

"I'm Rick; remember, this is just a story. Well, Pavel ended up on the west side of the Ural Mountains, near the Ob River. There was a unique place out there in the wilderness. A company of Spetsnaz guarded it—those are Soviet Special Forces troops, very tough guys. Most of their job was keeping people inside from getting out, although I don't know if anyone ever actually tried to escape. Inside the fences was a huge building. It might have been built in the Great Patriotic War—that's World War II to you capitalists—as an airplane factory. It covered about ten hectares—sorry, twenty-five acres—of land. Inside this giant building was a small American town. It had a school, a bank, a movie theater, a few shops, a baseball diamond, an American football field, and three dormitories—one for boys, one for girls, and a nicer one for the instructors. Everyone there just called it the Facility—that'd be 'Obyekt' in Russian.

"What they did in the Facility was teach young Russian boys and girls how to pass as Americans. It was mostly boys—about four to one, probably because they thought boys were better than girls in math and science." Natalie frowned. Had I said something offensive?

"All the classes were taught in English. In fact, the students were forbidden to speak Russian, even in the dormitories, which were of course bugged. They were taught a lot of American English, of course, but also US history and regular topics like mathematics and science. They were also taught religion. They wouldn't know until they went on assignment which religion they'd have, so they learned a little bit about all the major ones. Except Islam and Judaism, of course. They even had a Boy Scout troop there, and the boys earned merit badges the same way they would have in the States. There were special lessons on security topics—how to make sure the police or FBI wouldn't find out you were impersonating someone else, how to avoid being tailed, and so on. This was all for the Motherland, or the Rodina, as these Russian kids used to say before they could speak only English.

"The whole reason for the Facility was that it'd be easier to establish an American identity for someone who wasn't an adult yet. All you'd need was an existing American boy or girl whose identity could be taken over— no documentation would be expected. Of course, the original American boy or girl would have to disappear, along with their parents and anyone else who might know them well enough to spot an impostor. Because of that, they focused on kids who didn't have many friends or relatives. Kids with a single parent, almost always the mother, were prime targets. The usual method was to have the kid and his parent move to another town. A better job offer would suddenly appear, with the help of some of the Soviet sympathizers in the US. But the parent and kid who arrived for the new job were Facility graduates instead of the original kid and his or her parent.

"Every day when school started, the boys and girls at the Facility would pledge allegiance to the US flag and sing the 'Star-Spangled Banner.' They watched a lot of American movies and television, and the boys learned to play sports like baseball and American football. The girls learned how to use a modern kitchen and how to cook American-style food. I think they also had lessons on fashion—what girls wear in the US is very different from what a Russian girl would wear. After a few years, the boys and girls who did well could be put down anywhere in the United States and pass as a native citizen."

"What about those who didn't do well?"

I paused. "I don't really know. One day a kid who hadn't been keeping up just wouldn't be there anymore. Maybe they were used somewhere else in the Soviet Union as translators or where their knowledge of the US would be helpful. Maybe they knew too much and were just done away with. But this is just a story."

"Rick, what happened to Pavel?"

"Pavel did well in the Facility, not only in English, but in everything else, especially math and science. Meanwhile, KGB agents in the States were always looking for American people whose identities could be taken over by people from the Facility. About four years after Pavel was sent to the Facility, the KGB identified a couple of Americans—a woman and her young son—who were living in Northern California in a town called Fort Ross. They didn't have any other relatives—her husband had been killed in an accident in a sawmill, and both her and her husband's parents had died. The names of these targets were Emily and Ricky Burke. By this time it was 1957. Pavel was about fourteen years old; he would become Ricky, who was a few years younger. To become Emily, they picked a young woman named Irina Zherdev; she was about twenty-two at the time. The real Emily was twenty-nine, but Irina could pass for older, although I suppose no grown woman would really like to look older on purpose. The two of them would go to California and eventually become Emily and Ricky Burke. You understand that the real Emily and Ricky had to disappear. Permanently.

"They gave Pavel and Irina some specialized training, specific to that part of California, so they'd be able to fit into Fort Ross without any problems. Lastly, they were provided with temporary American identification papers; fake, of course. When they were ready, the KGB put the two of them, along with a KGB 'escort,' on a commercial flight to Rome, and from there to Mexico City. They were using Soviet passports with false names for this part of the trip. A KGB man met them in Mexico City and drove them to Puerto Vallarta, on the Pacific coast, where the two of them were put on a fishing boat. They took an eight-day voyage north and ended up in Half Moon Bay, just over the hills from where we're sitting now. The fishing boat came in late at night, and was met by a man who took Irina and Pavel up to Fort Ross. They were holding temporary documentation as Margie and Paul Thompson; these would be used until they took over the Burkes' identities. 'Paul' didn't actually have much identification, since he was too young for a driver's license, but 'Margie' had a driver's license and what looked like a real Social Security card, in a wallet with family photos and other ordinary stuff. I should have mentioned that the Facility had an area where the older students could learn to drive American cars; they even had to pass a driver's exam. Irina had done that, but Pavel didn't get to; he wasn't old enough yet.

"Anyway, Margie and Paul moved into a small house in Fort Ross that this person who met them in Half Moon Bay—we'll call him Uncle Peter—had rented for them. Peter worked for the KGB and was in charge of running the illegals in that area. Margie and Paul's cover story was that Joel Thompson—Margie's fictional husband—had deserted them and they were trying to start a new life without him. Margie enrolled Paul in the local school, where he made friends with Ricky Burke. Paul was pretending to be eleven years old, but as I told you, he was actually fourteen. Ricky didn't have any close friends, so Paul was able to get close to this lonely boy. They talked a lot, and Paul learned what Ricky liked and didn't like, and so on. Margie got close to Emily, who was a lonely person, and spent a lot of time learning similar things about her."

"Rick, why didn't you two just use the Margie and Paul identities instead of using the mother's and boy's?"

"Natalie, I didn't say this was me—this is just a story. Anyway, the Margie and Paul identities were very thin—there was no documentation for them in the birth registers, motor vehicle records, Social Security Administration, and so on to match the papers they were carrying. Irina and Pavel were going in as illegals—people from a foreign country posing as citizens of the US. They'd eventually need solid documentation to back up their claim to be Emily and Ricky."

"But if anyone looked very hard at the fake Emily, they'd surely find some discrepancies," Natalie argued. "I mean, the work and salary history, checking her fingerprints against other records, and so on."

"That's true—you'd have been good at the Facility. But Irina wasn't going to be put into a situation where she'd be examined closely—Pavel was. A child that age isn't expected to have much history, and has probably never been fingerprinted, so it'd be easy for him to pass later background investigations, since all his documentation would happen after he arrived in the States. Irina would eventually get married and live a normal American life — her only purpose was to help me—I mean Pavel—get into the country. She wouldn't put herself into a situation where she might be investigated in depth. But Pavel's assignment was to get into a senior position in the US armed forces. Because of this, he had to have a background that would withstand investigations for high-level compartmented security clearances."

"So what happened next?"

"Uncle Peter set up an attractive job offer for the real Emily, down in San Mateo. The job was authentic, but I don't know how Peter arranged it—probably it was some Soviet sympathizer who owned the business.

There are more people like that than you'd think. She happily made plans to move. Emily didn't have any friends in town close enough to try to look her up afterwards, so she and Ricky left Fort Ross without much fuss or notice. Naturally, they never got there—Irina and Pavel arrived instead of them, but using the Burke names. The two new "Burkes" blended into the community. About a year after they went down there, Irina—now known as Emily, of course—met a widower and eventually married him. His name was Byron Halsted; Pavel—I mean Ricky—changed his last name to Byron's."

"And you were fine with all this?"

I dropped the flimsy pretense that I hadn't been talking about myself. "Natalie, when I was torn away from my family, I wanted to rebel against the Soviet system. But a ten-year-old can't do anything, and if I'd revealed my true feelings, I'd have been disappeared. So I played along, survived the Facility, and got to the US. Since then I've only gotten more anti-Communist. The Soviets think I'm a deep cover agent working for them, but in reality I'm a very patriotic American. It's important you understand that."

"So you had no choice but to go along, at least until you could somehow separate yourself from whatever they had planned?"

"Unfortunately. As I told you, the KGB eliminated the kids at the Facility who didn't do well enough. I obviously didn't want to fall into that category. Natalie, these people are completely ruthless; Peter or someone who works for him murdered the original Emily and Ricky. Knowing Peter, I'd guess he did it himself—I think he enjoys that kind of thing. I wouldn't be surprised if he raped Emily with her son tied up and watching before he did away with them. He's a violent man, and very clever—it doesn't do to underestimate Uncle Peter.

"He was very happy when I got my NROTC scholarship and then got into the submarine force. But he wasn't planning on my getting an assignment like the one I'm on now. When I took this job I knew I'd have to convince him I'm still a loyal Communist, and that success in this job would enhance my chances of getting command of a submarine—that's the kind of mission I was put in this country to fulfill. I suppose they have a plan like having me bring my submarine into a Soviet port, but I haven't been told yet. I hope you understand I wouldn't do anything like that.

"At any time, if I'd screwed up academically or in any other way that would have significantly diminished my value to the KGB and the Motherland, he'd have had me done away with. I'm planning to outlive him; I may even take steps to make sure he dies way before I do. He's a cagey bastard, so I'll have to be careful. Right now, he seems to think I'm still a loyal apparatchik carrying out my mission. I haven't talked to him since I started at Federated, so I still have some explaining to do."

"What about Irina—I mean Emily?"

"So far as I know, Peter leaves her pretty much alone now—her job is basically done. She's just another American housewife, but much better off than most because Byron is wealthy. I think she's taken very nicely to the lifestyle Byron can provide, and has put her Russian background down the memory hole. Peter drops by now and then, like he did today, just to check on how things are going. And, I suppose, to remind her that he's keeping an eye on her." I suspected he also forced her into sexual submission to him, but why mention that?

"I meant, will you have to eliminate her too, along with Peter?"

"I don't think so, and I hope not. We got along—still get along—fairly well, and she's a decent person. The only reason I might have to do something is if I thought she'd turn me in, but I don't think she'd ever do it. She'd really be turning herself in at the same time and losing the life she has with Byron. And keep in mind, almost all the kids who got sent to the training facility were forced to go there, so it's not like she volunteered."

"What's she like?"

"Well, you met her—she's very attractive. She's in her late thirties now, although she's claiming to be seven years older to match the real Emily's age. I have to say she's treated me well over the years. I like her."

"It's a good thing you two never got together," Natalie murmured. "That'd be almost like incest."

My answer would be a good test of Natalie's sense of humor. "Actually, Natalie, Irina was my first sexual partner. The procedure at the Facility was to have the older students break in the younger ones, and I drew Irina. They believed sexual skills might be important to our mission at some point. Or maybe they just wanted to keep our morale up, and used that for an excuse. Anyway, that was before we were teamed up to come to the U.S."

"And you were how old?" Natalie asked incredulously.

"Probably around thirteen; I don't remember exactly. We didn't celebrate birthdays in the Facility."

"And I suppose you enjoyed it."

"Honey, I'd be lying if I said I didn't. Any young teenage boy who's initiated into sex by an attractive young woman is going to think he went to heaven. But she was nothing like you—there were no real feelings involved, just a mild affection for each other. And that all stopped when she met Byron. Irina—I mean Emily—takes her wedding vows seriously. Of course, when I was in junior high school and pretending to be a few years younger than I really was, I'm pretty sure I was getting laid more regularly than anyone else in my class."

"If that was an attempt at humor, you need to work on your routines," Natalie said, although she was smiling for the first time in this difficult conversation.

"Natalie, you're the only person I've ever told about this and, except for Irina and Peter, the only person in this country who knows about it or—I hope—even suspects it. My life is in your hands now—you could destroy me with a phone call to the FBI."

"What do we do now, Rick?" Natalie asked somberly. "Should I turn you in or do you expect me to work with you on whatever you're trying to do?"

"I want you to be part of my life from now on. I couldn't ask that of you without telling you who—or what—I really am. I have to leave what you do about that to your conscience. But what I'm going to do is try to eliminate this Soviet spy ring. After that—well, I don't know. The right thing to do is to tell the Navy who I really am. That'd be the end of my career, but it's what I should do. And before I do that, Peter has to be eliminated."

"But you're some sort of Russian spy! How can we have a life?"

"Natalie, I'm not a spy! I never have and never will do anything to help the Soviets, or to hurt my country—this country—in any way. I'm the most anti-Communist person in this state, except maybe Reagan. What I have to do now is finish this assignment and try to start a regular life. Hopefully with you, if I haven't turned you against me by telling you all this."

"Oh, I'm still with you, big boy, but all this Russian stuff you just told me has my head spinning."

"Look at it from my point of view. If a whisper of what I told you gets back to the Navy, I'll need a good civilian career opportunity. And an excellent lawyer."

Chapter 39

"**W**HAT NOW?" I asked, walking her back to the car.

She went on the offensive. "I still didn't get an answer about helping you. The two of us can do a lot more than you can by yourself."

That was true, but I was in enough danger that I didn't want to bring Natalie into it. Unfortunately, if we were going to spend most of our off-work time together, she'd be at risk whether she was actually helping me or not. And there was still the possibility that she might somehow be helping the Soviets. I didn't want to think about that too much, now that she was in a position to blackmail me.

"Are you actually serious about helping?" I asked, half-hoping she'd say she wasn't.

"You betchum, Red Ryder. Now let's figure out how I can lend a hand. Tell you what—why don't we start by you telling me what you've done so far?"

Well, why not? I'd already told her too much, so how could more hurt? As we drove back down to her house, I summarized the information I'd gathered so far, some of the analysis I'd done, and some of the problems—notably Detweiler's murder and the mystery of just who the hell Yolanda really was. Natalie bristled when she realized I'd been gathering information on her own income, debts, credit rating, and so on, but she realized I had to cover everyone. "Besides," I told her, "that was before I had any idea we'd be together again." She nodded reluctantly.

"Back to Arnold and whether he's the likely leak," I said as we pulled into her driveway. "I've been giving that some more thought. I still think the SSIXS and the ocean surveillance system are the big prizes for the bad guys, and Arnold has the most involvement in that. But the way the project's being run, almost everyone has access to the key documents for all the technology. So it could still be anyone. What do you think?"

She nodded thoughtfully. "That's the way it works in my department. Everyone gets a complete project update at the Monday meeting, and can get to most of the documents. How about telling me more about the research you've done on all of us?" I offered details about the information I'd already gathered, and mentioned that copies of federal tax returns for each person should be arriving shortly.

"What about telephone records?" Natalie asked. "If you could get a few months worth of outgoing and incoming calls for each person's home phone, you might uncover something."

I should have thought of that. How was she able to quickly figure out ways to identify people doing bad things? Was it a female thing or was she naturally talented in this area? Maybe she was working for the other side and trying to divert my attention away from her as a potential spy.

Nat was thinking out loud about how to organize the reports of both incoming and outgoing calls for everyone on the project. "We'll need the printouts to show the name and address of the person or business on the other end—that'll save us a lot of time. And payphones—wouldn't that be a way spies would contact each other? We've got to identify the payphones involved in calls to or from any of these people." Interesting— her colleagues were now *these people*—potential spies.

"Great idea, sweetheart," I told her, following her into her house. "I feel stupid for not thinking of that. I'm sure we can get the outgoing records, since that's what the telephone companies use for billing, but the incoming calls might be trickier."

"It's just a database sort," she said. "That's not part of your expertise, so trust me on this. It may take a little longer; but if Pacific Telephone needs more than a day or two, there's not enough pressure on them. In fact, they probably already have a program like that written to use when police or a federal agency asks for phone records."

"I'll get the request going through Navy channels," I promised.

"What about stuff they may have written down?" she asked. "I suppose they might have sneaked it out through security, and there's not much we can do about that unless we're willing to break into their homes, get access to their safe deposit boxes, and all that. I guess they could just put it into their personal safe at the office. Everyone in my group has one and probably everyone in yours."

"Phil doesn't have one; everyone else does. But the safes aren't a problem. I can get into them, except Andy's. And yours, I guess—I haven't tried any in your group yet."

"You're a safecracker as well as a submarine officer and an engineer?"

"And a marvelous lover, right?"

"No, really—where'd you learn to crack a safe?"

"I had some lessons before starting at Federated. But, Natalie, to be honest, I can only work a simple safe, but that means I can open everyone's in my group except Andy's. The trouble is I have to hang around in the evening until everyone's gone and I'm sure they won't be coming back. It'd be embarrassing to be caught with my hands in someone else's safe."

"Especially if it's by one of the roving security patrols who prowl around the building in the evenings." This was something I hadn't known. Apparently I'd had been lucky to miss those on the nights I'd stayed late to rummage through my co-workers' desks and safes.

"So now we're both working to catch some spies," she murmured.

"Look, honey, can you take a couple of hours off tomorrow? I want to get your alarm system installed. And we need to buy a pistol for you this week."

"What if I don't want an alarm system? And what if I don't like you telling me what to do?"

"If you want to work with me on this investigation, you're going to have to let me take the lead. And you need to start thinking about protecting yourself. Keep in mind that you may have attracted Pete's attention again."

She shuddered. "OK, OK. We'll do the damned alarm system and I'll even get a weapon. In fact, when we shoot again next weekend, I'm going to kick your ass. With my own pistol."

"I hope so. Both of us being decent shots may come in handy. Maybe we could find a range with pop-up targets to get us ready for a real-world situation."

She changed the subject. "Rick, why did Pete put so much pressure on me to break up with you? I still can't figure that out. And believe me, I've given it a lot of thought since we broke up."

"You may find this hard to believe, but the man doesn't confide in me at all, and we haven't seen each other much lately. I avoid him whenever possible—being in the fleet over the last seven years was a huge help in that. Before today, I'd only seen him twice since I was commissioned. So far as 'why,' I suppose he decided I was too focused on you to do well enough to get command, or maybe even that I'd give up the Navy just to be with you." Of course, if I'd done that, Pete would have found some way to punish me. Or do away with me.

"You almost did agree to give up the Navy—at least you offered to do it if it'd keep us together."

Actually, all I'd suggested was I could go surface Navy to minimize separation time. She'd rejected the idea, but it was nice of her to remember I'd offered, even if she was fuzzy on the details.

"Pete may still believe I'm on track to get a CO job, but now that he knows you're back in the picture, he may think he has to step in again. We have to be ready."

That sobered her up. "Rick, you have to promise to make sure Pete never gets his hands on me again. Can you do that?"

"If you and I are together all the time outside work, I'll be there doing my best. Just the thought of that son of a bitch attacking you makes me angry enough to kill him."

"It'd be nice to plan it out so we could eliminate him without running the risk of being linked to his death," she said thoughtfully. I was starting to think she was more cold-blooded than I was, and I'd assumed I stood second to none in my desire to eliminate Pete. But I'd just come up with an idea on how to get Pete to help me with my project before I eliminated him. Wouldn't that be sweet! I decided to keep it to myself for the time being.

Chapter 40

L ET'S GET over to your place," she suggested. "Before we go, I'll pick up what I want to wear tomorrow."

"Remember you need to take some time off tomorrow to be at home when your alarm system's being installed."

Natalie frowned. "Right now I just want to wind down from a very stressful day. That means you're going to have to focus on helping me relax. If it doesn't sound too weird, could we just cuddle tonight?"

"Absolutely, sweetheart."

She followed me in her car so she'd have it to drive to work in the morning, and we detoured for dinner, having walked out of the Halsted dinner in San Mateo. In my apartment, I explained again how to arm and disarm the system, took out my pistol so it'd be handy, and suggested we go to bed early.

Natalie woke in a good mood on Monday morning. She even fixed me a nice breakfast, creatively using the meager contents of my refrigerator.

It was hard to believe I'd been at Federated for just two weeks; it seemed much longer. I was ready to go at 7 am as usual, but Natalie was nowhere near ready. "I usually don't get to work until a few minutes after eight," she told me as she worked on her hair in front of the bathroom mirror. "You might as well sit and relax for a while, unless getting there early is so important you're going to leave me here alone."

"Honey, I have to make a phone call to my office back in DC—they left a message saying they have some of the information I've been looking for. I can't do that from my phone here, in case it's bugged, so I have to go out to a payphone. Just set the alarm for "*Stay*" when I leave and then change it to "*Away*" when you leave, OK? I'll see you at work."

I kissed her and left. A few minutes later, satisfied I wasn't being tailed, I was at a strip mall on Evelyn Avenue using an outside payphone. Sammon answered the phone himself. "Here's what I've got for you," he said, skipping any pleasantries. "First of all, the FBI isn't being cooperative about this Yolanda or Maria or whatever the hell her real name may be. The interesting part is they aren't denying she's an agent— they're just saying they can't talk to us about her until they get approval from higher up."

"The Director?" I asked.

"Probably. And that means he'll want something in return—like getting the fruits of our investigation in return for having whatever-her-name cooperate with us."

"Wouldn't that be a good thing?"

"Rick, I realize you're a submariner first with counterespionage coming in a distant second, and that you don't have experience dealing with other agencies. You have to understand the FBI isn't good at playing with others. If we let them in, we'll find out pretty soon that they're trying to run it. We don't want that." Pretty much what Admiral Robards had told me.

"So the best thing would be to withdraw the request and stay away from Yolanda so we can do things our way?"

"It's too late for that, bucko. Now that we've gotten his attention, I'm sure the FBI Director will try to find some way to make the Fibbies the heroes of this operation. They love to jump into situations where some other agency has done the groundwork so he can step in, take over, and claim all the credit. All we can do now is wait and see what happens. What next? Oh yeah—I wanted to let you know the tax returns will take a while longer. And I have something on this Natalie broad." He knew it irritated me to have him refer to Natalie that way, so he'd probably keep on doing it as long as he knew he was getting my goat. I kept silent, not wanting to encourage his sarcasm by letting him know it got to me.

"OK," he finally said, giving up on forcing me to lose my temper, "it looks like she got her clearance despite her association with a number of left-wing groups at Berkeley, which I'm sure you knew about. Our 'friends' at Langley—and I use that term very loosely—stepped in and convinced the FBI to grant the clearance. We don't know why, but presumably she did them a favor or two at some point."

That presented some interesting tactical questions—should I just ask her straight out about this or try some other way to learn what she'd been doing with the CIA? What kind of favors could she have supplied?

"I've got another request," I told him. "I should have brought this up earlier. I'd like to get several months of telephone calling records for everyone on this project, including Greenwood and Nielsen. I want both outbound and inbound calls, with the name and address of the other party identified for each call. Any calls to or from payphones should be flagged. One more thing on that—we need to have the phone company include any other phones at the same address. It could be whoever our leak is got cagey and decided to have a separate phone, maybe unlisted, to use for calls he doesn't want anyone to know about." I'd considered telling him this was Natalie's suggestion, but that'd be an unforced error.

"We can do that, but it'll take a week or so. I'll call our people in San Francisco; they have some contacts with the telephone companies there.

Pretty good idea, actually—congratulations on coming up with it." Why wasn't something as obvious as telephone call analysis a standard step to take in a project like this? I'd been wondering why I seemed to be reinventing the wheel. NIS should have already done some of these things I'd thought up in counter-espionage cases.

"Captain," I ventured, "it seems to me that a lot of the things I've been recommending should be standard procedures for a counter-espionage case like this. Why is it that the credit reports, tax returns, phone records—all this stuff—hadn't been done before I got here? Over the years, I'm sure NIS has developed checklists of things that have to be done in these cases. So why is it I'm coming up with basic ideas and relaying them to you, and then waiting to get something I'm pretty sure you'd already put together?"

A silence ensued. I was about to ask if he was still on the line when he spoke up. "Rick, you have to understand that you didn't complete the full training course—we didn't have time. Since we figured it'd take a few months for you to produce results, we decided to let you tell us what information you wanted. That way we'd get a sense early on about whether or not you could succeed. If you'd waited too long to ask for stuff, I'd have chewed your ass and demanded you do a better job. But so far, so good. OK?"

Actually, it wasn't OK. If they'd just supplied me with all the usual information right away, I could have been spending my time considering other areas to investigate instead of plowing ground they'd already been over. There was no point complaining to Sammon about that.

"One last topic, Captain, and it may be important. I've been thinking about what the Soviets might really want out of this project. If I could narrow down what they might be most interested in, I could do a better job of identifying who might be cooperating with them."

"And?" Sammon didn't sound interested in this line of reasoning.

"And I think it's *not* the Outlaw Shark hardware or software. They'd have to redo all that so thoroughly to fit their own weapons systems and electronics setup that they might as well start from scratch. I think the number one thing they want is to get into the SSIXS satellite system, either to find out what data we have on them or to screw up the system so badly we couldn't use it. Plus there's a lot of message traffic on SSIXS other than ocean surveillance that they'd love to get their hands on."

"So what does that tell you about who might be leaking?"

"There's one guy in my group whose work is almost totally focused on that area. The problem is that at Federated, everybody on the project has access to all the data. Maybe the phone records will help us narrow this down."

"Not bad, Halsted. Let me know how that works out. But don't drop the ball on the other areas, OK?"

"Sure. Now I have to get to work. And that reminds me of another point. Saturday I was at a pool party my boss—Andy Malone—gave. His boss, Lee Greenwood, told me I was in line to be promoted in a month or so to take over the department when Andy moves on to something else."

He snorted, "Are you jerking my chain, Commander? You've been there a couple of weeks and they're going to move you up over people who've been on the project for years?"

"I guess they know talent when they see it," I told him and terminated the call before he could put together a sarcastic retort. Hanging up on him for a change improved my mood considerably.

I was at work before eight, and was working on an outline of issues dealing with access to the SSIXS system when I looked up to see Yolanda smiling down at me. She came close to the desk so she wouldn't be heard outside my cubicle and whispered, "My boss is talking to your boss. I'm looking forward to working with you. We can talk later."

I didn't intend to discuss my assignment with her until I found out if J. Edgar wanted to join the party under our rules, so I played stupid. "Andy's talking to himself?" I mumbled vacantly, and received what I was sure was an obscene Latina gesture in return.

As Yolanda stalked off, I called South Bay Alarms and got Wes. I explained that a friend of mine owned a home in Cupertino and was in need of some robust alarm protection. "Is she a friend of Norm's?" he asked.

I admitted she wasn't, but stressed she needed to have the best. "I'll be paying for it," I told him, and gave him the address. "Is there any chance you could get out there this afternoon?" He told me he could be there at two. I promised he'd be hearing from Natalie to confirm.

Our weekly meeting began exactly on schedule and wasted almost two hours of our time. The only unusual thing was that Andy seemed to have his thoughts elsewhere; instead of micromanaging the meeting, he was sitting back and pretending to listen.

I sat next to Natalie for the first time. Since everyone seemed to realize we were now a couple, that didn't raise any eyebrows, just a nasty glare from Phil. While Owen was droning on about what he'd done last week, I passed her a note with Wes Sheeley's business phone number and the words "2 pm."

"It's for the alarm system. Call him and let him know if you can make it. It'll probably take several hours," I said quietly.

"Let's talk about this; we can have lunch together," she whispered back. "Maybe somewhere in town where it's more private." Why couldn't she just call him? She'd already agreed to the alarms. Perhaps I didn't yet fully understand female reasoning. Maybe I never would.

"OK, but at least call Wes before lunch so he knows whether to come out or not." Nat nodded absently.

An eternity or two later the meeting finally ended. It was eleven-thirty, so we decided on an early lunch and headed out in my car to a Mexican restaurant in downtown Sunnyvale. "Did you call Wes before we left?" I asked after we were seated.

"No, I wanted to talk first. I'm not sure I want an alarm system in my house. It seems—I don't know—kind of paranoid. And it's my house, after all." I'd made it clear I was calling the shots on her security if she was to be involved in my counter-espionage work, and didn't understand her attitude.

"We've been over this. It's your house and you can decide what you do with it. But if you want to be involved with this investigation, which might get nasty, you *will* get an alarm system. In fact, you'll do everything I suggest that has to do with your personal safety. Natalie, just think about Pete being involved on the other end of this. Do you see what I mean?"

"Rick, I'm terrified of Pete and I understand what you're getting at. But it seems like it's kind of giving in to fear to put in an alarm system." Next she'd be arguing that we shouldn't have nuclear weapons to deter a Soviet attack. She apparently hadn't shaken off all her left-wing views, but I should have realized that when she went on about global cooling a few weeks ago.

I tried again. "I want you to be safe. There's no guarantee that Pete won't come after you even if you decide not to work with me on the investigation. But if you do get involved with this, the odds go way up. You decide."

It didn't take her long. "OK, you were right and I was wrong on this. Let's get the damned alarm system installed," she said reluctantly. Not very gracious, and certainly not an apology, but a step in the right direction.

I suggested she call Wes and agree on a time. She came back a few minutes later. "OK, big guy. Wes will be at my place in ..." she glanced at her watch "... two hours. Let's finish lunch and you can take me back to work. What are we doing tonight?"

"Remember to have Wes leave the bill for me to pay. He'll give you good advice, so be sure to ask him about how to make it physically more difficult for anyone to get into your house. Do whatever he suggests. Now, let's see—how about a movie tonight? You get to pick, but choose somewhere local so we don't have to do a lot of driving."

"OK. Remember, tomorrow night we're going to the Homebrew Computer Club meeting up in Palo Alto." I wasn't really interested in Homebrew, but I'd read somewhere that it's wise to at least pretend you enjoy some of the same things your girl does. Homebrew might be a good place to start.

I took us back to work and went to my desk to start outlining a plan to detect when SSIXS information might have been compromised, and how we might nail down the source of the leak. I'd barely gotten started when my phone rang. "Rick Halsted," I answered, trying to sound polite.

"Rick, it's Emily." My "mom" must have been alone—when Byron was around, she always referred to herself as my mother.

"What can I do for you?"

"You can tell me what that scene yesterday was all about. Byron had no idea why Natalie should have reacted like that when Pete showed up, and frankly I don't either. I need a story to give him, so let me know what was going on."

"The problem was that Pete decided—eight years ago—that he needed to force Natalie to break up with me. You understand where his priorities lie. He was probably worried that if she and I stayed together it might compromise my Navy career."

"So?"

"So he assaulted her and forced her, with threats of more of the same, to break up with me."

"Assault? You mean sexually, or that he hit her?"

"Let's just say he was pretty brutal." She didn't need to know Pete had actually raped Natalie and threatened her with what would have been serial gang-banging if she didn't break up with me immediately.

"Oh, Rick, that's horrible."

Of course it was. "I think the best thing to do is to set it aside. The last thing Natalie needs is to have to go through that again talking with you or Byron. Come up with a story to tell him, such as ... he looked very much like a nasty uncle who used to treat her badly. I've got to get back to work, but if you have any questions, call me."

I hung up and the phone rang again within fifteen seconds. It was one of the security guards on the ground floor. "Mr. Halsted, you have a visitor, a Mr. Ralph Flynn. He says he's your uncle." I sighed; it could only be Pete. What were the odds that the only two people who'd been involved with my infiltration into the US would call one after the other? My initial reaction was that no good could come from this visit, but then I remembered my semi-brainstorm on how I might actually get him to help me nail the leaks within Federated. Talking him into it wouldn't be easy.

Chapter 41

H
IS SUDDEN appearance was both annoying and worrying. I was
irritated at being interrupted, and nervous that Pete had the gall
to show up at Federated, possibly linking himself to me.

Pete smiled cheerfully at me as I came out of the elevators, heading
for the visitor area where he'd been waiting. "Hey," he said, holding his
hand out. "I thought it was time I saw where you're working now."

I didn't take his hand. "This isn't a good time, Uncle Ralph, and it's
not really appropriate for you to come here."

"Come on—how about signing me in and taking me up to your
office?"

"Can't do that. The workspace requires a security clearance. If we
need to talk, I can take you down to the cafeteria. We've got to keep this
short—I've got a lot to do. Give me your driver's license so I can get a pass
for you." Pete wasn't used to backtalk from me, but it was time to start
training him to treat me with more respect.

When I took the license to the guard, I looked at Ralph Flynn's
address; it was a PO Box in La Honda, a very small town in the redwoods
south of Woodside and about ten miles inland from the Pacific. The
guard handed me an unclassified temporary badge. As I led Pete to an
empty elevator car I wondered if the address was fictitious or if it might
lead me to his den. While we were riding down to the basement level, he
started in on me. "Why the hell didn't you talk to me before you decided
to get out of the Navy?"

"Pete, I've got good news for you. I'm still in the Navy. In fact, I got
an early promotion to Lieutenant Commander. I'm here masquerading as
a civilian, doing counter-espionage work for the Navy. Obviously you
can't tell that to anyone, especially Emily."

That struck him as hilarious. "They hired a Russian mole to do
counter-espionage? That's just bloody beautiful." The elevator door
opened and he immediately quieted down.

We took a table where we couldn't be easily overheard, which wasn't
difficult—in mid-afternoon the cafeteria was almost deserted.

"So tell me more about this job," Pete urged me.

I explained the basic outline, leaving out details like who I was working for in the Navy, and exactly what the project was that might be penetrated. Then I hit him with my zinger. "It seems to me you could be helpful in this, Pete. Do you know if the KGB is involved in any espionage work here? If you could tell me which employees here are involved, I could come out of this a winner."

He stared at me uncomprehendingly. "Why would I tell you anything like that? There must be some good stuff here the Rodina could use. You'd want to turn in our guys to make yourself look better. Why should I cooperate?" It seemed he was admitting he knew who at Federated might be leaking data. And that there was more than one of them.

"Because if I'm successful here, I've got an inside track to get command of a nuclear submarine. That has to be more important to the Motherland than some dribs and drabs of stuff that won't be of any real military value. You have good odds of having a Russian commanding an American SSN. Keep in mind that these guys have already given you the information and probably don't have any future utility—all you'd be doing is blowing the whistle on them." Implicit in what I said was that I was still loyal to the USSR. As long as I could keep Pete convinced of that, I had a good chance of using him to actually help my counterespionage effort. And of staying alive.

"You know what I learned about you?" he asked, apropos of nothing. I shook my head.

"I was told that you're in the top 20% of the submarine officers your age. That leads me to believe that if you continue to perform well, you'll probably get command. Is that right?"

"Where'd you learn that?" I asked suspiciously.

"Friend of a friend." If this was true, Pete must have a contact somewhere in BUPERS. This was not good news.

"Look, Pete, assuming that's true, then if I stay in the top 20%, I probably will. I think there are about 150 in my year group still in submarines, and I'm guessing there'll be forty to fifty command openings when our time comes. If they all stay in, an officer in the top 30% should have a good chance at command. That makes it all the more important that you help me. If you don't, and if I can't figure out who the leakers are, I'll get a bad performance review, and that'd probably knock me out of contention."

He seemed to be thinking about the situation seriously, so I kept quiet. "What's your time frame on this?" he finally asked, surprising me. Maybe he saw the potential benefits and was taking my suggestion seriously. Or he was setting a trap for me.

"I only started a few weeks ago. I don't think my bosses will expect anything concrete for a while yet," I answered more or less honestly. "So if it takes you a month or so to get me the information, that'd be fine. But I need more than just names. You'll have to give me evidence that'll nail whoever's doing this, like copies of what they provided; written messages, bank deposit stubs, recordings of conversations—stuff like that. And here's another angle—what if the GRU—our cousins[60]—have people working on this project too? Wouldn't it be nice to screw up their operation and make them look like dunces? I'll bet they have agents working under the direction of their goons at the Soviet Consulate up in the City. It'd be sweet to hurt them and help my career, don't you think?"

"How would I know what the cousins are doing? Anyway, this is none of their business—the KGB is the Soviet agency responsible for intelligence!"

"Right, Pete," I said with a straight face. "The GRU would never dream of doing anything in the area of military intelligence. Come on— you know as well as I do—actually, you know better than I do—how nosy and intrusive those bastards can be. But the bottom line is that whether it's KGB or GRU involved in this, the best thing for the Rodina is to help me find them so I can turn them in and set myself up on the way to command. Think about it, OK?"

Pete sat uncharacteristically silent, obviously pondering my suggestion for a few minutes before he answered. "I have a guy with connections inside the GRU group up in San Francisco. You understand he has to be very careful asking questions—those are exceptionally suspicious people." Like he wasn't. But his response was more positive than I'd hoped.

He continued, "I could have him cautiously start to mention Federated in casual conversations with them. Maybe he could suggest they consider trying to penetrate the company to get information they can send back to Moscow. That might give him a clue whether or not they're already doing it. Is there anything in particular you'd like to have him mention?"

"Just submarine systems in general." I didn't want to give Pete hints as to what the US was working on. But as far as I knew, which wasn't saying very much, Outlaw Shark was the only submarine-related project in this aerospace company. "So can I look forward to hearing from you on this?"

"I'll think about it," he grumbled.

---

[60] Aka the "far neighbors," indicating the rivalry and the mutual distaste between these two organizations. Luckily for the United States, all our agencies work harmoniously without any rivalry or selfishness.

"While you're thinking, I want to tell you it'd be best if you didn't make any effort to contact Natalie. Just seeing you yesterday put her almost into hysterics, and I don't want that to happen again. In fact, I'll do whatever I can to make sure it doesn't. Am I making myself clear?"

He stared at me blankly. "Pete, why do you think she ran out of the room yesterday when you showed up? Could it have been what you did to her eight years ago?"

"I couldn't figure out why she ran out on the dinner yesterday just because I showed up. I haven't seen her for years. Have I done something to offend her?" This was an example of his sense of humor.

"Pete," I said, reminding myself to try to remain cool. "Back in 1967, you hit her hard enough to knock her down. You raped her. And you threatened her with a gang rape if she didn't break up with me. Doesn't that seem offensive enough? And why were you focusing on her anyway?"

"OK, lad, let me lay it out for you. First of all, back in the day it was Emily who told me you were dating that girl. She was excited about it, probably because she wanted to see you find the right girl. But I knew Natalie's name because she was on the Coordinating Committee at Berkeley. We like to keep an eye on groups like that." I could believe that; in fact, I was confident that various Soviet agencies provided funding and other help to the leftist groups at Berkeley and other leading universities. There was no point asking Pete to verify that.

"I knew who she was, but I'd never met her. I kept a low profile with those groups and gave whatever advice and help I could behind the scenes. I'm sure you understand why. But after Emily told me you were getting serious about her, I knew I had to do something. I mean, besides the possibility she'd distract you from your studies, there was the fact that she was in the leadership of the progressive groups at Berkeley. I worried that even if you were still doing OK and got into the nuclear program, having a fiancée or a new wife who was associated with groups like that might hurt your chances of advancement in the Navy. So I decided I had to approach her and try to find a solution." This was all plausible, and Pete might actually be telling the truth, although that was always a long-shot bet with him.

"I understand all that. Let's get to what you actually did to make her leave me."

"Well," he smiled, "It was kind of ironic that you were involved with a left-wing girl like that—I mean, here's a stalwart but secret Communist masquerading as a normal American boy, and he ends up falling for a girl who believes in the same ideals he does. But he can't reveal who he really is, and has to keep up the pretense that he's anti-Communist." It wasn't a pretense, but giving Pete a sniff of that would be harmful to my life expectancy.

"Understand this," he went on, "my original goal was just to have a friendly chat with the girl. I introduced myself as a friend of the movement. Then I gave her the pitch. You know—advised her that it'd be wise to walk away from this little romance. But the stubborn bitch told me it was none of my business. I'd done a little research in advance—we have a group at the Consulate who spend their time digging up dirt on college professors, senior military officers, executives at big companies, and so on. As it turned out, we had some info on her dad that could have ruined his career. So I told her that unless she broke up with you—immediately—we'd make sure he lost his position at the university." That meshed with what Natalie had told me. I waited patiently for him to go on.

"She was still balking, so I had to step it up." That sounded ominous, but after all, she'd already told me what had happened.

"So what'd you do, Peter?"

"Well," he said defensively, not meeting my angry glare, "I had one of the guys from the Committee standing by so no one could disturb us. I knew he had the hots for Natalie, so I decided to threaten her with being forced to have sex with him unless she promised to dump you the very next day."

"Peter, Natalie told me you raped her, and that Johnny Ross—you may know him as Giovanni Russo—helped hold her down. Now is that true, or is it not?"

"OK, OK. The problem was that it didn't seem to me that, even after what I'd already threatened, she was scared enough. It might have taken her too long to get up the nerve to walk away, and by that time maybe it'd be too difficult for both of you. So I figured if I did her and threatened to keep on doing that until she dumped you, it'd solve the problem faster."

"So you were doing us some kind of favor? Is that your story?"

"Look," he growled, "just keep in mind you're working for me, not the other way around. And if your memory is any good, you remember what'll happen if you make me angry."

"Pete, listen carefully. You're in a position to be able to take the credit for running a Soviet mole who ends up commanding a US nuclear submarine. The way things are, it makes a lot more sense for you to be doing what I recommend, rather than the other way around. So are you going to help me out or not?"

He glared at me, and stood up. Then he shook his head and sat again. "Maybe you're right on this. I'll let you know in a week or so what I can do to help you on this. I've gotta bump this up the line to see what my boss thinks is right to do."

"Peter," I said firmly, "if you want the credit for what I'm going to do here, you'll do what I say, not the other way around."

"Or what?" he laughed.

"Or I'll go to the cousins and tell them I'll be working for them. Then the GRU will get all the credit, and you'll be the guy who blew the opportunity to make the KGB the winner in the gold medal Olympics for stealing US secrets."

Chapter 42

I NSTEAD of getting angry, he seemed to be amused. That made me uneasy. "Hold your horses," he smiled. "I've got something to show you." He pulled an envelope from his inside jacket pocket, extracted a photo and tossed it on the table. It was two women, both blonde, sitting at an outdoor restaurant table. One was middle-aged and the other looked to be in her early twenties. Both were attractive and seemed happy. The photo seemed to be somewhere in Russia, based on the Cyrillic lettering on the signs and the crummy Stalinist architecture.

"Why are you showing me this?"

"It's your mother and sister, lad. They're now living in Tambov, just southeast of Moscow. Very nice place, from what I've been told."

I stared at the photos. It'd been so long, but they roughly matched my fuzzy memories. "What about my father?"

"Sad news, I'm afraid. He died about eight years ago; some sort of industrial accident. I'm sorry I had to tell you that." His voice actually sounded as though he *was* sorry, but Pete was an excellent actor. If he were telling the truth, my father would have died about the time I was a senior at Berkeley.

It'd be wise to behave as though I believed these two ladies were my family. "How are my mother and sister doing?"

"Quite well, partially thanks to you. They're in a nice apartment and they both have good jobs. Those benefits are a reward for your success here so far. Your little sister, by the way, is now a doctor—a radiologist, I believe. And I understand she's seeing a young man—another doctor at her hospital—and that they're considering marriage." Radiology, I thought, would be a busy specialty in the Soviet Union, which was notoriously lax on radiation safety standards. US submariners joked that Soviet submarines didn't need bunk lights; the crew glowed in the dark.

I stared at the photo. The KGB was quite capable of faking a picture by finding a couple of women who looked vaguely like my mother and sister might after all this time. I also realized that if the picture was real it was a threat—if I failed in my assignment, they'd be punished.

"And I've got a written message from them. It was in Russian, of course, so this is the translated version." He handed me a slip of paper.

Dearest Pavel,

> *We've missed you so much over the years. Your father and sister, and I, of course, kept hoping we'd see you again, but so far, that hasn't come to pass. Your dear father passed away a few years ago, but Larissa and I are still thinking of you and hoping you're well. The State has been very good to us since you left, and has told us it's the fine work you're doing for the Motherland that has made this possible. We are both doing well, so perhaps that is some consolation for our separation.*
> *We know you won't be able to reply to this letter. Please realize that Larissa and I keep you in our thoughts daily. Perhaps through some miracle we can all be re-united.*

Your Loving Mother

This did nothing to prove—or disprove—that the women in the photo were actually what was left of my family.

Pete picked up the picture and the note and slipped them back into his pocket. Just as well; it wasn't like I could do facial analysis on the photo to see if they could be my family. Or put it on my desk at work.

Resuming our prior conversation as though nothing had happened, he asked, "How long will that take? I mean, for you to get command of a submarine?" he asked.

"It'll be another six years before I'm in the promotion zone for full Commander. That's about the time they start final screening for CO candidates. Before I can be considered, I have to complete my qualification for command and serve a successful tour as XO. And before that, I need another sea tour as either Chief Engineer or as Ops/Nav. And I have to be certified as qualified to be the Chief Engineer, whether I get that job or not."

"What's that Ops/Nav part mean?"

"It means I'd be the Navigator and in charge of the Operations department. Either NAV or ENG usually has the third officer job, meaning third in seniority behind the CO and the XO. When you come up with the data I'm asking for—including whatever the GRU is doing here—I'll have an inside track for getting the jobs I need to qualify for command. Come on; I'll get you signed out of here so I can get back to work."

Chapter 43

AFTER PETE had left I sat at my desk for a while pondering my options. I was pleased Pete hadn't completely balked at my demand that he turn over the names of any Federated people who were feeding Outlaw Shark information to the KGB. Of course, once I had the names, assuming he'd really supply them, I couldn't just tell Sammon I'd identified the culprits. I'd need the detailed evidence I'd asked for. And, more importantly, a plausible explanation as to how I'd gotten that data. That would be a challenge.

More importantly, I needed to get ready to take Pete out. I had to wait until he either supplied the names of the traitors or made it clear he wouldn't. In the meantime, it'd be nice to locate his den and do some very careful reconnaissance to see how to get to him. I was hoping the DMV would have a real address in addition to the PO Box on his driver's license. The bastard probably had multiple licenses under different names and addresses, but I had to start somewhere.

I picked up the phone and started to dial the NIS number in San Francisco before my brain kicked in, telling me not to make that call from a possibly monitored company phone. I trudged down to the cafeteria and called NIS. I got Martinez again and asked him if I could speak to Ryan Philpott. Luckily, he was in.

"Agent Philpott, this is Commander Halsted. I called to ask you a favor. I've got a license plate number for someone who's been following me. I wanted to know if you could run a trace on it. I'd like the name and address of the owner." He was agreeable, so I gave him the Studebaker's number.

"How long do you think that'll take?" I asked.

"I should have it for you tomorrow. I have a contact at DMV who gives good turnaround time. What did this person look like?"

"I only saw him in my rear-view mirror," I lied. "He looks like a fairly big guy—not tall, but strongly built. Not young, but I can't guess how old he might be. White hair, worn in what looked like a crew cut. Ruddy complexion. That's about all I could see."

"OK—I'll have it for you tomorrow. Should I call you?"

"I'll call you. How about sometime in the afternoon?"

"Should work. If I'm out of the office, I'll leave the info with our yeoman."

"Thanks, Ryan."

"One more thing, Commander. Let me know what comes of this, will you?"

"Of course," I said, not knowing whether or not I was lying. It'd depend on the tactical situation.

I had enough time to finish my preliminary notes on SSIXS security issues before I had to leave to get to Natalie's. I wondered if it'd be appropriate for me to call and see if she needed me to pick up anything on my way. That'd be the thoughtful thing to do, right?

"Hello?" she answered

"Hey, honey, it's me."

She was quiet for a few seconds, and finally asked hesitantly, "Who is this?"

This might be her sense of humor, which I was still learning. Two could play at this, assuming it was a game. "I was calling my girlfriend Tiffany. Isn't this 255-4683?" I asked, making up a number just one digit off from hers. "Sorry for bothering you." I hung up.

A few seconds later, my phone rang. I gave it four rings and then picked it up, saying politely, "Rick Halsted. How may I help you?"

"Very funny," she said, but she was laughing. "Tiffany? Really?"

"I called to see if I should pick up anything on the way over."

"Well, you won't need a change of clothes or your shaving kit. I brought those back here with me from your place. Let's see—how about picking up some Italian sausage links—the spicy kind—and a bottle of Chianti. And a loaf of Italian bread. I'll whip up a quick dinner."

"What are we going to see?" It was a movie night, after all.

"Actually," she said hesitantly, "I'd like to push the movie back. You and I have to spend some time talking."

This was scary, based on our past history, but I resolved not to panic. "OK, honey. What are we going to talk about?" I was trying not to sound anxious.

"Don't worry—it's not like eight years ago. It's just some things I have to tell you about myself. All you have to do is relax and listen. Trust me—it'll be fine."

It must be something important, but worrying wouldn't do any good, so I should just take Nat's advice and relax. Good theory, but I wasn't sure it'd work out in real life. "I'll see you in about an hour," I told her and hung up.

An hour later Natalie handed me a Jack on the rocks as I walked in with my grocery bag. "I'll take this, and you take this," she smiled, kissing me on the cheek. Peeking into the bag, she asked, "Where are my flowers?"

"Shit!" I explained.

"Don't worry—I was just pulling your chain. Flowers are always nice, but you shouldn't bring them every time. That'd make it seem too routine. Just surprise me once in a while. Actually, often would be OK."

That sounded reasonable. Then I remembered what I'd meant to ask. "Honey, how'd the alarm installation go?"

"All installed. My pass code is 0928 and the password is Sailor Boy. It cost $235."

"Sounds good," I said, reaching for my briefcase to get my checkbook out. "Were you satisfied with the work? Does the system operate OK? Do you have your pager yet?"

"Yes, yes, yes, and no," she told me as she started cutting up the sausages.

"What was the 'no'?"

"That was 'no' to you paying for the alarm installation. This is my house and I'll take care of the costs of maintaining it. Are we clear on that?" The words were severe, but her expression was cheerful.

"Sweetheart, I told you I'd pay for it. You only got it because I insisted, and one of the conditions I made was that I'd cover the expense. Believe me, I can afford it."

"Rick, I know what you make as a recently-hired engineer ..." Her voice trailed off. "You're still getting paid by the Navy too, aren't you? You're drawing two salaries, you bastard."

"Yep," I said. "And I still don't make as much as you, even with two paychecks coming in. Maybe I should retire and let you take care of me."

She smiled, but ignored my suggestion and went on with dinner preparations. "You can put the Italian bread in the oven—set it at 250 and take it out after ten minutes, then butter it and add a little garlic powder. And I have a little surprise for you after dinner and before our talk."

Dinner was fine; the spicy sausage added a nice touch, and the Chianti I'd picked based entirely on its price level went down well.

As we were finishing dinner I said, "Guess who dropped in to see me at work today."

"Ronald Reagan, thanking you for your support?"

"Nope; none other than Pete. He came as Ralph Flynn, with a driver's license to match. It appears he may live somewhere near La Honda. Tomorrow I may get his address—I have someone running his car license plate number through DMV."

"What did he want? Why did he show up at Federated?" My news had naturally made her nervous.

"I think he wanted to chew my ass for getting out of the Navy without his OK. And to remind me he was in charge. I may have turned the

213

tables on him." I explained how our conversation had gone, thinking it'd amuse Nat. It didn't.

"Rick, I don't like it that he showed up like that. It's like he's showing he can intrude into your life—our lives—whenever he wants and do whatever he wants."

"Honey, as soon as he gives me the information I asked for, he's expendable. But I'm not expendable to him—it'd be a big feather in his cap to be running an illegal who ends up commanding a US submarine. I'll track down where he lives and figure out some way to eliminate him. Then neither of us will have to worry about him."

"And then what? You get charged with his murder?"

"I'm pretty sure I can figure out a way to do it without being suspected."

"I guess that rules out driving up alongside his car and shooting him in the head," Natalie observed, surprising me with her capacity for mordant humor.

"At least in Mountain View," I agreed. I didn't want to come to the attention of Detective Fehler again.

"How about what you wanted to discuss?" I wanted to change the topic.

"After dinner, big boy. And remember, I told you to relax. I'm still all yours."

Chapter 44

I HELPED her with the cleanup, resolving not to say a word about the talk. I'd leave it up to her, and try not to reveal how worried she'd made me.

As she put the last dishes away, she said, "Close your eyes."

Could this be "the talk?" I shut my eyes and heard her trotting off down the hallway and then coming back. A few seconds later, she said "OK," and I opened them. She was holding a large pink zipper bag.

"Nice bag," I said, not sure what my reaction should be. Was it a fashion accessory that my Y chromosome rendered me incapable of recognizing?

"Look inside," she suggested with a smile, unzipping it. There was a pistol that looked very much like mine, nestled in with ear protectors, a cleaning kit, and four boxes of ammunition.

"My timing was good on this. Now that we know Pete may show up anywhere at any time, I'm glad I have this. It's like yours, but with a slightly smaller grip and lighter trigger pull. You're officially challenged to a shooting match this Saturday."

"Accepted. Is there a bet involved?"

"There is. I'll tell you on Saturday before we start shooting." She seemed very pleased with herself, maybe with good reason. Last Saturday she'd shot almost as well as I had, and now she had her own weapon, chosen to suit her better. I should be careful about the bet; she might kick my ass around the block at the range. Maybe it was time to move to a pop-up range.

"Was that what we were going to talk about instead of having movie night?"

She took the bag from me and set it on the counter. "Nope. Let's go over and sit down while I explain some things to you. All I ask is that you try not to judge me too quickly. Let me get through the whole thing and then you can ask all the questions you want. And remember I love you."

She led me to the couch and sat a few feet away, facing me. "Rick," she began after a deep breath, "I didn't tell you the whole truth when we had that first conversation down in the cafeteria." I guessed she must have been referring to the answers she gave on my first day at Federated

215

about her security clearances and disentangling herself from her lefty friends. Whatever white lies she might have told me would surely be nothing compared to me telling her I'd resigned from the Navy, not to mention the tiny issue that I was a Soviet sleeper agent.

"I told you that after I learned what really went on during the Tet Offensive, I disengaged from the Coordinating Committee and my other activities." I nodded, and she went on, "That wasn't exactly true. I *wanted* to get out of all that, but I was approached by someone who asked me to stay in and report what was going on. So I stayed on for the rest of the school year and the first part of the next year before I actually stopped going to the meetings.

"I didn't tell you all this at first because ... well, I didn't have any idea we'd get back together, and anyway I was supposed to keep all that secret. But you've been so straightforward with me—confiding in me that you're still in the Navy and the whole 'Facility' thing—that I feel ashamed I haven't told you everything."

I waited, adopting a facial expression I hoped looked like patience.

She hesitated, but went on, "In winter term, after I left you, I was taking a course on 'American History in the Cold War' to satisfy part of my liberal arts requirement. By February, just after the Tet Offensive occurred, we'd gone through the Marshall Plan, the Korean War, and the beginning of the mutual assured destruction strategy. After Tet, our professor assigned a major paper based on what went on there. I told you about the talk I went to and the research I'd done about it, so I wrote a long paper—and a really good one, if I say so myself—that concluded it was a major tactical victory for the US, but a strategic loss because of the biased views of the major media. I think I told you all this before.

"Anyway, a week or so later I got a note from the prof asking me to meet him during his office hours. I showed up and he congratulated me on my paper. He gave me an A+ on the paper and guaranteed me an A for the course. Then he asked how someone with my radical reputation would write an essay like that, so I explained what had happened. It turned out he was a closet conservative. That was a surprise." I was amazed a Cal history professor was a conservative, and could certainly see why he'd prefer to be "in the closet" at Berkeley, a Republican-hostile environment.

"So," she resumed, "he asked me if I'd mind meeting with an acquaintance of his. I agreed, but couldn't figure out why he'd asked or what he was getting at. A week or so later I got a call from someone who called himself 'Roger Wilcox.' He said he'd gotten my name from Dr. Johansson and wanted to know if we could meet for dinner at a hotel. It sounded a little fishy, and I wasn't eager to meet a strange man in that situation, but he sounded harmless, so I agreed. I did call the hotel and ask for Mr. Wilcox's room, but they said they had no such person registered, so either it was a false name or he was staying somewhere else."

I could see where this was going, especially since it appeared the CIA had been responsible for Natalie getting her security clearance despite her radical record. And the "Roger Wilcox" name was pretty funny—drop the last letter and it'd be Roger Wilco[61]. "Over and out," to use a phrase you'd never hear on a military voice radio[62].

"I can see what you're thinking," she smirked. "OK, Mr. Smart-Ass, let me finish my story before you jump to a conclusion too soon. I decided to take a chance and at least meet with him. Roger, or whatever his real name was, turned out to be somewhere in his fifties—way too old for me, in case you were worried about that. We sat in the bar for about half an hour. He gave me a summary of all the lefty things I'd been involved with at Berkeley. I have no idea where he got all this stuff, but it was pretty accurate. Then we spent a while talking about my Tet paper. He was really interested in my change of views, so I told him the whole background, and how I was so disillusioned with the anti-war effort that I was going to get out of all those activities.

"At dinner he got to the point. He asked me to stay on the Coordinating Committee and give reports to him on what was going on. He was particularly interested in whether outside people—not students or staff at Cal—were involved, and what they'd said or done. In return, his agency would give me what he called a "monthly stipend" of two hundred dollars. He also said that his people—he never told me what governmental agency he worked for—might be able to help me after I graduated. I suppose that's one reason I was able to get my security clearance."

"And obviously you took him up on his offer," I observed.

"I didn't actually make the decision right away. I felt kind of bad about informing on people who trusted me. I know this is difficult for you to believe, but some of the people on the Committee were actually honest and honorable, and were doing what they believed was best for the country."

It *was* hard to accept this, primarily because I didn't believe they had any patriotic feelings at all. But that's just me.

---

[61] "Roger" means you understood the message and "Wilco" means you "will comply" with it. "Wilco" *includes* the "Roger," since you can't comply unless you understand.

[62] "Over" means you've completed your message and have handed the circuit "over" to the other party for a reply. "Out" means you've completed your message and are going off the circuit. Despite the movies, "Over and out" is redundant, contradictory, and is used only by amateurs (or film writers).

"Anyway, I finally decided to go ahead with helping them. I was disillusioned by what I felt was the betrayal of the movement—you know, actually supporting our enemy. And maybe this was naïve, but I figured that anyone who wasn't involved in anything actually treasonous wouldn't really be hurt by my passing on information about what was going on."

"How long did this go on, sweetheart?"

She looked down, avoiding my gaze. "I stopped partway through the next school year. I didn't really need the money and I was tired of spying on people who assumed I was their friend."

"Did you ever hear from him again?"

"He called me a couple of times after I told him I didn't want to do that anymore; he tried to persuade me to keep on doing it. He even offered an increase in the money they were sending, but I still said no."

"And then what? Did they keep on contacting you?"

"Of course they did. After paying me for over a year, their attitude was that they owned me, or at least owned the right to demand I keep on helping them."

"Who are 'they'? Did they ever tell you what agency they were from?"

"I always assumed they were CIA, but I don't know for sure. I actually asked Roger a few times, but he'd just pretend I hadn't said anything." Since the CIA had stepped in to ensure she got a security clearance, I was sure she was right. I could understand why she hadn't told me all this earlier. After all, when I'd suddenly showed up at Federated, neither of us had any reason to believe we'd resume our relationship. And this wasn't the kind of thing you'd tell a casual acquaintance. Or a former lover.

"So you haven't had any contact with the CIA—or whatever agency this guy was from—since college? No money, no reporting to them?"

"Actually," she admitted. "I still get calls once in a while from them. I got one about three months ago—maybe July or August." That would have been about the time I was selected to infiltrate Federated. Coincidence? Perhaps, but I was becoming more suspicious as I aged.

"What'd they ask?"

"They wanted to know what kind of projects I was working on. I told them I was on a submarine-related project, and that I still wasn't interested in working with them again. They were kind of pushy."

What might the CIA do if they really wanted to get Natalie working for them again? A nasty idea occurred to me. "Honey, let's go for a stroll outside."

She looked at me suspiciously. I held a finger to my lips and helped her up from the couch and out to her back yard. Once we were outside and well away from the house, I whispered, "I think it's possible that the CIA—or whatever agency it is—may have decided to bug your house."

"Bug it? Put some kind of listening device on my phone? But even if they did, we were just talking—we weren't on the phone." She said that at normal volume, not taking my obvious hint to keep things quiet. I put a finger over her lips.

"Softly, baby. Look, some phone bugs work even when the phone's hung up, like a listening device." I'd just realized that if someone were listening to our conversations here, they might have heard enough to know my real origins. Not a good thing.

"You're talking like some kind of paranoid. Why would the government want to listen to whatever's going on in my home?" At least she was whispering now.

"They might hope to learn something that'd give them enough leverage to get you working for them again. Or maybe our friend Pete decided it'd be nice to know what's going on here. There are all kinds of possibilities."

"I don't *like* the idea that my house may be bugged," she hissed emphatically.

Then you shouldn't have started playing with the CIA, I thought to myself. At least I'd had my place checked for bugs. Of course, the very helpful Ryan Philpott might have actually *installed* a bug while I assumed he was searching for someone else's listening equipment. How would I know? If NIS wanted to keep an eye—sorry, an ear—on me, that'd be an easy way to do it.

Natalie whispered, "Well, I think we should figure out whether or not a bug's installed here. What do you think we should do?"

I was thinking I should carry that little bug detector with me everywhere. But of course that assumed it was actually a detector instead of a dummy device Philpott had planted on me. I was definitely getting more paranoid by the day. I wondered if there was a spy shop in the area where I could buy a reliable bug detector.

"Well?" she asked impatiently. I was pondering my next suggestion when my pager went off. It was Sammon's office number. It was almost eight here, meaning he was still in the office at eleven back in Virginia. This'd have to be important for him to be calling me now.

"Excuse me, honey. I've got to go to a payphone and answer this."

"Just use my phone," she suggested.

"Your phone may be bugged, remember? I'll be back as soon as I can."

I leaned over to kiss her, but she averted her face. "I can't believe you're walking out on me. We were in the middle of an important talk."

"I'm not walking out on you. I just have to answer this page and I'll be right back."

"Don't bother." She turned and walked back into the house, stationing herself at the front door. I had no idea why she was so angry at such a minor thing.

Not having any good exit lines, and unsure why she'd been so annoyed, I took my hanging bag and shaving kit from her bedroom and left without another word. As I got into my car, it occurred to me that getting Natalie angry with me could have some serious downside consequences. She knew too much that could hurt me. Did this mean I should knuckle under and let her win all the arguments? Of course not.

Chapter 45

I DROVE miles up Stevens Creek to find a safe payphone. Just as I was getting out of the car, my pager went off again. Thinking Sammon must be in an impatient mood, I checked it and saw Natalie's phone number on it. An apology or more angry words?

First things first; I'd get business out of the way before deciding whether to call her back. I dialed the toll-free number. "Captain, it's Rick."

"About time. Good thing you have that pager. I suppose you were at Natasha's—sorry, I meant Natalie's—playing kissy-face and forgetting all about your work."

"Not at all. We were just having a discussion about how some agency—I think it's our buddies at Langley—was running Natalie as an informant for a year or so while she was still at Berkeley." I had to admit the "Natasha" was amusing.

"No shit? I suppose that explains how she got her security clearance so easily."

"Could be. She also told me when she was at Berkeley they were giving her some money each month as an incentive to help them. Do we have any friends in Langley who could check up on that?"

"Sounds like you don't entirely trust your little playmate. Trouble in paradise?"

"No trouble, but I'd like to verify her story." Sammon didn't need to know about Natalie's temper tantrum.

"As I think I said when we first met, I admire a man with a suspicious mind. But isn't it a little cold-blooded to be investigating a young woman with whom you seem to be emotionally involved? Or, based on how seldom you're in your apartment, maybe 'shacked up' is a better phrase."

"Checking her out thoroughly is my job, Captain. I'll be very happy when I can clear her and focus on other suspects. And I still didn't get an answer from you on whether we have someone inside the CIA who can verify that story. I should have mentioned that her contact, back in

1968, called himself 'Roger Wilcox.' Maybe that name can be linked to a real person."

"Pretty funny name," he chuckled. "I've got a contact or two who might be able to shed some light on that. I'll get back to you on that. Let's get back to Natalie. Seems to me you're spending a lot of time with her; maybe too much. So tell me this—have you revealed any classified information to her? And have you totally forgotten how information security works?"

Answering only the second question, I said truthfully, "No, Captain, I haven't forgotten." He'd have been better off asking one question at a time. I had given her classified information, since my naval status was probably at the Secret level. On the other hand, my bizarre personal history wasn't classified—the government has to know about something to classify it.

"All right," he said grudgingly. "Now I'll tell you why I paged you. I found out a couple of hours ago that J. Edgar decided he wants in. They finally verified that they placed this woman—Yolanda or whatever her real name may be—inside Federated as part of a counterintelligence operation. They seem to be interested in getting you to pass information on to them. I got the impression they think you may be able to deliver more information than she can, or at least something they aren't getting from her."

"Do you know her real name, her educational background, anything like that?"

"Not yet, but I've been promised a dossier on her will be hand-delivered to my office tomorrow morning. In return I had to send over the same kind of information on you."

That made me a little uneasy, but I couldn't think of a good reason to object. I could picture some FBI analyst back in DC starting to go through my background looking for anomalies. I was pretty sure they wouldn't turn up anything suspicious, since I'd already been cleared for compartmented access, but the downside was frightening.

"Here's the reason I had to reach you tonight. I'll be flying out your way tomorrow. There's a meeting tomorrow evening with you and me on one side and Yolanda and some senior dweeb from the FBI in DC on the other. We'll be talking about how to work together going forward."

"From what you said earlier I'm assuming the Fibbies will try to set it up so they get the lion's share of the credit and make most of the decisions."

"That's their style, all right. I don't really give a rat's ass about who gets the credit. The Admiral and the people who matter in my command chain will understand what we've done. The decision-making may be an issue. The way I intend to go into this is to point out that since you're in the more senior position in the company, and have more experience to understand what information is valuable and what isn't, you should be telling Yolanda what to do instead of vice-versa. But I'll be surprised if it works that way. What I'm guessing will actually happen is that you'll each do what you think best and from time to time you may share information with each other. Or not."

"Where and when do you and I get together?"

"Meet my flight from DC tomorrow. I get into SFO on United at about five o'clock. We'll need to talk before the meeting. The FBI guy will be renting a suite at one of the airport hotels and we'll use his room for the meeting."

"Don't you think it's a little strange that we'll be meeting with the people who told me you aren't to be trusted?"

"That'll make it more fun. By the way, I found out how the Fibbies found out about your part in the operation. Want to guess where they got it?"

It had to be somebody inside Sammon's operation, unless the admiral or his staff were guilty of the leak. "Debbie?" I asked, hoping to get a chuckle from him.

"Got it in one. She has an FBI boyfriend and apparently blabbed too much in their pillow talk. Now guess what I'm going to do with her."

I was pretty sure he wouldn't have her killed. Only one answer made sense. "You'll keep her on without letting her realize you know she was the leak. Then you can plant false information with the FBI whenever you want."

"Excellent, grasshopper! I see some of your training took."

"Anything I need to bring?"

"Just a good defensive attitude. Don't be afraid to stand up for what you think we should be doing. I'll have your back. See you tomorrow evening. I'll buy dinner."

He hung up and I stood for a moment, pondering whether or not to call Natalie back. Hopefully she wanted to apologize for her nasty behavior. Feeling in a forgiving mood, I dialed her number.

"Hello?" She sounded properly chastened.

"It's me, returning your page." I was trying to sound aloof, but didn't think it was working.

"Please come back. I don't want us to spend tonight apart after an argument. My dad told me it was important that a couple never go to sleep still mad at each other." Interesting advice from someone with his sexual orientation.

I must have hesitated. "I'll make it worth your while," she whispered in a sultry voice.

"I'll be there in five minutes."

Chapter 46

S HE WAS waiting for me, leaning against the door and apparently posing as a hooker. "Hey, sailor. Want a good time?"

I did and it was, just like all the nights since we'd reunited. I'd made it more likely to work out happily by not revealing I wouldn't be able to go to the Homebrew meeting Tuesday evening. I woke Natalie up at six, explaining I had to get into work early today, since I'd be leaving early. The darling insisted on fixing me a nice breakfast; now I might spoil her appetite with my news.

I took her outside again. If there were ears in the house, they wouldn't need to hear this.

"Honey, I found out on my call last night that I have to go to a meeting this evening up at SFO. I'm going in early, since I'll have to leave work early to pick up my boss. He and I need to talk before the meeting."

"What's the meeting about?"

"I'm not sure yet." This was technically true so far as the details went, but despite my trust in Natalie, I didn't want to let her know I was meeting with the FBI and my NIS boss. Not to mention Yolanda—God knows what conclusions my girl might jump to if she found out I had an evening meeting with that beauty.

"Who is your boss anyway? You've never told me."

"He's Jack Sammon, a Navy captain. Former naval aviator, served a tour in Moscow as a naval attaché. Probably speaks better Russian than I do, since I haven't said a word in that language for twenty years."

"Does he know you and I are together now?"

"He knows I'm spending a lot of time with you. I'm sure he'll have a lot of questions along that line when I meet with him." I was feeling pleased I'd gotten away with breaking my promise to attend tonight's computer geek meeting. Prematurely, as it turned out.

"You realize you promised you'd go to the Homebrew meeting with me." She didn't sound happy.

"I wanted to go," I said almost truthfully. "But duty calls. When's the next one?"

"Two weeks from now, as you know very well. Will you make that one?"

"Unless something else comes up that I can't skip. Gotta go now. Meet for lunch?"

"Fine," she said grudgingly. But her goodbye kiss was slow and sincere.

I was at my desk before seven, and got to work proofreading the draft version of my proposed agenda for our Norfolk submarine visit. At about eight, I heard someone come into my cubicle. I looked up to see our lovely departmental secretary. This was the first time I'd seen her in the office before 8:30. Today's outfit was very conservative, with a skirt down almost to her knees and an opaque white blouse buttoned to her neck. She might have decided to show a little less skin for meeting with her boss—and with mine—tonight. Was that a touch of malice in her smile?

"I'm looking forward to our meeting tonight," Yolanda said.

There didn't seem to be any point in playing dumb with her anymore. "Seven o'clock, I understand. My boss and I will see you two at your boss's hotel, right?"

"How about you and I go up together? We can talk on the way."

"I'd like to, but I can't. I'm leaving early to meet my boss—you know, the guy you told me isn't who he seems to be—when his plane comes in. He and I will need some time together before the meeting." I'd tried to be honest, since we'd probably end up working together to some degree, but maybe I'd sounded rude. As I was considering whether to say something placating, she spun on her heels and stalked away, her usual way of ending our conversations.

I'd barely gotten back to work when I realized someone was standing in front of me again. "What now?" I asked irritably, continuing my writing.

"Jesus, don't bite my head off." It was Lee Greenwood smiling down at me.

"Sorry, I thought it was someone else. What can I do for you?"

"Come up to my office. There's something I want to discuss with you."

I tucked away my papers in my safe and followed him. His office was on the executive level, the sixth (and top) floor. The opening elevator doors revealed a décor that was palatial compared to the utilitarian areas we ordinary people had. The floors were plushly carpeted and the walls paneled in dark wood. The dozen or so young women sitting behind the desks in front of each executive's office apparently were chosen for beauty. Very impressive.

Greenwood led me to his office, pausing to introduce me to his secretary. "Laura, this is Rick Halsted." She was a lovely green-eyed redhead.

"A pleasure to meet you, Mr. Halsted," she smiled. "I guess we'll be seeing a lot of you up here." What was that supposed to mean?

Greenwood's office was as imposing as I expected and included its own conference area with a large coffee table and several leather sofas. "Have a seat," Greenwood offered expansively as he took a seat on a sofa. My alternative would have been to assume the position of "parade rest" in front of him. But, acting like the gracious person I sometimes simulate, I thanked him and sat across from him.

I wasn't kept waiting long. "This shouldn't be much of a surprise to you, Rick," Greenwood began. "At the pool party I told you that you'd soon be bumped up to acting manager. That'll be happening sooner than I'd anticipated, since Andy will be absent from the office for several weeks. Once he gets back, he'll be taking over another project. You'll be promoted effective today to take charge of the department."

"Is Andy OK?" I was worried that he might have a serious problem. I still wasn't an admirer of his non-existent management skills, but I'd warmed to his personality at the pool party.

"He's decided to take a couple of weeks and go away with Cindy. I think they're going to Maui." Greenwood hadn't answered my question.

Since the pool party I'd given some thought to this "promotion." There had to be a hidden agenda here. After only a few weeks they had no way to know if I could handle a management job, so what was their game? The most likely answer was that Greenwood wanted to shield Andy from any failure in the program. With him not involved in day-to-day decisions, they could blame problems on me. And if things turned out well, Andy could take the credit as the original manager of the project. It was time to feel Greenwood out a little.

"Is this an actual promotion, or just a title change?"

"Well, there's no immediate salary raise involved, although you can expect one in a few months if your performance meets our expectations. Your title will be 'Acting Manager' for the time being. But your authority over the project is real." This meant some of the people I'd be managing were making more money than I was, but at the beginning of my submarine career, I'd had the same situation with my chief petty officers. Of course, that was because a seasoned submarine CPO was much more valuable than a non-qualified junior officer just out of school. I wasn't sure that analogy would transfer well to Owen and Wayne, let alone Arnold.

"How do we handle this with the group?" I asked. "I'm guessing they already knew this was going to eventually happen, since it got around at the pool party pretty quickly. Wayne has already let me know he didn't think someone as new to Federated as I am should be promoted instead of him. I can deal with that situation, but some backup from senior management would be helpful."

"All you have to do is carry on doing what Andy did," Greenwood told me. He said that like it was a good thing. It was time to push the envelope.

"Look, Mr. Greenwood—if I have management responsibility, I should have the authority to do things the way I think they should be done."

"But you just got here. You don't have enough experience to decide how things should be run. You need to clear your decisions through me."

"If you think that's the case, you shouldn't give me the responsibility. Sorry to have wasted your time, but thanks for considering me." I stood up and walked toward the door.

I took two steps—one more than I'd thought I'd have to—before Greenwood grudgingly said "Hold on! Let's not be too hasty here. You have to understand that it's not reasonable for us to give authority to make what may be crucial decisions when that person hasn't managed a department before."

"Is that what was worrying you? I was a division officer or a department head on two nuclear submarines. I managed over twenty people when I was Main Propulsion Assistant, and about the same number when I was Weapons Officer. Both those jobs required technical expertise as well as the ability to motivate people to do their best, sometimes under a good deal of pressure. On my last boat I was fifth in seniority out of sixteen officers. I'm guessing I have more management experience than Andy." That was definitely low-hanging fruit.

Greenwood apparently wasn't used to being talked to like this; he was making a visible effort to control himself. "It's not the same kind of management," he insisted. "There's a lot of paperwork and other burdens."

"Do you think the Navy minimizes paperwork? On the nuclear propulsion end alone, I spent probably fifteen to twenty hours a week just on the logs and reports that Naval Reactors required. My typical workweek was sixteen hours a day, seven days a week. Isn't that enough experience?"

Instead of answering, Greenwood changed the subject. "Next item," he said, "we got approval this morning from the Navy to send a group to visit the *LOS ANGELES* on Monday and Tuesday of next week. They'd specified four people, but we can call Nielsen and see if we can add one more body, if you agree. Since Andy won't be going, that'll mean the three engineers can go, as well as you and Natalie."

"I definitely want all the engineers to go on this. I think it's important for team-building as well as giving them a good look at a submarine environment." I wanted to get back on topic. "Is there anything else I need to add so you'll feel comfortable I can manage a group of five people?"

There was a pause as Greenwood apparently tried to decide whether to boot me out or to promote me.

"OK," he finally said. "I'm appointing you as acting manager, reporting to me directly. Do things your way and we'll see how it goes. This takes effect immediately. Any questions?"

I wanted to ask if one of the factors in my promotion was his belief it'd give him an in with Harris Booth. Instead I asked, "Would it be possible for you and Andy to convene a team meeting this morning to give them the news? If you make it clear you're completely behind me on this, it'll get me off to a good start. Before the meeting, can we call Lieutenant Commander Nielsen and make sure it's OK for five of us to do the tour? I'd like to be able to tell Owen, Wayne and Arnold that they can make the trip."

"Andy's already gone," Greenwood said. "But I'll be glad to come down and introduce you as their new boss. Now let's call Nielsen and see if we can get approval for the extra people." That turned out to be easy; Nielsen agreed without any argument.

"Have Yolanda arrange your flights," Greenwood told me. "Nielsen will have a van from the shipyard meet your group at the Norfolk airport on Sunday evening. He'll be phoning you later today so you two can finalize the agenda. You'll all fly back Tuesday evening. Now let's go down and let the group know you're their new manager. Any other question?"

"I think I'm all set. Let's go give everyone the good news."

Chapter 47

GREENWOOD led me out of his office, pausing in front of his secretary's desk. "Laura, will you please order a set of new business cards for Mr. Halsted, with the title 'Acting Manager'? If we can get them by the end of the week, that'd be very helpful. And arrange with Security to get a new ID card for him with a silver stripe." I got a warm smile from her, which would have been interesting in other circumstances.

Once down in our office space, Greenwood asked Yolanda to have everyone gather at the conference table. He told them, "I wanted to let you all know that Andy is taking a new position at Federated. Rick will be taking over as acting manager of this department. I'm sure you'll give him the same support and enthusiasm that you did for Andy." Actually, I was hoping for more enthusiasm and support than I'd seen under Andy's regime.

"Rick," he went on, "would you like to say a few words?"

I'd been trying to think of something good to say about Andy but had given up. "I'm sure this is at least a small surprise to all of us, including me. I'm aware I have less time on this project than anyone else in this room. Nonetheless, I'm in charge now. While respecting what Andy's done, I have my own way of doing things. I'm open to suggestions or criticism, so feel free to approach me with any concerns you might have. You should know a few things right away. The first one is that we've received permission from the Navy to bring five of us out for the submarine visit that's coming up next week. Natalie and I were already on the schedule, and Andy won't be joining us, so Owen, Wayne and Arnold are invited to come with us. I strongly encourage each of you to come, but this isn't mandatory. Anyone who doesn't want to go, please let me know, but you can expect I'll try to change your mind. I think you'll have a much better perspective on the project once you've spent a few days on a submarine. We'll be leaving sometime Sunday, probably early in the morning, spending two days and two nights in Norfolk and then flying back Tuesday evening. Because of this trip, next Monday's meeting is canceled. Any questions on that?"

"Is there room for one more?" Phil asked.

"Sorry, no. Commander Nielsen really wanted only four, but Mr. Greenwood persuaded him to let us bring five. Suit and tie won't be needed. Casual clothes—like slacks and a short-sleeved shirt—will be fine. You should bring a sport coat or blazer just in case. Any other questions?"

"How much actual management experience do you have?" Wayne asked. The sarcastic edge in his voice let me know he wasn't happy with reporting to me, not a surprise after his "go screw yourself'" comment at the pool party.

"I ran two large departments—Main Propulsion and Weapons—on two different submarines. Each time I had about twenty people reporting to me. And I was Vice-President of my eighth grade class up in San Mateo." Of course, Main Propulsion was a division, not a department, but why confuse them?

"Now, the second thing," I said. "It seems to me we spend a lot of time at the Monday meetings rehashing stuff we've done instead of focusing on what roadblocks we're running into and figuring out how to solve them. I think we should reorient the meeting to problem solving. Each person in this group will put together a short written summary of any issues affecting his part of the project. These are due by noon on each Thursday, and they'll be distributed that same day so everyone has time to review the information ahead of time. This afternoon Yolanda will give everyone a standard layout for these summaries. I'll be talking to Natalie to see if she'll ask her group to do the same thing."

"I'll bet she will," I heard Owen whisper.

"I'm sure I didn't hear that," I smiled. "Now, here's what'll happen at the Monday meetings starting on the first Monday after the Norfolk trip. Everyone will have received and read the summaries of what each person is doing and what the problems are in that area. I'll prioritize the items, and we'll go 'top down,' solving the most crucial problems first and working our way down the list. Questions?" There weren't any, although I saw a few sour expressions at the requirement for a new written report.

"OK, next. And last, actually. I'll be holding a one-hour brown-bag lunch tutorial once a week. It'll cover basic submarine information, focusing on what you need to know for this project. Attendance is voluntary, but I'll contribute toward the food cost, so I need to know who'll be showing up. The first one will be tomorrow; to get ready for the submarine visit, we'll discuss submarine attack procedures. That should help you see how our project will fit into these procedures. Now, any questions? Any of you can come to me at any time if you have something you want to discuss in private."

There were no questions, and everyone except Yolanda went back to their desks. "Can we talk?" she asked, using her Mexican accent.

"Sure, come over to my cubicle."

I headed for my cubicle, but she called after me, "Wrong one, boss man. You're over here now." She led me to what had been Andy's cube. The safe door was gaping open, showing it'd been cleaned out too. I'd never know what he'd kept in there. Yolanda had already moved everything from my old cubicle into my new one, except for the contents of my safe. Had Greenwood let her know what was happening before everyone else was told?

I sat gingerly behind the desk in the much more comfortable chair I'd inherited. I had to admit the polished mahogany desk was a nice upgrade from the battered steel relic I'd been using. "What can I do for you?" I asked.

"Let's talk about the travel reservations first. Federated normally flies on United. I already have you and Natalie booked on a 9 am departure on Sunday, sitting in coach. You have to be a VP or above for the company to pay for business class or first class. But the airline offers an upgrade to business class for $20 per person. You'd have to pay that out of your own pocket. It'll be deducted from your next paycheck."

This seemed like a good opportunity for morale improvement. "Upgrade Natalie and me; I'll pay for both of us. And see if you can get the same deal for Owen, Wayne and Arnold. If you can, I'll pay for that too. How about the flight into Norfolk?"

"That's a one-hour flight. You'll be landing at Washington National at 5:45 pm and the connecting flight leaves an hour later. It lands in Norfolk just before 8 pm."

"Skip the upgrades on that; we can rough it for a short flight. Can you get the return trips upgraded also?"

"I should be able to. I'll let you know in an hour or so." She looked around to make sure no one was near. "And we need to talk again about tonight's meeting. Can we go down to the cafeteria?"

"Give me a minute. I'll join you down there."

When she left, I dialed Natalie's phone. "Hey, I have some news for you," I began.

"You mean about being made manager, and Andy moving to never-never land?" I'd been looking forward to surprising her, but apparently the word was out.

"We can talk about it at lunch. Remember I have to leave early today to make it up to SFO."

"I wanted to take you to dinner to celebrate your promotion, but you've got that damned meeting. How about tomorrow night?" she asked. "I'm so proud of you!" That was more like it.

"Sounds good. And I'll have some news about our trip to Norfolk. I'll see you at lunch."

"OK. Remember I love you."

233

"See you then, honey." I headed down to meet Yolanda.

The morning rush for coffee and pastries had abated; I found Yolanda at a table a good distance away from anyone else. She didn't waste any time, and went without the Hispanic accent. "I talked to Owen, Arnold, and Wayne," she said. "Arnold's claiming he doesn't want to go. The other two are interested, so I booked their flights."

"Good old Arnold. Did he give you any hints as to why he doesn't want to go?"

"Not really, but if I had to guess, I'd say he's nervous about dealing with a bunch of people he doesn't know. You know how shy he is."

I nodded. "Who's close to him? If either Owen or Wayne is friendly with him, they could try to persuade him to join us." Did I really want Arnold's company? No, but I thought it'd be a good team-building experience. I'd also like a chance to see how each of the three behaved during the submarine visit. If one of them was spying, their questions during the visit might provide a tip-off.

Yolanda moved on to the topic of tonight's meeting. Unsurprisingly, she wanted me to tell her what our agenda was, but I could truthfully tell her I didn't know yet. "Sammon and I will probably discuss that at dinner," I told her, and decided to change the subject. "Tell you what—this afternoon could you take Arnold aside and urge him to come along on the trip? I think it'll work better coming from you, and it's really for his own good."

"Better coming from me because the little weirdo has the hots for me?"

"Certainly not! What I meant was that he might resent my promotion, so the suggestion coming from someone else would go over better."

"Of course that's what you meant, boss," she said sarcastically. "But I'll try it. And remember you have to give me the template for this weekly report you want from everyone so I can distribute it this afternoon like you promised." She got up and walked away. I wasn't sure whether she'd been insubordinate or helpful.

Waiting until she'd disappeared into the elevator, I went to the payphone and dialed the NIS office in San Francisco. Ryan wasn't in, but had left a message for me. The address for the car license was the same PO Box in La Honda that the Ralph Flynn license had shown. I wondered how I could track that back to a physical address without having it get back to Pete that someone was asking about him.

I went back up to work, producing a draft of the outline Yolanda would distribute to the department. I had time to call Nielsen and set up the agenda for our two submarine days next week. At 11:45 I went down to the cafeteria to meet Nat.

She greeted me with a brief but passionate kiss. "I'm so proud of you," she whispered, ignoring the whistles from some of our fellow employees. We had a quick lunch, during which I explained how I wanted to handle the dreaded Monday meeting to make it productive.

"About time," she said. "Everyone in my group hated Monday mornings because they were such a waste of time. I think this'll make it better, and I'll make sure my people do it the same way."

I explained my idea for lunchtime tutorials in submarine operations, and suggested that if any of her people were interested, they'd be welcome. "I'll be there for sure, and I'm guessing all or most of my people will come along," she assured me.

After lunch I had to start going through a manual Yolanda had produced detailing the responsibilities of a department manager. A quick flick through its table of contents had revealed a dismal list of required reports that rivaled the anal retentiveness of Naval Reactors. I was starting to understand why Andy had always seemed to be in a bad mood.

A little before five, I put all my work away in the safe (now changed to my own combination), and left without saying a word to anyone.

Chapter 48

I'D ASSUMED that going northbound at rush hour would give me less traffic, as most of the traffic at that time of day was outbound from the City. It was better than southbound, but it still took me more than forty minutes to go the twenty-seven miles up to SFO. After parking, I went into the airport and consulted the United Airlines board to identify the gate where the flight from Washington National would be landing.

The flight was going to be a few minutes late, so I sat within view of the gate and waited. At about 5:15 the passengers began streaming out of the gate. Sammon was near the head of the line.

"How was your flight?"

"Sucked. Are you ready for this meeting?"

"I will be once you tell me what you expect to happen."

"Let's go to my hotel. We can have dinner and I'll give you my best guess as to what the Fibbies are going to want. You and I also have some other things to discuss." That sounded ominous.

I drove to the airport Marriott, where he checked in and ordered two steak dinners and a bottle of wine to be sent up to the room. When we got there, he set his briefcase on the bed and opened it up. I'd brought up my own, with some goodies for Jack in it.

He went to the mini-bar and pulled out four miniature bottles of Jack Daniel's and emptied them into two glasses over ice. "Here's to success—and outwitting the Fibbies," he toasted. "Now let's get started; we've got a lot to cover before the meeting."

I'd thought he'd start with the FBI meeting, but he had something else in mind. "First of all, I wanted to tell you in person that I'm very satisfied with the work you've been doing here ..."

"Thanks, Captain," I said, pleased at the compliment.

"I wasn't finished. I'm still concerned you're too involved with Natalie. If you two are getting close, it's going to affect your ability to investigate her as a suspect."

"Based on all the information I have, she's eliminated so far as I'm concerned," I assured him.

"I guess I need to be more direct. I'm worried that you two are so involved that you're not exercising good judgment in anything that relates to her. To me, her history is shouting that she should be a prime suspect, no matter what the CIA says. And all you can think about is love, right? You aren't being objective about her. And you should face the possibility that she might be playing a game of her own—maybe she's not as crazy about you as you seem to be about her. Keep that up and you'll blow this mission. And your career."

I needed to divert him. "I know what I'm doing. When I get more of what I need—like those phone records and income tax returns I asked for—I can narrow this down. Let me show you what I've done on that. I brought a copy of my spreadsheet so you can see how the information's shaping up." Actually, his comment about her not being as entranced by me as I was by her had struck home. The romance had rekindled pretty damn fast and I wasn't that irresistible.

I opened my briefcase and pulled out the copy of the big spreadsheet I'd put together on everyone with knowledge of the project. "This shows the background information and details on cash flow for everyone except Lee Greenwood and Tim Nielsen. Detweiler was going to get info on them, but he was killed before he did anything about it."

Sammon took his time going through the data. "This is good work, Rick. Based on what you know so far, who are your prime suspects?"

"The problem is that everyone on the project basically has access to all the data; there's no compartmentation whatsoever. I was leaning toward Andy—the former manager of the group I'm in. He makes more than anyone else, but is behind on his mortgage and has a crappy credit score, as you can see. That'd make him vulnerable to someone—like the KGB—offering cash for secrets. Phil Boyce is in pretty much the same position. Everyone else seems to be living within their means, but that doesn't make them invulnerable to offers of extra cash. No one in Natalie's group caught my attention. And Lee Greenwood is someone I'd like to believe is guilty of something. I just don't like the guy. But as I told you, I don't have any details on him."

"What do you mean, the 'former manager'?"

"Sorry, I forgot to tell you; Andy's moving to a different project. Today I was promoted to acting manager of the group. I told you a week or so ago that might happen."

"Tell me more about that. I'm not knocking you, but it seems very strange to take some guy with only a few weeks at the company and make him a manager."

"I agree. A big part of it is that Andy wasn't doing a good job. He has basically no engineering or scientific knowledge; he does have poor people skills. He got the job, I think, because the VP in charge of the group is his father-in-law. It might have become clear to senior management that the project wasn't being managed effectively, so Andy got moved sideways to manage another project."

"But why did they pick you instead of someone who's been at Federated for a while?"

"I spoke up at a meeting a couple of weeks ago pointing out that the project should be extended to SSBN's. That got me a few brownie points. Then there's the feeling around the company that the other engineers in the group aren't what they consider 'management material.' So that left me. One other factor may be that Greenwood seems to believe Harris Booth and I are buddies, and that I can put in some good words about Greenwood with him."

"I'm still not clear why it's you instead of someone else in the company. But congratulations. Now back to work—what are the next steps you have to take?"

"The income tax returns should shed light on everyone's cash situation, but I think the detailed phone records I asked for last night would be the most important thing I could get right now." What I was really hoping was that Peter would come across with detailed evidence nailing the person—or persons—who were giving info to the Soviets. But since I couldn't count on that, my investigation, like a Broadway show, must go on.

"I realize you've only been here a few weeks, but it'd be nice to get this all wrapped up by February at the outside. We'll have the phone record stuff next week. One of the SF NIS guys will bring it to you." Before he could go on, there was a knock on the door. Sammon opened it and let in the room service waiter, who arranged our dinner on the coffee table.

"We can talk more later. Now let's just enjoy the meal. But one word of warning—you're not out of the woods on this Natalie thing. We'll talk about it later."

I decided to push back a little. "You know, Captain, if you don't trust my judgment on this job, just tell me. I know that'll put my Navy career into the crapper, but I can resign and keep on working here."

He laughed at me. "I might can your ass off this project, but you can forget resigning. Remember the fine print on your commission? As a Regular Navy officer, you serve 'at the pleasure of the President.' And I happen to know that President Ford would be pleased if you stay in for a while. Maybe quite a while. So you don't have the option to put your uniform in the closet and become a civilian. Keep that in mind. Maybe it'll be an incentive to finish this job off, make me and the Admiral happy, and go back to your career in glow-in-the-dark sewer pipes."

We finished the meal in silence.

Before we headed for the meeting, I thought of one more topic to bring up.

"Captain, a group of us will be going to visit the *LOS ANGELES* on Monday and Tuesday. Can NIS do anything to make sure everyone on the boat knows that I'm supposedly a civilian?"

"All taken care of, bucko. Since you'll be there two days, the duty section briefing idea won't work. Later this week I'm going down to meet with the CO and XO on how to treat you. It'll work out fine. Now, before we go, have a quick look at the file on your secretary." He handed me a slim folder.

Flipping through it, I saw that Maria Vega was, in fact, her real name. She had a degree in psychology from University of Arizona and a law degree from Texas. She also was, if I could believe the FBI dossier, fluent in German and Russian.

As we left his room for the meeting, Sammon finally offered some guidance on how to handle it. "Don't volunteer anything to them. Let me do most of the talking. Try to situate yourself where you can see me. And, depending on the Fibbies, I may decide to break off the meeting and leave. If I do, just follow me."

Chapter 49

THE FBI people were in the same hotel, a couple of floors above Sammon's room. We got there precisely at 7:30, as agreed.

The door was opened by a tall ruddy-faced man in the FBI uniform of a dark suit, white shirt and rep tie. Sammon immediately broke into laughter. "Connor! Haven't seen you since Moscow. This should make the meeting easier."

Unsmiling, Connor said, "Hello, Jack. I assume this is Commander Halsted. Come on in." As we entered, Yolanda—or Maria—was a few steps behind him, still wearing her unusually conservative outfit. No clothing short of a burqa could hide her voluptuous figure, as Sammon's reaction to her confirmed.

Connor turned to me. "I'm Connor Healey, Commander. I'm Deputy Assistant Director of the FBI, in charge of the counter-espionage group. Thanks for coming."

Meanwhile Jack had finished checking Yolanda's credentials. "You're the young woman who told Commander Halsted that I wasn't to be trusted," I heard him say as he handed her ID back to her.

"Actually, I told him you're not what you seem to be, Captain, and that you're not a good guy. So far as I know, that's still correct." I had to give her credit for standing her ground.

He smiled at her. "Should I call you Yolanda or Maria? I'm a little confused, since you're not who you seem to be either."

"Yolanda's fine," she said grudgingly. "I'm used to answering to it."

He turned to face Connor. "I'm guessing you're the one who put that bug into her pretty ear. If we can't get over that misunderstanding, this meeting is going nowhere."

"It's not exactly something I can overlook," Healey told him.

I stood watching, having no idea what Jack might have done, except that whatever it was, Admiral Robards knew about it and didn't consider it a problem. Sammon stared back impassively.

"Tell you what, Jack," Healey offered. "Let's get started on how we might work together on this project and if we get to a point where your escapades in Moscow come to bear, we can discuss it then. How about we move over to the table?"

Healey's room was a suite with a separate dining area. Four places were set at the table. Sammon took a seat on the right side, so I moved left and sat opposite him. Healey sat next to me, with Yolanda next to Sammon.

Sammon started things off. "I'd like to find out what the FBI has accomplished on this, and we'll be glad to share what Rick has done so far. How does that sound?"

Healey hesitated, and Sammon went on, "But first, we have a decision to make. I think one of the main points will be who'll be running the operation at Federated. I assume you'll want Yolanda running it and I'll want Rick to be in charge. So let's talk about that first."

Before Healey could open his mouth, Yolanda spoke up. "I agree with Captain Sammon that we should decide that first. My suggestion is that Rick run it. He has a better technical background than I do, understands the submarine-related issues, and is now managing the project for Federated, so that makes more sense." I kept my jaw from dropping open.

Sammon grinned. "Sounds like Rick will run it, by a three-to-one vote. Or would you care to make it unanimous, Connor?" Healey grunted unhappily; he apparently wasn't a popular vote kind of guy. Notice that nobody asked my opinion.

My boss was on a roll. "Rick would like to show you something he put together to give us a good handle on the potential of each of the Federated people to be susceptible to bribery. I think you'll find it helpful."

Taking my cue, I removed my spreadsheet from my briefcase and unfolded it on the table. "This is a copy; the original is in the safe in my apartment. What you see here is a list of all the people directly involved in the project, and notes on the key components of their financial status. As you can see, I don't have data on Lee Greenwood, the VP in overall charge of the project, and Tim Nielsen, the Navy officer monitoring the project. I'm still waiting for past income tax returns, but other than that it's fairly complete."

Healey and Yolanda looked at the chart closely. "So the two guys most likely to peddle secrets for money are Andy and Phil?" Yolanda asked me.

"Right, so far as this data tells us, and so long as money is the motivation. But we have to keep in mind that even those with good credit scores could still want extra cash, so we can't really eliminate anyone based on this. And there's no way I know to quantify the likelihood someone's doing this for ideology or being blackmailed. Andy's no longer on the project, but most of the good stuff has been available for a while, so if he's one of our spies the damage could already be done."

"Rick," Sammon suggested, "why don't you explain your theory on what the Soviets might really want?"

I went through my explanation as to why I thought the SSIXS penetration would be the primary target for the KGB. Neither Healey nor Yolanda offered any reaction; it was like I hadn't spoken at all.

Jack asked sarcastically, "Should Rick say it more slowly so you two can understand?"

"We've been concentrating on the hardware, but if Rick's right about the Soviets not being able to make direct use of that technology, this might be a useful tack," Healey conceded.

"Can we see your work products?" Sammon asked with a tone that would have sounded polite for someone who didn't know him.

Healey hesitated. "We don't have any actual documentation for what we've done." I thought the "we" was an exaggeration; Yolanda was probably responsible for whatever real work had been done.

"OK," Sammon said cheerfully, picking up my spreadsheet copy. "Let us know when you have something to contribute."

The only result of the meeting had been to agree that Yolanda and I would share information and that I'd be nominally in charge. I was sure both sides would keep some juicy tidbits to themselves, and Yolanda would continue to do what she thought was best, without much regard for my opinion. I'd reciprocate, of course. Sammon's escapades in Moscow were never discussed.

We left just before nine, after Sammon and Healey thanked each other for being there and agreed we were looking forward to thwarting whatever it was that the Soviets wanted from the Outlaw Shark project. No real sincerity was evident on either side.

As we walked down the corridor toward the elevator, I muttered, "What a waste of time."He smiled. "Welcome to the wonderful world of inter-agency cooperation. Actually, it went better than I thought it might. I've got a red-eye flight back to Dulles in about two hours. We can talk in my room for a while before I have to go."

Chapter 50

BEFORE Jack got going on a topic of his own, such as ordering me to break up with the only girl I'd ever loved, I got up the nerve to ask him exactly what had happened in Moscow that had gotten the Fibbies so skeptical of him.

He was silent for so long I thought he was ignoring me. "I guess I can tell you about it," he decided. "But keep it to yourself."

"Fine," I agreed. "I won't even tell Natalie." That was intended as a joke, but all it got me was a sour glare.

"It started about four years ago, a few months before I went to Moscow. The DNI—it was Admiral Hughes at the time—called me in. He told me he'd just gotten a call from the Superintendent of the Naval Academy. One of their first-class mids, who was going to be commissioned in three months, had come directly to him and told him a fantastic story.

"This mid claimed he was a Soviet illegal. Said he'd been trained in some huge secret facility in Russia where he and other kids, both boys and girls, were given immersion training for several years in speaking English and in American culture. He told the Admiral he'd been flown to Canada on a false passport and then taken across the border. He took over the identity of a kid in western Massachusetts, whom he assumed was done away with. An older female illegal became the 'mother,' taking the place of the real one, who'd also been disappeared. There was a KGB officer who ran them and, he supposed, other illegals in the area as well. This mid had turned into a patriotic American, and felt the right thing to do was to turn himself in. The Superintendent—Vice Admiral Calvert— passed this to DNI right away. He'd had the foresight to tape the whole conversation, or we'd have probably thought he was playing a prank on us."

He had my complete attention. This mystery midshipman was probably at the Facility when I was, although he'd be younger than I was if he was passing for a 22-year-old four years ago.

"So what happened to this guy?" I hoped I sounded casual.

"It turned out the Admiral should have taken more aggressive action to keep him under surveillance. I suppose he was so surprised by what this mid had claimed that he wasn't thinking through the situation. He dismissed him and asked him to report back later that day. The kid vanished."

"Did they find him?"

"Maybe. Four days later a body showed up in Baltimore harbor."

"Suicide?"

"Probably not. The head and hands had been removed with a saw, according to the autopsy. Not much was left in the way of clues; you probably know that Chesapeake Bay has a large crab population. The blood type matched our mid, but there was no way to positively ID the body. Now tell me why you think he disappeared."

"Either he told someone he'd spilled the story, or the Admiral has a leak in his office. But I'm guessing the first one. Whoever he told must have been someone assigned by the KGB to keep an eye on him. He either passed it on or took direct action right away."

"That was an easy one. Now guess what we did next."

"You went to the midshipman's home to talk to his parents."

"Parent. No father, only the fake 'mother.' But she'd flown the coop by the time we got there. Or maybe they did away with her and hid the body somewhere. We dug through that house pretty thoroughly and found something interesting."

I kept silent. Sammon went on, "We looked at his high school yearbook photos. They were definitely the same guy. But then we looked at his junior high school photos. Our future midshipman was using a different name, and the guy with the name we knew him under looked totally different—blond and medium height as compared to our midshipman, who was taller with black hair."

"So that's when the switch was made—he showed up at high school using the name of the other kid. But wouldn't people have known him already under the original name?"

"Nope. The high school was in a different state. My guess was they did away with the blond kid and let this guy, who was probably the Russian illegal he claimed he was, take over his identity, but move somewhere far away from anyone who'd know him. And the 'mom' was no doubt the same woman who'd come over with him."

"How does this tie in to your Moscow assignment?"

"Well, this was considered very important—the idea of having these people infiltrate into key positions scared the crap out of Naval Intelligence. DNI decided that since I was going over as naval attaché, I should try to ingratiate myself with the KGB. The idea was that I'd pass them phony classified information on naval aircraft and electronics and see if I could gain enough trust to learn a little about this place where the kids were trained. I'd be acting like a traitor, motivated by money and—how do I say this?—pleasures of the flesh. Once I'd passed on information they wanted, they might take me into their confidence, at least enough for me to learn a little about this illegals program. Hopefully I'd get an idea of how many there were, how long they'd been there, and so on."

He went on to tell me that, after arriving in Moscow, he briefed the senior military attaché (an Air Force colonel), as well as the Ambassador, the Deputy Chief of Mission (the number two diplomat in the embassy), and the CIA station chief (aka "cultural affairs" officer). The four of them, but no one else at the embassy, understood that Sammon would be making what seemed like improper contacts with the KGB. Naturally each of them would exhibit a high degree of disapproval of the forbidden conduct Sammon was about to engage in, but would subtly thwart any effort to have him shipped back to the US in disgrace.

A few weeks later Jack attended an embassy reception and was introduced to a senior KGB officer from their First Directorate[63]. He'd made sure to frequent bars where he was clearly looking for young Russian women, so the KGB was almost certainly aware of this "weakness" in his character, and had made this known to his new KGB friend. A few days after his encounter with the KGB officer, he got a call from a young woman named Taisia, who said she was a cousin of the officer, and suggested he meet her for dinner.

The date had gone very well, ending up in Taisia's apartment, where he spent the night. Sammon had violated rules by bedding the young beauty, although his being unmarried minimized the blackmail possibilities. "Taisia was one of those classic Russian buxom blonde beauties," he sighed. "Kind of like Julie Christie in that Russian movie, but with a better figure."

It wasn't long after that that he was approached by his KGB friend, who asked if he'd enjoyed his time with the blonde. After enthusing about his time with her, Sammon made it clear that in return for more time with her, and perhaps some cash, he'd be able to supply information on USN aircraft capabilities.

The KGB had been, as he'd hoped, very interested in ESM[64] systems in US naval attack aircraft, something Sammon had a thorough knowledge of and could discuss intelligently. Before going to Moscow, he'd prepared a sanitized version of the manual on the newest system being put into service in F-14's and planned for the new F/A-18 aircraft that'd be joining the fleet in a few years. His version of the manual had lower than actual performance characteristics in key areas and didn't mention some of the advanced features of the system. "We didn't actually want to help the Soviets, so I needed something that looked

---

[63] The Foreign Intelligence directorate within the KGB.
[64] ESM = Electronic Support Measures. This equipment detects and analyzes electronic signals, such as radar.

authentic and would be accepted by them. We'd kill two birds—giving them bad info and maybe providing me with the credibility to learn more about this illegals operation," he explained. He didn't need to mention that if the Soviets had a copy of the real manual, he'd have been toast.

By the time Connor Healey arrived to become the new Legat[65], it was common knowledge within the US embassy that Sammon was too close to the KGB, and he'd made it no secret that he was spending nights with Russian women. Some staffers knew he'd passed sensitive US data to the Soviets. Healey, not being in the loop on the deception operation, took it as gospel. In his mind, Jack was a traitor to the US and dissolute on top of that, putting his sexual pleasure ahead of the interests of his country. He'd complained to the DCM and even to the ambassador directly. Both had listened to him solemnly, and promised to do what they could to get Sammon shipped back to the States, but there always seemed to be a reason why this action would have to be delayed.

Jack went on, "After about a year of this, and supplying a few more doctored-up classified papers to them, I started getting invitations to parties with just KGB people there, not counting the girls they brought in for recreation—no other non-Russians. We'd have all-night drinking and sex parties, and I was able to get a couple of them drunk enough to say things they shouldn't have.

"One of those guys knew about the illegals program. He wasn't directly involved in it, but knew some of the specifics. The people who knew the details—like the names and locations of the illegals—would never get in the same room with anyone they hadn't known a long time and whom they thoroughly trusted. I'm pretty sure a lot of the top KGB officers weren't even aware of that program. One night I sat and drank with him for a long time—from midnight until about dawn. He got smashed and I didn't, at least not totally. I'd made up a story with details about a non-existent US program to take young people with Russian or Eastern European ancestry, polish up their Russian, and send them into the USSR. The hard part was coming up with a good way to create a new 'person' in a society as tightly organized as the USSR. I claimed we had someone inside the Soviet bureaucracy that administered the nationwide internal passport program. When I was there, there were gaps in that system, and my story was that our mole in the Ministry of the Interior was able to create passports for the people we were inserting. My story was all bullshit, unfortunately, but my KGB

---

[65] Many US embassies have an FBI agent as their legal attaché ("Legat"). They set up liaison with local police and security departments, particularly in areas such as terrorism and organized crime.

buddy lapped it all up like it was gospel. Of course, he had to come up with a description of a similar program.

"He looked around to make sure no one else could hear us. Fat chance—they were all either passed out or in one of the other rooms enjoying the young women who'd been brought to entertain us. Anyway, he told me about this huge indoor facility somewhere east of Moscow. He told me hundreds of young people—mostly boys, but with a number of females—had been trained there and sent to the US. He said their American English was perfect, and that they'd spent years studying US culture, slang, and so on. A tightly compartmented organization—he claimed he didn't know much about it—worked with Soviet agents in the US to introduce these illegals. They set them up with their new identity, and managed them into positions where they could either become military officers or get a job in a US security agency—CIA, FBI, NSA, you name it. The women, to the extent they had a mission, were to attract the interest of the same kind of men; senior military, security agency, or even Congressmen or Senators. He thought most of them were just there to fill the role of a single mom until the boys got old enough to operate on their own."

I asked, "So what did you think? Did you believe what he said? It sounds to me like he might have been bullshitting you just like you did to him."

"I believed him," he admitted. "I know it sounds far-fetched, but it seemed to me it was just the kind of thing the Soviets would try. When you think about it, it'd cost a tiny fraction of what they spend on weapons systems, and it could have an enormous payoff. I mean, suppose one of these moles, if they really exist, succeeded in getting into a senior position in the military? If they set the identity up carefully enough, these guys would probably get a high-level security clearance without a problem."

"Pretty scary, if it's true," I agreed.

"You better believe it. Anyway, since coming back to the US, one of my projects has been to try to identify one of the deep KGB agents who manage these projects. I suspect they have several scattered around the country. Certainly at least one for New York, one for the DC area, and one out here for all the high-tech stuff. Maybe there are dozens of them."

"How could you possibly find one of these people? They must have really good documentation, and probably don't do anything that'd bring them to the attention of NIS or any other counter-espionage agency."

"Probably," he agreed. "But they've got to screw up once in a while. Everyone makes mistakes. In the meantime I look for anomalies in the illegals themselves."

"Like?"

"What we've started doing, on a going-forward basis, is to more deeply investigate the background of everyone applying to the Naval Academy or NROTC, going back to when they were ten years old or so; we figure the Soviet 'replacement' would have to be at least that old. We check yearbook photos and even interview people who knew this person when they were younger."

I hated to ask this next question, but had to know. "What about trying to identify those who've already got commissions?"

"We're doing that too, but it's a long process and it's tougher to find a witness who has a good memory of what they looked like twenty years ago. It'll take us years to get through them all, and for a lot of them we'll never be sure whether they're real or not. But the list isn't as long as you might think—anyone whose records show he was in the same town from birth until joining up probably can't be an illegal; there'd be too many people who'd know he couldn't be who he says." This meant I was on a shortlist. Had I been in a school picture in Fort Ross as "Paul Thompson" along with Ricky Burke? I couldn't remember.

"And what about illegals who want to get into government? Or get into senior positions in the Army or Air Force, for that matter?"

"Don't care. My job is the Navy and the Marine Corps, so I stick to that."

"This sounds like a long-term project. You'll never get them all; you might not get any."

"We'll get some. I've got a few good leads right now. Sooner or later we'll find one of these illegals, and that may lead us to the KGB contact, which in turn could get us the rest of the pack that guy's running. Maybe even to some of the other regional KGB guys." Jack had already found one illegal, but didn't realize it yet.

"I've gotta go," Jack said, picking up his briefcase. "Drop me at the United departure area. I'll be in touch."

A few minutes later I was driving south, wondering whether I should be rooting for Jack to succeed in his hunt. Finding Pete seemed to be a long shot, but if he succeeded, I'd be in a dangerous position. If Pete ended up in NIS custody, I was pretty sure he'd yield up whatever information Jack wanted. Pete would experience "better living through chemistry" with some of the drugs I was sure the government had available.

As I drove, my worries about Sammon's investigation were temporarily replaced by speculation on why Yolanda had been so eager to yield control of the joint project to me. Her reasons made some sense, but she'd clearly pissed off an Assistant Director, who must be many levels above her in the FBI hierarchy. Maybe she'd drop some hints to me.

My original plan had been to drive to Natalie's and stay there overnight with her. But when I got to her house at about 10:30, it was dark and there was no sign of her car. Maybe the Homebrew meetings had informal get-togethers afterward; I envisioned my lovely girl surrounded by dozens of horny computer geeks. Sitting around waiting for her seemed too desperate, so I headed back to my apartment for a rare night alone.

Chapter 51

I GOT TO work early on Wednesday. There were three workdays of this week left, and most of my group would be in Norfolk on Monday and Tuesday next week. I wanted to make sure the group learned to do things my way. My first submarine lecture was scheduled for today; that might be a good start. Arnold had agreed to join our trip; another good indicator.

Almost as soon as I'd gotten to my desk, the phone rang. It was Natalie calling from her home, upset that I hadn't come back to her place last night. My explanation—that I'd found her place vacant and didn't know how late she might be—didn't seem to mollify her. I supposed Pete reappearing in her life had been a big enough shock that her moods might be volatile until we solved that issue.

Before starting to catch up with Andy's delinquent paperwork, I organized my lunch session for today. Yolanda had let me know that for work-related meetings like this, we could have lunch brought up from the cafeteria and charge it to the department budget, saving me a few bucks. As it turned out, everyone but Phil from my department was going to attend, as would Natalie and her whole group.

We started promptly at noon; no time like the present to get these people used to doing things exactly on schedule. Yolanda had set out food and drink on a side table, and everyone helped themselves before sitting down at the conference table. Planning ahead, I wrote a few words on a sheet of paper and stuck it into a folder, making a mental bet with myself that I could use it to good effect.

Using the big whiteboard, I'd drawn the layout of a submarine attack center. "Today," I started off, "we'll talk about submarine versus submarine scenarios. We obviously can't use a Harpoon for a submerged target, so this is a torpedo-shooting situation. This is one of the primary missions for US submarines, so we practice it a lot and get pretty good at it. The key is detecting the enemy submarine before he knows we're in the area. This all depends on who's making less noise. Right now, our newest boats have a 5 db advantage over the quietest Soviet submarines." Then I had to explain how decibels are calculated. I hadn't expected Natalie's group to understand this, but Owen and

Arnold had a good grasp of it from their EE studies. The others had a difficult time accepting the non-intuitive reality that a 98 db sound level is twice as high as a 95 db level. "Got it?" No, they didn't, but were nice enough to pretend they did.

Back to the tactics; pointing at my diagram, I explained where the CO, the XO (acting as Fire Control Coordinator), the weapons officer, and the firecontrolmen would be, as well as the manual plotting party. "The consoles are called 'Pos 1,' 'Pos 2,' and 'Pos 3' for shorthand. On *BOWFIN*, the Weapons Officer—that was me—sat at Pos 1. As you can see, there's no room for a 'Pos 4,' so the Outlaw Shark system will have to be accessed at one of the three existing positions. Now, back to our submarine vs. submarine scenario: you need to understand that we use only passive sonar when we're hunting another submarine. If we went active, we'd be advertising that we're in the vicinity. Here's the problem: with passive sonar, all we know for sure is the bearing of the target at any given time. The range, speed, depth, and course are unknown. So we do a lot of TMA—time and motion analysis—to establish these unknowns."

I explained how TMA worked, both the manual plotting methods and the "stack the dots" algorithms that were built into the fire control system. I drew examples of what a bearing plot looked like, and explained how to maneuver to get an Ekelund range[66]. "Once we get a decent solution, we're ready to shoot. You'll see how the fire control team works when we go to the tactical trainer next Tuesday. While they're working the problem, you should be thinking about how our systems will fit into the way the fire control team works. Now let's talk about the weapon we'd use."

I gave them basic information on the capabilities of the Mk 48 torpedo, assuring them it was a reliable and deadly weapon. "There are a lot of options in how to program the unit, plus it's wire-guided, so as long as the wire's intact, we can steer it where we want, have it speed up, slow down, and so on."

"What if your target solution is wrong?" Owen asked.

"It's never *exactly* right, but it doesn't have to be. If we get our unit into the right neighborhood it'll do the rest of the work. It has significant homing capabilities, so if we lob it out in their general area, we have an excellent chance of getting a hit. That's why they say that 'close' only counts in horseshoes, hand grenades and homing torpedoes." And nuclear weapons, of course, but I wasn't going to bring that up.

---

[66] Ekelund ranging is a technique for maneuvering your own submarine across the target's line of sight and using the change in the before and after bearing rates (measured in degrees per minute) of the target to estimate range.

Arnold, of all people, had a question. "What happens next? I mean, after you shoot."

"As soon as our unit goes into the water, the target submarine will realize there's an enemy submarine in the area. It'll begin evasive action, possibly fire some decoys, and almost certainly will launch its own torpedo in the direction ours is coming from."

"Then what do you do?"

"Depending on how its torpedo is set and how far away the bad guy was when they shot, the best thing is either to physically stop the submarine in the water by backing down and then going quiet, or to turn and run at high speed. If the weapon uses passive homing—where it looks for noise from its target—going dead in the water will probably cause it to lose contact. We also have devices we can use to spoof the incoming torpedo."

"Does that really work?" Natalie asked.

"It's supposed to, but I've never actually had a live torpedo fired at me." That drew a few chuckles, but not from Natalie.

"Now, any more questions?"

"How many people are on one of those?" Tammy asked.

"I think the allowance for the *LOS ANGELES* is about 120 people. That's twelve to fourteen officers, maybe a dozen chief petty officers, and about 90 lower ranks."

"How do they all fit in?"

"The submarine is bigger than you might think. If you put it on a football field, it'd be as long as the complete field, including the end zones. And it's more than thirty feet tall—about as tall as a three-story building. Unfortunately, almost all that space is taken up by propulsion machinery and other equipment, so it really is pretty cramped living despite the total size."

Owen asked "Don't you get claustrophobic? And how long have you been underwater without coming up?"

I handed him the folder. "The answer's in there."

He stared at the scrawled note I'd put in there and muttered, "You wrote 'No,' and '62 days.' How'd you know what I'd ask?"

"Everyone asks those same questions," I assured him, earning me a few laughs.

I spent a few minutes with the perspective diagrams of the layout of the *LOS ANGELES*, which had some notable differences from *BOWFIN*. I explained what the purpose of each compartment was, and gave a short lesson on how to refer to directions on the boat (port and starboard, forward and aft, etc.)

"Next Wednesday, I'll ask Owen, Wayne and Arnold to each take a few minutes and give their impressions of the submarine visit and how it impacts our project. If Natalie would like to say a few words also, that'd be very helpful."

"Let's you and I talk about that," she said. That probably wasn't all we'd be talking about; I was pretty sure she was still irritated about me not waiting indefinitely at her house last night.

Chapter 52

THE REST of my work-week had its ups and downs, just as I'd described submarine duty to Natalie. On the good side, Natalie had either forgiven me for not waiting outside her house or had set it aside for use in later arguments.

On the bad side was being a manager at Federated. The paperwork burden seemed to grow every day. I spent most of my time on the management reports Andy had been neglecting for months. It took me the rest of that week to catch up on budget analyses, staffing summaries, and other very boring paperwork.

On Friday I got a visit from Laura, Greenwood's lovely administrative assistant. She had my new business cards and the complete attention of the men in the room. For whatever reason, the title on the cards was "Manager," rather than the "Acting Manager" title I'd been told I'd hold. My conscience suggested I point this out, but I resisted that impulse. She also gave me my new security badge with the silver stripe. I was surprised and a little worried that I was pleased to get these. It wasn't like this was my career.

Friday evening and Saturday Natalie and I relaxed, if you can count the four-mile run and a long session at the gun range as relaxing. She didn't actually kick my ass in the shooting, but did very well. She beat me in two out of five sets at 25 feet but lost all five at 50 feet.

Sunday morning we got up early to head for the airport. Owen, Wayne and the reluctant Arnold got to the boarding gate shortly after we did, and seemed happy I'd paid for their upgrade to business class seating. Owen and Wayne began their flight by taking full advantage of the free drinks, rationalizing that they were on East Coast time.

The flight to DC was uneventful but very comfortable; I hadn't flown in such luxury before. The connecting flight to Norfolk was a severe downgrade, as we all had to sit in coach seats for the short flight. Nielsen was waiting for us with a Navy van. He took us to the VOQ, which was actually better than I'd feared—maybe the equivalent of a "Motel 10," if such a thing had existed. Naturally, Natalie and I were assigned separate rooms; I was on the ground floor and she was on the

257

third. After we dropped our luggage off, Nielsen drove us to the Officers' Club for dinner, paid for by Federated, via my expense report.

At dinner Nielsen told us that our morning would consist of a thorough tour of *LOS ANGELES*, focusing on the control room and the spaces set aside for electronic hardware. It wasn't clear whether we'd have access to the propulsion spaces. In the afternoon we'd go to one of the diving trainers, where he thought it'd be interesting to have our civilians handle the fairwater and stern plane controls. "You can be the Diving Officer," he suggested to me.

"Nope," I answered. "Natalie, Arnold, and I need to spend time after lunch with the radiomen and fire control techs to make sure we understand how the SSIXS download information will be loaded into the Outlaw Shark hardware. And if I do show up at the trainer, I'll be the OOD unless you persuade me you're qualified as a submarine OOD. You can be the Diving Officer." He seemed to think his surface "water wings" were equivalent to submarine dolphins.

We'd spend Tuesday morning at the attack trainer, where the *LOS ANGELES* officers, sonarmen and fire control techs were already scheduled. Since my group already had an overview of the tracking procedures, this should be interesting for them. We'd leave after lunch to catch a 2 pm flight to DC and then our flight back to SFO. Everyone, even Wayne, seemed to be looking forward to their first time on a submarine and to learn how their work might eventually fit into the submarine tactical world. I was interested in seeing if I could get back aft to check out the new reactor system (an S6G instead of the venerable S5W the boats I'd served on had used). I was also curious to see if the much larger internal volume[67] of the *LOS ANGELES* would translate into more room for the people, or if it'd be crammed with additional equipment, cramping the habitability even further. I was betting on the latter.

As he dropped us at the VOQ, Nielsen told us, "Tomorrow we start with breakfast at the club. We're due at the boat at 0815, so I'll be here at 0645. It'll be a long day."

It might be a long night too, I realized. Natalie and I had spent almost all our nights together over the past few weeks, excepting my MIA last Tuesday night. I was wondering how to approach her about how she wanted to handle things tonight when she whispered in my ear as we walked into the VOQ, "Ten o'clock sharp, sailor. I'm in 312."

We all walked to our separate rooms. I thought I caught a sardonic smile from Owen, who might have overheard Nat. When I got into my

---

[67] The displacement of a *LOS ANGELES*-class SSN was almost 40% more than that of a long-hull *STURGEON* class boat. Very little of this larger volume went to crew habitability.

room, I still had half an hour to go. I showered again, brushed my teeth and read for a while before creeping upstairs to join Natalie. A fun night ensued, although we were both asleep by 2 am.

I got up early to sneak back to my own room. I wasn't under any illusion that the other people on the trip—except maybe Arnold—didn't realize Natalie and I were lovers, but there was no sense rubbing their noses in it. At 0630 I was out on the front porch of the VOQ. The three other men were out there a few minutes later; Natalie showed up at 0645 on the dot, looking innocent and refreshed, just as the van arrived.

After breakfast, Nielsen took us to the docks. I'd never been to Norfolk, having been a Pacific Fleet sailor for my entire Navy career except for Submarine School in New London. It seemed most of the Atlantic Fleet was here, from aircraft carriers down to minesweepers. *LOS ANGELES* was still at the Newport News Shipbuilding docks, across the James River from the naval base. We took the naval base ferry to the other side and passed through security, arriving at the pier where she was berthed.

And there was the *LOS ANGELES*. Obviously longer than my last boat by at least fifty feet, she was also beamier. No commissioning pennant or US ensign was flying, as she hadn't yet been commissioned. Shore power cables were running from the pier into the boat, so it was likely the reactor was shut down. If so, maybe we could get a bow-to-stern tour.

"Big mean-looking sucker," I heard Owen whisper to Wayne.

Nielsen, wearing working khaki, led us across the brow. He saluted the topside watch, asking "Permission to come aboard."

I was next and followed a similar procedure, but without saluting, since I wasn't in uniform. The other four strolled on board the submarine without any effort to request permission, earning a hard stare from the topside watch and embarrassing me. I should have explained some of the naval customs they'd encounter.

As Arnold straggled on board, a master chief petty officer came up through the weapons loading hatch. He saluted Nielsen, who returned it, and then turned to me. "Are you Mr. Halsted? I'm Master Chief Lister, the Chief of the Boat. I understand you're Qualified." It's important when saying that word to pronounce the capital letter clearly.

"Qualified on *PERMIT*, then went to *BOWFIN*. Good to meet you, COB. I'd like to introduce you to our group. We're all from Federated Aviation, and we're working on a submarine-related project. We'll be here today and tomorrow morning. We'll try not to get in the way of ship's work."

After the introductions, the COB said, "Let me take you below, Mr. Halsted. Before we get started, the CO wants to talk to you." He motioned to the topside watch. "Cutler, get TM2 Barkis up here to give a topside tour to our guests. They can come below when Mr. Halsted comes back up to get them. Come on, Mr. Halsted, if you still remember how to get down a submarine's ladder."

"I'll manage," I assured him, heading down the hatch after him. I slid down the twelve-foot ladder just to show him I could.

"Follow me, sir. CO's stateroom is just forward of the control room."

The boat hadn't yet acquired the "lived-in" aroma of an operating submarine—a mixture of hydraulic oil, amine, ozone, and human odors. Despite its size it already appeared crammed with more than enough equipment to fill up the extra space. Lindsay stopped at the captain's stateroom and rapped twice on the closed door. "Captain, I'm here with the manager from Federated."

From inside I heard, "Is that Halsted out there? Get your sorry ass in here!" It was a voice from the past—it had to be Larry Bourne, my XO when I arrived on *PERMIT*. Lister laughed, gave me a thumbs up, and headed back topside.

I opened the door. I'd been right. "XO! I mean 'Captain'—it's great to see you again." It was indeed Bourne, who'd kept unrelenting pressure on me not only to qualify as quickly as possible, but to excel. He'd been a difficult but rewarding person to work for.

I'd reported to *PERMIT* more than five years ago, straight out of Submarine School after a year of nuclear power training. He'd called me into his stateroom for what he called my "welcome aboard" talk. He'd started, "Well, George ...," I'd already known it was a Navy tradition that the junior officer on board—which was then me—is often addressed as "George." No one I talked to ever knew why this name had been picked; I suspected it came from the phrase "Let George do it." The XO went on to congratulate me on my appointment as the new SLJO for the boat. This acronym had been new to me, but he explained it meant "Shitty Little Jobs Officer." In short order I became the Welfare and Recreation Officer, the Voting Officer, the Blood Drive Officer, the Drug and Alcohol Inventory Officer, and the Savings Bonds Officer. These were naturally in addition to my two real jobs—Main Propulsion Assistant and, most importantly, qualifying for as many watch-stations as I could. These would start, he told me, with EOOW, OOD Surfaced, Contact Coordinator Surfaced, and Engineering In-port Duty Officer. Those would be the first steps to eventually Qualify in submarines. "Stay ahead of this schedule and you and I will be fine. But you're already delinquent, so get to work! Until you qualify for these jobs, your shipmates have to do your share of the work, and you're just a waste of good oxygen." That launched a year of very little sleep. Despite this scary beginning, I came to regard him as an outstanding XO and even a friend. And now here he was in what must be the most desired command billet in the Submarine Force.

Shaking my hand, he told me, "I'm not officially the commanding officer until the boat's commissioned, so you should just call me 'Commander.' But what the hell—I like the sound of 'Captain' and it'll be official next month. Now sit down; we have to talk before you bring your gang of potential spies aboard."

I sat and he went on, "I had a visit from Captain Jack Sammon last Thursday. He told me he's in Naval Intelligence and that you're working on some kind of super-secret project to unearth possible security leaks. He said you're masquerading as a civilian and are working at Federated on this project, but that you're really still on active duty. Oh, and he mentioned you were spot-promoted to Lieutenant Commander. Is this all correct?"

"It is. I didn't exactly volunteer for the job, but I had a chance to back out and decided to go for it." I filled him in on the project and why ONI was worried about the KGB penetrating it. "This visit seemed like a good idea, both to give the Federated people a better appreciation of the submarine environment, and to see if any of them act suspiciously while we're here. On that topic, I'd appreciate it if your people who are talking to the Federated employees let you know if they seem unusually curious about something that seems outside their need to know."

"That won't be a problem. We already passed the word on that, thanks to the hints the Captain gave us. Everyone on board knows, or will know soon, that you're a submariner, but only the XO and I are aware of your real status. Let me bring him in." He knocked on the connecting door and then cracked it open. "XO, come on in. We need to plan out today's events."

A tall dark-haired Lieutenant Commander came in, eyeing me suspiciously. "I'm Commander McGonigal, Mr. Halsted. Welcome aboard." He didn't sound very welcoming.

Captain Bourne cut in. "Rick's the same rank you are, Kevin, so ease it up a little." OK, it was true we were the same rank, but McGonigal probably had at least five years seniority on me and was, I was sure, on his third sea tour[68].

Bourne went on, "Rick's working on a tough problem. The three of us have to figure out how to handle this visit. He's got four civilians with Top Secret clearances standing around topside, and we've got to host

---

[68] An submarine officer's first sea tour is normally about four years, beginning with his first submarine (his 'qual' boat) and possibly involving transfer to a second boat after qualifying. After a shore duty tour, the second sea tour usually involves serving as Engineering Officer("ENG") and/or Navigator ("NAV"). The third sea tour is the XO tour, and the fourth will be in command, assuming the officer gets selected for those two opportunities.

them today and tomorrow, knowing one or more of them may be spying for the Soviets. At the same time, we have to be cooperative, because these people are designing the systems we'll use for OTH targeting with those new Harpoon missiles. So how do you suggest we handle it?"

I decided to step in and save the XO some awkwardness. "Here are my thoughts, Captain. Even though the people I brought have TS clearances, they don't *need* answers to a lot of the questions they might ask. They have no 'need to know' on classified info about main propulsion, sonar, torpedoes, and so on, so act accordingly. While we're here, let me be the hard-ass who tells them they may not an answer to something they're may be curious about. How does that sound?"

Bourne and McGonigal exchanged glances. The XO spoke up. "That'll be fine. What else?"

"Who'll be giving us the tour? And can we go into the propulsion spaces? I see you have shore power cables, so I'm assuming the reactor's down."

"We've assigned our WEPS, Joe Emerson, to your group as guide. We thought we'd go to the wardroom to start with; he's put together a presentation to give your group an overview of the boat. He'll go through the perspective view of the compartment layouts and the equipment in each area in some detail. Then we'll start the tour forward and work aft, beginning at the upper level. Radio is out of bounds for the general tour, although the two people you mentioned can go in there—with you—if necessary to work out the SSIXS data download issues. So far as the propulsion spaces, there's no reason you can't go all the way to the EPM[69]. As you said, the reactor's down, so we don't have to get into the dosimeter issue. Let me get Joe here to meet you before we get started. And remember—nobody except the CO and I know you're still on active duty."

I'd realized that WEPS was a Submarine School classmate; Joe and I had been in the same section for tactical and diving trainers, and we'd gotten to know each other fairly well. Some might think it was stretching coincidence to have my former XO be Commanding Officer of this ship and a Sub School classmate on board also, but the Submarine Force isn't all that big. Since there were about 120 from my year group still on active duty, I was likely to run into at least one of them on any boat I visited.

A knock on the door and there was Joe, not looking much changed over the past six years. "I'm looking for someone who knows this boat

---

[69] EPM = Electric propulsion motor, located at the very aft end of the submarine. If main propulsion is lost, this motor can run off the submarine's battery to provide propulsion at slow speed. Very slow speed.

well enough to give a tour," I said before he could say anything. "Could you point me to someone who could handle that?"

He recovered quickly. "That'd be me, you civilian carpetbagger. It's good to see you again, Rick."

After thanking the CO and XO for their time, Joe and I excused ourselves so I could fetch my people. Before I headed topside, we paused to spend a few minutes catching up. Joe's big news was that he'd gotten married a few years ago and he and his wife were expecting their first baby. "Julia's a little overdue," he frowned. "She was expected to deliver last week, so it could happen anytime now. But fill me in on your group and what they expect." Joe was out of the loop on my real status, so I gave him the fictional story.

But we needed to make sure we didn't give away info we shouldn't, so I tried what I hoped was a subtle approach. "Joe, all these people have TS clearances, but that doesn't mean they need to know everything. If they ask questions that you think might be iffy, keep your eyes on me. If I don't want you to give them highly classified data, I'll shake my head or frown. If I just stand there, go ahead and tell them. I might cut in once in a while to say they don't need to know those details. OK?"

Joe nodded.

"I'll go topside and bring the group down. Besides me, there are two electrical engineers and one industrial engineer in my department, plus Natalie, who's the manager for the programming side. And Nielsen, of course, if he wants to come along."

"We'll meet you in the wardroom," Joe said. "It's on the middle level, about where it was on the *STURGEON* boats. I'll give an overview briefing, your group can ask questions, and then we'll start the tour. We should finish about lunchtime. Your group, the CO and XO and a few other officers will be there for the noon meal."

I headed topside, collected my people and led them to the weapons loading hatch. "I'll go down first," I said. "Watch what I do. Face toward the pier, take hold of this metal frame and then put your left foot on the top rung. From there on down, it's like a normal ladder. Natalie, you come down after me and then everyone else in whatever order they want." I didn't want the males gathering at the bottom of the ladder to watch Nat come down. Maybe that wasn't entirely rational.

Once they were all down, I said, "OK, we're on the upper level of the Operations Compartment. This compartment makes up the front 40% of the boat's length. The aft part of the boat is all propulsion and engineering equipment, including the nuclear reactor. You're going to see the entire boat today; that's a rare privilege. Usually visitors, even senior officers, are only shown around this compartment. We'll go down to the wardroom now—that's where officers eat, do paperwork, and sometimes watch movies. The WEPS—Weapons Officer—will be our guide today and he's going to start by explaining the boat's layout so you'll have a better idea what you'll be seeing. I know we went over this a few days ago, but it'll be good to hear it again before we start the tour. Now follow me, and watch your step. We're heading forward on the port side."

I led them forward and then down the ladder (which they called "stairs") to the middle level, and then back to the port side to enter the wardroom. They'd goggled at the complexity of the control room as we passed through; they'd learn the details of that area later.

Besides Joe, the CO, XO and COB were waiting for us. Introductions were exchanged and we all took our seats.

Chapter 53

"**W**ELCOME to *LOS ANGELES*," Emerson said to my group. "I'm Joe Emerson, the Weapons Officer—you can call me 'Joe' or just 'WEPS.' I'll give you a summary on what you're going to see, and then we'll head to the upper level and work our way all the way through that level, back down to this level to do the same thing, and finally the lower level. After that, we'll take you through the propulsion spaces."

Joe had a slide presentation prepared. He began with an organization chart, showing the different departments on the submarine and laying out the chain of command. Next he explained the perspective diagram of the boat, covering all the compartments. "You'll see all this starting in a few minutes, but I thought it'd be helpful to show how the different areas are laid out and where specific equipment is."

After that, he went through the mechanics of how the boat dived and surfaced, with diagrams showing how the main ballast tanks functioned. Then we got a quick overview of the various sensor systems—visual, radar, ESM and sonar—with an emphasis on the latter. Joe continued with a high-level description of the electrical, atmosphere control, hydraulic, air, and trim and drain systems. His last section was what I'd call "nuclear power for people who never took a physics or chemistry class." I assumed Owen and Arnold had had those courses, and maybe Wayne, but wasn't sure about anyone else. If they hadn't had these courses and weren't comfortable with basic concepts like atomic structure and isotopes, it'd all be way over their heads.

"When we tour back there, will we be in any danger of radiation?" Nielsen asked, showing he hadn't understood Joe's nuclear power explanation.

"Not a bit. First of all, the reactor is shut down right now; the boat's drawing its power from a shore connection. But even if the reactor was critical[70], you could spend months on board and get less radiation than you would from living in a place like Denver, Boise, El Paso, or

---

[70] A nuclear reactor is deemed to be "critical" when the nuclear reaction becomes self-sustaining.

anywhere else that's several thousand feet up, where the atmosphere's thinner and lets in more cosmic radiation." Most of my group probably thought a "critical" reactor was judgmental.

"If there aren't any more questions, let's get started with the tour. It'll take almost two hours, so if anyone needs a head call, do it now." He paused, realizing from the blank stares that the visitors had no idea what he'd meant. "I should have said that if anyone needs to use the toilet, let me know."

No one responded, so Joe led us out of the wardroom and up the ladder to the upper level. We went forward all the way to the sonar equipment space, taking a peek into the ESM cubicle on the port side. "Here's where I assume the hardware for the Outlaw Shark system will live. Right now about 70% of the space is taken up, most of it for the sonar system computing equipment. We keep getting new stuff to install. If you let us know how much rack space you'll need for your equipment, we can reserve room for it."

Natalie spoke up. "We're going to have a UYK-7 dedicated to Outlaw Shark. I see you have one here already. We'll need the same amount of space for ours, and maybe room for tape drives, depending on what we learn about the data downloads."

"We can do that—I'll contact the shop people here and tell them we need space set aside for another UYK," Joe answered. He made a note in his wheel book[71].

"Is there a way to pass that on to other 688-class boats?" Nielsen asked. "We need to make sure each of them has room for it."

"Newport News is keeping track of all the modifications we put in, so they can add them to the standard plans. That shouldn't be a problem," Joe assured him.

Our next stop was the sonar room. "The equipment's shut down now, but at sea we'd have three or four sonarmen on watch at all times. A lot of what they do is handled by computer-driven visual displays, but they still use their ears a good part of the time," Joe told us. He explained the major sonar systems—the sphere in the bow, the conformal array, and the towed arrays.

Leading us further aft, he took us into the control room. Everyone had walked through here a couple of times already, but none of the equipment had been explained. "OK," Joe started, "this is the control room and attack center. It's the focal point for most everything that goes on while we're at sea. Over there in the forward port corner is the ship control station. Those two yoke wheels are used to control the

---

[71] These green-covered pocket notepads are carried around by officers, chiefs and senior petty officers to make notes of tasks that have to be completed. I don't know why they're called "wheel books."

submarine's depth and angle, as well as the course we steer. The one on the right usually controls the rudder and the fairwater planes—those fins you saw sticking out of the side of the sail. The left-hand station controls the stern planes, which are used to control the boat's up or down angle. The chair behind the controls is where the diving officer sits, and to his left is where the Chief of the Watch mans the ballast control panel[72]. That panel operates the main vent valves to let us submerge, controls the high pressure air for blowing the tanks when we surface, raises various masts, and has the controls to pump and flood the trim tanks to balance us properly. When you go to the diving trainer this afternoon you'll be operating these controls. You'll get a better understanding then of how it all works."

He led everyone to the periscope stand and raised the #1 scope. Everyone got a chance to look through it, rotate the view, and experiment with different magnifications. For some reason, this is a big event for civilians touring a submarine. If they'd ever had to spend hours "dancing with the fat girl" they wouldn't think it was so entertaining. Those who weren't on the scope could watch the video monitor where the view through the scope was shown.

They got a look at the navigation area before we turned to the fire control system. Joe lit it off and showed what the operator would do to line up the dots for a fire control solution. "Down here on the bottom, these 'course,' 'speed,' and 'range' knobs are used to try to stack the dots. You'll get a much better idea of this tomorrow morning when we're in the attack trainer. The one we're going to is actually a *STURGEON* trainer, since the Navy doesn't yet have one for the *LOS ANGELES* class. But they're both Mk 113 systems, so there's no real difference. Now we'll head aft so I can show you where the radio room is. We won't go in there now, although I understand some of you may see it this afternoon."

A few minutes later we headed back down the ladder to the middle level. We went to the Chiefs' quarters all the way forward and then aft through the various berthing compartments. Joe told us that there were bunks for only about 80% of the crew. "This means the non-rated guys and a good chunk of the E-4's will be hot-bunking." He explained how that worked, earning a horrified look from Natalie. "You're telling me that three people share two bunks? That's disgusting!" Perhaps, but it was also a good incentive to advance in rate so you have your own bunk.

On our left side as we headed aft were the officers' staterooms. Joe led us into one. "Three of us—me, the MPA, and the Chop—sleep in here. As you can see, we have one desk, so if it's being used you have to go into the wardroom to do paperwork. Which there's a lot of." Then he had to explain that the "Chop" was the supply officer, and that the oak

---

[72] aka "BCP"

leaves on his collar looked, with a stretch of the imagination, like a pork chop, hence the nickname.

"Looks pretty comfortable," Natalie said, peering into one of the bunks. "A reading light and what looks like an air conditioning vent. But there's not much vertical room; if you sat up, you'd bang your head." Very true, and many times I'd done that.

From there we went to the galley and the crew's mess. From the aromas, I'd known for a few minutes that our lunch was going to be "J-5[73]" —grilled steak. As we neared the galley, my civilians recognized it also.

"Wow!" Owen said. "Something smells great!"

"The submarine force has the best food in the Navy," Joe explained. "We have an extra monetary allowance for food and get better cuts of meat. When you've been submerged a few weeks, meal time can be a highlight of the day. When we finish our tour you'll be able to decide for yourselves at lunch how good the food is."

Now it was down to the lower level. As we went down the ladder, Wayne asked hesitantly, "Are we underwater now?"

"You've been below the waterline since you were halfway down the weapons loading hatch," I smiled. "Now you're more than 20 feet underwater." That didn't seem to make him feel better as Joe led us forward to the torpedo room. The boat hadn't yet loaded out its weapons, so all the skids and tubes were empty. "This is the main working space on the lower level—aft of here is the auxiliary machinery space and the freezer and cooler for all the food. The only hard limitation on how long we can stay at sea is food, so we have to cram in as much as possible before heading out."

He briefly described how torpedoes were loaded into the tubes and fired, opening the breech door of #2 tube so everyone could look into it. "The tubes are 21 inches in diameter and a little over 20 feet long. The inner and outer doors are operated hydraulically, and we also have hydraulic equipment to help load the fish into the tubes. When we get the Harpoons, they'll come in a capsule that fits inside the tube. Any questions about the torpedo room?" There weren't any questions. "From here we go back up to middle level and then head aft through the reactor compartment and into the engineering spaces."

Joe led us up a level and then back through the crew's mess to the watertight door leading to the tunnel through the reactor compartment. "Remember," he told us as he spun the wheel on the door, "the reactor's shut down, so there's absolutely no radiation here. To get through these watertight doors, the best way is to put your head and one leg through and then go through." He demonstrated; everyone managed it, with the

---

[73] As you might expect, each Navy menu item has an alpha-numeric designator.

usual awkward style going through for the first time. When everyone in front of me was in, I followed and shut and dogged the watertight door behind us.

"You can see the reactor through this thick glass port in the deck here. When it's been shut down a while, it's OK to go into it, but every entry has to be documented, so we won't do that." None of the Federated people seemed enthused about actually entering the reactor, so that was probably just as well.

"Joe," I said, "Your reactor seems to sit lower than what we had on *BOWFIN* or *PERMIT*. Is that something to do with the natural circulation?"

"Sure is," he agreed. "We can run on natural circulation if we're going two-thirds speed or slower. Anything faster than that and we have to use the main coolant pumps. Having the reactor lower lets us use gravity to help the coolant flow back from the heat exchanger."

"Nothing like the weakest force[74]," I agreed. Physics humor is hilarious.

Everybody ducked through the next watertight door, showing a little improvement over their performance on the first one. Joe said, "We're now in the aft compartment. It's the biggest on the boat in terms of cubic feet. As I told you earlier, we generate electricity and power to the main shaft by flashing water into high-pressure steam and then running the steam through turbines. The first set of turbines—the SSTG's—use steam power to produce all the electrical power we need to operate propulsion equipment, electronics, and what we call the 'hotel' load—the air conditioning, AC electricity, lighting, and so on. The second set—the main turbines—are connected mechanically to the propeller shaft through reduction gears. When the steam leaves the main turbines, it's lost most of its energy and is sucked into the condenser. The condenser has sea water running through its shell, which cools the steam, turning it back into water. This creates a vacuum that helps keep sucking the steam into the condenser. Then the water goes back through the heat exchanger with the radioactive primary coolant, flashes back into steam, and goes around again. Everyone got that?" Probably nobody had understood everything he'd said; I could see their eyes were getting a glazed look.

Joe took us up to the Maneuvering space, explaining what the four people standing watch there did, but he was starting to lose the civilian portion of his audience through information saturation.

"How about we head forward for lunch?" I suggested.

---

[74] As compared to other forces of particle physics—the strong interaction, electromagnetism, and the weak interaction—gravity is by far the weakest.

"Don't you guys want to see the EPM?" Joe asked plaintively. It really wasn't that interesting.

"I'm up for lunch," Owen admitted. "What kind of beer do you guys serve?"

I gave Owen the bad news. "Alcohol, except for medicinal purposes, has been banned from US Navy ships for over sixty years now. You can have iced tea, milk, or bug juice." I decided not to let my group, or even Joe, know about the occasional swim calls and steak barbecues with beer I'd enjoyed on my midshipman cruise on *TUNNY* back in 1967. After all, that was in a combat zone. And what goes on there ... you get the idea.

Chapter 54

W E ARRIVED at the wardroom as the steward was finishing setting the table. "Mr. Halsted," he said, "the Captain asked that you sit on his left and that the other men sit with a vacant seat on each side so they can mix with the other officers. The lady will sit next to the XO over here." I wondered if putting Natalie next to the XO was McGonigal's idea.

I explained to my group that submarine dining was "family style," so everyone would help themselves as the platters were passed around. "Normally the Captain goes first, then the XO, and then it just goes around the table. If special guests are here, the Captain and XO may defer to the guests. Oh, and the tradition of the wardroom is that there are no discussions of politics, religion, or ... uh, the fairer sex." Natalie gave me a sidelong glance of amusement as she took her seat across from me.

"You never discussed any of those things when you were in submarines?" Owen asked skeptically.

"Of course not," I said, raising my hand in the Boy Scout salute. "That would have been against the unwritten rules."

Joe, no dummy, slid in on Natalie's right side as the others took their seats. Within a few minutes five other officers straggled in and introduced themselves. The NAV, Larry Kudlow, sat on my left and the ENG, Frank Bowland, took a seat next to Wayne. Three junior officers filled out the table, sitting among Nielsen and the men from Federated. Joe and I handled the introductions. The officers seemed more interested in Natalie than in anyone else from Federated; an attractive young woman in a submarine wardroom is a rare and welcome occurrence.

The XO came in, followed by the Captain. Everyone stood except for my civilians. Natalie came to her feet quickly after she saw us rise, but the three men remained seated, looking puzzled. Another failure on my part to teach them proper naval etiquette. Bourne shook his head in mock dismay and winked at me.

The stewards came in with platters of steaks, fresh vegetables, and French fries. They brought them to the CO, who whispered to them. They turned, offered the first choice to Natalie, the next three to the

Federated men, and then back to the CO and XO. I got my normal turn in the rotation.

Before we began eating, Captain Bourne said, "I'd like to welcome our Federated visitors on board. We're looking forward to helping you move forward with your project. Rick, would you introduce them?"

I did, and Captain Bourne resumed, "Everyone here should know that when I was XO on *PERMIT*, Rick Halsted came on board as a brand new non-qual. He'll be the first to tell you that I made his first year onboard pretty damned difficult, pushing him all the time to do better. And he met my goals, which I can tell you doesn't happen very often. His last job before he got out was WEPS on *BOWFIN*. Just keep in mind he's Qualified. Help out him and his group so we can figure out how to aim Harpoon missiles at the bad guys."

While the stewards were serving, the conversation stuck to unclassified topics, focusing on the civilian group's reaction to the tour of the boat. Natalie and Owen offered some compliments on the tour, but Wayne and Arnold stayed silent. I understood Arnold's social skills were limited, but Wayne was starting to piss me off with his attitude.

"Rick, what's your impression of *LOS ANGELES*?" the CO asked.

"Well, Captain, I was on the commissioning crew of *BOWFIN*, so I know how things go in those hectic last few months. You seem to have everything under control, and the boat's in great shape—looks like you could go to sea on short notice if you had to. What I noticed most was that despite the fact this boat has lots more internal volume, there's actually less room for people. NAVSEA[75] must have come up with a ton of ideas on equipment they just had to add. And now here we are demanding more room for our equipment."

He nodded. "Yep, it's amazing how little 'people space' we have in a boat this large. Joe probably told you about the hot-bunking situation. So far as being ready to go to sea, we're loading torpedoes later this week, and the Chop's planning the first major food load-out. The Naval Reactors people are almost through with their certification—the new natural circulation system on the primary coolant loop was the first production model of its kind, so they had to write whole new sections in the RPM[76], based on the *NARWHAL*[77]'s operations. You can imagine what a hassle that was." I could indeed.

---

[75] NAVSEA = Naval Sea Systems Command, the Navy bureaucracy responsible for the design, construction and maintenance of all naval vessels and their various systems.

[76] RPM = Reactor Plant Manual. Produced by the Naval Reactors organization, this is the bible detailing exactly how naval nuclear reactors are to be maintained and operated. Stray from it at your peril.

[77] *USS NARWHAL* (SSN 671) was the first submarine to use natural circulation in its primary coolant system.

As lunch went on, I noticed Kevin McGonigal was devoting his entire attention to Natalie. He had no wedding ring. Natalie seemed to be pleased by his interest in her, but I supposed that'd be natural. I turned my attention back to the Captain and we talked amiably through the main course.

The meal was soon over. "That'll be all," the Captain told the head steward. "Shut the door behind you."

As soon as it was shut, leaving just the officers and my Federated group in the wardroom, he asked me, "Have you seen anything so far that'll cause a problem with your project?"

"If we can wedge another UYK computer into the sonar equipment space, I think we'll be in good shape. I still don't have any idea what sort of input console you'll have in the attack center to pass on the targeting information to the Harpoon missile. I think the McDonnell-Douglas people are designing that."

"Now that leads to an interesting topic. Do you think we'll actually shoot at an over-the-horizon target based on the information we get from your system?"

"Captain, that'll be your tactical decision, but I'm having a hard time imagining you'd lob a missile based on only the ocean surveillance data in the Outlaw Shark system. I'd think you'd like to have a sonar contact—it'd have to be convergence zone at that range—and maybe some ESM[78] data also to verify it's a warship out there."

"From what I know about these ocean surveillance systems—mainly satellite stuff—the data isn't actually real time," the CO said thoughtfully. "If that's true, how do we get real targeting information?"

"Based on what I've seen of the data you'll get, you won't have a good targeting solution unless you use other systems to get an accurate bearing and verify it's an enemy ship. And then you'll have to do TMA to get a range estimate, because it's almost certain the surveillance data will be too outdated to shoot on. But that's today's technology. Once Harpoon goes out to the fleet, the ocean surveillance systems will have to be massively upgraded. I suppose that could include getting NTDS data from surface ships as well as satellite and SOSUS[79] information. But even with the existing data you'll at least have some idea of what ships may be in the area."

---

[78] ESM = Electronic Support Measures. This involves passive analysis of electromagnetic transmissions and, based on their characteristics (frequency, pulse width, etc.), identifying the vessel or aircraft making those transmissions. A submarine has a mast with antennae to detect these signals.

[79] SOSUS = Sound Surveillance System, a network of undersea hydrophone cables linked to shore stations. Deployed in key locations around the world, its primary task was to identify Soviet submarine activity.

"You're saying it'll take pressure from the CO's to get the system to where the targeting information might be sufficient."

"That's what I think. One other point—you may know that the initial Outlaw Shark rollout is scheduled just for SSN's, probably starting with the 678 boat[80]. But we recommended it also be rolled out to SSBN's so they can use it to help them make undetected transits to and from their patrol areas. Not to mention its value once they're in the area. That went to OP-02 several weeks ago."

Captain Bourne smiled sardonically. "Someone figured out that'd increase your sales."

"Including SSBN's was actually Rick's idea," Natalie told everyone.

"You adapted quickly to life on the outside," the Captain said with a straight face. "Now let's move on to what we have to do this afternoon. We have time booked on the diving trainer to orient you civilians on how to operate a submarine. What else needs to get done?"

I answered, "Natalie, Arnold and I need to talk to the senior firecontrolman and the senior radioman. We have to figure out how the surveillance data that comes in will be downloaded onto the storage devices—what the data format will be, how much storage might be required, and so on."

"I'm on that," Joe said. "The chief radioman and our first-class firecontrolman will meet you here at 1300. I can take Commander Nielsen, Owen and Wayne over to the diving trainer and the three of you can join us when you finish here."

I agreed and thanked Captain Bourne for his hospitality.

"Glad it worked out. Now the ENG and I are going to have a talk about departmental training. I'll see you and your gang tomorrow morning at the attack trainer."

Joe and his little group—Nielsen, Owen and Wayne—left for the diving trainer, which was across the James River on the naval base. He'd given me directions on how to get there once we'd finished our meeting to discuss the data download issue.

He told me, "Until you get there, I'll handle OOD and the BCP. Commander Nielsen can try his hand as Diving Officer if he'd like to."

---

[80] This was *ARCHERFISH*, the first of the 'long-hull' *STURGEONs*.

Chapter 55

I T WAS a few minutes until our meeting, so I asked the stewards to bring some iced tea. "What are your priorities for this meeting?" I asked Arnold and Natalie.

Not surprisingly, Arnold had nothing to say. Natalie needed to know the expected volume of data, how it was organized, and how often it'd be updated.

"Here's what'll probably happen," I answered. "The chief radioman should have outlines of how the data's organized. The volume per download is going to depend on how long it's been since we last interrogated the satellite, as well as changes in volume of output from the different reconnaissance sources. On most operations, a boat will interrogate the satellite a couple of times a day, but on others, there may be long intervals between downloads."

We'd just begun to discuss what this might mean for computer data storage requirements when we heard a knock on the open wardroom door. A chief in khakis and a first-class in dungarees peeked in. "Mr. Halsted, I'm Chief Warren and this is Petty Officer First-class Tompkins. We're here to answer some of your questions on the data downloads for ocean surveillance."

I introduced Natalie and Arnold and we sat down to work.

"Chief, could we start with what you understand about how the surveillance data will come in and what the layout of the data will be?" I asked.

He opened a folder he'd brought with him. "Here's a copy of the preliminary message layout. You can see that for each contact there's a DTG[81], lat and long, and a classification code indicating nationality and ship type." He'd prepared several copies, and handed one to each of us.

---

[81] DTG = "Date/Time group." This is a ten-character data set indicating the month and time, along with the time zone. Example: A reference to 1 pm (London time) on September 19 would be SEP191300Z. The "Z" indicates Greenwich (London) mean time, which is the standard time used in naval messages.

The sheet also showed how to decode the ship type abbreviation and also had a list of the letter designations for different nation's naval ships.

"I don't understand these letters at the bottom," Natalie said.

"Civilian and naval ships have prefixes. The two most common for civilian ships are 'SS,' meaning steamship, or 'MV,' meaning a motor vessel, usually diesel powered. In the case of navies, we can tell which country a ship belongs to by its prefix," I explained. "For example, our naval vessels are always prefixed with 'USS,' meaning 'United States Ship.' The Brits have 'HMS' for 'Her Majesty's Ship,' the Japanese have 'JSDF for 'Japanese Self-Defense Force,' and of course the Italians use 'AMB'." I waited patiently and wasn't disappointed. I could sense Warren and Tompkins smirking.

"So what does 'AMB' stand for?" she reluctantly asked, probably suspecting correctly that I'd set her up.

"Really, Natalie," I said condescendingly. "Everyone knows that's 'Atsa My Boat.'" This earned me a dirty look, but I was sure she was laughing inside.

"How about the Soviets?" Arnold asked, speaking up for the first time in this meeting. And with a good question.

"They use 'SVR' in this database," Chief Warren answered.

"So," Natalie said, "getting back to the data volume estimate, it looks like there'd be 18 characters for the latitude and longitude, plus ten for the DTG, two for nationality, up to four for the prefix, and two for ship type. Including the spaces in between each set of info, that looks like 40 bytes per item. Chief, do you have any idea of the number of ships that might be reported at a time?"

"Well, ma'am, that'll depend on where you are and on how the submarine operating authority—COMSUBPAC or COMSUBLANT—decides what's relevant to a given submarine. For example, he might decide to include everything 200 miles in front of a given boat that's transiting—traveling from one place to another—but only 50 miles behind and on each side. The rules will be different for a boat that's on station; that means in the area in which it'll operate for a while. Some ocean areas, like around choke points—Strait of Gibraltar, GIUK[82] gap, Panama Canal, Straits of Hormuz, some of the passages between the Indian and Pacific ocean—may draw more attention than other areas. And I suppose the CO of a boat could ask for different data limitations based on his own situation."

---

[82] The "GIUK gap" refers to the gaps between Greenland and Iceland and between Iceland and the U.K. Soviet Northern Fleet submarines have to transit through this gap to get into the Atlantic.

"Rick," Natalie asked, "how many ocean-going ships are there? I mean, not just naval ships but also cargo ships, tankers, passenger liners—everything?"

"I think I read once that there are over 40,000 ocean-going ships of all categories, but that was several years ago."

"So to store the info for every ship, it'd take over a million bytes," she decided after some mental math.

"More, actually," the Chief interjected. "A ship will probably be reported several times by different sources, or by the same source at different time intervals."

"Say that's true," Natalie replied. "One 9-track tape can hold at least 5 megabytes, so it sounds to me like one tape drive could easily handle all the data on every ship within several hundred miles of each submarine. If, for example, there were two hundred ships within the defined area for a given submarine, you'd only be talking 30 kilobytes. That's a high-end estimate, based on 3 reports per ship and 50 bytes per line. If course and speed were added to the data, that'd be just seven more bytes per line. It sounds like we won't be overwhelmed with data volume. That's good news."

"Miss Natalie," the FTG broke in, "where's this tape drive going to be? And who maintains it—I mean mounting tapes and so on?"

There was no way Natalie could know the answer for the second question. "I think that's you, Petty Officer Tompkins," I said. "We'll be putting another UYK-7 in the sonar equipment space just for Harpoon targeting, and the tape drive has to be near it. That seems squarely in your bailiwick, since it'll be part of the fire control system. So far as tape mounting goes, you may want to rotate different tapes on a daily basis to have proper backups and so on. But that's for Ms. Montaigne to recommend." You'll notice I was careful to avoid the use of "Miss," which I'd learned (the hard way) from a young lady in DC was considered demeaning by many young women. I wasn't sure if Natalie shared this opinion, since I rarely addressed her by her last name.

"Chief," Natalie asked, "how often will you be getting these messages?"

"Well, ma'am, normally we try to copy the fleet broadcast three times a day. Sometimes we can't do that, because we have to stay deep for some tactical reason, but it's rare that we don't do it at least daily."

"How do these messages come in? I mean, what's the data transport rate?" Arnold piped up. Maybe he'd been paying attention all along.

"They come in encrypted, usually via the SSIXS satellite. That's a 4.8 kbps connection. We have to be at periscope depth to stick up an antenna for that one."

"So that's 600 bytes per second," Arnold mused out loud. "Based on Natalie's estimate, we could expect it'd take less than a minute to get the data." This was the most I'd ever heard him talk.

"Sounds about right for an average situation," Chief Warren agreed. "But if there's a lot of traffic in the area, it could be several times that."

Arnold asked, "Can we see inside the radio area?"

Warren looked at me; I frowned. He took his time, putting on an expression of deep thought. "You know, I can't think of anything you'd see in there that'd help you in what you're doing."

I didn't want Arnold to think we were picking on him, so I cut in. "If it'll make you feel any better, access to that space is very restricted. Only a few people on the submarine are cleared to go in there, so it's not as if you're being picked on. On *PERMIT*, I only went in there a few times as part of my qualification and on *BOWFIN* I only went in when I was checking rig for dive in that area. Now, do we have any other questions or issues on this? If not, thanks for your time, Chief Warren and Petty Officer Tompkins. If anything pops up you'd like to talk to us about, we'll be at the diving trainer for the rest of this afternoon and at the tactical trainer tomorrow morning. Here's my card so you can contact me if something pops up later." Natalie and Arnold took the hint and handed their business cards to Warren and Tompkins.

The three of us left the boat, caught one of the ferries to go back to the Naval Station, and went south to the building where the trainers were situated. It didn't take us long to locate the diving trainers, all of which were on the third floor. The second one showed us an interesting view of Nielsen pretending he was the Diving Officer, Joe manning the BCP and acting as OOD, and Owen and Wayne wrestling with the plane controls. Joe was prompting Nielsen on which commands to give.

I took a few minutes to explain to Natalie and Arnold what was going on. Even he seemed interested as he noticed the trainer taking up and down angles while Owen and Wayne continued their losing battle to maintain depth and angle.

Joe saw us and motioned for us to come in as he shut down the current problem.

"I've gotta get back to the boat," he told us, handing me the headset to communicate with the petty officer running the trainer. "It's set up now so you're back on the surface. How about you take over at the BCP and as OOD? It's time to rotate these guys. Owen wants to shift over to stern planes. Wayne can take a rest and Natalie can run the bow planes. You can show Arnold how the BCP works. I didn't do the 'angles and dangles' yet—I thought you might want to do that when everyone's here." And he was gone.

I spent a few minutes showing Natalie and Arnold where the controls were on each of the two stations. "Push in to go down, pull back to go up. Keep an eye on this dial that shows the speed—the higher the speed, the more responsive the planes are, so at higher speeds—anything above two thirds—you have to be really careful.

"Now, this is important. I'm sure Joe already told the three of you who've been here, but it's worth saying again for everyone. When the Diving Officer—that's Commander Nielsen—gives a command, you repeat it back word for word, so the OOD and Diving Officer know you heard the order correctly."

Natalie nodded happily, taking a seat at the fairwater planes control, as Owen moved over to stern planes. "Arnold and Wayne, come give me a hand with the BCP. I'll show you how to trim the boat. Take a look at the controls and let me know if you have any questions."

"Diving Officer," I said, loudly enough for everyone to hear me, "All hull openings indicate shut. Submerge the boat. Make your depth 200 feet. All ahead two-thirds. Make sure you and the planesmen have your seat belts fastened." I sounded the diving klaxon twice.

"Submerge the boat. Make my depth 200 feet and all ahead two-thirds aye," Nielsen said grudgingly, giving me a look indicating he didn't like taking orders from me.

I opened the vents and watched Nielsen. "Stern planes," he said firmly, "Ten degree down-angle. Ring up all ahead two-thirds."

Owen pushed on his plane control and then turned the engine order telegraph to "Two-thirds," but didn't say anything. I gave Nielsen a few seconds and then barked, "Stern planes, repeat the order you were given. Word for word."

"Ten degree down angle and all ahead two-thirds," Owen muttered sullenly. I saw the telegraph indicate that Maneuvering had responded to the speed order, but Owen didn't say anything.

"Diving officer, has Maneuvering answered the speed bell? I didn't hear the stern planesman verify that."

Nielsen peered at the engine order telegraph. "Maneuvering answers all ahead two-thirds."

"Next time I want to hear it from the planesman."

"What do I do?" Natalie asked. I didn't say anything, waiting again for Nielsen. He didn't seem to know what to say, so it was my turn again. "Natalie, the fairwater planes aren't below the surface yet. Just relax and wait for an order from the Diving Officer."

"Come left to 275. Use twenty degrees rudder," I told Nielsen. That'd give her something to do.

"Fairwater planes, left twenty degrees rudder and steady on 275," he relayed, and Natalie echoed the command as she turned the yoke to the left.

"All ahead full," I told Nielsen. It'd be interesting to see how the plane operators reacted to the greater sensitivity the boat would have to movement of the planes. This time Owen properly told us that Maneuvering had answered the full bell.

As I'd expected, we overshot the 200-foot ordered depth, over-corrected up to 170, and then finally got more or less steady on depth. "Now," I said in my official OOD tone, "it's time for angles and dangles[83]. Make your depth one thousand feet. All ahead flank. Twenty-five degree down bubble," I ordered. "Diving Officer, don't overshoot. Test depth isn't that far below a thousand." The trainer cabin took a very large down-angle; a good thing everyone had their seat belts on.

Peeking over Owen's shoulder, I saw we were close to a thirty degree down angle. I gave a significant look to Nielsen, who responded well. "Stern planesman, you're at too steep an angle." Owen pulled back and the angle went to about fifteen down.

"Diving Officer, give me the angle I want and give it to me now," I said firmly. "And I should warn you that going down to a thousand feet will make us too heavy—the hull compresses as we go down, making us less buoyant. I'd recommend you pump about 15,000 pounds from the auxiliary tanks as we start down. It'd be embarrassing if you took us too deep. Just tell the Chief of the watch." I pointed at myself.

Nielsen hesitated and then said, "Chief of the watch, pump 15,000 pounds from the auxiliary."

Correcting him diplomatically, I said, "Pump 15,000 pounds from auxiliaries to sea, aye sir." I turned to the BCP and punched the appropriate buttons. A few minutes later I announced, "15,000 pounds pumped from auxiliaries to sea, sir. BCP is secured."

"Very well," Nielsen answered, seeming happy at the "sir" from me in my COW role.

I beckoned him over and whispered, "Start bringing the boat back to a zero bubble at about 900 feet. Otherwise you're likely to overshoot." He nodded.

---

[83] "Angles and dangles"—extreme up and down angles—are used routinely when going to sea after a period of time in port. This helps make sure that everything on board is stowed properly so that in an emergency situation objects won't go flying around the submarine.

We ended up pausing temporarily at 970 feet, then going down to 1040, and finally were porpoising plus or minus ten feet from the ordered 1000, which really wasn't bad for untrained operators at almost thirty knots. Natalie and Owen were learning to coordinate their actions and to keep an eye on each other's plane indicators so they could adjust properly.

This went on for a few hours, with everyone rotating through the different positions, including putting Nielsen on the planes and letting each of the Federated people take turns as Diving Officer. Two hours later we'd all had enough fun, but everyone, including even Wayne, seemed to have enjoyed their simulated submarine ride.

Chapter 56

A FTER OUR fun at the diving trainer, we headed back to our quarters. On the way I kept quiet, listening to Natalie and the four men discussing their "submarine day." What they really needed was to be severely sleep-deprived and then go through the same exercise for six straight hours, with the unique aroma of a boat that's been submerged for months seeping into them. Then they'd have had one-third of a real submarine day.

Everyone except Wayne was enthusiastic, and even he'd seemed interested and involved at the diving trainer. Nielsen seemed to think he was now virtually qualified in submarines as a result of walking through *LOS ANGELES* and a few hours in the diving trainer. I should have initiated a major flooding casualty when he was playing Diving Officer to give him some humility.

Natalie and I had decided to go to the Officers' Club on base for dinner, hoping the rest of the group would join us. "Who's up for dinner at the club?" I asked. "The food will be decent, and we won't have to worry about trying to find a good restaurant off-base."

Natalie nodded, but none of the men said anything. "Look," I said, "I'll be down here in about an hour. If anyone wants to come along, be here then. If you decide on the club, I think slacks and a blazer or sport coat would be fine."

We all went our separate ways and, as usual, I was down slightly early. Natalie and Arnold showed up, but Wayne and Owen were MIA and Nielsen had begged off, leaving a note at the front desk saying he'd pick us up in the morning. Natalie had brought a nice little black dress with her, which did an excellent job of showing her off; even Arnold noticed.

The Breezy Point Officers' Club was north and east of the dock area, with an excellent view of the waterway to the north. The club was quiet, but it was a Monday night. I'd put on my miniature gold dolphin lapel pin to improve the odds the bartender would serve us without asking for military ID, which I couldn't display in front of Arnold.

The three of us took a seat in the bar area. I went over to order the drinks; white wine for Natalie and my usual Jack. Arnold asked for a

Shirley Temple, but I substituted a similar-tasting but alcoholic drink. He needed loosening up.

We'd only been there a few minutes when someone tapped me on the shoulder. It was Captain Bourne. "I've got a table in the dining room with Marge and Kevin. Why don't you guys join us?" They were at a table with four chairs, but McGonigal was pulling over another table to make room for us to sit with them. It was good to see Bourne's wife; Marge had taken on the job of den mother for the single junior officers on *PERMIT*, and we'd become good friends.

Introductions were made, although Arnold was too timid to say much or meet anyone's eyes. When musical chairs finished, I found myself sitting next to Marge with Natalie next to Kevin across from me. I like Marge, as I proved by kissing her cheek before I sat down. I'd still have preferred being next to my girl.

"Marge," I told her, "I'd like to get the secret formula you use to keep from getting older. You look years younger than the last time I saw you, and that must have been three years ago."

"You're as full of shit as always, Rick, but it's good to see you. I can't believe you got out of the Navy. I had you pegged as a career submariner."

I shrugged. "It seemed like a good idea. And it's more relaxing—I have a lot more time for personal things, and I can usually get a good eight hours of uninterrupted sleep every night." Actually, since reuniting with Natalie, I rarely got more than a few hours of continuous sleep, but I wouldn't complain about that.

"And," Marge responded, "you can probably also plan ahead more than a day or two for things like vacation, dinner with friends, and so on. Maybe you should have a word with Larry."

"Not a chance. He's got the best job in the Submarine Force; I'm guessing he'll be working his way up the ladder pretty quickly. And before you say it, we both know you may not see him much over the next couple of years, but after that he'll have mostly shore duty. Then you can have a real life just like me."

"Very funny. But you're right about Larry having the *LOS ANGELES*. It's a real feather in his cap."

"And in yours. I don't know all the ins and outs, but I'm betting that a savvy wife has a lot to do with a man's success in this Navy."

"Maybe," she smiled. "But I'm not allowed to give details about the secret women's network to anyone of the male gender, including Larry. Now tell me about this girl of yours."

"What girl?" I asked innocently.

"Natalie, over there."

"Why would you think she's my girl?"

"Really, Rick. All I have to do is see the way you two look at each other. But I warn you, Kevin fancies himself quite the ladies' man, and it looks like he's doing his best to impress your Natalie. Now, I've asked you once politely to tell me about her. Don't make me ask twice."

"There's not much to tell. Natalie's the manager of the IT group that's working on this project. I'm managing the engineering side. She's actually senior to me, since she's been a manager longer. Let's see ... she has an IT degree from Cal Berkeley, she's single, she's fluent in French, she likes Italian wine and French food ..."

She swatted my arm sharply. "Rick Halsted, you know very well what I want to know. How did you two meet ... when's the wedding set for ... that kind of stuff."

"Sorry, Marge. No plans yet. But someday, if I have enough Jack Daniel's in me, I might tell you how we met and all that other sappy stuff."

She was starting on her retort when one of the waiters called out, "Captain Bourne? Captain Bourne? Sir, if you're here, you have a phone call."

He grimaced and got up. "What now?" he griped as he walked toward the telephones. A few minutes later he came back and, still standing, beckoned to McGonigal, who reluctantly tore himself away from Natalie. The two of them talked for several minutes; it seemed McGonigal was arguing with Bourne. Then the Captain motioned me over.

"Halsted," Bourne said, "I've got a great opportunity for you. That was Joe on the phone. Julia's gone into labor, and he's heading to the hospital with her. That means we'll need someone to be WEPS during our tactical training tomorrow morning. Can you handle it?" McGonigal's frown told me he'd argued against this, which was a good reason to want to do it.

"I can handle it, but wouldn't it be better to have one of your wardroom instead?"

"I'll tell you what, Halsted. How about you let me make the decisions on training my officers while you use your tiny brain to decide if you're still competent to run a fire control exercise?"

"I can handle it, Captain, and I'd be honored to."

"Great. Meet us at the attack trainer at 0730 tomorrow for a briefing. The rest of the Federated people don't need to be there until 0800. We're going to run two or three problems and cut you guys loose in time to get your flight back to DC. Any questions?"

"Can you tell your XO to stop hustling Natalie? She's mine." I didn't actually say that. I just shook my head and went back to the table. Marge had moved next to Natalie, taking McGonigal's seat. The two of them were deep in conversation. McGonigal had noticed this too, and now seemed doubly pissed off. Things were looking up.

We all ordered dinner and a few bottles of wine, and had a nice relaxed evening, with Arnold taking more than his share of the wine and beginning to display a personality. After dinner McGonigal moved over to the vacant seat on Natalie's left, directly across from me. Looking him over more closely, I decided his face was what a female might call "ruggedly handsome," and he seemed to have a couple of inches on me (that's a reference to height). Could it be Natalie found him attractive? I certainly didn't.

After dinner Captain Bourne collared me and pulled me away from the table. "I see my XO's making a high-speed run on your girl," he frowned. "What are you going to do about it?"

"Why does everyone think she's my girl? We're managers who happen to be working on the same project," I protested.

"If that's the story line you want to use, you should let Natalie in on it. She filled Marge's ear with details of you guys getting back together. I had no idea when you introduced her that she was the same girl you used to moan and groan about when you were on *PERMIT*."

"I don't remember doing anything like that."

"I'm not surprised. Remember the night after we finished that ORSE[84] in 1972? You and the ENG had been working your asses off practicing all the possible casualty drills they might inflict on us. I think each of you were getting about two hours sleep a night, and that was in port. You may remember that Marge and the kids had gone back to Indiana for a few weeks, so after the ORSE I took you up to the Ballast Tank to congratulate you on how well you'd done. You snorkeled down an entire fifth of Jack and gave me the whole sorry story. I have to say, you were pretty pathetic. At least you didn't break down and cry on my shoulder, and thank God for that. Now the two of you end up working at the same company? What are the odds on that?"

"Pure chance, Captain. You know my Navy role on this project, so unless Jack Sammon somehow knew all about my history with Natalie and decided it'd be fun to see what happened if we met up with each other, there's no way to explain it."

"Damn strange, though. It's like one chance in a million."

"I'm not complaining. So far it's worked out very well."

"But what if your lovely Natalie is one of the spies you're looking for?"

---

[84] ORSE = Operational Reactor Safeguards Examination. The ORSE is a multi-day in-depth inspection of each nuclear-powered vessel's ability to deal with various propulsion casualties and emergencies. A poor mark in an ORSE can spell career doom for the CO, XO and Engineering department officers.

"Nothing I've seen so far indicates she might be. But if she is, I'll have to do my duty." In reality, if she was one of the spies, or even if she was innocent but got angry at me, I was screwed, blued and tattooed in many ways.

"Back to my original point, Rick. I'd advise you scoop up Natalie before Kevin talks her into something you'd resent. He's tireless and usually successful in his pursuit of young ladies."

I had no idea on how to "scoop her up" without starting a drama that might end badly. Young women often find it flattering for their male companions to resent another man's attempts to seduce her, but don't appreciate any action that'd stop these attempts. Why is that? Anyway, Natalie seemed to be enjoying McGonigal's company, which was more than I could say. I was considering asking her if we could just talk for a moment when she got up, smiling politely at McGonigal.

"I enjoyed talking with you, Kevin. I'll see you tomorrow morning at the tactical trainer." Then she turned to me. "Shall we go? It's been a long day." I agreed. I paid for the dinner and drinks for everyone, over Bourne's protests, which went away as soon as I explained Federated was actually paying. The three of us headed back toward the VOQ. Arnold seemed to have gotten on the outside of more alcohol than he was used to, and was actually talkative, although incoherent, on our walk back.

Chapter 57

ON THE walk back to the VOQ, we let Arnold stagger along a few feet ahead of us, giving him an occasional hint on where and when to turn. Whatever conversation Natalie and I might have was none of his business. I wasn't about to bring up McGonigal as a conversational topic, but Natalie had no such compunctions.

"Kevin's kind of an interesting guy," she said. I thought this was an attempt to get me to vent my jealousy.

"All submariners are interesting, sweetheart." A lame reply, but better than giving her an opening to taunt me.

"Mmm," she said noncommittally. "He told me tomorrow you're going to be part of the ... what did he call it? 'Fire control party'?"

"That's the team that'll run the tactical trainer problems tomorrow morning, and it looks like I'll be playing WEPS. Did McGonigal seem to be pleased that I'm joining them?"

"Not really. He doesn't seem to think you're up to it."

"I guess we'll find out tomorrow morning. Since I'll be busy, Captain Bourne—or maybe someone he'll appoint—will explain the details of what's going on to you and the other Federated people. We'll run two, maybe three problems before we have to leave to catch our flight." Time to change the subject back to Kevin. "Did you have a good time tonight?"

"I did, especially talking with Marge. But Kevin got a little old after a while; he's one of those men who thinks he's being subtle when he keeps touching you. A little pat on my hand, then a hand on my knee and all that. I think it's supposed to make you feel you're already intimate."

"Did he try to touch you somewhere you didn't want to be touched?" I asked reflexively.

"Don't be a dick, Rick," Natalie said, chuckling at her own wit. "If he'd tried that, you'd have heard a loud smacking noise when I slapped him. But he did ask if I'd be interested in going with him to someplace for drinks and dancing."

"We'd better pick up our pace. I don't want you to be late when he shows up at the VOQ to pick you up."

"I'll tell you what, big boy. Why don't I just stay in the VOQ and we'll see if you can make me glad I turned him down?"

A great idea. We were coming in sight of the VOQ and Arnold was faltering, so I caught up with him and helped him into the lobby. He couldn't tell me what his room number was, and there was no one at the reception desk. I propped him on a couch and left one of my business cards on his chest with his name written on it. Hopefully whoever showed up at reception would take him to his room.

"My place. Fifteen minutes," Natalie told me and disappeared into the elevator. I looked at my watch. Only 9:45, and I expected to be kept busy tonight. I was.

In the wee hours of the morning, before going back to my own room, I told Natalie I'd have to leave the VOQ at about 7:15, and that she should coordinate the rest of them arriving at the tactical trainer—in the same building as the diving trainer—no later than 7:55. "I'll put a wakeup call in at the desk for 6:30 for everyone." Natalie frowned. "Except you, of course. Tell everyone to leave their luggage at the front desk, so they won't have to lug it all the way to the trainer. We can pick it up here on our way to the airport."

Arriving on time at the trainer, I found the whole fire control team assembled. I'd met all the officers except for the Chop, who'd be working on the plotting table. I spent a few minutes talking to the firecontrolmen who'd be in the tracking party and then sat in front of one of the BSY-1 terminals to reacquaint myself with the controls while I waited for Captain Bourne to kick off the meeting.

Instead, Kevin McGonigal started things off. "Before we get started on the first problem, I wanted to make sure everyone knows that Joe Emerson's wife went into labor last night. She and their new son are doing fine, but Joe's going to spend the day doing the things a new dad has to do. Since WEPS won't be here, we're going to have a civilian handling his duties. Rick Halsted, formerly WEPS on *BOWFIN*, will be our stand-in today. Captain Bourne was XO on *PERMIT* when Rick qualified, and assures us that he'll do fine. Any questions?" That had been more gracious than I'd expected. Maybe Kevin was apologizing, in his own non-humble way, for making a high-speed run on Natalie last night. Interestingly, he'd put the burden on the CO for any mistakes I might make.

My group came in shortly after 0800, led by Nielsen. Natalie gave me a rueful shrug, probably because they were late, and inclined her head toward Owen and Wayne. They seemed to be suffering from some sort of self-inflicted ailment. I remembered *TUNNY*'s XO on my midshipman cruise in 1967. He'd noticed my hangover-induced reluctance to go to sea in very bad weather after a night of way too much San Miguel beer. He explained to me "if you're going to hoot with the owls, you've got to scream with the eagles." Wayne and Owen didn't look ready to scream, although I was considering it. Arnold, I was surprised to see, seemed as bright-eyed and bushy-tailed as I'd ever seen him.

The squadron staffie who'd be running the exercise, a lieutenant commander, came in and gave us an outline of what the exercises would be. "This is the scenario: NATO and the Soviet Bloc are at war. So far it's non-nuclear. Heavy armored battles, supported by tactical air, are going on in the Fulda Gap region of Germany. *LOS ANGELES* is the northernmost element in a barrier patrol of US and British submarines whose mission is to prevent Soviet submarines from entering the North Atlantic traffic lanes. The rules of engagement allow you to make a pre-emptive attack on an enemy submarine. You're operating south of Svalbard in about 2800 feet of water, shallowing to as little as 1000 feet to the east. It's late summer, so the area is ice-free. We expect Victor II's and Charlie's, submarines you should be familiar with, and possibly some Tangos. They're diesel powered, but are quiet and can operate for a week in between battery charges. The sound velocity profile for your area has been downloaded to your fire control displays. You have Mk 48's tube-loaded in all four tubes. Your threat axis[85] is between 050 and 110. When the problem begins you will be at 350 feet, one-third speed with primary coolant pumps off-line, on a course of 075. Your towed array is streamed. Any questions?"

There weren't, and we all took our places. As I sat down, the XO asked, "WEPS, what are your recommendations for depth, course, and speed?" I wasn't sure if he was putting me on the spot for his own reasons, such as making me look bad to Natalie, or if Bourne had put him up to it. I glanced at the SVP and turned to face him. "XO, I recommend we go to 570 feet, the axis of the sound channel[86], and come right to 170 so our towed array will have a good look toward the center of the threat axis. We should slow down to minimum speed and let them come to us."

McGonigal retorted, "Being in the sound channel increases our chances of being detected." A true statement, but ...

"We're supposed to be one of the quietest submarines in the world. Let's use our acoustic advantage to make sure we detect them and fire on them before they realize we're here," I replied. Behind McGonigal, I could see Captain Bourne talking to the Federated group. No doubt he was telling them what a tactical genius I was.

---

[85] The "threat axis" denotes the general direction from which the enemy is expected to appear.

[86] A sound channel occurs when there's a layer of decreasing sound velocity above one of increasing velocity. This provides longer sonar detection ranges because the sound is trapped in that channel.

Without comment, McGonigal gave my depth, speed and course recommendations to Frank Bowland, the ENG and battle stations OOD. If my recommendations put us in a bad tactical situation, the blame would come down on me.

As usual, the first ten or fifteen minutes passed without us gaining a sonar contact, so I turned to see how the other Federated people were doing. Wayne seemed to be asleep, and Owen was fighting it. "XO, can I get up for a minute? I need to see how my team is doing up there."

He nodded and I went up to drag Owen and Wayne out into the hall. "Listen," I told them, "your behavior is unacceptable. I don't give a shit what you did last night or how hung-over you are. You're here with a client and you have to make a good impression. Now start pouring coffee down your throats, go back in there, and circulate around. Show interest and ask questions."

"What if we don't want to?" Wayne mumbled truculently.

"If you don't, I won't physically force you to." Although that was a tempting idea. "What I can—and will—do is to write a performance evaluation saying that neither of you can be trusted to act appropriately with clients. That'll put the stops to any hopes you might have of advancing at Federated. It's your choice." I turned and left them there in the hall.

Stopping next to Natalie, I whispered, "Just had a confrontation with the bad boys. They're supposed to start sobering up and talking to the plotting party. You and Arnold should mingle also; ask some questions."

"Is there anything I can do to help them?"

"If you have any aspirin—extra strength would be good—that'd probably help. All my stuff's back at the VOQ."

"I'll see what I have," she answered, opening her purse.

Just as I got back to my seat, a report from sonar of an unidentified contact bearing 068 came in. As usual, the problem started developing slowly, but everything accelerated as we moved on. I noticed when I turned around to address McGonigal that all four Federated people were clustered around the plotting table, apparently asking questions about how the fire control solution was developing. Wayne and Owen still looked like hell, but hopefully could articulate a sentence.

The tempo was getting quicker and the fire control solution looked good. Sonar had identified the target as a specific Victor II whose signature had been recorded by the *RICHARD B. RUSSELL* several months earlier. We had it on a course of 196, speed twelve knots, and an estimated range of 11,500 yards, close to the results of the Ekelund ranging. "Good solution," I told the XO.

"WEPS, what are your recommendations for torpedo settings?" I went down the list, starting with my favorite (anti-circular run—it's nice to know your own unit won't attack you).

McGonigal ordered the Mk 48 in Tube 2 to be made ready in all respects. A few seconds later I reported "Unit in Tube 2 is warmed up and tube is flooded."

"Open outer door on Tube 2," the CO said firmly and loudly.

"Open outer door on Tube 2, WEPS aye," I said, and a few seconds later, "Outer door is open on Tube 2."

"Firing point procedures," Bourne announced. This meant that at his next command I'd press the firing button on my control panel. I looked at my display. "Possible target zig to the left!" I snapped. I was sure the squadron puke had waited until the last possible second and then zigged the target to see how we'd respond.

"Shut outer door on Tube 2 and secure from firing point procedures," Bourne sighed. I repeated the command and verified the outer door was shut. Five minutes later we had a new solution with our target now on course 158. "Looks like your torpedo settings are still good, Mr. Halsted. Open outer door on Tube 2."

I repeated the order and, a few seconds later, verified that the door was again open.

"Firing point procedures!" Bourne snapped and then under his breath, "Again."

My line of dots remained arrow straight; my finger was poised over the "fire" button.

"Match bearings and shoot!" barked Bourne. I stabbed the "fire" button. Five seconds later a voice in my headset announced that Tube 2 had fired normally and the wire seemed to be streaming properly.

We waited to see if our target would detect the torpedo and fire a snapshot back at us; nothing happened immediately. Five minutes later the squadron puke reappeared and said the program had been terminated. "Good shot—it'd have been a hit in real life. Let's take a ten-minute break before the next problem."

"Not bad for a civilian," Bourne told me, clapping me on the back.

"Some things you don't forget," I responded. "Thanks for giving me the chance to play the game again."

He left to get some coffee and Natalie came up. "That was really interesting, honey," she smiled. I looked around, but no one was within earshot.

"Was someone explaining what was going on?" I asked.

"Captain Bourne gave us an overview at the beginning; it was kind of like what you'd told us last week, but with more detail. As it went on, I spent a lot of time at that table where they mark the lines—are they called bearing lines?—on the chart. That young officer they call 'Chop' explained how the bearing rates are analyzed. And when Captain Bourne had the submarine change course, Chop told us how you use the change in bearing rates to estimate the range. Sounds like it'd get complicated real fast if you were tracking multiple targets."

"That it would. It may happen after the coffee break."

Then came the second problem, which had us attacking both a Charlie and one of those nasty quiet Tango diesels. Bourne opted for a virtually simultaneous attack, shooting two units at the Charlie and one at the Tango. I was kept busy at my position alternating analysis between the two targets and recommending the torpedo settings for each, but it worked out fine.

We stopped at 11:30. Captain Bourne called everyone together, including the Federated people. "That went real well, even with a civilian pretending he's a real WEPS. I wanted to see if your people have any more questions, Rick."

Natalie had a few, and Arnold asked what happened if we were way off in our range estimate. I let McGonigal answer that one. Nielsen showed up just as the questions stopped.

Bourne looked at his watch. "Commander Nielsen's going to take you to lunch somewhere and then to the airport for your flight. Before you go, I wanted to thank you for coming out and learning a little about what submarine warfare is like. I hope it'll help you in your work on project, which is very important to the submarine force. If any questions pop up after you've left, give them to Rick. If he can't answer them, he can call the XO or me at any time. And before you leave, I have something for all of you." McGonigal handed him a small stack of cards.

"These are 'Honorary Submariner' cards for each of you, except Rick, of course. Tuck them into your wallet—or purse, Natalie—and use them to impress your friends." It seemed everyone was pleased to receive these. Good.

"What did those two do last night?" I asked Natalie.

"As near as I could tell—they weren't especially coherent this morning—they decided it'd be fun to find some 'sailor bars' in Norfolk. They apparently stumbled on a strip club and spent most of the night there. I think they got back to the VOQ around 2 am."

I had no problem with Owen and Wayne going out on the town, although it seemed a little weird for two married guys to go to a strip club. But not being able to function properly on a business day was totally out of line.

Chapter 58

THE FLIGHT back to San Francisco was relaxing, at least for three of us. I'd punished Owen and Wayne's bad conduct by cancelling their upgrade to business class.

"When you represent Federated, you're expected to handle yourselves professionally. The two of you made a bad impression on the *LOS ANGELES* officers and crew this morning. Think about that on the flight back; we'll talk more about it tomorrow."

They complained that I was being arbitrary, but I pointed out I'd paid out of my own funds to get their luxury seats on the eastbound flight. "If you want to pay your own twenty bucks for an upgrade, feel free. But I'm not going to pay after your behavior today." They actually tried to, but there were no vacant business class seats available. I'd succeeded in getting their attention. On the downside, the airline refused to refund me the money I'd paid for their upgrades.

We arrived at SFO at 6:30 in the evening after a 2:10 departure from Washington National. Natalie, Arnold and I, since we were sitting up front, were in the first group off the plane, while Owen and Wayne were stuck somewhere aft. Rush hour had died down enough that we got to Natalie's house by 7:30. She easily persuaded me to stay.

I left the next morning for my apartment to change into a business suit. Checking my answering machine, I found a message from Ryan Philpott, telling me he "had the package I'd ordered." That had to be the report of the outgoing and incoming phone calls. There was also a plaintive call from Beth, which I erased.

I was in my office by 7:30, before anyone else arrived. There was a stack of inter-office mail in my in box. I'd worked through about half of it when Yolanda arrived, sporting one of her more tantalizing outfits. "Welcome back, boss. Can you and I set aside some time? A few things happened you should know about."

"Meet you in the cafeteria in about ten minutes? I've just got a couple more memos to go through so I can make sure I haven't missed some deadline."

A few minutes later I was in the basement level outside the cafeteria and seized the opportunity to call the NIS office at Treasure Island. Ryan was in and verified that he had the phone records. "It's a pretty thick package—way over a hundred sheets of that large green-bar computer paper. I'll bring it down to Federated if you want." I agreed and he promised to be here within an hour.

I found Yolanda sitting at a table, apparently oblivious to the lustful stares of the male employees in the vicinity. "How did things go while I was gone?"

"Not bad. The big news is that yesterday Phil told me he was taking a job in a different department. I tried to reach you in Norfolk but you'd already left."

"Did he say why?"

"It's always about money with Phil. Or sex; I almost forgot that. I think he got about a five percent bump to take this other job. He cleaned out his desk yesterday and, I suppose, started at his new job this morning. I've got the paperwork filled out for your signature. You've got to fill out an evaluation form rating his work."

"Any other problems?"

"The biggest was that it was just me and Phil for the last two days. He spent most of it hanging around my cubicle and looking down my blouse. I finally had to shoo him away so I could get some work done. How was your trip?"

I gave her a quick-and-dirty summary, including my revocation of Owen and Wayne's upgraded seats on yesterday's flight. "It was a worthwhile trip; I think the people who went came away with a much better understanding of submarine operations. Thanks for the update; I've got to get up and re-attack the paperwork." I wanted to be at my desk when Ryan arrived.

Arnold had left a note on my desk saying Natalie had called, so I returned the call. "How about lunch?" she asked. "I just finished telling my group what we did in Norfolk. They all wish they could have gone. Thanks again for including me."

"You're very welcome and lunch sounds good. Let's do it in town."

"I'll do it wherever you want, sailor boy. Meet you in the lobby at 11:30." Should I take that first sentence literally? Before I could decide, the phone rang again—Ryan was in the lobby.

He gave me a bundle of 11x17 printouts that must have been two hundred pages and weighed five pounds. "These are sorted by home phone number; I wrote the name of the person with each number on the first page of every section. One of them—I think it's Greenwood—has two different phone lines in his house, so he has two sections. The printouts cover the last six months of calls. Enjoy yourself." It was going to take hours to go through that, and I wasn't looking forward to it. I was still pondering it as I crammed them into my safe. I didn't mention them to Yolanda, even though we were supposed to be sharing information. I assumed the FBI had run the same sort of request months ago. Maybe they hadn't been clever enough to get the identity of the calling and called numbers, as Natalie had suggested. If so, Yolanda had probably spent hours trying to find out who the other numbers represented.

At lunch I told Nat I'd received the printouts of the phone data for our colleagues. "Let's work on that tonight," she said immediately. "Maybe we can narrow things down."

I spent the afternoon on administrative paperwork, including my evaluation of Phil's performance. In the Navy, performance reviews are inflated upward to the point where if you rate someone "above average," you've sabotaged that person's chances of promotion. I assumed civilian life was different, so Phil ended up with an overall evaluation of "below average," based on his lazy work habits. All this, plus a report to Greenwood on the results of our Norfolk trip, took me until about six to finish.

Natalie came directly to my apartment from work, and arrived with a ready-to-go attitude. "Let's order some pizza while we work through these phone calls. How do you want to split the work up?"

"I'll call for the pizza and you go through the phone calls."

Ignoring that, she said, "How about I go through your people and you go through mine? I'll handle your five people plus Greenwood and you go through three. Should we even look at Andy's? He's not on the project anymore."

"Doesn't make any difference. He'd have done all his spying before he was transferred. I looked at the amount of detail, and the call volume is heaviest for Andy and Lee Greenwood. Your people don't make or receive nearly as many calls. How about I do your own calls, Andy and Lee, and you do the rest?"

It seemed this annoyed her. "Why would you look at mine? Don't you trust me?"

"I trust you implicitly, but Jack doesn't. If I can tell him there's nothing in your phone records to indicate you're a suspect, I'll have another reason he can stop nagging me."

"How does he 'nag' you?"

"Actually, he keeps suggesting that I shouldn't be involved with you. But that's not open for discussion, so all I can do is keep showing him evidence that you're not one of the spies we're looking for." His "suggestions" were more like direct orders, which I'd been ignoring.

"OK," she sighed. "Pepperoni and extra sausage. And some bread sticks." She sorted the telephone records into stacks by individuals while I called for the delivery order. I'd borrowed a few highlighters from the office so we could mark the calls we thought deserved more research.

"I've got an idea," I offered after calling in the order. "How about you and I go through your own printout together and use it as a template on how we'll label calls that need different types of investigation? Then we can each do our stack, since we'll have a standard way of dealing with the data."

Natalie's call listing actually wasn't very interesting. This was a good thing—an *interesting* call log would be one that was suspicious. We started with her outbound calls. None of these included calls to or from payphone numbers; calls like those would be indications of concealing the identity of the other party. Most of the calls were to girlfriends or to one of the people working for her. A few were to Ted Johansson, who was her boss at Federated. Several, up until the last month or so, were to men she'd dated. The inbound calls were even less out of the ordinary, so as far as phone records could indicate, Natalie looked clean. The bad news was that since we hadn't found anything suspicious, we still hadn't decided how to highlight the questionable calls.

"How are we going to know whether someone who shows up on a call list is a friend, a relative, or a Soviet agent?" Natalie asked. The answer was that we wouldn't, and we could hardly give each of these people a list of the names and ask them to tell us whether they were Soviet agents. Maybe these printouts weren't going to be as valuable as we'd hoped.

"Don't know," I agreed. "Let me look through a few and you do the same. Maybe we'll find some pattern. Any set of call records that show lots of calls to or from a payphone are suspicious. Let's make that our first criterion. Maybe as we work through them some other ideas will pop up." I picked up a random printout and started scanning it.

Natalie was flipping through her stack. "I'll start with Yolanda. I've always been curious about her."

We'd only done a few pages when the food arrived, so we took a break. "Anything pop out at you yet?"

"That girl has no social life," Natalie chuckled. "There aren't any calls to or from a local phone except for a couple of take-out restaurants. She does have a fair amount of calls from a number in DC that belongs to someone called Connor Healey. Maybe that's her boyfriend, but I don't see why she'd be involved with someone all the way across the country."

"Maybe they met out here and he got a job transfer," I offered. Natalie had no need to know about Yolanda's FBI status. At least Healey was smart enough not to place calls from FBI headquarters, now housed in the brand-new building that was named after Hoover. Imagine lobbying for a new building and suggesting it be named after you.

After dinner we kept digging through the files. I did find some payphone calls on a few of the printouts. One of our colleagues had placed several evening calls to a payphone on Lombard Street in San

Francisco. I realized I should have had detailed street maps of all the counties in the Bay Area. Tomorrow I could go by a gas station and pick up whatever they had. I might end up having to buy a Bay Area street atlas, if such a thing existed.

"Natalie, copy down this payphone number in San Francisco and see if it pops up on any of your lists." It was possible that if the same KGB (or GRU?) agent was running both people, he might use the same payphone for both, although that seemed like poor tradecraft. That led us to the idea of making a separate list of all payphone numbers, including the name of the Federated employee and the date and time of the call. If we got multiple hits to or from the same number, it might prove something.

"If you had a home computer, I could enter all this data and then sort it in different ways to identify matches," Natalie groused. Like I was going to get a home computer. Maybe she was hinting that she could take the files home and enter them, which might not be a bad idea.

"There's probably over two thousand calls in this set," I pointed out. "Would your computer have the capacity to work with that much data? You'd need ten digits for each phone number, four for the month and year, four for time of day, and two or three for a code identifying the employee."

"Call it twenty characters; that's 160 bits times 2000 calls, so it's over 300 kilobits. And we'd still need enough room in memory for a program to do the sorting. Let me think about that."

I didn't understand what she'd just said, but had to respond. "And how would we get any output from it? You've got no way to print from your computer, at least not that I saw."

"The worst case is I could sort and then download the data onto a cassette tape. Maybe I could somehow get that into our mainframe at Federated." I gave her a skeptical look and she shrugged. "Probably not a good idea, right?"

Chapter 59

THE NEXT few weeks were routine. Lee Greenwood wanted a lot of my time, including a two-hour session grilling me on our Norfolk trip and covering the same points I'd included in my trip report. The only upside to this attention was that, rather than just calling me and asking me to come up, he'd send the delectable Laura down to ask me in person. This was a morale raiser for the men in the office.

My new boss was a micro-manager who wanted me to ask his approval for every decision I made, despite having promised the opposite. I decided just to make and immediately implement my decisions, notifying him after the fact. I was pushing to see how much I could get away with. So long as he continued to believe I was a protégé of Harris Booth, I'd be bullet-proof unless I screwed the pooch with one of my decisions.

Natalie and I continued our work with the phone records. Mainly because we had no way to determine which names on the call list might be espionage-related, we were focusing on calls to and from payphones. The street atlas I'd bought had shown me that the San Francisco payphone number that two of our colleagues had each called several times was on the west end of Lombard, just before it became Richardson Avenue where it entered the Presidio. This didn't mean much to me at first. Then a minor brainstorm hit me as I realized this phone booth was only a few blocks from the Soviet Consulate on Green Street. It'd be easy to reach for KGB agents for surreptitious calls to or from whoever at Federated was passing secrets. Of course, a cautious agent would avoid making calls from such a handy phone, but maybe these guys were lazy.

On the first weekend after our Norfolk trip, Natalie and I decided to spend the day in the City. On the way to a seafood restaurant near Ghirardelli Square, we detoured to drive past the consulate and from there to the phone booth, which sat in an ARCO gas station. No one wearing a cloak or sporting a dagger was hanging out there at the time, but it did seem a very convenient location for its presumed purpose. I pulled over and used the suspect payphone to call Sammon, knowing he was usually in the office on Saturday. I explained the payphone situation and suggested he see if the phone could be tapped. He seemed pleased, and promised a tap would be in place within a few days.

Over lunch, Natalie brought up the possibility of her leaving Federated. There were, she told me, a few interesting opportunities surfacing at the Homebrew meetings.

I found this out myself when she dragged me to my first experience with these people. I'd never been in the Stanford Linear Accelerator facility, so at least the meeting would have one upside. Natalie was, it seemed, a favorite of many of the other attendees, probably because she was by far the most attractive female in the room. There were possibly four or five other women in the meeting I went to, although I wasn't sure of the gender of two of them. Homebrew was only a few months old at the time and was, Natalie told me, just getting to the point where the meetings were productive.

An older guy named Felsenstein—I never caught his first name— tried to moderate the session, but trying to maintain structure in this group of free spirits was a challenge. A lot of the talk centered on trying to set technical standards for personal computers. I sat patiently through the entire meeting, hopefully looking as though I was having a great time. Sitting next to Natalie was always nice, but the other stuff? Not so much.

When the formal meeting ended, Natalie dragged me to a bar on El Camino in Menlo Park. "The Oasis" was, she told me, where most of the interesting conversations took place. It seemed to me that the main point of going there was so the guys could all hit on Natalie. We spent a few hours there drinking beer and talking, although it was clear I was never going to be in the in-group of this club. The dweebs obviously resented my presence as Natalie's escort and presumed boyfriend. From the looks of them, dressed as I used to be before Debbie took charge of my wardrobe, their social lives were rather limited.

Chapter 60

ON A DISMAL Wednesday morning in November, dark rain drenching the parking lot, I received a call from the security guard in the lobby. It was Uncle Ralph again.

Once we were seated in the cafeteria, Pete began, "I've been thinking about this deal you proposed. I can see where it makes sense. But handing over the information you want demands a quid pro quo."

"Like what?"

"Well, our mutual goal is for you to get command of a nuclear submarine, preferably one of the *LOS ANGELES* class. 'State of the art,' you know. So we want to make sure there aren't any obstacles to you getting selected."

"Nailing the guys who are passing info to the Rodina will be a big plus in that area," I said with an edge of sarcasm.

"I hope that'll give you an advantage, Rick. But there's something else that might cause problems."

I waited him out silently.

"It's Natalie. I still feel that someone with a background like hers will make the Navy think twice about giving you command."

"Pete, she has a Top Secret clearance—not many Navy wives can say that. I don't see why she'd be any sort of obstacle to my getting command."

"That may be, although I suspect the Navy takes a closer look at the private lives of prospective commanding officers than you think. But Rick, it's not just Natalie, although she's a big problem. You need to understand you can't get married or even have a serious relationship. Ever. Period."

"Why the hell not?"

"Think it out, laddie. At some point in the future, once you've had command of a submarine, the Motherland's going to want you back so you can pass on all you've learned. You'll come back as a big hero and get the good life all the nomenklatura[87] enjoy. But you can't bring an

---

[87] The Soviet "nomenklatura" was made up of senior Party officials, who

American wife back to that—too much of a security risk and lots of bad publicity. So enjoy the American girls. Screw all of them you want to, but no serious relationships. And that's why Natalie has to go—she's become your top priority in life, instead of your mission."

I'd never really bought into what the Soviets thought of as my real purpose, but I realized Pete was right—if I actually were a loyal and successful mole here, I'd have to go back at some point so the State could reap the rewards of all I'd done. This would probably consist of years of debriefing sessions. Apparently, so long as Pete was around, which I hoped wouldn't be much longer, I'd be restricted to casual sex. And there was the minor thing that I'd have to walk away from Natalie.

"So you want me to dump her?" I asked with as much sarcasm as I could.

"In a manner of speaking, yes. But it has to be done so you can never change your mind and go back to her. It has to be a permanent solution."

"So you want me to cheat on her, or do something to totally turn her away from me?"

"Nope. I said *permanent*, in case you weren't paying attention. I want you to kill her. That's the only way I can be sure she'll be out of your life."

I just stared at him. I'd known Pete was capable of violence and murder, as exemplified in his vicious rape of Natalie. But I hadn't expected anything like this. Finally I was able to speak. "Pete, I can't and won't do that."

He actually looked sad, but he'd always been a competent actor. "Believe me, it'd be best if you did. The alternative is that I do it, because one way or another she has to die. You know as well as I do that you two would find your way back to each other so long as you're both alive. Look at how you managed to reconnect with her after eight years.

"Now, if *you* do it, you can make it quick and painless so she'll never see it coming. If I do it—well, it'll take a long time and it'll be ugly, but I admit it's the kind of thing I enjoy. I can promise she'll be begging me to kill her days before I actually finish her off. I can even mail you little pieces to show my progress. Maybe a finger, a toe, an eye—she has beautiful eyes, doesn't she?—and finally her heart. Or maybe her head. Would you rather have that happen, or will you do it yourself?" He was convincing as a murderer, as I was sure the ghosts of the original Emily and Ricky could testify.

I wasn't going to hurt Natalie in any way, but I needed to string Pete along until I could get whatever he was going to cough up on the people

---

got better housing, food, and other special privileges. It's taken from a Latin word, meaning to assign a name to someone or something.

giving up information to the KGB. "I'll tell you what," I offered. "After you get me the information you promised, we'll discuss how to do that. Obviously I don't want to, but I sure as hell don't want you torturing her."

"That's not how it works. First you kill her, *then* you get the information."

"No. You can try to kill us both off, but I'm not even considering killing Natalie until I've got the data you promised." And after that I still wouldn't be considering it. I'd be working out a way to eliminate Peter and get away with it.

"Rick, I've told you how it has to go. I need to know she's out of the way—forever—before I give you what you asked for. It'll take me at least a week or two to put everything together for you. In the meantime, give some thought to how you're going to do it. Run your plan by me; the last thing I want is for you to get nailed on a murder charge. That's why the smart thing would be for me to handle it, but because I've got a soft spot for you, I'm willing to give you a break on this. And Natalie too, when you think about it."

"I have no idea how to murder someone and get away with it," I admitted, marveling at Pete's belief he had a "soft spot."

"It's important to make sure she disappears completely. And set things up so that if she is found, it'll look like a random act of violence not tied to you. Make it difficult for the body to even be identified. You could take a walk with her in some isolated place, like down near Crystal Springs Lake in the evening, or somewhere in one of the county parks. Take her to an area where no one else is around. Then shoot her in the head from behind and drag the body somewhere where people won't stumble across it. I can give you a.22 pistol with a good silencer; you'll have to dump it after the operation. And bring me hard proof—like a Polaroid photo of her body and the bullet hole in her head, or one of her fingers. If you can do it, it's a good idea to cut off both hands and the head and put them somewhere where they'll never be found, or at least miles away from the rest of the body. Strip the body of any identification. If it's found, we want to make sure the police would have a hell of a time figuring out who she was." It sounded like he was talking from experience, which might include murders like that of the midshipman whose body may have turned up in Chesapeake Bay.

"Say," Pete said as an afterthought. "Are you any good with a pistol? We can hardly have you pulling off multiple shots with bullets going everywhere."

"I shot two clips with a Colt 1911 back when I was a midshipman." A true statement, but very misleading. I didn't want Pete to know about my upgraded skill level with a handgun.

"We'll talk later about the details. Just remember—Natalie has to die if you want to get that information you asked for. That's not open to negotiation, so get used to the idea. I'll be in touch." IIe walked out, leaving me wondering how I could protect Natalie from this monster.

Chapter 61

I HAD TO decide whether I should tell Natalie about Pete's insistence that she die. I suspected this might upset her if I didn't use all the tact at my disposal. Actually, I'd probably need more tact than I had.

This evening we'd agreed she'd come to my place, we'd go out for dinner and then spend the night doing whatever came to our minds. She'd be at the apartment by six.

All the way home I puzzled over how to present Pete's ultimatum to her. Her first reaction might be that it was a very sick joke. But once she realized it was serious, who knew what'd pop into her mind? She might think I was actually insane, or that it was a desperate attempt to have her break up with me, or ... I couldn't think of any others, but I was sure any reaction she had would be a very bad one.

I was still worrying about it when Natalie arrived. She looked so happy she almost brought tears to my eyes. I had to do whatever I could to keep Pete from getting his hands on her. My 20/20 hindsight had already told me I should never have approached Pete to turn in the Federated traitors. Too late now to do anything about that.

Pouring her a glass of white wine, I decided to let her enjoy the evening until after dinner. Then I could ruin her life.

The time went all too fast, and by eight we were back in my apartment. Natalie had, naturally, seen through my pathetic attempts to act normally. "OK, Rick, what's bothering you? You were mopey and distracted all through dinner."

"No matter how I do this, it's going to be tough for you to hear. Sit down; I'll get you a glass of wine."

"Make it brandy instead. A big one. Is this going to be a kiss-off?"

I put her drink on the table next to her and sat down. "It's not a kiss-off—you and I will be together for the rest of our lives if it's up to me. But it *is* bad news. You won't be surprised to hear this all starts with Peter. Today he showed up at the office and ... well, he told me that I couldn't ever have a serious relationship with any woman, and especially not with you. He thinks that eventually I'll be taken back to the USSR so I can be milked for all I know, and that being married, or even seriously involved with a woman, would make that difficult."

"So you have to convince him you dumped me? We could pretend that for a while until we manage to get rid of him."

"I definitely want to terminate him, and as soon as he gives me the proof I need to nail whoever's spying, I'll do it. The problem is that his demand involves more than you and I just separating."

"Like what? I don't understand."

This was going to be awkward. "Honey, Pete said that you have to die—otherwise, he'd never be sure we wouldn't get back together."

"Die? Are you saying Pete's going to kill me?"

"Actually, he suggested it'd be more compassionate if I did it. He said ... I'm not going to tell you what he said he'd do, but it's much worse than anything you can imagine."

"So the plan is that to make things better for me, *you'll* kill me?" She sounded incredulous.

"That's Pete's plan. What we have to do is find a way to convince him I killed you. Obviously, by then you'll need to be safely concealed until he's eliminated. He's promised me that as soon as I present absolute proof of your death, he'll hand over incriminating evidence proving who at Federated has been passing classified information to the Soviets. Once he does that, I'll take him out."

"I'll bet you it'll be harder to kill him than you might think. And more dangerous."

"Look, sweetheart, both of us want to get this problem out of our lives forever. Once Pete's eliminated, things will be a lot easier to manage." After that, what I thought was most likely was that whoever was above Pete in the KGB food chain would try to eliminate me in retribution. I was hoping no one from the KGB would be worried enough about Natalie to go after her.

She was clearly skeptical, but had more questions. "Exactly how do you plan to 'prove' you killed me without actually doing it?"

"I'm still working on that. He demanded photographic proof that you were dead, so we've got to come up with a photo that does that conclusively. And maybe some other item, like a finger or an ear. He's a smart guy, and won't be easy to fool."

"A body part? Where would you get such a thing?" she asked dubiously.

"I have no idea. Maybe I can find a way to get it from a police morgue." That sounded far-fetched even to me, but I needed to see how she'd react. The main thing was to convince her that I'd go to any length to protect her, squeeze the information out of Pete, and then terminate him. At that point, she could resume her normal life..

Natalie sat in silence for a long moment.

"You know," she finally said, "I'd never have met Pete if I hadn't met you. He's the worst thing that's ever happened in my life, and I thought you were the best. I'd give anything—even giving you up if I had to—if I could be sure Pete would never come into my life again. If you love me like you say you do, you'll find a way to do that. Until then ..." her voice trailed off.

"What? Until what?" I asked. Talk about déjà vu.

"Maybe we shouldn't see each other until this whole thing's resolved. Maybe I should just take a vacation and go away somewhere until you've gotten rid of that bastard."

"Honey, going away like that wouldn't solve anything. I'm sure Pete's keeping an eye on you somehow, and if you went away, he'd be likely to come after you and ... let's just say it wouldn't work out well."

She glared at me. "Look," she hissed, "maybe you've scared me enough about the vacation idea that I won't do that. But I'm sure as hell not going to loll around assuming you'll come up with some foolproof plan to fool Pete. I've got to take control of my own life. I'm going home now to think this whole thing over. I'll call you." She slammed the door behind her on her way out.

"That could have gone better," I murmured. Hopefully she'd come around to my way of thinking enough so that we could work together to devise as foolproof a plan as would be possible under these strange circumstances.

Chapter 62

A FTER SHE left, I sat trying to figure out how I could get the documents from Peter without endangering Natalie, let alone killing her or letting her be killed.

The toughest obstacle would be convincing a very skeptical and canny Peter that I'd had killed the only woman I'd ever loved. That would be based on my word, which he'd doubt, and on photographs he'd view with the utmost suspicion. The possibility of producing a body part that he'd believe came from Natalie seemed very remote, but maybe after a week or so to think about it, I'd come up with something.

"Concentrate on the photo part to begin with," I mumbled to myself.

My first problem was that I knew absolutely nothing about what damage a pistol shot would do to a human skull, or what that damage would look like. Maybe some library research was called for. It was too late tonight to hit a library, so I made a list of the possible wounds and side effects of a bullet piercing a human skull. I thought the entrance wound would probably be smaller and neater than the exit wound, but wasn't sure that a .22 such as Pete wanted to give me would have enough punch to exit, or if it'd just rattle around inside the skull. If the silencer slowed down the muzzle velocity, the "rattle around" outcome seemed more likely. What kind of holes would it make on both sides? How much difference would caliber and muzzle velocity make? Would Pete expect to see powder burns from a close shot? What kind of inside-the-head gunk, if any, would be expected around an exit wound?

Norm Connors, it occurred to me, might be a great source of help and advice here. Of course, I'd have to come up with an excellent story on why I needed to know how to convince someone from a photo that the victim was definitely dead.

I had lots of questions and very little information. Unfortunately, most of this didn't sound like stuff you'd expect to find in a public library.

Maybe I could connect with a local coroner or pathologist; again, Norm might be of help. Getting the expert's trust would probably be a prerequisite to grilling them on matters like this. I didn't want to be turned in as a potential serial killer, like that Zodiac[88] killer and his escapades in San Francisco years ago.

Sammon, or even Ryan Philpott, might know enough about handguns and ballistics to answer those questions, but I couldn't ask them about it without raising curiosity and suspicion in the minds of men who were trained to doubt everything.

Absent a brainstorm which was lacking so far, I couldn't come up with a way to produce a spare body part as evidence. Pete was probably savvy enough to be able to tell whether a finger, for example, had come from a male or a female. Avoiding the body part issue would solve a lot of problems, but that put the burden on me to come up with other evidence, probably photographic, that'd be so convincing that I could get away with it.

Until I could start actual research, I decided to try to "game out" how we might be able to fool Pete. I could put together a scenario and then try to look at it from his much more experienced viewpoint to see where the holes in my scheme might lie. Then modify the scheme and try again. If I could get Natalie to participate, her sharp mind might find inconsistencies or flaws that I couldn't see. Right now, however, it'd be best to leave her alone for a few days to calm down.

---

[88] The Zodiac killer was active in the 1960's in Northern California. He was never caught, if you don't count Clint Eastwood's triumph in the first Dirty Harry movie, in which the killer was known as "Scorpio."

Chapter 63

SEVERAL weeks later, I still hadn't come up with a foolproof plan for photographing a fake execution of Natalie. As a first step, I'd bought a high-quality Polaroid color camera (an SX-70) and practiced extensively with it to make sure I'd get a photo of realistic quality. The practice was necessary, since it was a finicky camera that seemed to have its own mind. Practice makes, if not perfect, then good enough. The camera itself was almost two hundred dollars; you don't want to know how expensive the film packs were.

Thanks to the Stanford library, I'd learned more—lots more than I wanted to know—about the gruesome results of a head shot. Depending on the caliber of the bullet, the wound could be quite small or horrifically large, with various types of skull contents leaking out.

It didn't seem wise to explain all this to Natalie. She was smart and logical, so I needed to have everything lined up so well that she'd trust me to do this properly. There wouldn't be any do-overs; we had to do it perfectly on our single opportunity. Another week or so and I thought I'd have everything in hand to get this horrific task out of the way, hopefully leaving Natalie and me unscathed and rid of the menace of Pete.

Clausewitz, or someone else from the 19th century, had said that no plan survives contact with the enemy[89]. I was to learn that only too well.

This had been a dismal time for me; Natalie and I had seen each other at work now and then, but hadn't spent any real time together, except for a dinner at which she tried to come up with an alternative to what I'd suggested.

She'd suggested that she just temporarily disappear and take a job somewhere else until the Pete mess was cleared up. I persuaded her this wouldn't work. There was no way she could put together, on short notice, a false identity that'd offer her any kind of life. She wouldn't have any educational credentials, so she'd probably be limited to menial jobs of various kinds.

---

[89] Rick should have known better. It was actually Helmuth von Moltke who coined that phrase years after Clausewitz died.

When Natalie realized that wouldn't work, she tried other options. "Maybe I could just book a room under a different name somewhere far away—Florida, Maine, somewhere in Canada?" she offered. "I could pay in cash so there's no identity trail, and just wait it out until you've taken care of Pete." She was back to the idea of solving the problem with a vacation, even though I'd explained that'd put her into immediate danger.

"Honey, Pete will be expecting something like that. We have to have convincing proof that you're definitely dead, or he'll take things into his own hands." Meaning that Natalie would be his plaything for a horrible interval until he finally killed her.

She glared at me and stayed silent for the rest of the dinner, after which she stalked out without a word. The next day she offered a weak apology, but told me—again—that we shouldn't see much of each other outside work. "For the time being," she added. That didn't help much.

I missed her badly, but was probably going to have to get used to that feeling.

My days at Federated were tolerable. I was seeing signs of morale improvement, and the Monday meeting seemed much more productive focusing on problems rather than recapping history. I didn't really care about any of that—my entire focus was on how to fool Pete into believing Natalie was dead. I thought I was getting close to a solution— just another week or so and I'd have the details worked out. But I'd run out of time and didn't know it until too late.

Pete called me at my apartment on a Wednesday evening in November. "We can meet tomorrow, or Friday at the latest. I've got all the stuff you asked for on these people at Federated. I'll hand over transcriptions of conversations with them, copies of checks written to them, and so on. You'll have more than enough to nail them. Are you ready on your end?"

"I could use another day or two," I hedged.

"All you're going to do is shoot the bitch," Pete snarled. "By now you've had plenty of time to figure where and how to do it. You know I'm going to need solid proof; don't try to pass off some half-ass photographs. Once I'm sure she's dead, I'll hand this material over to you. Then you can wind up this project as a big hero and go back to your real job—getting command of one of the newer nuclear submarines."

"How about next Monday or Tuesday? I'm kind of busy right now." That sounded lame even to me.

"Tomorrow or Friday. That's it. If you aren't ready I'll do it myself— my way. Now, how do I get the pistol to you?"

"Actually, I went out and bought one myself. It's a .38 revolver, not a pistol. It doesn't take a silencer, but for where I'm planning to do this, I won't need one."

"Have you ever shot it?"

"I went to a range in Cupertino and shot a few dozen rounds so I could get used to it." A true but misleading sentence. Of course, I'd shot dozens of clips with my 9 mm, but nothing with the .38 I'd gotten a few days ago under a false name. That would have been next week's goal.

"Is it registered with the police?"

"I didn't think that'd be a good idea. Anyway, my plan is to ditch it immediately afterwards."

"Don't ditch the weapon in one piece. Field-strip it and drop different parts miles away from each other, preferably in different police jurisdictions." I had no idea if a revolver could be field-stripped.

"Good idea. I'll do it that way." Or not—getting rid of a weapon before meeting with Peter might not be wise.

"Where are you going to do her?"

"I found a good spot—quiet and secluded. That's all you need to know." If I told him the "where" he might find a way to show up to witness the killing. That couldn't happen.

"Make sure you bring me something that convinces me you've done her."

"You'll be satisfied with the proof I bring. But Peter—don't jerk me around on this. You know my feelings for Natalie, so you have to hold up your end on this. Things will get ugly if you've forced me to eliminate her and you don't hold up your end of the bargain."

Pete went on as though I hadn't said anything. "Get some paper and a pencil. I'll give you directions to where we'll meet Thursday night." His directions started with what might be called the "city center" of La Honda—a two-block stretch. From there I was to head north on highway 84 and then west on gravel and dirt roads. Pete's directions involved using my odometer to make a series of turns on unmarked roads. "At 0.2 miles after that last turn," he finished, "pull over next to a white post on the right side of the road. My car will be parked nearby. There's a footpath heading uphill. The place I'll be waiting is a ways up that path. Be there at exactly 8 pm. I don't need to tell you to come alone." He hung up.

I'd start my journey with Natalie and end up alone. Really alone.

"Let's see," I mumbled out loud. "If I need to be at Pete's location by 8, I'll have to have finished with Natalie by no later than 7. It's only a few miles, but the roads suck and in the dark it may be slow going." This told me I'd have to take Natalie from her home no later than six— preferably earlier—to make sure I'd have time to do all that had to be done. I'd only have one shot at this (pardon the pun), so it'd be prudent to leave enough time so I wouldn't be rushed.

There were lots of things that could go wrong, but I thought I'd done all I could to minimize the probability of the whole plan crashing.

Now it was time to use my submarine training and check and re-check everything I'd need. I still had some items to buy and a few phone calls to make. The first would be the most difficult.

"Hello?" Natalie answered tentatively.

"It's me, honey." I could either build up to the message slowly or just smack her with it. "Tomorrow is it. You and I need to leave your house no later than 5:30 tomorrow, so you may have to leave work a little early."

A long silence ensued, until it got to the point where I was about to speak again. "I'm not sure I want to do this," she finally said, her voice breaking a little.

"There's really no alternative at this point, Natalie. We've been over this several times. You'll have to trust me."

"Maybe it'd be better if I just disappeared," she offered hesitantly.

We'd been over this ground before, but I was willing to plow it again. "If you use your real identity, Pete could track you down in no time. Then you'd be at his mercy, of which he has none. Or you could try a fake name and re-invent yourself, but you wouldn't have credentials to allow you to work at the level you are now. Maybe you could be a checkout clerk in a supermarket. And it'd have to be a long ways from here. You'd lose your home, your savings—everything."

"I know, I know," she sighed. After a long pause, she said, "I'll be here tomorrow afternoon on time. See you then." She hung up without a goodbye, let alone an endearment.

Chapter 64

THURSDAY MORNING. There was much I had to do before this evening. I phoned in to work with a fake sick call, telling Yolanda I might be out the next day also. I actually was sick at heart. Did that count?

I made a few necessary phone calls and spent the morning running around picking up everything I'd need for the horrible evening. Extra color film for the Polaroid, a powerful flashlight, an entrenching tool, ammunition, a new pair of outdoor boots ... the list wasn't very long, and I'd finished by lunchtime, with all my equipment packed into a duffel bag.

As the afternoon wore on, my anxiety and worries grew. I could think of dozens of ways I could screw this up, starting with failing to overcome Pete's skepticism. My preparations and proof had to be airtight.

After setting the apartment's alarm system, I carried my gear down to the car and started on the drive to Natalie's. I'd allowed for rush hour, during which traffic on major arteries slows to a crawl all over the Bay Area, so I reached her place at 5:15.

Natalie opened the door before I could press the doorbell. She'd apparently been watching out for me. "Let's get this over with," she said in lieu of an actual greeting. Her mood, as I'd expected, was grim and unforgiving. She was sure I'd gotten her into this terrible situation and, as usual, she was right. Without intending to, I'd put her into a horrible predicament.

The weather was gray and rainy, slowing us down. It took us about forty minutes to get to the entrance of Memorial Park. I'd seen a dark blue car behind us all the way from the 280 to the park, but it kept on going when we turned in. The visitor parking lot was empty; I breathed a sigh of relief. That'd make things a lot easier.

We pulled on rain parkas and trudged, with me carrying my duffel bag of equipment, several miles into the park and into the western "Primitive" area of the park, a large expanse that was totally wild, with no trails, signs, or other indications of civilization. I'd scoped this out last week. I led the way far into the Primitive area, almost to the western edge of the park and well away from anywhere other visitors might go.

"This'll do," I said as we reached a large clearing within the redwoods.

She looked around fearfully, tears rolling down her cheeks.

"Give me your pistol," I told her.

"Why? Are you going to shoot me with my own weapon?"

"You know very well what we're going to do here. Give it to me."

Reluctantly, she handed her 9mm to me; a clip was inserted, but the firing chamber was empty. I pushed the clip release, thumbed out the rounds and replaced them with several rounds from my pocket. Slapping the clip back into the handgrip, I pocketed the pistol.

I set my gear down on the ground and pulled out my revolver. I flipped open the cylinder to triple-check the load and then snapped it back into place.

"Do we have to do this? Does it have to end this way?" Natalie asked, her cheeks wet with tears.

"We've been over this, sweetheart. There's no other way." I raised the pistol and she lowered her head, staring blankly at the ground.

The sharp cracking noise of the shot was absorbed within the forest as Natalie crumpled to the ground. Only one shot was necessary. Looking down, I saw her huge green eyes open and staring at me. "I'll never love anyone else," I murmured as I knelt beside her. I had a lot to do before I was finished here.

Ten minutes later I had my color photos. They'd come out well, showing gory details of the entrance and exit wounds as well as some shots of her body lying limply on the forest floor. I put my equipment back into the duffel bag and headed back toward the park entrance without looking back. The rain was coming down more steadily now, making my mood even more depressed.

Looking at my watch, I was surprised to see it was a few minutes after seven. I couldn't be late at Pete's—the man was anal about being exactly on time. But so was I, leaving me little room to complain. I was in the car by 7:15, but in the gathering darkness and rain it took me longer than I'd thought to find the white post he'd directed me to. I might have missed it except for the Studebaker parked nearby. I could see a muddy trail leading up the slope and thought I saw a light near the top of the hill.

Glancing at my watch, I could see it was 7:50. If I was to be at the cabin by eight, I should probably start now. Going up that muddy path would be slow, but I could use the time to put myself into the role I had to play.

Chapter 65

THE PATH was worse than I'd expected. The rain had softened the ground to the point where my boots sunk in deeply, forcing me to pause to pull my foot out of the mud with each step. It took me until a few minutes before eight to reach the small cabin.

I'd intended to walk up to the door and knock, but a figure emerged from behind a tree. "Hold it right there!" he said sharply. It wasn't Pete. I took a close look and realized it was Johnny Ross, aka Giovanni Rossi.

"Johnny!" I said heartily. "Or is it Giovanni? Remember me?"

Apparently he did. "Hey, Rick. Too bad I had to give you all that shit back in the day. I had no idea we were on the same side." We hadn't been then and we weren't now, but why tell him that?

"Sorry, man, but I've got to take whatever weapons you have. Peter's careful about stuff like that. You don't mind, do you?"

"Here you go," I said cheerfully, hauling Natalie's 9 mm out of my pocket and handing it to him butt first. He looked it over briefly and pointed it in my direction.

"Come on in, Rick," I heard Peter call from inside the cabin. I stepped forward and Johnny fell into place on my left and slightly behind me. It was a cramped and shoddy little space, certainly not Pete's actual lair.

Behind the table Pete was smiling. "Let's see the proof."

"I've got to reach into my pocket," I said, not wanting to be shot for making a move Rossi might misinterpret. I turned slightly toward Johnny so he could see I was reaching into the breast pocket of my shirt. I drew out a sheaf of Polaroid photos and then turned back to Pete.

"I did what you said I had to," I told him, placing the first photograph face up in front of him. The color picture was a close-up of Natalie's head and upper body. Her eyes were staring vacantly, and around a hole in the side of her skull was a mess of blood and brains. Her mouth was agape, and a trickle of blood was running down her chin. I heard Johnny gasping behind me.

"That's the exit wound," I explained. "Here's a photo of the entrance wound. It's a lot smaller and cleaner."

"Jesus," Pete hissed, staring at both pictures. "That's her, all right. I never thought you'd have the guts to do this."

"You didn't offer much of a choice. The alternative was that you'd do it over a few days, throwing in torture and rape. This seemed like a better end for her. She never saw it coming."

I added a couple of other photos, showing her lying face-down on the forest floor.

"What'd you do with her?"

"We were in a remote area of one of the county parks here—a place way off the paths where almost no one ever goes. The park was completely empty when I was there; no cars in the parking lot, probably because of the crappy weather. Anyway, the ground around the redwoods is soft and easy to dig. I buried her about three feet deep. I moved a big fallen branch and some good-sized rocks on top to keep the critters away." I flipped down a final picture showing the grave site.

Both men stared at the pictures.

"Now it's your turn," I said. "You promised me the documentation—complete documentation—once I delivered my end of the deal."

"Just a minute, lad. What'd you do to make it look like she ran off on her own?"

"Her car's still at her house and she hadn't told anyone that she and I were going anywhere tonight. I told her it was a secret and she had to keep it quiet. Tomorrow they'll wonder why she's not at work, but nothing will happen during the weekend. Maybe early next week they'll get worried enough to send someone to check it out. It'll be a mystery. Now give me the documentation."

He hesitated, and then reached behind him and pulled up an accordion file from the floor.

"Here's all the stuff for the two of them. The first half is for one of them and the second for the other, and the sections are labeled indicating whether it holds check copies, transcripts of telephone conversations, actual data handed over, and so on."

I leafed through them and was impressed. The identities didn't totally surprise me; one was my prime suspect and the other had been number three on my list. If this was valid data that'd check out, I now knew who my two bad boys were.

"When do you plan to turn this stuff over to your boss?" Pete asked.

"I'll need to go through it and slip in some stuff of my own, like analysis of their phone calls and notes on their behavior at work. That'll probably take me a few days, so I'll hand it in early next week."

Now it was time to do something I'd been waiting a long time to do. First I turned to check out Johnny. He still had Natalie's pistol in his hand. I pulled out one of the papers from the folder and walked over to stand next to Pete. "Can you explain this?" I asked.

Pete peered at the paper as I pulled my .38 from my jacket pocket and pushed it firmly into his left ear. He froze.

"What's this all about, Rick?" he asked in a wheedling tone. He thought he could talk his way out of this.

I leaned over and whispered three words in his ear. Pete's eyes widened and he made a reflexive move toward what I assumed was his weapon. I squeezed the trigger and watched the other side of his skull explode out. What a satisfying moment that was.

I turned back to Johnny, who'd just pulled the trigger on Natalie's pistol and been rewarded with the soft "pop" sound of a snap cap practice round.

"Don't kill me, Rick. You and I go back a long way," he begged pathetically. The fact that he was still futilely pulling the trigger, apparently expecting a different result, took out a lot of the sincerity out of his appeal.

"All the way back to when you bragged about banging Natalie," I smiled. I shot him in his right shoulder and pried the useless pistol out of his hand. Better to disable him in case he had another weapon.

I went over to Pete and found a pistol in his jacket. It was a Colt 1911, the same type of weapon that'd been used on Detweiler. I put it in my pants pocket and turned back to Johnny, who was sitting on the floor, legs spread and moaning in pain.

"Now, Johnny, you're going to tell me where Pete's house is."

"I don't know. Honest!" he sobbed. I fired a round from my revolver, hitting the floor between his legs a few inches from his crotch. "Oops," I muttered, "I missed! Before I try again, give me the answer I'm looking for."

"I'll tell you! Just don't shoot again," he pleaded. "It's off Highway 84 south of La Honda. I don't know the address, but I know how to get there." I frisked him quickly, finding no other weapons, and tied his feet together to keep him out of my way for a few minutes.

I started by searching Pete's pockets. I wanted to find something that'd lead me to where he lived, in case Johnny failed me. There'd be, I hoped, more evidence, possibly including something that might identify me as a mole. He wasn't carrying a wallet, but I found a small black book, the kind used to list phone numbers and addresses in. I pocketed that and continued searching Pete, including inside his shoes. I drew the line at searching his underwear.

A thorough search of the small cabin didn't reveal anything, leaving only Pete's car to search for clues. Tucking the accordion folder, now also containing my Polaroid photos, under my arm, I clumped down the muddy path to the road, leaving Johnny moaning in pain behind me. I put the folder in my car and went over to the Hawk. A search there finally yielded his wallet, which was jammed under the passenger seat.

Going through it by the light of my flashlight, I didn't immediately see anything giving me his address; the driver's license was the same "Ralph Flynn" card he'd used at Federated, with the PO box address. The car registration was in a holder clipped to the visor, and that showed the same unhelpful address. The glove box was empty except for a couple of road maps, which I took, along with the wallet and registration.

Getting a little desperate, I unlocked the trunk. Apart from the spare tire, nothing seemed to be in there except for a large pipe wrench. I pulled up the carpeting and found … nothing. What next? Back into the passenger compartment, where I looked under all the seats, and under the carpet. I sat in the driver's seat for a few minutes, wondering if there was actually nothing here to find. I couldn't spend more time on this. In the very remote case that someone had heard the shots, I needed to leave the area.

I went back up to the cabin, untied Johnny's feet and helped him to stand. "Walk in front of me going down to my car. Then you're going to drive—with my pistol in your ear—to Pete's place." He'd be a poor driver with his right shoulder and arm out of commission, but that was certainly better than me driving while he sat figuring out how to overcome me.

Chapter 66

THE DRIVE to Pete's house took longer than I'd hoped. The rural area around La Honda didn't have much in the way of road signs or house numbers, and the rain hampered visibility. Johnny made a number of wrong turns, driving awkwardly with only his left arm functioning. After twenty minutes of driving around, we arrived at what Johnny assured me was Pete's place. On a twisty road leading east from 84, it was set back several hundred feet from the dirt road, and was shielded by a heavy growth of underbrush, making it invisible from the road.

I suspected it might be booby-trapped, and there was only one way to find out. "OK, Johnny, you lead the way in. I'll be right behind you." Actually I was about ten paces back, to minimize the chance I'd be hurt by whatever trap my radical friend might activate.

If there were traps, Johnny didn't seem worried about them. He climbed the front steps, walked to the front door and pulled it open. "Stop there!" I told him and walked up to about ten feet behind him. "OK, now go in." Johnny took several steps into the room without causing an explosion, and I had him halt again.

Then I forced a laborious routine of ordering Johnny to walk around the various areas of the house, open all the various doors, drawers, etc., and generally act as my mine canary until I decided it was safe. I was surprised at the neatness and cleanliness of the little cabin, but there were few personal touches here—other than clothes and cooking utensils, it looked like a vacant furnished house.

Now that my little radical had done what he could to help me, he'd become expendable. Letting Johnny live seemed counter-productive. If I released him, it was almost certain that people who shouldn't would soon know I'd done away with Pete. Besides, it wasn't like he was a great human being to begin with. So far as I was concerned, his part in aiding and abetting Natalie's brutal rape was enough for a death sentence. My thoughts must have showed on my face. "Come on, man," he pleaded. "I did what you asked. And I swear I'll never tell anybody what happened here." You shouldn't be surprised to learn I didn't believe him. I was sure that if I freed him, I'd have the Oakland chapter of the Black

Panthers and various Bay Area communist and radical organizations hunting me down.

"I really appreciate your help, Johnny. Now take a seat while I prowl around a little." I had to keep him immobilized, and I happened to have handcuffs and rope in my duffel bag. Always remember the "6P Rule[90]." In a few minutes I had him securely trussed to a wooden chair in Pete's kitchen. I thoughtfully added a tight gag, consisting of one of his socks, knotted around his neck and between his teeth. He didn't like this; I didn't blame him, having been able to smell the sock from several feet away, but I didn't want to put up with his whining while I looked around.

"Now be a good boy for a few minutes."

This was just a preliminary search for low-hanging fruit, which I didn't expect much of. There were all kinds of things I wanted to find here—who he reported to up the chain, what other illegals like me were being run by him, and so on. Most importantly, what could be here that would identify me as a Soviet mole? Tonight I could perhaps find a few nuggets, and afterwards, with proper precautions, I could search more extensively.

Without prying up the floorboards, tapping for hollow places on the walls, and other intrusive actions, I found nothing. After my cursory inspection, I decided it was time to leave for both me and Johnny. He wouldn't be coming back.

"Thanks for your help," I told him, more or less sincerely, as I undid his bonds. "Now we're going to get back into my car. I'll drive this time." Once he was in the car I tied his arms behind his back. His right shoulder and arm were probably causing him a lot of pain. Too bad. He was still gagged, so all he could do was give me a piteous helpless look and make a gurgling noise in his throat.

Twenty minutes later I was back at Memorial Park. I helped my prisoner out of the car. "I'll tell you which way to walk. Don't try to run—you won't be going very fast with your hands behind your back and you can't outrun a bullet anyway."

It took longer than it had when I made the same walk with Natalie, but it'd been lighter then and she hadn't had her hands tied. We arrived at the same place. "Look familiar from the photos?" I asked cheerfully. "Kneel down."

He shook his head violently, but awkwardly knelt when I raised the pistol. "Are you religious, Johnny?" He shook his head again.

---

[90] 6P = "Prior Planning Prevents Piss-Poor Performance."

"I guess it's up to me to do the rites. Tell Pete, when you see him in hell, that I wish I could've taken more time killing him. Rest in peace." I shot him in the forehead with no regrets whatsoever. Pretty good shooting today, I mused. Not counting Pete, two accurate shots, counting my shoulder shot into Johnny; three if I counted the deliberate near miss near his crotch. I didn't have time to bury him, so I dragged the body over to a nearby shallow ravine and rolled it in. I hoped all that'd be left in a few weeks would be a few gnawed bones. Walking back toward the parking lot, I found a suitable place deep in the woods, dug a hole and dropped in my revolver. I refilled the hole, scuffed up the area, and moved some loose branches over it.

Now it was time for my last stop of the day.

Chapter 67

G ETTING INTO my car, I reflected on today's events. All in all, everything had gone about as well as I could have hoped, with the unexpected bounty of getting rid of Johnny as well as Peter. I had the evidence I'd need to close out my covert assignment at Federated, had permanently solved the Peter problem, and might be able to uncover some valuable information in the late spymaster's cabin. On the negative side, I now realized that although I had proof of who the leakers were, I couldn't explain how I'd gotten it.

The rain had stopped, so I had an easy drive back to the 280 and then to Moffett Field. I used my military ID to get through the gates, drove to the VOQ and went to room 425, which I'd cleverly deduced was the correct room. Mostly because of the handwritten note that'd been on my car seat at Memorial Park when I'd returned alone after leaving with Natalie.

It was almost 10 pm; I knocked softly. After a few seconds the door opened slowly.

"Hi, sweetheart," I said. "Are you OK?"

"Better than I should be," Natalie said, managing a wan smile. She flowed into my arms for a mutually much-needed hug. "How about your end?"

"Pete's permanently out of the way and I have the information he promised. And there was a little bonus—your old buddy Johnny Ross was there too."

"And what happened to him?"

"Nothing you need to know in detail, but you won't be seeing him again. The Black Panthers will be looking for a new token paleface."

"You had me so scared out there. For a moment I thought you were really going to kill me." She was beginning to sob, and I didn't blame her. I was close to crying myself. I hugged her tighter and kissed her forehead.

"Sweetheart, I could never do anything to harm you. It's as I said there: I'll never love anyone but you. And you were so brave—I'm very proud of you. Now tell me how it went after we cleaned you up and you left."

"I used that path you pointed out. It wasn't easy going, but it only took a few minutes to reach the road. That NIS guy—Ryan—was waiting for me in his car. He drove to a service station so I could fix myself up—you really made a mess with the moulages and all that gunk. Once I looked human again, we went to a restaurant for drinks and dinner. After we ate, he dropped me off here. He'd picked up the suitcase I'd packed at my house, so I was all set." I'd blazed the path a week ago, once I'd discovered the best route from our kill site to Pescadero Creek Road.

I kissed her cheek and leaned back. "I wish you could've been there when I shot the old bastard. I was never so glad to do anything in my life. Before I pulled the trigger, I whispered 'She's still alive,' just to give him a thought to carry into hell. Then I shot him. And here's your pistol. It was never shot tonight, not counting the snap caps I put in. You should have seen Johnny's face when he squeezed the trigger and just got that little 'pop' noise."

"Did you have to hurt Johnny much?"

She didn't need to know about the shoulder shot, which must have been very painful, so I just said, "His death was painless, I promise you." Before that, not so much.

Natalie gave me a narrow look, but decided to change the subject. "How does the stuff Peter gave you look?"

"It looks authentic. I've got bank deposit slips, transcripts of telephone calls—lots of good stuff. I should be able to substantiate it with not too much work. And Johnny showed me where Pete lived; we can go back there and search for more goodies." I didn't really believe that we could authenticate the evidence easily, but it sounded reassuring, and that's what she needed after what I'd put her through.

"Who are—were—our spies?" I told her.

She nodded. "Pretty much who we expected. Say, did you get rid of that revolver you bought?"

"I never bought a revolver. Larry Unfeld did. I buried it in the woods in the Primitive area."

"Why did you buy that anyway? You're a great shot with your 9 mm."

"Because I like that weapon and want to keep it. It'd be too dangerous to keep the murder weapon, in case the police somehow get involved in this thing. And remember, my pistol's registered with the police."

She was silent for a moment. "Would you like a drink? This place has one of those mini-bar thingies." I nodded; I could use several right now. The stress level I was coming down from was giving me a monster headache, and my mind was swirling as I considered all the ways this plan could have gone fatally wrong.

Natalie handed me a water glass full of Jack Daniel's. No ice. Two deep swigs and I felt somewhat better. "Hey," I offered, "want to see your pictures?"

"I'm not sure," she managed to laugh. I was glad to see her mood lightening.

"Here you go ... I should say that Peter and Johnny found them absolutely convincing."

"They should have," she murmured, leafing through the photos. "What a mess it was with those calf brains and that fake blood, but the best touch were the moulages[91]. I'm glad I thought of those."

I was sure that had been my idea, but decided not to say so. I'd gotten the tip on these devices from the chief pathologist for Santa Clara County. Norm Connors had been a good person to talk to on how to produce a convincing fake bullet wound, and he'd referred me to the very helpful pathologist. The worthy doctor even told me where I could buy the revolting things and gave me some tips on what I could buy to make the leakage around the fake wound look real. I'd had no idea people ate calf brains.

"The moulages were the crowning touch," I agreed. "The 'exit wound' was very convincing."

I pulled out another photo. "This one's actually my favorite." It showed Natalie scowling and giving me the finger, both wounds leaking fake blood and calf brains. I'd made very sure not to include it with the ones I showed Peter. It coaxed another laugh out of her.

She relaxed and cuddled against me. "I can't tell you how relieved I am. That bastard Peter had been on my mind for years. I put him on a back shelf for a long time, but since he showed up at dinner in San Mateo, I've been a mess, mentally. And now he's gone forever, all thanks to you. Look, I know I've been really bitchy since he reappeared, and I took a lot of it out on you."

"That was reasonable, honey. After all, without my connection to Peter, he'd have never been in your life at all. So it all comes back to me."

"In life you take the good with the bad. And you're so good for me—better than I ever dreamed anyone could be. The only bad part was that Peter was part of your baggage, but now he's gone and it's just us."

---

[91] A moulage is an artificial patch—usually rubber or latex—that can be put on a person to mimic the look of an actual wound or skin condition. These are used by firefighters and other first-responders, as well as medical students.

Just us and maybe whoever in the KGB he reported to, I thought. But I didn't need to disturb Natalie's mood just yet.

We spent our first night together in several weeks, my first night without gory dreams of Natalie's torture ordeal with Peter.

Chapter 68

SINCE I'd skipped work the previous day, I needed to go in Friday. I persuaded Natalie that, with the stress she'd gone through yesterday, she could use a day off. We were up early, giving me time to drive her back to her house. "See you tonight," I promised, kissing her at the doorstep.

As soon as I got back into my apartment, I put Pete's folder in my safe. After a quick shower and a change into business clothes I was at work on time. Yolanda was already there, and came over to my desk as I was setting my briefcase down. "Are you OK now?" she asked. I couldn't tell if she was skeptical about my alleged sickness yesterday.

"Just fine, thanks. Anything I need to know to catch up?"

More or less cheerfully, she gave me an update on the very scant interesting happenings of the previous day. "Everyone got their reports in on time for the Monday meeting, and I distributed them yesterday," she ended.

I spent most of the day sitting at my desk and looking very busy, but my work had nothing to do with Federated. I was making a list of things I should be looking for in Peter's house, and of where they might be hidden—in the walls, underneath the house, the ceilings, and so on. I was going to need a hefty crowbar, a sledgehammer, a shovel, some large bags to carry whatever we found and, maybe most importantly, rubber gloves, so I wouldn't leave fingerprints all over the place. "And some disinfectant and scrub cloths, so I can get rid of whatever prints I might have left last night," I reminded myself out loud, earning a quizzical glance from Owen, who was walking by my cubicle.

At some point I was going to have to tell Jack that I'd identified the two guilty parties and had evidence to prove it. The problem I hadn't solved was the "how"—he'd surely ask where I'd come up with the various records Pete had so thoughtfully provided. I couldn't think of any explanation of how I could have come up with the information on my own. Pending a brainstorm on how I could explain this, the only road to success I could see on this was using the information to pressure the two people I knew to be guilty. Maybe Natalie would have some ideas.

At that moment my phone rang; it was Natalie. Must be some sort of mind reading. "Hey," she said cheerfully, "what do you want to do tonight?"

"I think you can guess."

"Get your mind out of the gutter, you animal. If you behave nicely, you might get lucky, but that's all I can promise." She paused for a moment. "I wanted to ask you more details last night about the information Peter gave you. Can you tell me a little about it?"

Not over a company phone, I couldn't. "Let's not talk about that right now. I have what you're talking about at my place. How about you come there at about six? I'll take you to dinner and afterward we can go over the documents. Later maybe I'll get lucky."

"I won't promise anything, horny dog. I'll see you at your place at six."

By the end of the afternoon, I was caught up on Federated paperwork and had talked with the three engineers who'd gone to Norfolk. Now that they'd had several weeks to absorb the whole thing, I wanted to see if they'd come up with any insights. Arnold had a few questions, Owen had one, and Wayne had nothing. That reminded me that semi-annual personnel evaluations were due next month; his wouldn't be very good. I wished everyone a nice weekend and left at 5:30.

Natalie was exactly on time, and hungry. We headed for the restaurant—Friday evenings in Sunnyvale equal crowded restaurants. Tonight it was Italian with a nice Chianti (no fava beans). We didn't talk about yesterday's events. Despite her slip on the phone call, Nat understood that absolutely no one else could know what we'd done.

Back in the apartment, I pulled the document folder out of the safe and put it on the kitchen table. "First," I suggested, "let's go through this and see what we got. I only had a quick look last night."

I watched her leaf through the data. She was thorough and went through both sets of information several times as I waited. Finally she looked up. "This seems pretty conclusive on both of them. We have transcripts of phone calls, evidence showing money deposited in their bank accounts—all kinds of stuff."

"And what would we do with that?" I asked.

"Well, we'd go to Federated security, or the FBI—someone—and show them the proof."

"How is that proof?"

"It shows what they stole, how they got paid for it, documents their phone conversations ..." She trailed off.

"It doesn't prove anything," I said, although from her expression she already knew that. "All we have is a set of data that could be made up out of thin air."

She thought a moment. "But the bank records could be verified. That'd prove something."

"It doesn't show where the money came from; those are all cash deposits. A canceled check from the Soviet Consulate would've been nice, but there's no actual proof in any of this. If this were a legal case, it'd be thrown out of court." This conclusion was based on my one term in Navy ROTC studying the Uniform Code of Military Justice, which had nothing to do with civilian standards of proof.

"But this isn't fair. You risked my life—and yours—to get this stuff. And now you're saying it's worthless."

"Sweetheart, it isn't worthless—it's priceless. First of all, we now know who the villains are. And the data Pete gave us is good stuff. If we can get information to back up what we have here, we can nail those two. And we can focus on just *their* phone calls, credit reports, and so on. We've eliminated eighty percent of the suspects." Including Natalie herself.

"That makes sense, but what do we do to nail down the proof on the two spies?"

"I can probably get taps on their home phone lines and maybe we can arrange for some kind of surveillance, but I'd be surprised if these two are still contacting the Soviets. I don't know yet what I can ask for without showing proof." I found myself yawning. "Look, baby, I'm more tired than I expected; maybe it's left-over stress from yesterday. How about we sleep on this? Tomorrow, if you feel like it, we can go out to Pete's cabin and search it to see what else we find."

"What if someone else is there? If the police found Peter's body, wouldn't they have the place 'staked out,' or whatever the phrase is?"

"There'd be no way to connect the body, even if they find it, to his cabin miles away. And even if they did, we'll know that when we drive by—if there's a lot of yellow tape and police cars, we just drive on by. And I doubt very much that Peter's body has been found. That place we met is very isolated, and it might be quite a while before anyone stumbles on that old shack."

She shrugged. "Let's talk about it in the morning. It seems a little creepy to be going through his home searching for stuff, but you may be able to persuade me. Shall we do the running and the gun range first?"

"It'll be Saturday, and that's our tradition. But let's sleep until we're both rested enough."

"You may not get as much sleep as you're hoping," Natalie smiled, unbuttoning her blouse.

I didn't get as much rest as I'd planned on; sacrifices sometimes have to be made. After running, breakfast, and an hour at the gun range, we headed up the 280 toward La Honda. I had my duffel bag, which included thin plastic gloves for both of us to wear, as well as two crowbars, a sledgehammer, and some other basic tools. Plus the disinfectant spray and scrub cloths to wipe down the place after we finished.

I found Pete's place without much trouble. We drove by slowly, and saw no signs of any activity. "Shall we go for it?" I asked.

"Why not? If there's someone official up there, we can say we were looking for a rental cabin that we might want to use on weekends."

No one was there. We walked in and Natalie got her first look at this place. "You know, Peter is—I mean was—a rough guy. But this place is really pretty well kept." She prowled through the few rooms and shrugged. "Now what?"

"Put these gloves on," I told her as I slipped my own pair on. "I'll look underneath the floors to begin with. How about you do a double-check for any possible storage space? Tap on the walls, cabinet backs and so on to see if there may be space behind them. I did a quick look-through the other night, but probably missed a lot." She nodded and we began what was to turn into five hours of fairly hard labor.

I pried up floor boards in each of the rooms and, using my flashlight, looked underneath to see if there was anything underneath. There wasn't. Then I found the little hatch to the attic; it had a pull-down ladder, which I mounted. The attic had only a few boxes, which I spent time looking through without finding anything interesting. I was crawling around the edges of the attic with the flashlight looking for other storage areas when I heard Natalie calling from downstairs.

"I found something!" she shouted.

I hustled down and found her in the bedroom. "I was going through the drawers in this bureau and realized the bottom of this drawer is fake." She pulled it off, revealing two good-sized journal books.

Natalie took one of the journals and flipped through it. "This looks like an encryption—maybe a letter substitution like those cryptograms in the newspapers. But the words are all five letters. What does that mean?"

"It means it'll be harder to break this thing," I said, looking over her shoulder. "Peter probably just strung all the characters together and put in a space every five letters to make it easier to read. If we can break it, we'll still have to figure out where to put the spaces, punctuation, and so on. With a regular cryptogram the very short words –three letters or less—can be used to determine what some of the letters are, but we can't do that. We'll have to do it based on letter frequency—'e' and 't' are the most common letters, and so on. How about the other book?"

Natalie opened it, looking at the first few pages. "Same thing, although it looks like the ink might be fresher in this one, and not as many pages are filled in. Maybe it's the current book and the other one is past history."

I took the two books and stuffed them into the trunk of my car. If we were interrupted here and had to leave in a hurry, they'd go with us.

Natalie resumed her search, but didn't find any more hidden compartments. I finished the attic and spent some time thumping all the walls to see if I could find a hollow area. No luck. "Let's call it a day," I suggested. "I forgot to mention it last night, but I have an address book that I took off Peter yesterday. We may be able to get some good information out of that. First let's make sure no one finds our prints in here."

We'd been wearing gloves since we started work, so all we needed to worry about was what I'd touched last night. Between the two of us, we had everything sprayed and wiped down within a few minutes.

As we drove away, Natalie was staring off into space, clearly pondering. Finally, she suggested, "Honey, let's go back to my place. I was thinking about this cryptogram thing and realized I might be able to use my computer to help decipher it. It'd be easy to get a numerical count for each letter, and that'd speed up the decryption a lot." That sounded reasonable to me—if we took a lengthy section, we should have a large enough sample that we could guess which represented popular letters. Morse code, which the Navy had relentlessly drummed into us, told me that the two most common letters are E and T (one dot and one dash, respectively), and the next four were A, I, M and N (each of which had two Morse characters). After that would be the eight letters that had three characters (D, G, K, O, R, S, U and W). The more rarely used letters should be obvious once we'd gotten the "top fourteen" identified.

Chapter 69

HALF AN HOUR after leaving Pete's cabin, we were in Natalie's computer room. She took the first ledger book and typed in the first entry. Then she began writing a program that would do letter counts.

"Go make a drink for both of us. Then you start on the address book while I work on this."

A few minutes later I was paging through the little address book. I opened it to the "H" page, where I assumed I'd find phone and maybe address information for me and for Byron and Emily. There were actually three entries there. The names and addresses were unreadable, probably encrypted in the same way as the journal Natalie was working on. Each entry had a ten-digit number in the format XX-YYYY-ZZZZ. If these were phone numbers, the XXY would be the area code, YYY the prefix, and ZZZZ the last four digits. None of these showed either a 415 or a 408 area code, which would be Byron's and mine, respectively. So these were also encrypted. Or my reasoning was screwed up. I decided to go with the first option. One of them began with "637" and another with "620." The third was "434."

I knew both my and Byron's area codes began with a 4, so if the 6 represented 4, it meant he'd added two digits to each number. "637" would be "415" and "620" was "408," which were the San Mateo and Sunnyvale area codes. I checked to make sure all ten numbers matched my and Byron's phones, and it worked. The "434" area code would be "212," which Natalie's phone book told me was the New York City area code.

"Natalie, is there an office supply or stationery store near here?"

"Go south on Stevens Creek for about a mile and there'll be one on your right hand side. Why do you have to go there?"

"Once you've figured out the code, we'll need to make up a separate decrypted address book. I think I figured out how to decrypt the phone numbers, but we don't want to write in the original."

"Pick up a half dozen or so letter-size memo pads, a couple of journals that are close to the size these are, and some colored markers while you're there. I'll probably end up transcribing the decrypted version into new journals, like you'll be doing with the address and phone stuff. I'm almost finished with the letter counting program; after that I'll write one that'll substitute in the letters we guess." We'd finally found a practical use for a personal computer, but I didn't think it'd be widely popular.

My round trip to pick up our supplies didn't take long. By late afternoon Natalie was almost finished with an initial letter substitution solution for the first entry in the journal, and I had a decrypted set of phone numbers—the decrypted names would have to wait. "Let's take a break," she decided. "My head's whirling and I'm hungry. I'll take you to dinner—my treat—and when we come back we can decide how much more we want to do tonight."

My head was also spinning. Even if we broke the codes so we could read Pete's journals and phone directory, what could I do with that? The more I thought about it, the more it seemed the only option I had would be to bring in Sammon and his resources. If Natalie and I were able to break the code on our own, it seemed likely that what we uncovered would have ramifications way beyond the Federated spy ring. Once we found anything like that, we'd have to bump our findings further up the food chain, so wouldn't it be better to do that starting now? Of course, the downside to that was that it'd immediately reveal more information about me than I wanted Jack to know. His first questions would focus on how I'd had any connection with Pete, and that'd inevitably lead back to my illegal true identity. This was a tough call, and if I decided to bump it up the line, I'd have to have Natalie's full and informed agreement.

Natalie drove us to an upscale steak and seafood restaurant on Stevens Creek. There was a backlog of people waiting for a table, so I took her into the bar and was lucky enough to find an isolated table.

After giving our drink orders, I explained my reasoning to Natalie. She was smart and intuitive, and might have a better way to approach this problem.

"It looks to me," I started, "that when we break these codes and read those journals, we'll find information that goes way beyond what I was brought here to solve. I imagine Pete not only had lots of contacts with the leftist groups in the Bay Area, but was also running several other people like me who were sent here from the Facility."

She nodded. "Makes sense. I can't believe that the only thing Pete was sent here for was to keep an eye on you. You told me that once you were in the fleet, you hardly ever saw him. So what was he doing with all his time? And we know he had contacts with the Coordinating Committee in Berkeley, and probably with all kinds of other radical groups in the Bay Area. Maybe he was working the whole West Coast."

"And if that's true," I mused out loud, "We may not want to get too far into decrypting. We could learn stuff we shouldn't know.'"

She nodded. "We still have our basic problem. Sammon—and I suppose everyone in naval intelligence—will immediately want to know how you knew Pete. And that leads to big problems for you; at least getting kicked out of the Navy, and maybe a court-martial followed by time in one of our finest taxpayer-financed institutions. You need to think about this. There's no reason you have to do anything right away."

"You're absolutely right. A day or two will make no difference. We can play with the code a little to see if we can break it. Or I should say, if *you* can break it. We both know the government probably has rooms full of nerds who do nothing but break codes all day long, and that they could probably do Pete's in a few hours. But it'd be a nice peace offering to bring ... maybe they'd cut me a little slack for years of loyal service."

"How about this—let's forget this conversation and just concentrate on relaxing and having a good time tonight and tomorrow? I'll bet I can keep your mind off that particular problem until Monday."

I agreed she could. She could distract me from almost anything if she put her mind to it, but this particular decision was going to be a major life-changer.

Dinner was excellent and Natalie's company comforting. But my mind was busily churning visions of how a wrathful Navy, realizing they'd been carefully training a Soviet illegal for years, would react to my revealing myself.

After dinner, we spent a few hours on the decryption, with Natalie doing the brunt of the work, and ended up with what seemed a good solution to the passage she'd typed into her computer. When we tested it on the next section of the same journal, however, it failed. Neither of us believed Pete could memorize multiple versions of the code, and we'd found nothing like a crypto "cheat sheet" in his belongings. Maybe some idea on how to approach this would pop into Natalie's mind. It certainly hadn't shown up in mine.

The translated passage detailed how he'd set up two new arrivals from the Facility in Portland. He hadn't put in information that'd allow us to easily identify the date or those people's new names. Maybe the decrypted phone book would yield some clues on that.

We spent a few hours with the next section. Natalie quickly found that the letter rotations had just moved down one character, so the letter that used to mean "A" now meant "B," and so on. Presumably we could replicate this with each section of the two journals, but each time was taking over an hour to make the new substitution table, apply it to the text, and then edit it to put in spaces between words and punctuation marks. Since Nat had no way of printing from her computer, we had to do a lot of manual work.

"A mainframe computer could do this in no time," Natalie decided. "Except for the spaces and the punctuation, of course. But until home computers have real computing power and a printing capability, it'll just be too cumbersome." I now thought her home computer was pretty slick; without it, I doubted we'd have gotten to where we were.

Chapter 70

I SPENT a good deal of my time on Saturday and Sunday pondering whether or not to kick this whole thing upstairs to Sammon. If I did, I might as well come clean about my true background at the same time, since his inevitable questions about the source of the documents would reveal that anyway.

Natalie and I had gone over this several times. She seemed to enjoy taking the opposite side to whichever way I was leaning at that particular moment. As a devil's advocate, she was fiendishly successful, forcing me to look at every angle, each pro and con ... you get the idea.

It all came down to how much I trusted Jack. If he'd stand up for me during the tempest that'd certainly begin as soon as the word 'Facility' left my mouth, everything might work out OK. If not, all I could do was bend over and assume the position. Please, sir, may I have another?

We went around and around on this. I changed my mind several times each day until on Wednesday, I finally accepted that the only sensible decision was to come clean with Sammon. I'd done what I thought was a good job in my assignment. Hopefully the positive points I'd earned would cancel out part of the shit-storm that was coming my way as soon as I confessed all to Jack. I decided to start it rolling early on Thursday. Natalie had spent the night, and wanted to be with me when I made the call. "For moral support," she'd said, offering one of her marvelous kisses to strengthen my resolve.

At seven my time, I dialed Sammon's toll-free number and shortly afterwards had him on the line. Natalie was sitting next to me.

"Captain, I've reached a point in this investigation where I think you need to come out here. I'll walk you through what I have and we can decide what to do next. I know who the two people are who've been passing info to the Soviets, and I have some documentation that'd help nail them. But I don't think I have enough to go into court with."

"That's great news!" he said enthusiastically. "Don't worry too much about legal proof; the legal system might not be involved with this. In cases like these, we sometimes find it's better to operate outside normal channels. To put it another way, someone who'll do this has, in my opinion, forfeited their right to be treated as an American citizen with all the rights and privileges that entails." I was pretty sure, from my elective course in Constitutional Law (a surprisingly interesting class) that the Supremes wouldn't agree with Jack. I did agree, although I also understood that the same rough treatment might apply to me, who'd never really been an American citizen at all.

"Tell me what you've got, but first I want to know *who* you've got." I gave him the two names. He whistled softly. "This might be fun," he said. "We'll have to carefully plan how to nail that first one." I explained the information I had on each of the two spies. "Where'd you get this stuff?" he asked.

"I'd like to cover that in person. When should I expect you?"

"I'll phone you back and let you know. Hopefully I'll get in tonight. Set me up with a hotel room near Federated."

"When you call back, use my office phone. I've got to leave for work in a few minutes."

"OK. See you tonight, hopefully. It'll likely be a long night, so prepare accordingly."

Natalie had heard most of what went on, but I went through it with her to make sure. She listened closely until I'd finished. "Look, Rick, I want to be with you when you meet with your boss. I can explain about how we broke the crypto code and offer some moral support."

"But ..." I was going to say that Sammon would be pissed at having a civilian, and a former suspect at that, joining our meeting. But once I revealed my background, Natalie's presence wouldn't matter. "Why not?" I finally decided. "He'll be angry at first, but once he learns the truth about me, you'll drop off his radar screen. And you'll impress the hell out of him when you show him how you used that home computer to help decrypt Pete's journals."

We went together to work, stopping en route for breakfast. "I'll leave work a little early today," she decided. "I'll want to go home and freshen up. Before I leave let me know the time and place of the meeting."

Sammon called me a few hours later. "I've got a flight. I'll be on United again; in fact it's the same flight I took last month, so you already know when it's supposed to land. Set up a hotel room for me; we can have dinner there later."

I made a reservation for him at a Marriott on El Camino and called Natalie to tell her where we'd meet and when I expected to get there with Sammon. "Give us half an hour alone before you show up," I suggested. "Call the desk from time to time so you can find out when we got there. I'll have the hard part out of the way before you get there. Jack will be so pissed at me by then he won't mind you showing up."

Just like my prior trip, the northbound traffic to SFO on 101 was slow but tolerable. Jack's plane arrived smack on time, which put us into maximum traffic jam time heading southbound. That gave us lots of time to talk, but I insisted we not talk about the proofs I had until we got to the hotel. This irritated Sammon no end. We got to the Marriott at about 6:30. Jack wanted dinner in the room, so I phoned it in, but asked for it to be delayed until 7:45. I ordered for three people.

"Want a drink?" I asked him. Planning ahead, I'd brought a bottle of Jack with me. I'd need it and he might too.

"Same as usual," he grumbled. "Then let's talk about why I'm here."

I poured a drink for each of us. "I've ordered dinner for us and someone who'll be joining us in a little bit, but I wanted to give you the overview first." I opened my duffel bag and began stacking information on the table—Pete's two journals, his phone book, the accordion folder with the information he'd given me, and my own spreadsheet on the various suspects.

I started with the folder, pointing out the various items of proof for the two spies. "How did you get this stuff?" was Sammon's immediate question, which I'd expected. "I got it from a man named Peter—I don't know his last name. I believe he was a Soviet agent working undercover on the West Coast, running spies of various kinds and doing who knows what kind of other dirty work."

Naturally, Jack wanted to know how I'd identified Peter. I took a deep breath. "Here's the situation, Captain. You and I were talking about this place in the USSR called the 'Facility,' where they train Russian kids well enough that they can infiltrate military and political organizations here. I'm a graduate of the Facility and Peter was what I suppose you'd call my handler."

I'd been expecting disbelief and shock from Sammon, but he just nodded. "I've been waiting to hear you say that, Rick. Or should I call you 'Paul Thompson'?"

"My real—my original—name is Pavel Nikolayevich Ulyanov. But I'm Rick Halsted, a loyal and patriotic American. How long have you known I'm an illegal?"

"Since a couple of weeks ago, when I found the sixth grade picture of an elementary school in Fort Ross. You, as 'Paul Thompson,' were in the back row, and a smaller kid labeled as Ricky Burke was in the front row. The next year neither of you were in Fort Ross, but someone looking like Paul Thompson was identified as Ricky Burke in a seventh grade picture at a junior high school in San Mateo. A few years later Rick Halsted was a sophomore at a Catholic high school in San Mateo."

"Why didn't you just bounce me off this project and bring me up on court-martial charges?"

"I trusted you. If I understand this 'Facility' thing correctly, no one volunteered for it. The KGB scooped up intelligent kids, trained them mercilessly and then shipped them to us. It seemed to me that a lot of these kids would resent what'd been done to them, and might be on our side. Kind of like that Academy mid. Besides, what could I have charged you with, even if I wanted to?"

I thought a moment. "Let's see. How about fraudulent appointment, aiding the enemy, spying, espionage ... there are probably more but those should be enough."

"I'm willing to bet you haven't handed over any classified information at all. Technically your appointment as a midshipman was fraudulent, but that wouldn't be a big deal. Basically, Rick, I was gambling that you'd become what you just said—a 'loyal and patriotic American.' Obviously, if I'd known this earlier, you wouldn't be on this project. But you've worked diligently on it and accomplished quite a bit. What I want to know now is how you got this stuff from Peter."

I explained how I'd pressured Pete into supplying the data to enhance my chances of getting command. His demand that I murder Natalie obviously shocked Sammon, but I had him laughing when I explained how we'd faked her death and hoodwinked Peter into giving me the data. I pulled out the photos and showed them to him, drawing some chuckles and headshaking.

"Then what'd you do?"

"Not a lot of choices at that point. I shot him in the side of his head. That was a great moment for me, and a better ending than he deserved. Think of what he did just where I was concerned; he murdered the real Emily and Ricky Burke, beat the crap out of me whenever my grades dropped below his very high standard, and years ago attacked and raped Natalie to force her to terminate our relationship. Lastly, he promised to torture and murder Natalie. And God only knows how many others he killed over the years. He absolutely had to go. I'm sure you'd have been happier if I'd kept him alive somehow so you could pump him for information. But Jack, I had no confidence I could handle him safely long enough to get help. He was a very dangerous man."

"I see what you're saying," Sammon admitted. "What else?"

"Pete had a helper there, a guy named Johnny Ross; at Berkeley he was one of the leading radicals, using the name Giovanni Rossi. I understand he was recently associated with the Black Panthers. After I shot Pete, I forced Johnny to take me to Pete's cabin. I thought Pete might have more information hidden there that we could use. At that point Johnny wasn't useful, and letting him loose would have been dangerous for me. I shot him too."

Sammon had been visibly shocked by my admission I'd killed Peter, and adding Johnny to the list had put him over the top.

"Where are the bodies? Have the police been asking you questions?"

I explained that Pete was rotting peacefully in an isolated cabin and probably hadn't been found yet, and that Johnny was pursuing a similar career path in a remote area of a county park. "Johnny had to go; if I'd just released him, I'd have been in danger of retribution and maybe nailed for Pete's murder. I should be fine; there's no physical evidence to tie me to either of them, in the unlikely case either body's ever found."

At that point, there was a knock on the door. Good timing. I went over, opened it, and brought Natalie in. "Natalie, this is my boss, Captain Jack Sammon. Jack, this lady, as I'm sure you realize, is Natalie Montaigne."

"Miss Montaigne," Jack smiled, "it's a surprise to see you, but a pleasure to finally meet you." Gracious words from someone who'd been pinging on me to dump her. He took her hand and then, the smooth bastard, leaned forward and kissed her cheek.

"Would you like a drink, Natalie?" I asked. "Dinner should be here in about twenty minutes." I brought her a glass of white wine as she settled on the couch facing Sammon.

She began, "Rick asked me to be here so we can discuss these journals we found at Peter's cabin. Honey, did you mention those yet?"

"No, we just got to the part about me doing away with Pete and Johnny. And I should say Jack seemed to appreciate the pictures I took of you the other night."

"Captain," Natalie said firmly, "Rick absolutely saved my life. He might not have told you, but Peter's threat was that if Rick didn't kill me, he would. But it'd include days and days of torture, until I'd be begging to die."

"Of course, if she hadn't been associated with me, she'd have never come to Pete's attention in the first place," I pointed out. "Natalie, can you explain to Captain Sammon how you started decoding Pete's journals?"

She went over to the table and picked up one of the journals. "We found these in a bureau drawer with a false bottom in Pete's cabin," she began. Handing it to Sammon, she went on, "You can see it's a substitution cipher like you'd see in the newspaper puzzle section. But all the letters are in groups of five, so there's no way to find a single letter word and know it must be an 'I' or an 'A'. I typed the whole first section into my computer and then had it total how times each letter was represented."

"What do you mean, 'your' computer?" Jack asked. "You mean you used a terminal at your desk at Federated?"

"No, my own computer. It's in my home office."

"I never heard of such a thing."

"They're pretty rare, but as soon as someone figures out how to make a capable one affordable and some geniuses write programs people can use, there'll be one in every home." Neither Sammon nor I believed this, but we nodded appreciatively.

"Using the computer, I broke the code on that first section, and then had to manually put in spaces and punctuation so it could be read," she went on.

Sammon took the paper she offered and read it. "So now you could do all the stuff in here? There's probably a lot of valuable details in there on who he's working with, who he works for, and so on."

"The bad news, Captain, is that each section may have a different substitution code. But if the second section is typical, it's really the same basic substitution as the first one, but just offset up or down the alphabet. Look at this list for the first section."

She handed him a single sheet of notebook paper with two columns. The first contained the letters 'A' through 'Z' and the second column was the corresponding substitution letters[92].

"Son of a bitch!" Sammon said with a grin. "The first couple of dozen letters in the second column spell out the three Russian words that 'KGB' stands for, with duplicate letters removed[93]. How does this relate to the second section?"

"It's the same sequence, except 'K' now represents 'B' and so on. If this same pattern holds true, there are only 26 different substitution tables," she explained.

"And if it doesn't hold true?"

"Then there are trillions of billions—it's 26 times 25 times 24 and so on—a really big number. But with the computer helping to identify the letter frequencies, it gets narrowed down pretty fast."

"You are a very smart young lady," Sammon said fervently. "Have you ever considered working for the government?"

That brought her first smile since she'd come in. "Not at all, Captain. Within a year I hope to be working at a start-up company making home computers. Getting back to the decrypting, I need to tell you that I stopped deciphering after the first section, except for doing enough of the second section to make sure it was just a shift of the same substitution table. I didn't want to find myself reading information that could get me in trouble. You won't need me anyway—I'm sure you have departments in the government that could break these pretty fast. Of course, once each substitution is solved, you'll need manual human effort to put in the spacing and punctuation."

---

[92] The Appendix shows Natalie's solution to the first and second encrypted sections.

[93] "Komitet Gosudarstvennoy Bezopastnasti" => K O M I T E G S U D A, etc.

346

"Rick, my apologies for pressuring you to break up with this young woman. She's a treasure, and a very good-looking young woman too."

Natalie's expression indicated she appreciated the compliments, but that she wasn't entirely on board with Sammon finding her attractive. I mean, the man must have been in at least his mid-forties—way too old to be interested in women.

At that point room service arrived with a folding dining table and the meals and wine I'd ordered (charged to Jack's room, of course).

By unspoken agreement, our dinner conversation was entirely social. Jack, when he wanted to, could be charming, and Natalie relaxed as the dinner went on. She offered her personal history and gave an edited account of our time together at Berkeley. Sammon probably knew all this stuff, and probably lots more, but acted as though it was all news to him. In turn, he related some funny stories about his days flying the E-A6B, mostly about aviator antics and practical jokes.

After the dinner had been cleared away and the waiters were gone, we got back to business.

"Here's where we are," he began. "You've both done great work up to this point. We know who the two spies are, and we have documents to back that up. As you probably realize, however, we don't have enough to take to a court. So we may have to do things a little different than how it'd happen in a regular court."

"I don't understand," Natalie protested. "I thought everyone was entitled to a fair trial."

"If it comes to a trial, it'll be fair; I can promise you that. The issue where things may get difficult is the evidence part. As I mentioned in the phone call this morning, we're going to try to find a way to get both of these people to confess based on what evidence we have in hand now."

Natalie and I looked at each other; I shrugged, not understanding yet what Jack was getting at.

Jack went on, "What you've given me is good stuff, as I think I already said. We're going to use that to give the impression that this is just the surface layer of what we have. An espionage situation isn't handled the same way that a civilian crime would be; lying to the perp is perfectly OK. So my basic approach will be to lay out the phone transcriptions, deposit records—all the stuff you came up with—and make them believe we have everything we'll need to convict. Neither of these people will have a lawyer with them; we're going to do it at Federated with no advance notice. It'll be a very nasty surprise to them, and when I mention that espionage is a capital crime, both of them should be very eager to confess with the promise of a life sentence instead of execution."

347

"California wouldn't execute someone for spying," Natalie protested.

"Nope, but the federal government would, and espionage is a federal capital crime. Look it up."

I had no problems with Sammon's approach. "When do you want to do this?"

"I think tomorrow; no sense in waiting. But we need to get Harris Booth up here, so let me call him and see if he can get up here." I understood why Booth's presence would be required—having a director of Federated at the proceedings would add legitimacy and probably also some intimidation.

"What if one or both of them insists on a lawyer before they say anything?"

"I tell them that execution is back on the table. What would you do if you were one of them?"

I saw his point.

Jack called Booth, who promised to be at Federated tomorrow for a 10 am meeting. He had use of a director's office there, on the sixth floor, naturally. I'd meet Jack there, but Natalie wouldn't appear. We didn't want anyone else at Federated realizing that she'd been involved in gathering evidence against the spies.

Chapter 71

NATALIE and I had been expecting a marathon session with Jack into the wee hours, but we were out of the hotel by 9:30. "My place," she decided. I left early enough the next morning to get to work by seven.

Jack had told me not to let Yolanda know in advance what was going on, despite our mutual promise with the FBI to cooperate fully. "She'll understand," he'd assured me. "It's important that she not have a chance to call Healey—he'd find some way to force a delay and screw up the works. Tell her she's there only on sufferance, and has no speaking role in this little play. Nor do you, for that matter. Having her there will give me cover with the FBI in case they want to complain about being left out. At the meeting you'll see a couple of FBI agents from the SFO office; Admiral Robards will arrange to get them there, but won't give them any details on what'll be going on. Their only job is to keep quiet and handle our boys when they become Federal prisoners. Got it?" I got it.

The early hours at work seemed to crawl by. I was both nervous and excited, and trying to hide it. At 9:45 I took Yolanda out into the hallway outside our room. "This whole thing is coming to a head right now. Sammon and I know who the two spies are, and we're confronting them—one at a time—this morning. The people there will be me, you, Sammon, and Harris Booth, who's on the board of directors at Federated. Harris may decide to call in the corporate head of security. There may also be a couple of your FBI colleagues there to escort each of them away when they become prisoners. We'll call in the guilty parties one at a time. Let's go." I didn't give her an opportunity to get to a phone and call Healey. She protested mildly, but came along willingly enough. I hadn't told her who the two spies were.

I escorted Yolanda up to the sixth floor. Laura, seated outside Greenwood's office, stared at us as we headed toward the directors' office Harris Booth would be in. I smiled politely and kept on walking.

Sammon and Booth were there at a conference table, as was a middle-aged man with a military haircut and two men in dark blue suits and rep ties, marking them as the FBI agents Robards had asked for. I introduced Yolanda to Booth. He introduced both of us to Chet Kunz, who turned out to be the head of security here, and to the FBI agents, Townsend and Koehler. Sammon was in service dress blue; I hadn't seen him in uniform since our first meeting at the Andrews BOQ.

"Here's what we're going to do," Booth began. "Captain Sammon has laid out the evidence you've supplied on the two apparent spies who work here. I've gone through them, and the captain and I have agreed on how to handle this. Neither of you two, nor you, Chet, need to speak. Nor do our two FBI friends. If something comes up that you think needs to be raised, let me know and we can briefly adjourn to discuss it. Understood?"

We all nodded. Booth turned to Kunz, handing him a slip of paper. "Chet, would you bring this person up here? Don't tell him any details; just tell him he's needed in a meeting here."

Five minutes later Kunz reappeared with a baffled Phil Boyce. As soon as he saw Sammon and Booth, Phil flushed and tried to turn around, but Kunz forcefully brought him to a chair at the end of the conference table.

"Mr. Boyce," Booth began formally, "do you have any idea why we called you in here?"

Phil shook his head. "No, sir, no idea at all." I thought he was lying, but it didn't matter.

Sammon spoke up. "I'm Captain Jack Sammon from the Naval Investigative Service. The gentleman to my left is Mr. Harris Booth, who is on the board of directors at Federated. The man standing behind you is Mr. Chet Kunz, who's in charge of security here. I'm sure you know Mr. Halsted and Miss Ramirez. The two men to your left are from the FBI office in San Francisco. As you can see, we'll be tape-recording this session.

"My specific job is counter-espionage. It came to our attention several months ago that the Soviets were trying to obtain technical information about the Outlaw Shark program that you were working on until recently."

He took a folder out of his briefcase. "Mr. Boyce, I have some things to show you. Let's start with these." He put two sheets of paper in front of Phil. "The top one is a deposit slip showing that $3,000 in cash was deposited to your checking account in August of this year. The second sheet shows the same amount deposited in September. Would you tell us the source of these funds?"

Phil had turned pale, but managed to shake his head. "I have no idea," he stammered.

Sammon gave him an evil smile. "And here is a transcript of a telephone call. It originated from a payphone near your home in Gilroy. The other party was at a payphone a few blocks from the Soviet Consulate in San Francisco. The conversation, as you can see, involved classified information that had been requested by the called party. Do you have any comments on this?"

Phil shook his head and tried to say something, but nothing came out. Sammon placed another sheet of paper on top of the stack.

"This, sir, is a copy of the US Code regarding the punishment for espionage. As you can see, the punishment for espionage is death." Sammon sat back and waited.

"Why are you telling me this?" he managed to ask.

"Because you're guilty of espionage. Would you like to see more proof? I have a briefcase full." He probably did have a full briefcase, but most of it had nothing to do with Phil.

Sammon went on without waiting for an answer. "Now, Mr. Boyce, this is your one and only chance to avoid being executed. If you give us a full and complete confession, including facts that we will cross-check to make sure your testimony is correct, you will not be executed."

Phil was crying now; I couldn't blame him. I doubted he realized yet that he'd be committed to life imprisonment without parole. A little heavy for $6,000, but that's what happens when you play at treason.

He began stammering out his confession, tears running down his face. Sammon guided him carefully through it, getting details in chronological order of how the whole thing had started, how he'd contacted the Soviets at the Consulate, how meetings were arranged, what information had been exchanged ... all the way to the bitter end.

"Mr. Townsend," Jack said to one of the FBI agents, "will you take charge of our prisoner? Mr. Cruz has a holding area where you can stay with him while we finish our work up here."

When Phil had been escorted out, Jack suggested, "Let's take a break for a few minutes." He turned to me. "When we're ready for the other one, would you like to get him yourself?"

"I certainly would," I said enthusiastically. This would be sweet.

Yolanda leaned over to whisper to me, "Who's next?"

I hesitated a moment, but told her; she'd find out anyway in a few minutes.

Chapter 72

O UR BREAK lasted about ten minutes, and everyone resumed their seats.

"Would you like Mr. Kunz to help you bring in the next person?" Booth asked me.

"I don't foresee any problems." If there were, I could handle them.

Standing up, I straightened my tie and buttoned my suit coat. I was ready, mentally and physically. Shutting the door behind me, I walked purposefully down to Lee Greenwood's office, where Laura offered a tentative smile. She was clearly confused about what I was doing on the sixth floor. "Is he in?" I asked.

"Yes, but I think he's busy," she answered.

I smiled and walked past her, opening Greenwood's door without knocking.

He was on the phone, and shot me an irritated glance. Finishing his conversation quickly, he hung up the phone. "What are you doing in here, and what do you mean by coming in without an appointment and without knocking?"

"I was up the hall with Harris Booth and he suggested I invite you down to join us." A true statement.

Greenwood immediately brightened as he stood. He walked to his clothes stand, put on his suit coat and buttoned it carefully. "Is he in the directors' office?"

"He is," I said cheerfully. This was going to be fun.

Reaching our room, I opened the door and held it for Greenwood to enter. He walked in confidently, but froze as he saw not only Booth, but also Jack Sammon, Kunz, Yolanda and the remaining FBI agent. He turned as if to go out, but I was in his way. Kunz moved to the door, shut it and stood against it.

Greenwood looked around, but there was no way out, so he apparently decided to bluff it out and see what happened. "A pleasure to see you, Mr. Booth," he said, taking a seat at the end of the table. I had to admire his poise, considering the circumstances.

"This is business, not pleasure, Mr. Greenwood," Booth answered without standing. "Let me introduce Captain Jack Sammon of the Naval

Investigative Service. Captain Sammon will be running these proceedings. The gentleman to your left is Special Agent Koehler, from the FBI San Francisco office."

"May I ask what Mr. Halsted and this secretary—Miss Ramirez—are doing here?"

Yolanda stood, looking Greenwood directly in his eyes. "I am Special Agent Maria Vega, Federal Bureau of Investigation." That must have been a sweet moment for her. I smiled at Lee, but didn't say anything.

Booth got things rolling. "Mr. Greenwood, I want to make sure you understand this isn't an adversarial situation between you and Federated. We're looking for your help to clear up some important matters dealing with corporate security, and think you could be of help. You must understand that no matter what you say or admit, Federated will take no action against you. It's important that you cooperate, and we assure you that the company won't punish you in any way. Captain Sammon will be asking the questions. Are you ready, Captain?"

Sammon glared at Booth. "As I told you, I do *not* agree with Federated allowing this person to escape liability to you. He needs to be held accountable."

"We've been over this, Captain. It's in the best interests of the company to find out exactly what happened, and if Federated has to allow Mr. Greenwood to escape consequences for his actions, that's the price we pay to find out what information has been compromised."

Sammon muttered something, probably obscene, under his breath.

Greenwood surprised me by asking, "Would it be possible to get that agreement in writing?"

"Certainly," Booth agreed. "Rick, would you bring in Mr. Greenwood's assistant? Have her bring her steno pad with her."

A few seconds later I was at her desk. "Laura, could you bring your steno pad down to the directors' office? Mr. Booth is going to dictate a letter."

I ushered her into the office we were using. Laura had chosen to wear a mini-skirt today, which I was sure Sammon and maybe even Booth appreciated, despite their advanced age. She paused, obviously confused by the presence of a naval officer and Yolanda, whom she knew only as a secretary several levels below her. "Take a seat near Mr. Booth," I suggested.

She took the seat and crossed her legs, showing a good deal of very fine thigh, as everyone in the room noticed. Booth dictated a letter clearly stating that Federated would take no action whatsoever against Lee Greenwood based on his testimony today. "Bring in a draft so I can double-check it," he suggested. "The signed copy will be addressed to

Warren Hodgkins, with a copy to the company's general counsel and another to Mr. Greenwood."

A few minutes later Laura was back with the draft. Booth scribbled a few changes and handed it back. The very efficient little redhead came back quickly with a smooth original and a photocopy. Booth signed the original and passed the photocopy down to Greenwood, who read it carefully.

"Thank you, Laura," Booth said politely, although his gaze wasn't into her eyes. How could a man who must be in his mid-fifties be interested in a young woman like Laura? It was like Sammon's obvious admiration of Natalie last night. The blushing Laura made her way out of the room and quietly shut the door behind her.

"Let's get started, Mr. Greenwood," Sammon told Greenwood. "As Mr. Booth said, I'll be running these proceedings. Make yourself comfortable; you may be here for a while."

Sammon repeated the same counter-espionage preamble as he had for Phil and pulled out the deposit slips for Greenwood. Placing four sheets of them in front of him, he explained, for the benefit of the tape recorder, that they showed deposits of $5,000 at one-month intervals. "Can you explain why you received these funds, and from whom they came?"

Greenwood looked carefully at the documents. Cautiously, he said, "I received these funds from an outside party not related to Federated in any way. They represent compensation for various services I performed for them."

"What was the nature of these services?"

"That is none of your business," Greenwood told him calmly.

Booth cut in. "Lee, please give Captain Sammon whatever information you can. You know very well that Federated is holding you harmless for whatever you did in relation to the matters Captain Sammon is raising."

"I can say that this was in return for providing information on various technical issues that the purchasers were interested in," he answered reluctantly.

"What specifically were these 'technical issues' on which you provided information?" Sammon asked.

"They concerned various aspects of the Outlaw Shark project."

"More detail, Mr. Greenwood—I need you to tell me exactly what you handed over."

Greenwood reluctantly listed technical information he'd passed over. Many of them were related to the SSIXS system and details of the ocean surveillance system data. Just what I'd suspected.

"Do you have any idea as to the nationality of the people to whom you furnished this information?"

"I suppose they were Russian," he said hesitantly.

"By that do you mean they were from the Soviet Union?"

"I assume so."

After almost half an hour of detailed questions, nailing down the details of what Greenwood had passed to the Soviets, Sammon told him, "I think I have all I want here, Mr. Booth."

I could see Greenwood sag in relief; now it was over. Not quite.

Sammon turned to the remaining FBI agent. "Mr. Koehler, please take Mr. Greenwood into custody."

Greenwood's eyes bugged out. I liked that look on him. "But Mr. Booth, you said I'd be held harmless for whatever information I provided!"

"I promised, Mr. Greenwood, that you'd be held harmless by Federated. And so you will. But the federal government, represented here by Captain Sammon, is bringing you up on felony charges of espionage and perhaps treason. If I'm not mistaken, conviction on those charges is punishable by the death penalty."

Greenwood was led, stumbling in shock, out of the room as Sammon and I smiled happily. Yolanda ... Maria, whatever ... was elated. "Can I call Mr. Healey to report this?" she asked Sammon.

"Absolutely, and be sure to tell Connor how thankful I am for all your help," Sammon said. I was pretty sure that was sarcastic. The FBI, so far as I knew, had contributed zero to solving the Federated spy problem, but I had no doubt they'd find a way to garner the lion's share of the credit. Sunday's San Francisco Examiner would no doubt have a headline celebrating the FBI's brilliant work in this counterintelligence coup, complete with a photo of Connor Healey, master of counter-espionage. NIS, I had learned, wasn't interested in publicity.

Chapter 73

S AMMON pulled me aside as the meeting broke up. "Let's meet in the cafeteria in a few minutes. Harris wants to talk to you first. Good work." He patted me on the back and left.

"Close the door, Mr. Halsted," Booth suggested. "We have some things to discuss."

He took a seat on one side of the conference table; I sat facing him.

"First, I wanted to thank you for not embarrassing me here at Federated. Jack persuaded me that if I became your 'sponsor,' as I suppose we'd call it, I wouldn't regret it. I was worried at first, because I really didn't know you. If you'd done a poor job, it would have hurt my reputation. No lasting damage, you understand, but I don't like being embarrassed.

"Anyway, within a couple of weeks I heard from none other than Lee Greenwood that you were doing outstanding work ..."

I interrupted, the first time I'd dared to do that to a flag officer. "Admiral, all I did was point out the obvious—that the Outlaw Shark system would be valuable on SSBN's as well as SSN's."

"May I continue?" he asked sarcastically. I thought I saw a smile in there, but wasn't sure. "Your work here at Federated has been fine. But I think you know as well as I do that one of the reasons you were promoted when Malone got pushed aside was that Lee thought he'd gain status with me through the promotion. The smarmy bastard kept sending me reports on how you were doing, no doubt hoping he'd get brownie points. But your work has been first-rate throughout. I'm just talking about the official Federated work. On your NIS job, it seems you've done at least as well, if not better. Jack told me back in September he thought it'd take until early next year before you'd have any results, but here we are before Thanksgiving and it looks like it's all wrapped up pretty nicely."

"Thanks, admiral. I had some luck on this, but as a novice in the spook business, I'll take whatever I can get."

Booth poured himself another cup of coffee. "You've been in the Navy long enough to know there's almost always some bad news to go with the good."

"And the bad is that I have to leave Federated," I volunteered.

"Unfortunately. The company can use people like you—you wouldn't believe how hard it is to find someone who can effectively manage people *and* a complex technical project. One or the other is easy to find, but not both. But this thing today, with a vice president being hauled off to a federal lockup and being tried for espionage and probably treason—some of that shit's going to land on you." I nodded; I'd figured that out a few weeks ago.

"On top of that, you can imagine what'll happen when we appoint a VP to take over Greenwood's job—no one in his right mind would feel comfortable having a manager who nailed the previous VP on a federal felony charge. All in all, you're going to be radioactive in this building within a week or so."

"It sounds like it'd be best if I resigned." This wasn't difficult; I'd decided some time ago that I wasn't on board with the Federated culture.

"That would be best," he sighed. "I'm pleased you're taking it so well. And it's obvious from what Jack told me that you'll have to resign your commission. He didn't give me any details, and went out of his way to say you'd done absolutely nothing wrong; that was just the way it was. But there may be an upside and a bright future for you somewhere else." Yes, and Reagan might run as a liberal Democrat. I kept quiet to see what'd come next.

"I have contacts in various companies, mostly in California. I'm assuming that since you were brought up in the Bay Area, you'd prefer to work in this area." I certainly did, if only because of Natalie.

"As it happens, I have a long-time friend—he's in the same camp at my men's club—who took over as CEO of a start-up telecommunications company several years ago. They're growing by leaps and bounds, and Gus told me they're having trouble finding the right person to manage what they call 'Field Operations.' I don't know much about the company, except it's headquartered near SFO, operates nationwide and, as I said, is growing rapidly. The job would be based in Burlingame, but would require substantial travel around the country. Since you're a proven manager—both here and in the Navy—and are an electrical engineer, you may be just the person they're looking for."

That did sound interesting. "How would I pursue that?"

"I took the liberty of setting up an all-day set of interviews for you a week from next Wednesday. You'll be busy next week; Jack will tell you about that. In the meantime, put together a resume and a list of references. Be sure to use me as a reference, and Captain Sammon as well. I'm going back down to San Diego today; I'll mail you my letter of recommendation. And one thing I should have mentioned—I've set it up so that when you leave Federated, even though it's technically a 'voluntary' departure, you'll get six months of severance pay." That'd be more than I'd earned by actually working here.

"I really appreciate that, admiral. And thanks for helping me find a new opportunity." We shook hands and I left to join Sammon down in the cafeteria.

"Your job here is done," he started, "and you've done it very well. Ordinarily you'd get an outstanding fitness report that'd put you on the fast path to command. But you and I know that can never happen."

"Are you saying President Ford isn't interested in me anymore? Just a month or so ago he couldn't do without me."

"Nope. Apparently he's prejudiced against Russians, the narrow-minded bastard. Your resignation from the Navy is considered to have been offered and accepted, effective today. You're now a real civilian."

This was what I'd expected. After telling Sammon about my real background, there was no way I could stay in the Navy even if I wanted to. Which, I suddenly understood, I didn't. Submarining had been challenging and interesting, but I didn't want any more sea duty.

Sammon went on, "Harris has probably already told you this, but you can't stay at Federated. The chances of finding a VP with big enough balls to have a subordinate who tried to get his last VP hanged for espionage are pretty low."

"You think they'll really hang Greenwood?" I assumed Sammon would honor his promise to Phil that he wouldn't get the death penalty.

"Not a chance. The presidential election race is starting up. Ford wants to get re-elected—I should say 'elected,' since he was never elected President in the first place—and one way to help achieve that will be to take the credit for bashing a Soviet spy ring and then showing compassion by letting the bastards rot in a federal prison. How about dinner tonight—just the two of us—and I'll explain some things. I think you can look forward to a happy civilian career, plus you've got Natalie. A very impressive young woman."

He went on, "I'll be busy this afternoon. I've got to finish the paperwork related to this whole fiasco to get our bad guys officially into the system. Ryan will be down with several teams of people to get what's left of Peter to the morgue and to search the two cabins; you'll need to lead them there. Another team will show up here later today and spend the weekend going through everything in Greenwood's office and wherever that little shit Boyce hung his hat, as well as both their homes. After this afternoon, I'll be ready for dinner and more than a few drinks. What's the nicest spot in this area to eat?"

If he was paying, we might as well go top drawer. "Let's try Alexander's Steakhouse; it's on El Camino in Palo Alto. How do I meet up with the NIS guys this afternoon?" I wondered out loud.

"First, have a nice lunch with Natalie so you can tell her what happened this morning. She was very helpful, and deserves to know. You can also break it to her that you're going to dinner without her. I'll cut you loose after dinner so you two can spend the night together, as I assume you've been doing routinely. So far as the NIS is concerned, Ryan will show up in the lobby here at 1:30. You need to lead them, in your car, to the cabin where Pete is currently and to his 'home.' They'll transport the body to the morgue at Moffett Field for an autopsy and cavity search, go through both buildings and their grounds thoroughly, and report back to me. It'll take them a couple of days for the search, so we won't know everything they found for a while. I'll see you at seven at the steakhouse."

It was already past noon, so I went straight to Natalie's office and whisked her out for lunch. She was eager to hear what had happened in our little star chamber session, and gratified that Phil and Lee were now Federal prisoners. I told her, "I agreed to meet Jack for dinner tonight. He wants to discuss some stuff. I assume it'll mainly be about how they're going to debrief me. And I suppose we're celebrating—as of today I'm no longer a naval officer." Why did that last sentence send a twinge to my heart? Separation anxiety, I supposed.

"How about your status at Federated?"

"I volunteered to resign. There's no way I could hang on here. After neutron-bombing a vice president, nobody would want to have me working for them."

"So you're going to be totally unemployed?" She said it like it was a bad thing.

"You make enough to support both of us. I've always wanted to be a beach bum."

Natalie decided that was a joke, and laughed politely. "When will you leave Federated?"

"I'll write up a letter of resignation, suggesting today be my last day of work." I paused and thought. "I have no idea who to send the letter to. I don't think Lee gets mail in the federal slammer."

"Send it to the corporate general counsel—the guy who's head of the legal department," she suggested. "Harris Booth will probably have notified him what happened to our little buddies we sent away. Copy Harris and the head of personnel on it."

By mutual unspoken consent, there was no more talk about Federated, the Navy, or my counter-espionage project. I did tell her about the upcoming interview with the telecomm company in Burlingame. "Sounds like it might be challenging and maybe even fun," I told her.

"I hope so," she said. "See what you can find out about the culture of the company—its personality. That's what can make the difference in whether you're happy there or not. So far as tonight goes, you might get back before me. I've got a dinner with the Steves." She had to remind me that she was referring to the 'little Steve' I'd met at the Homebrew meeting and his partner 'big Steve.' Apparently, they were interested in Natalie as a potential employee of this fantasy company they were planning to start so they could fulfill the huge pent-up demand for a personal home computer.

Chapter 74

THERE WERE a lot of things to do in the next few hours. But first I had to help Ryan and his colleagues find Pete and his two cabins. He was, naturally, right on time arriving in the visitors' lobby, where I was waiting for him.

"You lead in your car," Ryan suggested. "I've got a little caravan following me to take care of all the stuff we have to do. First we'll go to the place where the body is, and then to the other cabin. And if possible, lead us to the other body—it'd be best to get it out of there before someone stumbles on it." I led our parade to the cabin in La Honda where I hoped Pete's body still reposed.

It'd rained more over the last few days, so we had a sloppy trek up to the little cabin. I'd thoughtfully shut the cabin door behind me to minimize the critter-fest damage to my old friend. I pointed out the Studebaker and explained I'd done a cursory search on it.

An NIS team carrying a stretcher and a body bag trudged up after me. Two of the NIS people were equipped for searching the cabin, carrying tools like the ones Natalie and I had brought to Pete's cabin a few days ago.

Pete didn't look much different, but had a more pungent aroma. Ryan peered at him carefully, examining the entrance wound in his ear. "Nice shot," he commented sarcastically. Not much of a compliment. When you've got the muzzle stuck into a guy's ear, it's hard to miss.

The stretcher team slid him into the body bag, lifted him onto the stretcher, and made their way downhill without incident, an accomplishment in the muddy conditions. The two-man search team began their work, and Ryan and two other agents followed me down to our cars to follow me to the home cabin.

I spent a few minutes there explaining what Natalie and I had done yesterday in our search, but I was pretty sure they were going to pretend we hadn't done anything and start from scratch; probably a good idea. Once their search was underway, I went, with Ryan following me, to Memorial Park. After a long walk and a short search, we found what was left of Johnny—less than I'd expected after only a week. There were apparently a lot more hungry animals here than I'd thought. My job in La Honda was over, so I headed back for my last hours at Federated.

363

I wrote out a long-hand version of my resignation letter and walked toward Yolanda/Maria's desk to have her type it up and distribute it. She was cleaning out her desk; her job here was also over. The three men in the department were staring, obviously having no idea why our gorgeous secretary was history.

I helped her take her few personal items down to her car. After I loaded them into her trunk, I thought it'd be nice to shake her hand in thanks. But the voluptuous girl slid up against me for a delicious hug and a kiss on my cheek. "Thanks for bringing me up to the meeting. I know you did all the work on this, but today's results will probably keep Connor from firing me." Another kiss on the cheek, and she turned to get into her car. "Maybe we'll meet again someday," she smiled. It'd probably be best if we didn't; I couldn't imagine Nat being happy with having Yolanda/Maria reappear in my life.

Back in the building, I picked up my draft resignation letter and went up to the sixth floor to see if Laura was still perched outside Greenwood's former office. She was, looking forlorn and confused. I gave her the draft and asked her to type it up, addressed to the general counsel. "I'll have it for you in a few minutes," she promised. "But why are you resigning?" She still didn't understand what had happened to Greenwood.

"Lee was terminated today, and I was part of the reason for it," I explained. "I'll be persona non grata around here because of that, so I'm saving Federated the trouble of making up a reason to fire me."

"Lee's gone? I mean, I saw him escorted out, but didn't know what had happened."

"It's safe to say he won't need this office again. Some people will be showing up to search his office, just so you know. You ought to talk to whoever assigns the executive secretaries here," I advised. "Someone will be moving into Lee's job; you should stake out the job here for yourself. It'll probably happen pretty soon."

I waited while she finished, then signed the letter and left. Laura had promised to send the original to the general counsel, with copies for Harris Booth and the personnel manager. She'd forward all replies to my apartment.

Just to see what their reaction would be, I went back to our working space and asked Wayne, Owen and Arnold over to my desk. "I've resigned from Federated; this is my last day here. I just wanted to say goodbye and wish each of you the best of luck. I enjoyed working with you." That last sentence was difficult to say with a straight face.

The three of them stared back at me; Owen and Arnold just seemed shocked, while Wayne seemed to be enjoying the situation. "Who'll be the new manager?" he asked.

"I have no idea, and no one asked me for any recommendations."

"Were you fired?" Wayne asked hopefully.

"Nope. I'm leaving voluntarily." The unspoken missing phrase was "before they tell me I'm no longer welcome here."

I had absolutely nothing in my desk or safe that was personal, so I left without waiting for best wishes from anyone, took the elevator down to the lobby, and tossed my security badge onto the desk of one of the guards in the lobby.

Back in my apartment, I sat and took a moment to review the day. Today had been a resounding success, thanks mostly to Jack and Harris Booth, in getting confessions from our two spies. On the downside, I was unemployed and, not counting the interview Harris had set up for me, without immediate prospects of a job. I had plenty of cash to get by—probably I'd be fine for almost two years if I had to fall back on my savings and severance pay. I wondered if I'd get a separation allowance from the Navy. That was reserved for people who left involuntarily, typically by being passed over for promotion one too many times. But if mine wasn't involuntary, what was? I certainly hadn't asked for anything that had put me in this position.

Enough pondering, I decided, and headed for dinner.

Chapter 75

JACK AND I arrived at the steakhouse simultaneously, showing how well the Navy trains its officers in punctuality. He was in a good mood. "Everything went smooth as twenty-year old brandy. Our two perps are not so happily installed in a Federal facility in San Francisco. Little Phil is very depressed, and our friend Lee is insulted with the quality of his accommodations. Wait until he gets moved to Leavenworth." Imagining Greenwood's reaction to the reality of prison life cheered me up immensely. Maybe he'd find a nice boyfriend.

As dinner started, Jack updated me. "The teams searching the cabins didn't find anything in the one where you shot Pete. The other cabin was more rewarding. I know you and Natalie spent some time searching there, but our guys found some fake piping. It wasn't connected to the plumbing system; that's where the old bastard stowed a lot of the good stuff. We found a set of cards that probably represent the different substitutions for the letter codes in the journals. Natalie was on the right track; it looks like all of them are what she thought— different rotations of the starting point on the same sequence of substitutions. We also found correspondence and some photos. Here's one the team loaned me to show to you." He produced the photo that Pete had claimed was of my mother and sister.

"Pete showed me this a few weeks ago," I told Jack. "He claims it's my mother and sister, and that they're now living a comfortable lifestyle, at least by Soviet standards, in Tambov. Assuming this is really them, and not two people that look enough like them to fool me, the implicit threat was that if I screwed up—like by killing Pete, for example—they'd be punished."

"What do you think? Are they possibly your family?"

"Jack, I have no way of knowing. The older lady looks similar to how I remember my mother, but that'd be true even if they were fakes. The younger one? No idea. When I last saw my sister, Larissa was about seven years old."

"We could try to get them out for you," Sammon offered.

"Jack, how could you do that? And why?"

"We could tell the Soviets that we have the two spies and that we'll minimize the negative publicity if they send over the women. Of course, we'd have to persuade J. Edgar's boys to cancel the publicity spectacle they're probably planning."

"I loved my family dearly, Jack. I have a hard time believing any of them are still alive, but if they are, how would it be good for them to get sent here?"

Jack didn't answer. I looked at him closely. "You're thinking if we got them over here, we might be able to find out more about the Facility, aren't you?" He shrugged.

"Jack, first of all, my mother and sister would have no way of knowing anything about the Facility unless they were specifically briefed on it, and the KGB wouldn't give closely held information like that to someone who had no need to know. Or, suppose these women are KGB fakes; they'd come loaded with disinformation about the Facility to send our whole counterespionage effort off in the wrong direction. The bottom line is that if they're really my family, they won't know anything. If they do claim to know something, they aren't my mother and sister."

Sammon's smile broadened. "It's a shame you won't be on our team anymore, Rick. For an amateur, which is what you really are despite our training, you cut right to the heart of the matter. I'm 99 percent sure they're fakes. If they happen to be real, the only reason the KGB would let them go would be to use them against us somehow. So getting them out isn't an option. I'm sorry."

I thought he actually was, but wondered why he'd brought it up at all. "Jack, you're setting me up for something, aren't you? I thought we were finished—I'm now out of the Navy, or at least so you tell me, so I can't work for NIS anymore. Right?"

"Almost. You're definitely out of the Navy. I've got your separation papers back in DC, along with a check for your involuntary separation. Your discharge is on honorable conditions, which will make you potentially eligible for some benefits down the road, as well as helping you get hired somewhere. And you can use me and Admiral Robards as references while you look for a job. But you still owe us something."

"Which is?" I thought I knew what he was talking about.

"You need to be debriefed, bucko. You'll spend most of next week at a safe house in DC. We've got to get all the information we can about the Facility."

"How is that done?" I was visualizing being strapped into a gurney while various chemicals were introduced into my system to make sure I answered completely and truthfully. Maybe goons with clever torture instruments would show up when my memories slowed down.

"You'll be interrogated in detail by three or four of our experts in this area. The whole thing is on a friendly basis, if I can use a word like that to describe a highly-classified and thorough debriefing. The main goal is to extract all you know, even subconsciously, about the Facility and its training. The house is a nice comfortable place, and the techniques we'll use don't involve coercion of any kind. We'll use some drugs that have been found to stimulate memories, and maybe some light hypnosis, but you needn't worry about that. And you should expect some local follow-up sessions, but they'll just be a day or two, probably on weekends."

This made sense, and didn't sound too bad. "What are the travel arrangements?"

"I've got a first-class round-trip ticket for you from here to DC, leaving early Monday morning. You can spend the weekend with Natalie, join us for a few days in DC, and be back with her before next weekend. Harris told me he has a job interview lined up for you week after next; you'll be back in plenty of time to prepare for that. The trip is all expenses paid, including what we call a 'consulting fee.' Since you're no longer in the Navy, you'll be paid a daily fee of $500. Transportation, meals and all that miscellaneous stuff are on us. Someone will pick you up at the DC airport Monday afternoon. Your consulting fee starts today and ends on whatever day you arrive back in the Bay Area. So dinner's on you." He reached into his coat pocket and handed me an envelope; it was my plane tickets and itinerary for next week. There was no address or phone number for where I'd be in DC; not a surprise.

"Tell Natalie all about this if you want. That should reassure you that you'll be treated fine; the last thing we want is a pissed-off young woman going public on NIS abuse. All you have to worry about is a lot of long boring question and answer sessions."

"Jack," I asked, "who killed Detweiler?"

"I don't know ... yet. Maybe the answer will be in one of those journals. I'm guessing Pete did it, but unless he put it into one of the journals, we'll never know."

I paid the bill and shook his hand. "Will I see you while I'm out there?"

"Probably. If my schedule doesn't change, you should. I'll be on the same flight back with you, since there are so many loose ends to clear up here that I can't get out until Monday." Of course, he could take a Sunday night red-eye flight, but then he wouldn't be able to keep an eye on me and make sure I was going to show up for my debriefing. We said a temporary goodbye outside the restaurant.

Chapter 76

MY WASHINGTON debriefing trip went fine, so far as I could tell from the memories I was able to summon. Probably due to the drugs, there were long gaps in my recollection of what had happened in the safe house. I got back to the Bay Area late Thursday afternoon, and was met by Natalie. She'd had another meeting with the Steves, and was bubbling over with excitement.

As we drove down the 101, she explained, "They've all but offered me a job managing the group that'll write the operating system for 'little Steve's' new computer. At first it'll be just me, but I'll be able to add one or two people once we start selling them."

I tried what I hoped was an encouraging and supporting smile, and waited for more.

She went on, "the job wouldn't start until February, or maybe a month or two later. I guess they're still doing the incorporation paperwork for the company. They haven't got a name picked out yet, and they can't file the paperwork until they do. Got any name ideas?"

"Not my expertise, sweetheart. But whatever it is should stand out as something unusual. Something plain vanilla like 'California Computers' doesn't have any zing to it. Maybe something like 'Genie' or 'Wizard'? Don't they have a sales or marketing expert?"

"I think 'big Steve' is taking that role. He's an interesting guy— always coming up with ideas that sound off the wall until he explains them. Very strong personality, good public speaker." And probably smooth and handsome, I thought jealously. I'd been hoping for a taller version of 'little Steve' who was, although probably a genius in his field, socially awkward.

"What kind of raise will you be getting in this new job?" I asked. She might have to support me, after all.

Natalie stared at me as though I were an idiot. "I'll be making about half what I earn now at Federated, and very little in the way of benefits. A start-up like this can't afford competitive salaries."

"I hope you're getting a pile of stock options. And they'd better turn out to be worth something."

"I'll get a good chunk of options that vest three years after I start. But you have to understand how risky start-ups are. Most of them fail. I have a good feeling about this one, so I'm willing to roll the dice. And even if it goes belly-up, I'll have a better resume to find my next job."

"Sounds risky," I said thoughtfully.

"That's great, coming from someone who spent seven years running around underwater with a nuclear reactor radiating everyone on board." She paused a moment. "Let's talk about this later. Right now let's get to your place—I've slept alone the last four nights. I hope you've been eating your Wheaties."

I'd spent the last four nights alone too, so I was more than ready, Wheaties or no. An hour and a half later, I left Natalie dozing in my bed while I threw on some clothes and went down to check my mail.

I had three envelopes from Federated. One was a copy of my resignation letter, one contained my severance check, and the other was a letter of recommendation from none other than Warren Hodgkins, the CEO of Federated. I'd never seen Hodgkins, let alone met him, but he'd written a glowing testimonial to my leadership ability, hard work, and "immeasurable contributions" to the success of Federated Aviation. Maybe I should withdraw my resignation and offer to take Greenwood's place. Or maybe not—Natalie would probably not appreciate me having Laura as my personal assistant. The fine hand of Harris Booth was evident in both the severance check (a little over $5,000 after federal and state income tax, Social Security, etc. were deducted) and Hodgkins' letter.

Also in the mailbox was a envelope postmarked San Diego containing an enthusiastic letter of recommendation from Harris Booth. The old gentleman had gone out of his way to make sure I had a soft landing after leaving Federated. Of course, I *had* helped minimize the negative effect to Federated of two of their people selling secrets to the Soviets. If the FBI, for example, had been the prime movers in uncovering the spies, there'd have been much more adverse publicity, and that might have affected Federated's future government contracts.

Back in the apartment I found Natalie fully dressed and ready to go to dinner. "I'm starved," she announced. "And since you're unemployed, I'm buying dinner."

I opened my briefcase and produced a fat envelope. "How about I buy?" I tossed her the envelope.

She opened it; her eyes widened. "What the hell?" she muttered, pulling out a thick sheaf of currency.

"That should be thirty-five $100 bills; my 'consulting fee' for the time I spent with the NIS people back in DC."

"You'll take an income tax hit on this," Natalie said, still holding the bills.

"Nope. Jack told me it wasn't taxable income." Actually he'd said, 'The IRS will never find out about this,' but didn't that mean the same thing?

She handed me one of the bills and put the rest back into the envelope. "Put these in the safe," she said firmly. "We can talk money over dinner."

We did. It seemed the Steves were trying to round up an equity investor to put up $100,000. This would, they'd calculated, allow them to run the business until the second version of their "home computer" was ready for production. At that time, they assumed, based on the success of the first version, they'd have no trouble getting additional financing. They were offering 10% equity in the company to this investor.

"Looks like we're almost four percent of the way with my consulting fee," I joked.

"Rick, I could probably put up $25,000. If you could match that, we'd be halfway there. And if I had to, I could get a second mortgage on my home and get another $40,000 or so. I really don't want to do that, since my salary will be taking a big hit."

"You'd better tell me more about this 'first version' they're making."

That lit her off for at least half an hour. Apparently 'little Steve' had designed what he called a computer, but which appeared to me to be just a circuit board. Whoever bought the board would have to buy a television monitor for a display and a teletype keyboard for inputting data or programming. The Steves had no plan to farm out circuit board manufacturing, so 'little Steve' would be personally assembling and wiring every one of them. "The parts cost for each board should cost less than $30, and they can be sold for over $500!" Natalie told me enthusiastically. Apparently there were a large number of people who'd pay $500 for a circuit board and hundreds more for the television and keyboard, just because it was a "computer."

"What will this computer do?" I asked naïvely.

"Whatever the owner programs into it."

"Look, let's go back to the $100,000. If that's what the Steves need, we can't approach them with half a loaf. How about we set that aside for a day or two? I've got to concentrate on putting together a resume for my job interview Wednesday. I've never written one, and I don't have the slightest idea how to do it."

"You're a lucky man, Rick. I happen to be an expert on resumes—I've actually written one. After we run and shoot tomorrow, we can go to the library and find some books on resumes and put together a draft. Once we fine-tune it, we can take it to a print shop and probably get a hundred or so printed in a few hours."

We found plenty of references in the library, including books on common interview questions and how to handle them. By Tuesday I thought I was ready for my first civilian job interview.

Chapter 77

ON WEDNESDAY, I woke up early. Natalie was up already and prepared a very nice breakfast for me. She'd laid out the suit, shirt, and tie I should wear. The night before, she'd had a good time role-playing as an interviewing executive. She'd worked up a series of questions I'd probably have to answer, the first one being why I'd left Federated after only a few months of work. The recommendation letters from Hodgkins and Booth would be helpful, but didn't really address that question; we worked on it until I had a response that was both truthful and satisfactory. I'd also spent hours at the Stanford library researching the telecommunications industry and its technologies.

The interviews were scheduled to begin at 9:30, so naturally I was parked outside the headquarters building by 8:45. It was a one-story building on a side street off the Bayshore Freeway close to the southern runways of SFO airport. Not a very impressive headquarters.

Seven hours later I walked out, pleased with how things had gone. I'd been interviewed by my potential boss, George Stavropoulos, plus the heads of marketing, engineering, and purchasing. The top guy in finance was out of the office, so I was interviewed by his "number two." He turned out to have been the weapons officer on *TUNNY* during my first-class midshipman cruise. He hadn't recognized my name or, for that matter, my face, but quickly remembered who I was after I explained when we'd run into each other. My last half-hour was with the CEO, Gus Graham, who told me I could expect to hear from them within a few days.

I went over the whole day with Natalie over dinner. She wanted every detail of each of the interviews. "Sounds like you did great—I really like your answers."

"Couldn't have done it without your help. Other than my Rickover interview to get into the nuclear power program, I haven't had any experience in something like that. Luckily these guys were polite and friendly, unlike the good admiral. And the company sounds really interesting—they're so new they're still developing their procedures and policies."

Back at her house, she urged me onto the couch next to her. "We have some more talking to do. I really want to see if we can somehow get the money together to invest in this new company. I'll get a brandy for you."

Nursing my drink, I waited for her sales pitch. She was direct. "We need to decide this before someone else steps up with the money. I told you I could put in $25,000. How much could you invest?"

I had over $50,000 in my savings, now that I'd received the severance pay from both Federated and the Navy. But with Natalie taking a big pay cut and me maybe starting a new job with uncertain prospects, I wanted to set aside enough to handle expenses for at least a year. I'd given some thought to the issue of investing in what seemed to me to be a pipe dream. I wasn't a true believer in the market for personal computers, but Natalie was. For all I'd put her through, she deserved some support from me.

"Nat, I can put in $25,000. With your contribution, we're halfway there. I don't want you to take a second mortgage, and I want to keep a cushion in savings. Once my apartment lease runs out in about three months, maybe I can rent a room from you. In the meantime ..."

"You can move in with me whenever you want. I've always wanted a 'kept man.' Obviously I'm not going to charge you rent. But certain services will be required, if you understand my meaning."

"I suppose I can mow your lawn, weed your flower beds ..."

"I'll give you a list of the services I require, and they'll be limited to things I know you can do well. Meanwhile, you left us at the point where we were halfway to the amount we'd need to be the investors for this company. As you pointed out the other day, that's no good—if they need $100,000, they'll go to someone else."

"Natalie, tomorrow evening you and I are going to have dinner with my folks. I want you to make a pitch to Byron explaining what this new company is all about and why you think it may take off. Fifty thousand bucks doesn't mean that much to him, but I can assure you that as soon as he puts on his professional businessman hat, he'll be skeptical. He'll insist you convince him this is something that offers a good chance of success. He didn't get where he is by handing out money for hare-brained schemes."

It was still early in the evening, so I called Byron and suggested we'd take them to dinner tomorrow night. "We have something we want to discuss with you," I told him, not having realized until the words were out of my mouth that Emily's immediate reaction would be that we wanted to announce marriage plans.

After dinner the next evening, we went back to Byron and Emily's house. The first words out of my mouth were, "As I said, we have something we'd like to talk to you about. Sorry, mom, but it's not marriage plans. At least not yet. This is a business deal that Natalie will explain to you."

And she did, brilliantly in my opinion. She laid out the reasons why she thought a large number of people would want a personal computer, both for home use and for business. When she'd finished and answered a number of probing questions from Byron, he sat back and sipped his brandy for a moment.

"Here's what we'll do," he finally said. "I'll have my attorney create a new company—totally independent of my stores. I don't know whether it'll be a corporation or a limited partnership; that'll depend on how we minimize the tax bite if the company takes off. We'll call it 'Whimsical Investments' or something along that line. I'll put in $50K and you two together will put in the other $50K. In return we'll get a seat or two on the corporate board of this new company. Whatever we make on the stock will be split 30% each to me and Rick, and 40% to Natalie. She gets a bigger share because she brought us the deal and because she'll be one of the key managers in the company. I'll get the Steves to throw in a 'most favored nation' pricing for all current and future products of the company. That way my stores can make some good money selling these gadgets."

"That's not fair," Natalie protested, beating me to it. "The split should be based on the amount of money each of us put in—50% to you and 25% each to me and Rick." I noticed Emily was nodding in agreement with this.

"Take it or leave it," Byron laughed. "Without you, we wouldn't be in this deal. And you're taking the additional risk of leaving a better-paid job to something you think will work. For doing that, you deserve a little extra."

"*Here's* what we'll do," I said. "I agree with Byron that Natalie should get a larger share because she brought the deal to us. And Byron should get a large share because he's providing half of the cash. So here's the deal: 40% for Natalie, 40% for Byron, and 20% for me. Now *you* take it or leave it."

They took it. The three of us were about to become what I later learned were called "angel investors"— people who fund risky startups. This made the us the primary initial investors in the company. Byron was almost as enthusiastic about the future of home computers as Natalie, making me wonder if I was the one who was missing the bus. I didn't care about my slightly low share of the gains, since I doubted we'd ever see any money out of this.

The next day I got my expected job offer from the telecomm company, at a salary about 50% higher than what I'd been earning at Federated. Taking into account the loss of my Navy pay, my total monthly income was lower but, I hoped, with a lot less stress in my life.

377

The major lingering worry was that someone higher up on Pete's food chain might step into my life and either end it or make things much worse.

Jack called me a few days after I'd started my new job. "Thought I'd let you know that our spooks got all the way through deciphering those journals Natalie found. Her work was a big help, by the way. We found a number of names and, through decoding that little phone book you lifted from Pete, were able to find out their addresses. A lot of them were Facility graduates; we're tracking them down now. He also had some notes that led us to the person he reported to. Rather than take this guy in, we've set up a tight monitoring system, hoping he'll lead us to other people at his level."

"Jack, I've got to tell you, I'm pretty nervous about having this guy suddenly appear in my life. I'm sure you understand why. Now that I'm out of the Navy, all I am to them is someone who could cause them—or already has caused them—a lot of harm. They may want some revenge."

"We won't let him get anywhere near you, Rick. We've got eyes and ears on him every hour of every day."

"Just keep me informed, OK?"

"You can count on us. On a more cheerful note, how'd your interview go?"

"I already started. Looks like a good company with a lot of challenges. I think it'll be fun to work there."

"Keep some weekend time open for us. There are some follow-up questions based on your DC visit that we'd like to explore further, probably in a few weeks. Your regular consulting fee will apply, naturally."

"Give me some warning so I don't make plans with Natalie that I'll have to cancel. Otherwise I'm fine with that."

"Rick, thanks again for the excellent work you did for us. You helped eliminate a major threat to national security. I'm just sorry we couldn't do more to give you a softer landing. I was doing what I was ordered to do, but it kind of stuck in my throat having to terminate your Navy career and leave you on your own."

He was about to terminate the call, but I had one more nagging question. "Jack, what about Detweiler's killer? I'd sleep a lot easier if I was sure I wasn't going to pop up on his 'to do' list."

"There was nothing in the journals about that. I wish I had an answer, but I don't. If you see anything suspicious, give Ryan a call."

I was finally ready to begin a normal life. I hadn't had one since I was ten years old.

Epilogue

F IVE YEARS after all this happened, I look back on 1975 and marvel that Natalie and I survived. We'd had a generous helping of sheer luck that allowed us to deal with Peter. Without his baleful presence, we felt liberated.

Shortly after starting my new job, I moved out of the Carillon apartment and into Natalie's home. I told Natalie the main reason I moved in with her was because the commute was better going up the 280 to Millbrae instead of the 101. She persuaded me, in her own fashion, that there were better reasons for us to be living together. Ryan Philpott took over the apartment. Based on the information from Pete's journals, NIS had learned there were also KGB espionage operations going on at several other high-tech companies in the South Bay area. This led them to establish a small branch office in the South Bay—Ryan and one other agent. My former apartment was a good fit for Ryan, with its safe and alarm system. Not to mention the availability of many young women.

Natalie left Federated in early 1976 to take a lower-paying but much more challenging job at the start-up computer company the two Steves had started. They'd chosen a fruit name, by the way. Not that there's anything wrong with that. The company's start was rough, and Natalie worked very long hours, often seven days a week.

In August 1976 Natalie and I were married in a small ceremony at Byron and Emily's house; Jack flew out to be my best man. Byron gave away the very lovely bride, and Beth Haggerty was maid of honor. Just kidding on that last one. Nat's work hours had become almost normal. I was actually spending more time on the job than she was, counting my five or six days of travel each month. Once she cut her workload to sixty hours a week, we had time to enjoy being together.

By that time Nat's company was selling the computers as fast as "little Steve"—the only person knowledgeable about the circuit boards—could produce them. I'd apparently been wrong about the demand level for these gadgets. They were already working on a much-improved successor which would have an integral keyboard and much more flexibility for adding memory and storage capability. Even better, they'd farm out the actual manufacturing, eliminating the production bottleneck they'd had with the first model. Natalie was able to start building a staff, delegating some of the work she'd been handling personally.

The next four years were good for us. Our combined incomes allowed us to live as we pleased while still increasing our savings. Then things changed for the better.

Early this year—1980—Natalie's company went public. The investment Natalie, Byron and I had put in became a fantastic sum for each of us. On top of that, Natalie's stock options alone made her (us?) a millionaire several times over. She told me there were hundreds of people in that startup who became millionaires when the stock went public, and I was sure Nat was in the top ten. She no longer works, and I'm planning a very early retirement. Natalie reached her goal of financial independence at a fairly young age. "You'll never need to work again," Natalie tells me almost daily, rubbing in the prediction I'd scoffed at. She's achieved her dream of having enough money to stop working and do whatever she wants, and she's still in her early thirties.

We spent some of the money on a new home in Portola Valley, not far from La Honda. It's in a redwood grove, and is modestly sized compared to what we could afford—the property covers only a few acres. Natalie loves it, and is now starting to think about where she'd like to travel.

She's already planning a months-long tour of European art museums, a theme outside my area of interest. When I resign, which will be soon, we can plan a slow and luxurious trip. After that, I can show her Hawaii, where she's never been, and possibly interest her in East Asia.

She's had fun the last four years teasing me about our "nukular" President. Pointing out that Jimmy never served on a nuclear submarine doesn't stop her sarcasm. On the bright side, she'll be voting for Reagan this fall. Quite a change from a once-raging leftie campus radical.

I've lived a rags-to-riches story—a poor boy from rural Russia becoming a wealthy man in the US, and married to the girl of his dreams. "From peasant to plutocrat capitalist," I can say with some pride.

My nights used to be consumed with pitiful dreams of Natalie. Now my dreams seem to be of Russia. My strong and stubborn father, my tender and loving mother, and my mischievous little sister whirl through my night thoughts. All dead now, I believe. Images of the two Tambov ladies also float through my dreams, weeping in frustration because I didn't believe they were what was left of my family. Sometimes Peter's there also, grinning at me and promising awful vengeance.

But when I awake, there's always Natalie—all I need in life.

Appendix

Natalie's letter count program totaled the number of times each letter appeared in the substitution code for Peter's first journal entry. Assuming the decrypted text would be in English, she knew that the letters that showed up the most often would be E, T, A, O, I, M and N. Applying these to the encrypted text, and after some trial and error, she came up with the following table. It shows, for example that the letter A is represented by a K, B by an O, and so on. Sammon realized that reading down the "First Entry" column, the letters spelled out the Latin alphabet version of the Russian name of the KGB (*Komitet Gosudarstvennoy Bezopasnosti*). Letters that had already been used were skipped; the letters in parentheses are the letters already used. Once all the letters of the KGB name have been used, the remaining letters are inserted in alphabetic order. The "Second Entry" column shows how the code for the second entry was altered by moving down one letter.

Original Letter	First Entry	Second Entry
A	K	X
B	O	K
C	M	O
D	I	M
E	T	I
F	E	T
G	(t) G	E
H	(o) S	G
I	U	S
J	D	U
K	A	D
L	R	A
M	(st) V	R
N	(e) N	V
O	(no) Y	N
P	B	Y
Q	(e) Z	B
R	(o) **P** (astnosti)	Z
S	C	P
T	F	C
U	H	F
V	J	H
W	L	J
X	Q	L
Y	W	Q
Z	X	W

About the Author

This is Gerry Young's first fiction book. He was previously published by Prentice-Hall in 1978, as the co-author of *Computer-Assisted Business Planning*, and as the author of a major chapter in Dennis Chambers's book *The Entrepreneur's Guide to Writing Business Plans and Proposals*, published by Praeger in 2007.

Gerry attended Oregon State University on an NROTC scholarship, graduating in 1964 with a bachelor's degree in Chemical Engineering. Entering the submarine force upon graduation, he served on four submarines over a five-year period, working at various times as Weapons Officer, Engineering Officer, Senior Watch Officer, and Navigator, in addition to other assignments. After leaving active duty, he remained in the Naval Reserve. As a Reserve officer, he earned a postgraduate diploma with distinction from the United States Naval War College and in 1993 was awarded the VADM John T. Hayward trophy for best performance by a non-resident student. He commanded two Reserve units and retired as a Captain.

In 1971, Gerry earned a Master of Business Administration degree from Oregon State University, standing first in his class. He has been the senior or chief financial officer at four companies, and has held responsible positions in finance, strategic planning, information technology, mergers and acquisitions, human resources, and general management. Most of his experience is in telecommunications, starting with Southern Pacific Communications (now known as Sprint) and including six other telecomm companies. He's also worked in transportation, small business consulting, and automotive manufacturing. Gerry has executive experience in the United States and Western Europe. He has taught financial management at the upper-division university level.

Gerry is working on a second novel, tentatively titled "*The Hormuz Incident*." It's set in 2013 and involves an operation to insert SEAL's into an Iranian naval base to forestall an attack on US carrier groups in the area. The fictional insertion would be done from USS OHIO, an SSGN fitted out to handle operations of that type.

Gerry and his wife Joyce live in Michigan. They have two married children.

www.ingramcontent.com/pod-product-compliance
Lightning Source LLC
Chambersburg PA
CBHW051550250626
47157CB00001B/252